ROCK AND ROLL CHILDREN

AN 80S HAIR METAL GARAGE BAND STORY

ROCK AND ROLL CHILDREN

AN 80S HAIR METAL GARAGE BAND STORY

SEAN FRAZIER

SF

STAGE FRIGHT MEDIA

Published by Stage Fright Media
For more information on this book and its author:
stagefright.us/rock-and-roll-children

Editing by Kristen Tate – www.thebluegarret.com

Custom art by David Boller – www.virtual-graphics.ch

Book cover and interior design by The Book Cover Whisperer:
ProfessionalBookCoverDesign.com

Library of Congress Control Number: 2020915762

ISBN: 978-1-7355817-2-9 Paperback
ISBN: 978-1-7355817-1-2 Hardcover
ISBN: 978-1-7355817-0-5 eBook

Printed in the United States
FIRST EDITION

This book is dedicated to all the garage band wannabes, has-beens, and never-weres. The kids and the dreamers. Some make it, most don't, but the journey is worth it either way.

SET LIST

1 - FADE TO BLACK 5
2 - HIGH SCHOOL 29
3 - LACK OF COMMUNICATION 45
4 - MAGIC POWER 53
5 - FLAMING YOUTH 63
6 - WORKING MAN 72
7 - WHERE EAGLES DARE 79
8 - THIS BOY NEEDS TO ROCK 87
9 - YOU CAN'T STOP ROCK & ROLL 98
10 - ON WITH THE SHOW 105
11 - I WANNA BE SOMEBODY 122
12 - BRINGING ON THE HEART BREAK 138
13 - I WANNA ROCK 145
14 - MIDNITE DYNAMITE 159

ACKNOWLEDGMENTS

FIRST AND FOREMOST, I would like to thank my wife, Lonnie, for her unwavering support in everything that I do. She helped me in so many ways, for such a long time, it's hard to think of life before her. Thanks for always being my rock, my sounding board, and my conscience. I love you.

I would also like to thank my kids – Joshua, David, and Kyle – for being so much fun growing up, and for letting me grow up with you, but also, equally important, for being amazing, compassionate young men. Love you guys.

Thanks to the bandmates: Bob, Ronnie, Jak (Robert), and Mike. Without y'all we wouldn't have had this adventure and this story. It was such a fleeting moment in time (in the grand scheme of things), but it left an indelible impression in my mind and in my soul. This story is really for you.

Thanks to the friends that helped me/us along this journey: John, Andy, Jeremy, MikeE, SeanE, Ricky, ToddS, ToddO, Harold, BobS, JoeP, JoeH, Rich, Ali, Brian, Steve, Dave, Tom, and Scott (RIP, my brother).

Thanks to Mom and Bo for always putting up with and guiding me, even through my "teenage angst" period. An additional special thanks to my mom for always letting me be myself growing up. She let me wear my Kiss T-shirt for my third grade school picture day (see my cover bio picture). How cool is that?

A major thanks to all of the musicians who inspired me (us) along the way. Queensrÿche, Anthrax, Armored Saint, Y&T, Ronnie James Dio, Van Halen, Metallica, Ratt, Mötley Crüe, TNT, AC/DC, Ozzy Osbourne, Kiss, Iron Maiden, Judas Priest, Accept, Krokus, Twisted Sister, Fates Warning, Pantera, Slayer, Testament, Quiet Riot, Loudness, Stryper, Black Sabbath, Deep Purple, Rush, Triumph, Queen, Hanoi Rocks, Night Ranger, Dokken, the Scorpions, Def Leppard, Whitesnake, and W.A.S.P.

Special thanks to all of the talented local bands that showed us the way: Kix, Wrathchild, Child's Play, the Ravyns, Crack the Sky, and many others.

My deepest gratitude to Mark Schenker and Brian Forsythe from Kix for being such great guys with big hearts and rockin' souls.

Sean Frazier
Fall 2020

═══ FOREWORD ═══

I DECIDED TO BECOME a musician after seeing the Beatles on Ed Sullivan when I was around five years old. I had no clue as to how I was going to do it, but I was determined. Music was a big part of my life growing up, and I never lost sight of wanting to do it as my "job." Famous bands of the '60s and '70s such as the Beatles, the Rolling Stones, Cream, etc., seemed out of reach, so I aimed a little lower and began searching out musicians my own age at school. After learning to play guitar well enough to play with others, I went through a few different band configurations and eventually started playing gigs, parties, and jam sessions whenever I could. Soon I was playing in top forty cover bands and making a little money but up until then, I never looked beyond the point of playing in a cover band, having fun, and making a little money playing someone else's music.

One night at a 7-Eleven in Frederick, Maryland, I ran into Ronnie Younkins, who I knew from other bands in the area, and he told me about this band he and Donnie Purnell were putting together to write original songs and get a record deal. It never occurred to me that I could actually do that! So the Shooze was born, December 1977, in my parents' basement. It would still be two more years until we'd find Steve Whitman to complete the original Kix lineup. We still had to play covers, but we'd mix our originals into the set. As we began to play more and more and build a following, we would team up with other local bands to do shows. One of these bands was Face Dancer from Baltimore, who had a record deal with Capitol Records. That's when we realized that maybe it was possible to do that ourselves. We really looked up to those guys as an inspiration and motivation. We eventually asked their manager, who was responsible for getting them their record deal, to manage us and get us a record deal too.

We finally got signed to Atlantic Records at the beginning of 1981, which was roughly three years after first getting together. Our first single release from the first album was "The Itch," so that's the first song of ours I heard on the radio. Of course I was excited – that was a whole new experience and level of (perceived) success. My older brother was living in Reno at that time and heard it on his local station and somehow managed to record it on cassette, which he sent to me. He was so excited he turned up the volume when it came on, so the recording was completely distorted.

It was not easy getting to that point either. Those three years were a lot of work! A lot of grueling, nonstop touring in a van up and down the East Coast, playing dive bars and music venues. Vans and trucks breaking down in the middle of nowhere in the middle of the night, club owners refusing to pay us, and their bouncers threatening us and throwing us out when we tried to demand our pay. We always had a good work ethic and learned early on to give it 100 percent, no matter how many people were there. Starting out back in the Shooze days while still doing covers, there was a venue in Leonardtown, Maryland called the Wharf where we'd play six nights a week, five sets a night. The club owner ran the place with an iron fist and insisted we go on exactly on time for each set no matter what. The weekends were always packed, but on a Tuesday night we were lucky if there was one drunk passed out at the bar. We still gave that one drunk our full show and Steve attributes those types of situations to helping him relax as a frontman and to let his sense of humor carry him through.

I'm sure other areas in the country probably had their own collection of great local bands, but we did have a lot around the Mid-Atlantic area too. There was an abundance of music venues back then. Not only around Baltimore and DC, but also out in the sticks with places like the Mountain View in Smithsburg, Maryland, a cinder block building where your shoes would stick to what was once carpet on the floor; the 11th Frame Lounge in Martinsburg, West Virginia; Shiley Acres, a BYOB outdoor venue in Inwood, West Virginia, with thousands of drunken rednecks in a field; the Old Mill in Williamsport, Maryland, where Steve made his debut as the new singer; Cross Creek in Warrenton, Virginia, a biker bar where we had our soundboard smashed with a bat by a drunken biker; and the list goes on with many more around the Baltimore area too. Like I said, it's definitely not easy working your way up as a musician in the music business.

I always take it as a compliment when someone says they were influenced by me or I see a band and the guitar player has copped my look. When Poison came out, it bothered Steve that Brett Michaels stole his stage persona, but for me, that would've been the ultimate compliment. Like Face Dancer before us, we eventually filled that spot as an inspiration to younger bands in the Maryland area, to give them hope of the possibility that one day they too could get a record deal just like us!

PROLOGUE

THE STORIES IN THIS book are, for the most part, true, although some have been changed for the sake of continuity (or the fact that I can't remember all of the details) and some names have been changed to protect the innocent (or sometimes the guilty). These events were amazing in retrospect but at the time just seemed normal. The need to fit in. The need to escape a repressive life built in the shadow of the Cold War. The need to spread our wings and set off on a life that didn't, at all, look like the life of our parents or their parents before them.

Their life of get up, go to work, go to sleep, do it all again, held no appeal for us. The older I got and the more I settled into that routine, the more I realized that this was the dance of every generation. This is what every new crop of youngsters tried to do to separate from their seemingly dead-eyed parental units.

Writing these stories down allowed me to revisit this time in a way that I hadn't before. Sure, I've thought of these events from time to time over the years and reminisced with these friends over beers or at cookouts, but writing the stories down has allowed me to relive some of them, for better or worse. But mostly for the better.

The older I got, and the more I spent time with other musicians from all over the world, the more I realized that these stories were universal. Everyone has them.

In every town, in every state across the US, in every city throughout the world, these kinds of stories played out. Kids from all kinds of different backgrounds and walks of life got together in garages and basements to make noise and, eventually, some music. We all started off with the same dream, to be like our heroes. In my case, that was Rob Halford from Judas Priest, Bruce Dickinson from Iron Maiden, Geoff Tate from Queensrÿche, John Arch from Fates Warning, Elton John, or Freddie Mercury (believe me, this list goes on and on). For others, it might have been a pop music star like Madonna or Whitney Houston.

We would see our heroes playing in front of sold-out crowds, making loads of money, doing the thing that they loved. And we wanted that. We wanted to *do* that. We wanted fame, sure, and we wanted the money. But what we really wanted was the girls. Everyone (well, almost everyone) initially got into a band to impress "the chicks." But we stayed because we fell in love with the art of making music. Ninety-nine percent of the time, the dream of playing in front of sold-out crowds and actually getting paid never really materializes. Many of us, like me, gave it a really good shot and still ended up doing the nine-to-five dance our parents did.

Don't get me wrong. I have (and have had) an amazing life. I have a wonderful wife (who took this entire journey with me, by the way), three amazing kids, three adorable grandkids, and enough adventures for one lifetime, maybe even two. But the fact is, I didn't hit the big time, and I didn't realize "the dream." At least not "the dream" as I saw it through my seventeen-year-old eyes. "The dream," as I found out much later, can take many forms. Once you've realized that it doesn't have to be about making money or getting girls and is really all about the music, you realize that you can live that dream until the day you die. Maybe that is writing songs, strumming on your guitar on your front porch or in a coffee shop in front of three people, or maybe it's just you, alone, singing in the shower.

The music gets in you. It *is* you. And once it is part of you, it never leaves. To this day, when I find myself humming a tune, if I'm aware enough to realize it's not someone else's melody, I will try to "jot it down" by recording it on my phone. I have hundreds of these little vignettes. Most will never become songs, but some will. The point isn't what I do with these melodies, the point is that I *create* them in the first place. They are really for me and no one else.

When my friends and I were growing up in rural Maryland, none of us had much money, and we didn't see many appealing role models to us to grow into. It was the '80s, the time of Reaganomics and recessions. Kids our age were the first generation to see fewer opportunities than our parents after the revolution of the '60s and the industrialization of the '70s.

We channeled that fear and anger into rebellion. Rebellion of spirit and rebellion of music as we set out to thumb our noses at the establishment – and our overbearing, overprotective parents. In this arena, we didn't see any boundaries to what we could accomplish. That is the gift, and the hubris, of youth. We were also very lucky to be surrounded by so much good music, not only from around the world but also from our own backyard. Bands like Kix, Wrathchild, Child's Play, and many others showed us it could be done and that it could be done here, in our little backwater community surrounded by farm fields and closed minds. This dynamic, the pull to fit in *and* the push to break out, was what drove us.

Every day.

1

FADE TO BLACK

Godamnit! Fuck!

My usual playlist of cuss words reverberates through the oversized two-car garage. I had set aside this day to take care of some overdue basic maintenance on my first love. Well… one of my first loves. Truth be told, music is really and truly my first love, but the dark beauty who had simultaneously excited my dreams and haunted my nightmares (and my wallet) was a close second back in the day. I had committed myself to installing a rebuilt alternator in my '68 Camaro, and she is fighting me, as usual.

As I try to tighten the alternator on the mounting bracket, my socket wrench slips, causing the alternator to drop down, right on my left hand's index finger. *"Ouch! Fuck!"* The wrench hits the garage floor, sending even louder reverberations right into my eardrums. This car and I had seen and done so many things together. She occasionally let me down or left me stranded (less lately), and it was usually a power thing – hence the alternator replacement. This is the umpteenth time I've replaced it, but she is my road warrior. My heavy metal missile.

Today it is just her and me. She and I. Surrounded by metal. Not just car metal, but heavy metal. You know – *the* music. The music that makes life bearable when it otherwise wouldn't be. The music that on most occasions makes it ok to get out of bed and get moving. Or ok to deal with all of the things that life throws your way. This is *my* music. My wife has much broader musical tastes and sometimes mocks mine. "You are so stuck in the '80s." Or "My god, why are you still listening to those people screech?" But it is still my music. Always has been. And while my musical tastes have also broadened over the years, I am never so at peace as when I am elbow deep in grease and blasting Dio's "I Speed at Night." Heavy metal became part of my DNA many years ago and is fused into my being.

I compose myself and pick up the socket wrench and drop it on the workbench. I then stick my left index finger in my mouth, grease and all, to soothe my hurt. I pull my finger back out, shaking my entire hand, trying to quell the sting. Once the pain subsides, I decide it's time for a break. I head inside the house and wash the grease off my hands in the half bath near the garage entrance.

The house is quiet. But that's normal now that the kids have moved out and it is just me, the missus, and three senior dogs that spend more time sleeping than moving. When I hit the kitchen floor the dogs stir a bit, thinking they might get fed again. They meander over to their food dishes and give me that we-haven't-eaten-in-days look. It's hard for a fifteen-year-old German shepherd to pull off the puppy dog eyes, but she still manages. Unfortunately for them, the 'yellow moron' – a boxer mix that makes up for his lack of brains in undying, unconditional love – has left a slight bit of kibble wrapped in wet food on the side of his bowl. The shepherd, the smart one of the bunch, looks down at the yellow dog's bowl and sees the evidence. Now she knows there will be no second breakfast, so she shuffles herself into the living room and onto her hundred-dollar, special-order, geriatric dog bed, lying down with a big *humf.* I look at her and smile. "Foiled again, huh, old girl?" She looks back at me and does the shepherd eyebrow thing – the thing that makes you believe that they're really paying attention to what you said and thinking it over. For a moment I can almost believe that she's thinking, "Next time, I'll clean up that yellow asshole's bowl myself. No evidence." I laugh a bit at this and then proceed to put water on for tea.

A few moments later, the teakettle makes a loud, rattling, whistling sound as though it's gonna jump right off the stove. I take off the kettle and proceed to concoct my caffeine fix. I'm not a coffee guy, never have been. When I was little, my grandfather would drink coffee all day long, and I used to love the smell. I would wait while it brewed, taking in a big inhale of the coffee aroma as it wafted around the kitchen. One day my grandfather let me try some. Big mistake. I went right to the sink and spit that shit out. "Doesn't taste very good, does it?" he'd asked, laughing. "No. No, it doesn't," I replied. I'd had coffee ice cream and loved it, but it was mostly sugar and milk with a little coffee flavoring. My grandfather liked his coffee black. Nothing in it. No sugar. No milk. So from that day onward, I hated coffee. Yet I still loved coffee ice cream.

I take my tea (Earl Grey with lots of sugar and a dash of half-and-half) and head back to the garage. I stand there, staring her down. "You gonna come quietly, old girl, or are you gonna keep fighting me?" I, of course, know the answer. She's gonna fight. She would always fight. From the day I got her, she was a nightmare. A beautiful, sexy nightmare. All kinds of issues from electrical gremlins (that persist to this very day!), to water leakage, to starter problems. You name it, and she did it. But I love her anyway.

Growing up, I was always surrounded by Fords. My stepdad was a mechanic and was a Ford guy through and through. Back then, way back in the '60s and '70s, you were either a Ford guy or a Chevy guy. Couldn't be both. I had grown up driving Fords. Surrounded by Fords.

I learned to drive on a beat-up F-150 farm truck. That truck had power, but that was about it. It was little more than an engine with seats. It was a three-speed on the column, which was weird, but I didn't know any better. At the time it seemed normal. The grossest part to me was all the rust. The car was barely held together by orange and brown patches of rusted-out metal. I had heard that the truck started out white, but there was little evidence of that by the time I was learning to drive. It was so bad that the floorboards on both sides of the cab were rusted straight through. You could see the grass and dirt fly by as you careened through the fields. I remember wondering if I could pull a total Fred Flintstone and stick my feet into the dirt to stop the truck if I needed to or, on the flip side, whether I was going to slip off the bench seat and fall through the floor and run myself over.

That truck wasn't the only Ford around 'the farm.' I use the term 'farm' loosely since, while we had a lot of acreage, we were only sporadic farmers. There were several Galaxies, mostly '64s plus one '65, and a few Fairlanes. Our back field was a Ford graveyard. My stepdad had a need to 'collect' these cars. To hoard them. But the collected hoard mostly consisted of rusted-out buckets of junk, with only one of them (two, if we were lucky) running at any given time. Most of the time, my stepdad was stealing parts off of one to get another running in what I saw as an ultimate, unwinnable game of whack-a-mole.

When it came time for me to actually buy a car – using the money I had saved from years of baling hay in the summer, picking corn in the spring, or chopping wood in the winter – my stepdad was shocked when I didn't take one of the Fords but instead went out and spent my good, hard-earned money on a "piece of shit Chevy" as he would say, often. My stepdad and I didn't see eye to eye on much. He was only ten years older than me, so our relationship was more like siblings than father and son. We would always fight, sometimes physically, and created a lot of tension in the house. I loved my stepdad – still do, to this day. He is a good guy, but we didn't quite understand each other.

The one area of passion that we did share was cars. Even though I had gone to the dark side, my stepdad appreciated the fact that I wanted a muscle car and not one of those foreign "pieces of shit" (those would come later too). That would have been worse. He also appreciated the fact that I wanted to do most of my own work or at least try to. That being said, the criticism was constant. And the "black beauty" didn't help at all. Every time she broke down or left me stranded (and she did that a lot), my stepdad would snicker and say things like, "Yeah, you wouldn't catch me dead driving that thing," or "I've never had a car that left me hangin' like that car does to you," which of course was a total lie. He had been stranded by his precious Fords many, many times. Every time, he'd beat the shit out of the car (his temper was legendary), leaving it in even worse shape when he was done.

I had acquired the Camaro in the summer of '84, before my junior year. She was for sale, sitting on the side of the road in front of a large farm right up the road from where I lived. The car had been sitting out there a couple of years and, while I wasn't enamored at first, it kinda grew on me, much like the weeds that grew up around it. I would pass it while riding the school bus, which my mother drove. Every day I'd see it. Sitting there. All alone. The price started at two thousand or best offer but kept dropping steadily. And no wonder. It was a mess. It was black, at least on paper. The car was mostly primer grey. It had rally racing stripes so faded as to be barely visible, and the hideaway headlights made the front of the car look menacing (in a good way).

I had gotten my license earlier that year and was typically driving whatever car was running around the farm. I was tired of playing Russian roulette with the cars and needed something of my own. I was going to have to get a job soon, a real job that would require real transportation, and this might as well be it. I lived so far out that public transit was nonexistent. A car was the only way to get around. I had managed to save up eight hundred and fifty and, when I passed the Camaro one day and the price had changed to one thousand or best offer, I knew I could make that deal. That afternoon, I rode up on my bike (no Fords were running at the time) to buy the car. The old farmer took the eight-fifty with such speed that it probably should have set off alarm bells, but it didn't matter.

I had a car. *My* car. And I knew I could fix it up. My stepdad had an awesome set of tools.

I did manage to fix it up over time. At first, just enough to get it on the road and then bits and pieces over the years. I did a complete overhaul about ten years ago to get her back to the shape god intended. The car is pristine now and probably looks even better than when it came off the showroom floor in the spring of 1968, right around the time that I was entering this world myself.

I walk over to the work bench in my garage – a decent Craftsman rig but silver, not red – and put down my cup of tea. I bellow, "Hey, Siri, play my metal playlist." The first guitar riff from Accept's "Balls to the Wall" rips out of my garage speakers. I look over, throw up my metal horns, and exclaim, "Fuck, yeah!" I pop my head back under the hood and get to work.

A few hours later, I've finally won the battle of the alternator and am in the process of putting the car up on jacks in the rear so I can replace the back brake drums. As I start wrestling with the passenger-side rear drum, my iPhone starts to ring. It's in silent mode, like always, so it's vibrating on the top shelf of the tool chest in the back of the garage. It's making an awful racket – enough to be heard over the loud music. I stop what I'm doing, head over to the tool chest, and look at the phone dancing among the parts. My hands are covered in grease, so picking it up seems like a bad idea. The name that comes up is "Mike." The phone stops after three vibrations and then starts again. It rings a few times, then goes silent. I am trying to place the name. "Mike?" I think. "Hmm. Which Mike?" I knew a few Mikes.

I go back to working on the car. The house phone starts to ring...

and rings for a long time. It's very loud. I look up from the rear of the Camaro and strain to listen. I order Siri to stop the music, and "Lack of Communication" by Ratt comes to an abrupt end. I can now hear the house phone ringing clearly. I haven't heard that phone ring in months and have almost forgotten what it sounds like. I'm sure it's a telemarketer. They are the only ones who have called that phone in the last five years.

I walk over and wipe my hands on some shop towels and look down at my iPhone again. Three missed calls from someone named Mike. I wipe my hands a bit more rigorously (I know better than to go in the house, touching surfaces, full-on grease monkey – the wife would kill me) and head inside. The house phone, which had stopped, now starts ringing again, and this time I answer it. "Hello?"

I don't hear anything right away. Then I hear someone say, "Hey, Sean."

The voice is quiet, but I know in an instant which Mike it is – high school bud Mikey.

"What's up, brother?" I exclaim. "Long time no talk." Mikey's voice hasn't changed at all. Not at all.

Mikey lets out a sigh. "Uh, yeah. I know it has been a while."

Mikey is talking in a very somber tone, which is not like him – he's usually a ball of energy. I can sense that something is wrong. Very wrong.

Mikey continues, "Hey, so, I've got some news. It's Bob, man. He's uh... he passed away. Last night."

I don't know what to say, but I hear my voice responding. "Oh my god. Oh my god. What happened?"

Mikey sighs deeply but seems to regain his composure a bit. "He… he was… well, he was struggling. Not sure if you knew. It's always harder around the holidays for him, I think. I don't know. I thought he was doing better, but you know Bob. Hard to tell what's going on" – he stops and sighs heavily again – "what *was* going on inside that head of his."

I wonder why Mikey, rather than Bob's wife, is calling me with this news. But then it hits me. Bob and Mikey had stayed in our hometown and had stayed close – closer than the rest of us could. Hell, their houses are only about a half a mile from each other. Plus I imagine his wife is having a hard time – I can't imagine having to call all of Bob's friends and break this news.

His voice trails off a bit, and I manage to say, "Oh my god, I had no idea." Not that I would. I hadn't spoken to Bob in a few years. Not really. Of all my friends, Bob was the least social media–inclined of the bunch, so it was harder to keep in touch with him. People don't call each other anymore. It wasn't that he didn't have the aptitude – after all, he was an electrical engineer with a dual degree in computer science – but he did have a thing about privacy. Bob chimed in only sporadically on group texts and never had a Facebook account. He wasn't exactly a conspiracy theorist but close to it. "The man is always listening," he would say whenever we would get together. The group would laugh. Bob would laugh too. It was a joke, right? At least we always thought it was. The group text chat that had been going since the beginning of time had been pretty dormant for the last little while. I knew Bob had become a little more distant lately, but I just chalked it up to us growing older and being busy. But – suicide? "What the fuck, Bob?" I think and almost say out loud. Bob was the friendliest, most down-to-earth guy. Always had a smile on his face. "What the fuck?"

My mind is spinning, but I manage to jump back into the phone conversation. "Why didn't he call? Did he call Jak? Anybody?" I'm starting to get emotional and tear up a bit. I had known this guy since the sixth grade.

Mikey continues, "He didn't really want to tell anyone. You know how he is. Very private. He didn't tell Jak, but we ran into him and his wife at Panera. Bob and I were grabbing a quick lunch, and I think they could tell something was off. It was one of Bob's rough days and they asked if anything was wrong, you know, in that way."

My mind is still racing, all of these images of Bob swirling around. "Why didn't anyone call me?" I think. Not that I could have done anything from three thousand miles away, and I certainly wasn't a psychiatrist after all, but Bob was one of my best, and oldest, friends. I would've gotten on a plane in a heartbeat. I would've done anything if I had known that my friend was in pain. Hell, I would've camped out at his house for as long as it took. I would've crawled through fire for that guy.

I right myself a bit. "Ok... shit... I mean, we can catch a flight. We could be there tomorrow. Where is he? Does his family need anything?" My mind goes immediately to his wife and son.

"I don't think so. Everyone is pitching in, so they're good. As good as they can be." Mikey stops for a moment and takes a long, exaggerated breath. "It'll be good to see you guys. I'll text you the details for the viewing and the funeral and everything."

"Ok. I'll text you once we make travel arrangements. How's his wife doing? Hell, his son?"

"I talked to Ann. She says the kid's ok, but she doesn't sound good. It's been hard on him though, all of it. They were so close." He's quiet for a minute. "I think she wants you to say a few words at the funeral. Are you ok with that?"

"Of course. Whatever they need." I'm shaking.

"Well, I've gotta go. Text when you guys get in." Mikey hangs up the phone.

I stand there with the phone to my ear for a few seconds, stare at the receiver, and then slowly hang it up. I am still in shock. I sit down on my wife's new easy chair, unaware (or not thinking) of all the car grease that is being wiped against the new upholstery. My mind is swirling with memories. Lots of memories and a few regrets. Things I haven't thought about in years. Bob, my god. A good guitar player but a better human being. "The world needs more of those people, not
fewer," I think. "Fuck!"

My wife enters the kitchen with an armful of groceries, her phone snug between her shoulder and her ear, talking to one of her friends. "I told her that she should try that out before she plunks down money on it. I will never..." She stops as she sees me sitting in the chair and gives me a puzzled look. "Hey, I'm home and have to put these frozen things away before they melt. Let me call you back in a few. Ok. Got it. You too. Bye." She eyes me up and down and can tell I'm a bit dazed. "Car got the better of ya again? You know, you could always just take it to a real mechanic."

I look up at her with a weary smile. "Ha. It's not that. Mikey just called."

"Mikey?"

"You remember Mikey. From high school. The skinny kid."

"You were all skinny back then."

"Heh. That's true. The little guy who couldn't sit still."

"Ahh, that Mikey." Recognition dawns on her face. "What did he want?"

"He called to say... hmm... He called to tell me, I mean us, that Bob is... well, he's..." I take a long, deep breath. "He's gone."

"Gone where?"

I give her a slight smile. "He's gone from this earth, as in he's passed away." A tear starts to stream down my cheek.

"Oh my god! What happened? How?"

"Apparently he's been struggling. Had been for a while. I had no idea. I just don't get it. He's got a great family. Had a great job, a house. Everything. I just don't fucking get it."

"Depression is a hell of a thing. Doesn't matter what you have, when it gets a hold of you..." She pauses for a bit. "He never said anything?"

"You know Bob. He's never been a sharer of feelings. Plus, we haven't talked a lot since we moved. It's hard being three thousand miles away. Everyone has their lives and we're all so busy. We don't think about these things. On top of all that, he doesn't do Facebook."

She finally puts down the bag of groceries. "What are you gonna do?"

"Gotta go look into flights. See if we can get back there tonight. Although that's gonna be tough. Worst case, tomorrow."

I get up slowly and move through the living room. I sigh a deep sigh and look up at a couple of photos midway up on the built-in shelf. The first photo is of a group of long-haired kids. Metal kids. I pull the photo down and stare at it for a long while. I put the photo back and head into my office. I get on the ol' computer and start looking at flights.

I emerge from my office an hour later with a photo album. I attempt to sit down on the couch, but my wife stops me in my tracks. "You better go clean up first. Dinner is just about ready."

I drop the photo album on the couch. "Whatcha makin'?"

"BLT salad. Go get cleaned up."

"Yes, ma'am."

I head upstairs and get undressed. I get in the shower, lower my head, and let the water run over and around me. I spend a long, long time under the hot water. Much longer than usual. I need it – after all, I am filthy from working on the car – but that isn't why I can't get out. I can't stop thinking about Bob. About the music we played and the things we did. I haven't thought about these things in years, at least not in more than a passing way, but now it is hitting me like a… a two-ton… heavy thing. I can't escape it. Me, Bob, Jak, Mike, and Ron. The whole crew. We had really done some extraordinary things and didn't realize it at the time, not really. Thinking back on it now, I can't help but wonder, "How in the hell did we pull that shit off? What the fuck were we thinking?" I start laughing.

I slowly emerge from the shower. The entire bathroom is filled with steam, and I can't see anything. I grab a towel and dry myself off, wrap the towel around my waist, and walk to the sink. I take my hand and wipe the condensation from the mirror. For a second

I can see my face in it – my old, grizzled, fifty-year-old face with my full-on, grey 'winter beard.' I've grown this beard for the last ten years or so, when it got cold. It is fifty-five degrees today, cold by Northern California standards. I think how useful the beard will be when I head back to Maryland, where the temperature is sure to be much colder. I'm not looking forward to that. I never do. Even when I travel East for work, which is quite often. Usually I know that at least I'll be back to seventy and sunny by the weekend. But this time, I'm not sure how long we'll be gone. Maybe we could head back by Saturday, Sunday at the latest. I booked us on Southwest, who doesn't treat you like a terrorist if you buy a one-way ticket.

I find myself staring at a fogged-up mirror again, and again I wipe my hand slowly across the glass to reveal my face. This time, it is my 1985 face. The wrinkles have faded ,and my unmanageably long, curly dark hair trails over my shoulders. This is how I looked when Bob and I, along with a group of ragtag misfits, were about to take on the world, or at least our little corner of it.

I can't stop thinking about it.

I finally manage to get dressed and head back downstairs. I sit down at the table just as my wife brings out the salad. I've been upstairs for a lot longer than I expected.

She tries to make small talk, but she can tell that the news is weighing heavy on me. "The kids are coming over this weekend. Do you think we'll be in Maryland long?"

"Not sure. Depends on how things go, I guess. Should be a quick turn, I think."

"Did you book flights?"

"I did. First flight out of Oakland. Seven a.m. Direct into BWI, so we'll be home – er, back in Fredneck – late afternoon."

"Ok. I've got an appointment tomorrow I need to cancel. I'll also need to schedule a pet sitter."

We both start eating, for the most part in silence.

After we finish, we clean up and then retire to the living room. I pick up the photo album I left on the couch and start looking through it. My wife sits down next to me and rubs my head. I start to smile as I turn the pages and look at the photos. Most of them are band shots – some from live shows, some goofing around in a graveyard, some up against a brick wall (very '80s metal poses). I stop at a faded picture of me as a very small child, probably two or three, holding a wooden bed knob in my hand, singing into it.

"Ha. My mom took this pic."

"Always the performer," she says as she smiles.

"Or noise maker. Either one?" I shoot her a slight smile back.

I move on to a picture of a skinny white guy with a tiny 'fro, holding a funny-looking blue guitar. He barely fills out his 'skintight' spandex. "Bob." I tear up as I start laughing.

"What a fucking goof. A boy and his Kramer. I remember when he got that guitar. He thought it was the coolest thing."

My wife looks over at the picture and starts to smile. "I remember that picture. And the hair! Wow! Who did that to him?"

I chuckle a bit. "Oh, yeah. The hair." In the picture, Bob is sporting quite the Bob Ross perm. "We gave him so much shit for that. So much shit."

"That guitar is pretty though." She tilts her head to look closer.

"Pretty obnoxious, really. He got it about the same time he got that ridiculous perm. He had camped out all night in front of this music store. I think it was called Venemans? Vermins? Something like that. Anyway, they had this sale every year where they would have their prices so low that every broke-ass musician would come from miles around and camp out, overnight, for a chance to get inside the next day and get a good deal on whatever equipment they needed. We bought so much junk at those sales." I shake my head. "Bob thought that guitar – a Kramer Voyager, maybe – was the best thing in the world. I don't even remember if he went there to get that or if he just happened upon it while the madness was swirling around. That place got crazy."

"How did you guys meet? I don't think I ever heard you talk about that." She moves over to pet the comatose dog at her feet.

I continue to laugh as my eyes well up with tears. "Hmm, you know… I dunno." I pause for a moment. "He was just always there. I think it was sixth grade. In middle school, we were always just around each other. We had lots of classes together, but I think the first time we talked was at a Coke break in the sixth grade."

In the '80s, in our middle school, we did this Coke break thing, and it was a big deal. Every class had a designated thirty minutes to have a Coke and a reprieve from class. It was also another thing that got held over our heads. If you got suspended from Coke break, that was a big fucking deal. Even though you could only buy one Coke (for a quarter, of course) and it was only an eight-ounce bottle, we waited all week for Coke break. It was a chance to have a Coke, sure, but it was also a chance to sit down, almost like elementary school recess, with your peers and shoot the shit. It was long enough to talk about D&D campaigns and strategies, sports or, more likely, the girls. We were just starting to notice the girls and their, ahem, attributes. These days, every school in the country has a wall of vending machines and anyone with a dollar can buy a Coke. Back then, it was special. It was an event.

"He and I were also in the band together in middle school. We both played sax. I think he played tenor and I played alto. His sax was 'bigger' – that's all I remember, and he never let me forget it. He was a scrappy kid with short hair and matching outfits. I think it was Garanimals or some shit. We'd rock out to 'Jingle Bells' and 'Ode to Joy.' The same shit most middle schoolers play. But I always wanted to start a rock band, so when I got to high school, I decided the school band was not for me and I quit that scene. I was always trying to get a rock band off the ground. I'd ask anyone who would listen if they wanted to join. Bob was always a good listener. He had wanted to play guitar, but his parents were pretty conservative and wanted him in the marching band instead. He worked out a deal where he could do both as long as he kept his grades up."

I turn the page and let out a deep sigh. "Even in middle school, we used to make up band names and make flyers to try and recruit people into the 'band.' It was so goofy. We'd sit in Ms. Shelley's music class and fuck with the recorders, playing 'Highway to Hell' from AC/DC or 'Iron Man' from Black Sabbath. She hated us – most of the time. On Fridays, she'd let the kids bring in records to play. Bob and I almost never got our records chosen. You can imagine why."

"Yes, I can," she says slyly.

"Back then, there were probably four or five people in that school that could even carry a tune. Nobody, I mean nobody, played or even listened to rock. Bob was different. He liked all the bands that I liked. Rush, Kiss, Van Halen. Especially Van Halen. He had just started to play the guitar, so we really didn't have a working band for a few years, but we pretended we did and it didn't stop him from trying to play 'Eruption' – on an acoustic guitar. With nylon strings." I break into a wide smile. "Our 'band' had, like, ten members. Everyone wanted to be in the 'band.' We'd meet at recess and discuss band things, but there was no band, not really. It was more of a social club. But I really wanted it. Badly. I just wanted to play… For as long as I can remember. Bob was a good sport and he was up for anything."

I continue to flip through the photo album and land on a very faded Polaroid of me and Bob sitting in front of an Apple II computer in the school guidance office. Me in my jean jacket, jeans, and my messy hair. It was a middle period where the Jewfro was trying to figure itself out. Bob was in his matching blue Garanimals shirt and powder blue jeans with his short, scraggly hair sticking up all over the place. We were typical middle school dorks.

"Ha, look at this one," I blurt out. "He and I also got to get out of our last period class on Tuesdays and Thursdays to go to the guidance office to do data entry. We were the only ones interested in the computer, and we were so bored. I was usually getting into trouble, so they'd pull us out of class and we'd tinker for about an hour. It took us about ten minutes to enter the data – we fucked off the rest of the time, mostly playing games. We did, however, always keep our eye out for the master grades password – you know, like *WarGames*? But our school wasn't nearly that sophisticated."

"Oh, I remember." My wife looks at me with a melancholy sadness. "You need anything?" she asks softly.

Not looking up from the album, I respond, "No. I'm good. Thanks."

I stop on yet another piece of memorabilia. A flyer. *The* flyer for *the* event that defined my childhood. At least my high school years. The flyer is for a rock show at our high school. An event to raise money for the prom committee that our motley crew was somehow able to pull off. While it felt like magic at the time, now, some thirty years or more later, it seems even more magical. More improbable. How many teenagers are ever able to do something like this?

"Man, we sure shook the pillars of heaven, didn't we, Wang?" I say as I close the photo album. I shut my eyes and let out a big sigh. I finally get up, with a creak in my fifty-year-old back. "It's late, and we have to get up super early in the morning." I reach my hand out to my wife. "You ready to head up?"

"Yeah, what time are we getting up?"

"Four or four thirty. Flight is at seven."

"Ugh, early. Ok. Better let the dogs out one last time. I'll meet you upstairs."

"I'll be up in a bit. I have to get a few thoughts down for what I'm gonna say at the funeral."

"Ok. Don't stay up late. You can always finish it on the plane."

"I'll come to bed soon," I say, knowing that I won't get much sleep tonight. My head is swimming, and I can't stop drifting back in time. Back to when I was young, poor, and full of hopes, dreams, and whatever it is that gives kids the ability to ignore any obstacle.

I hope that I will get to tell some Bob stories at the funeral.

Me and others. We all have good ones. Some (most) wouldn't be appropriate for a family audience, but I think it will be important not just to honor who he was but to lighten the mood a bit and let folks know that if Bob was going anywhere it was "up." He was a good guy.

I slip the flyer out of the photo album and carry it with me as I shuffle around and turn off most of the downstairs lights. The whole house goes dark. The only exception is the Christmas tree – still up even though it's February. It's a fake tree – the first one we've had in many years.

We had been doing so much travel and had just gotten back from Italy before the holidays, so it made sense to have a fake tree. Less worry about fires, dogs knocking it over, etc. The tree was pretty plain, by design, with simple bright white lights. We'd decided to only put on the handmade ornaments, the ones made by our kids and our grandkids. It's a nice tree for a fake. It looks kinda real from a distance, not like a pole with green pipe cleaners attached. The tree light also shines over the menorah that sits in front of it on a table. It's a visual representation of the schizophrenic religious situation in my household. A little of this, a little of that. It is all the same, basically, anyway.

I pass by the tree and into my office. "Hey, Siri, turn on the neon light," I say as I enter the room.

"Ok, got it!" she says.

A red glow takes over the room. The neon light is an arcade Atari sign from back in the day, which bathes the office in an eerie red glow reminiscent of an '80s arcade.

I sit down at my desk and drop the Prom Aid flyer right in

front of me. "Look at those fucking kids." I hit the spacebar on my keyboard. The screen lights up and asks for my password.

"Shit!"

I've forgotten to put on my Apple Watch. My password is twenty-eight characters long, with numbers and special characters (as it should be), but I'm going to have a hard time typing it in this light. I give it a shot. Third time's the charm! The screen brightens, competing with the red glow from the Atari sign.

"Machines have no conscience," I think although I'm not exactly sure why.

I fire up Safari and jump into a new Google doc page. I stare at it for a bit and then I type.

"A few words about my friend Bob…"

I stop. I stare at the screen for about a minute. It feels more like forever.

I continue typing. "1985. That was a good year. '85 into '86 was when the whole world exploded for a bunch of scrappy, long-haired kids. When we finally got to realize our dream and play a rock show. A *real* rock show."

I stop typing, and my eyes drop back down to the Prom Aid flyer sitting on my desk. I smile and manage to produce a little chuckle. "Look at those skinny-ass kids," I say quietly as I pick the flyer up and study it even closer. Our buddy Jer had made this flyer for our show. "If you're gonna play a big show, we have to have a professional flyer. We have to put this thing up all over our county," Jer would say to us constantly, usually waving his arms for effect. Jer was good like that. He sweated the details. He had made this flyer on his family's new Macintosh.

We had taken some band pictures in the town graveyard (of course we did – if you had a local graveyard, that's where all the metal bands were taking their band pictures!) and Jer had decided to use one of these shots for the flyer. In the picture, we all had our menacing 'metal faces' on and were posed to the hilt. We were showing off our newly acquired assortment of spandex and ripped-up T-shirts, some with logos (either bands or musical gear) and some without. My outfit was fairly monochromatic and consisted of black-and-white spandex, with alternating black leopard-print stripes, and a ripped black shirt over a ripped white shirt, both shirts procured from the girl I was dating at the time.

On the far right of the picture, our bass player, Mike, was wearing a pair of black-and-red-striped spandex that almost looked like a demonic barber pole and a Yngwie Malmsteen *Rising Force* T-shirt. Between Mike and I was Jak, one half of our twin guitar attack. He was wearing spandex with a blocky pattern of black and white, seemingly prison issue, and a Live Aid T-shirt peeking out from underneath a sleeveless jean jacket. To my immediate left in the picture was our drummer, Ron. He was a good-looking guy and he knew it. He managed to capture the androgyny of '80s hair metal perfectly. In the picture, he was wearing red snakeskin spandex with a slim red belt off kilter across his hips, a ripped-up black Zildjian T-shirt, a red bandana, and black gloves. That's how you knew he was the drummer – the gloves.

To Ron's left was the second half of our twin guitar attack, my buddy Bob. I sigh as I look at Bob's image intently. He looked so nervous. Bob was a great guitar player but was never fully comfortable with the whole putting-yourself-out-there-in-spandex thing.

And in spandex, you definitely put yourself out there. There was no mystery about what was going on in those things. Bob was wearing black-and-white leopard-print spandex and a sleeveless, ripped-up Triumph shirt. Triumph was his absolute favorite band. I remember being a little pissed at him when he brought his spandex to the "clothing reveal" practice before we did the photo shoot because my spandex were also leopard print. They weren't exactly the same, but they were close enough, and we were really trying to make sure that our outfits were unique. I guess that was too much to hope for in our little town. We all had to get our spandex at the same shop in the mall.

The top of the flyer had our band name, ONYX, in a big, computer-generated font. Below the picture were the details about the show. "One night only – High School Auditorium – February 28th, 1986." 1986 felt like so long ago. Around the edges of the flyer were 'celebrity' testimonials. These were all made up, of course, since no one had seen us play at that point, save for the people who would drop by our band practices – and none of them were celebrities. The handwritten testimonials said things like, "One of my favorite local metal bands" (attributed to the drummer from Wrathchild) and "One of the best up-and-coming local metal bands" (attributed to Brian Jack of Child's Play). To my knowledge, neither Wrathchild's drummer, Shannon Larkin, nor Brian Jack ever said these things.

I think it must have been Jak's idea to add these to the flyer. He was always the promoter. We did, however, have one testimonial that might have been real, by Andy from Lynx: "These guys kick ass!" Andy was a friend of the band, and a previous bandmate for most of us, but I'm still not sure if he ever said this either.

Sometimes you have to embellish when you are just starting out. Fake it till you make it.

"Whew, man. What a fucking wild ride." I drop the flyer back on the desk and stare straight ahead for what feels like forever.

All the memories keep flooding in…

2

HiGH SCHOOL

I woke up as the cassette player in my alarm clock whirred to life and Iron Maiden's "Rime of the Ancient Mariner" roared from the speakers. "Water, water everywhere and all the boards did shrink. Water, water everywhere, nor any drop to drink." Ugh. "I am not ready for this," I thought, staring at my ceiling.

I'd had a hard time falling asleep the night before. Partly because my mom insisted that I go to bed at 10 p.m. – after all, it was a school night. But I was seventeen years old. Who the hell was she to tell me when to go to bed? I was practically an adult. Practically. And partly because of the overall anticipation. The next day was the first day of my senior year. It was both terrifying and exciting.

During the summer, I stayed up and listened to music or played computer games well into the wee hours of the morning on many (most) nights. This was my only downtime. On this particular night before the big day, my brain was still buzzing and I needed to listen to some music to calm it down. I could never fall asleep when the music was playing – my brain would be carefully following every note, every word in a song – but it would relax me to the point where I could finally sleep and then I would turn off the music before succumbing. I was in bed by 10 p.m. but didn't drift off to dreamland until well after 1 a.m. I had made it through quite a few songs and landed on "Rime" as the piece that would send me to sleep. Halfway through, I was finally able to stop the tape and shut it all down. My brain, my body. Everything. I could finally let it all go. The next morning, however, it was not so easy to get moving.

My mom yelled up the stairs and broke me out of my morning trance. "Let's go! Get a move on. You're gonna be late."

She knew I wasn't moving because she didn't hear my feet hit the floor. My bedroom was directly over the kitchen, where she spent most of her time sitting at the table, chain-smoking Marlboro Reds. This was an important 'first day' for her too. My mom was a school bus driver. I was sure she was dreading yet another year of putting up with the dunderheads that graced the school's transportation system. She had been driving a school bus since I was in elementary school. I didn't know how she'd done it for so long.

"Ok. I'm up," I yelled back. I wasn't really vertical, but I was at least partially awake. It was just taking me a while to get moving. I was groggy. First day back into the school routine was going to be hard, even though I had gotten up early plenty of times during the summer to work the farm – feeding livestock, baling hay, picking sweet corn. It was a way to earn a little extra money since my real job, busboy at the Captain Hook Inn, didn't pay very well and I had lots of expenses.

I had a car habit and a computer habit to support, but more importantly a music habit. A *big* one. At the beginning of the summer, I had put a PA system on layaway at Music World. A Peavey XR-600B with two massive three-way speakers (they weren't really massive but seemed that way to me at the time) – a really professional setup. Earning the money for this setup was not easy, and one of the main reasons my summer blew by like the breeze. I ran from job to job, with the occasional band practice and extracurricular outing squeezed in. Oh, and also the occasional car breakdown event. You've never known despair until you've broken down on a back country road, in the middle of August in the Maryland heat. We didn't have cell phones back then, so you were walking with your thumb out, sometimes for hours. If I'd had to rely solely on my restaurant income, I would have been well into my thirties before I laid my hands on that PA.

Did I need that fine piece of equipment? Not really. The "band" was just a loose affiliation, and the rest of the group didn't seem very motivated to play out – or do anything for that matter, at least not anything beyond getting together in Bob's basement and fucking noodling on a couple of tunes and farting around with Atari or Dungeons & Dragons or whatever else distracted them. I was different. I knew from nearly the time I could walk and talk that I wanted to be a performer and I wanted to sing. I didn't know why at first, it was just a feeling, but as time wore on I gravitated toward being front and center – the frontman of a heavy metal band. I wanted to be David Lee Roth.

We didn't have cable at my ramshackle farmhouse, but my friends did, and Bob would record all the metal videos on his parents'

Montgomery Ward VCR. He had bought it for them for Christmas the year before, using his employee discount. His mom would record her "soaps," and his dad would record his fishing shows or whatever, but we only recorded metal videos. After band 'practice,' we'd sometimes drop down on his couch and watch Mötley Crüe's "Shout at the Devil" or Ratt's "Round and Round" or Van Halen's "Hot for Teacher" or Quiet Riot's "Metal Health," and I'd study their moves and play them over in my head. Sometimes I would stand up and act them out, as long as Bob's parents weren't home. Back then, the videos were creative and told stories – sometimes related to the songs, sometimes just a story the director wanted to tell – but either way they were entertaining and we got to see the band members in action during a time when we were too young, or too poor, to go see them play live. I was pretty good at the singing part too. Not great, but I could hold a tune and would sing along, at the top of my lungs in the Camaro with the likes of Bruce Dickinson and Geoff Tate. While I couldn't sing like them, trying to mimic them forced me outside my comfort zone and made me a better singer. Always pushing.

"The PA. I have to get the PA," I kept thinking. The PA was another forcing function for me. It wasn't just a collection of circuits encased in a wooden frame, wrapped in rubberized fabric, it was also a metaphor for my evolution into a performer. It would force me, and the band, to get off of our asses and get out and play shows – to get in front of people and perform. I wanted to perform more than anything, and the PA was a way to be heard, both figuratively and literally. Using my current setup, I couldn't be heard by myself, let alone by others. The PA would make all the difference. "Have to get the PA."

But, alas, today was about school. Finishing it up and getting the fuck out so I could live my dream. I had it in my head that I was going to move to LA the second I grabbed my diploma. The Camaro would be in the school parking lot, packed and ready to head west. The Sunset Strip was where it was all happening, and I had to get out there, had to be part of that scene. I was laser focused on getting a band together to play – that was the first step.

"*Must. Get. Up,*" rang inside my head. I had to get up. I had to prepare. When you go out to bale hay or pick corn or bus tables, you don't worry about your hair or your clothes. No one gives a shit what you look like in the farm fields or neck deep in dirty dishes, but at school? Everybody cared, but self-conscious me cared most of all. The way you looked on the first day would set the tone for the rest of the year. I wasn't ready for this.

As I was mentally preparing myself to get out of bed, I looked around at all my wall art. There was a blacklight poster of Van Halen's debut album and another from *Women and Children First*. My Twisted Sister poster wasn't even really a poster but a magazine pull-out with the creases still showing. Must have been from *Circus* or *Hit Parader* or some other metal rag. I had a few of these pull-outs plastered together as a collage on the far wall, featuring bands like Ratt, W.A.S.P., Mötley Crüe, Dokken, Y&T, all of the LA Strip bands as well as full representation from the European metal establishment – Judas Priest, Krokus, Accept, TNT, and Whitesnake.

The side wall and my ceiling were my homage to Iron Maiden.

They were my favorite. A *Number of the Beast* poster alongside a three-by-six-foot, spray painted Iron Maiden logo took up most of the wall, and there was an "Up the Irons!" poster directly above my bed. My friend Mikey and I painted the gigantic logo over the summer when he stayed over one night to get high and listen to music (a regular occurrence). My mom was soooo pissed when she saw it, which was very shocking to me. My mom was pretty forgiving when it came to my rebellion since she was kind of a rebel herself. She listened to Led Zeppelin, Frank Zappa, and Black Sabbath and was pretty open to the music I listened to, but apparently spray painting the bedroom wall was where she drew the line. She had asked me to cover it up, but frankly, the walls in my room were crap anyway so I told her I would get around to it… eventually. I never did.

"*Get up!*" my mom yelled as she banged the broom handle against the kitchen ceiling (my floor).

"Ok, ok! I'm up!" I yelled back. This time I was. I jumped out of bed and shuffled across the bedroom floor, heading to the bathroom to take a quick shower. It had to be quick. Real quick. Apparently we had the smallest hot water heater in the world. I would be lucky to get five minutes of hot water before it would turn ice cold, and I mean *ice cold* – being pumped from a natural underground spring. After my shower I hopped out, dried off, and stood in the front of the mirror. I wiped away the condensation to reveal a skinny kid with a mop of wet hair.

My hair was so curly that it looked six inches shorter than it really was when it was dry. I hated that. My hair also had a mind of its own. I had learned early on that there was nothing I could do with it or to it to make it comply. I just had to let it do its thing. At the end of junior year, my hair had been a mess. I was determined to grow it long (I was a metalhead, after all!) but it had decided it just wanted to grow up, not out, so my head looked like a dark brown Q-tip.

I had received a notice over the summer that I was to report to the school on August second to get my senior picture taken. Senior pictures were a big deal, and I wasn't going to show up with my hair looking the way it did, so I skipped it. I would rather have no picture than a picture where I looked like that, in perpetuity. The funny thing was, by the end of August, my hair had dropped under its own weight and finally qualified as long. Long hair was the goal, tall hair was not. At this point, my hair was looking like Marc Storace's from Krokus but even a little longer, which was awesome or at least the best that I could hope for.

As I stared in the mirror, making sure everything was as it should be, I noticed another funny thing. Apparently all those days in the fields baling hay had paid off. I had one hell of a tan going on. But shit, this didn't matter. I was a teenager, and all I saw were the flaws. I was too skinny. My nose was too big. I had a nice little pimple cluster breaking out near my nose. "Perfect," I thought, "and on the first day. Fuck!" The kids on the bus used to tease me about my nose all the time. It's amazing how those little teases can burrow their way into your mind and never let go. "Ugh, do I have to do this?" I thought.

I just wanted to go back to bed. After a few minutes of staring and then thinking that this would just have to do for the first day of senior year, I put on some deodorant, threw on my safe-for-school metal outfit, which consisted of ripped-up jeans, a ripped-up T-shirt, a jean jacket, and a pair of slip-on, black-and-white checkered Vans. I went flying down the stairs and into the foyer, ready to head out to school. My mother barked at me (morning ritual) as I tried to slip past the kitchen and get out the front door. "Are you riding with me today or are you driving?"

"Driving, of course." There was no way in hell I was gonna roll into school, on the first day of senior year, in a school bus. "Why would she even ask?" I thought. When I was little, having my mom driving the bus was pretty cool. As a teenager, it was basically the same as riding with your mom to school in her station wagon. So *not* cool.

"You better make sure that heap starts before I leave," she said with more than a little disdain for the car I held dear. "Otherwise you're gonna be stuck here. Your dad has left already and there will be no one to give you a ride."

"Stepdad," I thought to myself. I wouldn't ride with him anyway. I never did. I'd walk first. But today I had to drive. I had to pick up my friend Mikey. We had plans – our usual pre-school ritual, which was especially important on opening day. We would stop by the High's, get two dollars' worth of gas and two blue raspberry Slush Puppies for breakfast. Not the breakfast of champions, but something where a splash of rum wouldn't be easy to notice. We had to set the tone for this year. Our senior year.

"It'll be fine. I'm sure she'll start."

I wasn't sure. I wasn't sure at all. It was fifty-fifty with the old girl and less than that if it was raining. At least it wasn't raining. I walked outside, admiring the 1968 Camaro as I did every morning since I got it. The black parts (not nearly as many of them as there should have been) shimmered in the morning sun. The primer and patches of Bondo? Not so much. But it was a cool car. *My* cool car.

I ran my hand down the side, got in, and said a little prayer to myself, taking a deep breath as I turned the key. For a brief millisecond there was nothing, and then the motor started to turn over and sounded like a groundhog digging in the dirt until the engine fired up with a loud, almost guttural, grunt, launching a large cloud of black smoke behind it. "Whew," I thought, "she started. It's gonna be a good day."

I raced the Camaro down the long dirt driveway – it was about a quarter mile but seemed much longer thanks to the shitty condition it was in – and out onto the main road. I squealed the tires, not out of pure power but because they were, in fact, "bald as a baby's ass," as my stepdad would always say. I headed down the road to pick up my buddy Mikey.

Mikey was one of my closest friends, both in terms of hanging out and proximity. We both lived in the 'country,' about a mile apart. He was also a metalhead. The little guy was five foot nothing, weighing about hundred pounds soaking wet, but he was a good kid and up for just about any adventure. I believed even then there wasn't anyone else I would want to have next to me in a bar fight, and this belief would be confirmed in later years – several times. What Mikey lacked in stature he more than made up for with tenacity. In between all the work, keeping the jalopy running, and trying to finagle some band practices when and where possible, Mikey and I had managed a little mischief over the summer. We'd get together and go to parties or hang out at my house listening to music and getting high or drunk or whatever we could get into.

This morning, though, was going to be our inaugural senior year adventure. Mikey's dad liked rum, dark rum, and drank enough that he couldn't always remember when he finished off a bottle, so Mikey was known to lift a partially drunk bottle from time to time. He and I would sometimes find a way to consume this bottle, usually before school, in a very unorthodox way. Typically this would involve a large blue raspberry Slush Puppie from High's, which was the Mid-Atlantic version of a 7-Eleven but with much better food and frozen beverages. A Slush Puppy was kind of like a Slurpee, but the ice pieces were bigger, causing a much greater chance for brain freeze, and the flavors were more diverse. But we weren't looking for diversity. We were looking for blue raspberry. The shit would turn your entire mouth blue, tongue and all, and was pretty much a big blue flag to school administrators that these kids were up to no good. But we didn't care. It was quickly becoming a tradition. We had already been caught once the year before, but the blue raspberry mess was so overpowering that the vice principal, Mr. Holt, could not use the sniff test to determine, with any certainty, that alcohol had been consumed. Thank god they never had breathalyzers in high schools in the '80s. If they had, we would have been totally fucked.

I pulled the Camaro up in front of Mikey's house, where he was already standing outside waiting. He was looking around and clutching a gym bag, like a drug dealer. He had long hair and was wearing a black sweatshirt all covered up by a camo jacket and skinny jeans. (Skinny jeans didn't exist back then, but Mikey was skinny and was wearing jeans so, yeah, skinny jeans.) No, not suspicious at all.

Mikey opened the car door and jumped in. "Hey, man."

I shot back, "Yo, bro" – our usual morning greeting ritual.

"I've got it," he exclaimed.

"Hell, yeah! How much?"

"Enough. About half a bottle."

"Half of a fifth? Would that be a tenth?"

Mikey looked at me with a puzzled expression.

"Never mind," I said. "On to High's, my friend."

I took off down the main road. About ten minutes later, I pulled into a gas lane in front of the High's.

Mikey looked over at me. "You gettin' the goods?"

"No," I replied, "I'm getting the gas. You're gettin' the goods."

"Alright, alright. Can I borrow a buck fifty?"

"Shit. Dude, you know the drill. I gotta put two dollars in the Camaro. I have two dollars. I can't put fifty cents in the car. That won't get us anywhere. Hold on." I went rooting through the ashtray. I was never a smoker so it was only slightly grody from the previous owners. I pulled out a handful of coins. "Twenty-five, fifty, seventy-five, eighty-five, ninety-five, a dollar, a dollar twenty-five – that's what I've got."

"Ok. That should be enough."

"You said you needed a dollar fifty."

"Yeah. I have a few coins."

"Why do you need a dollar fifty anyway? The Slush Puppie is a dollar."

"You know, for incidentals."

"Incidentals. What the fuck, incidentals?"

"You know. Like gum and shit."

"Here." I handed Mikey the change. "Slush Puppie, por favor. Sans incidentals."

"Roger."

"Oh, and here." I handed Mikey two dollars. "Give them this for the gas. Gas, not gum. Not incidentals. Capiche?"

"Yeah, yeah. Gas. Gotcha."

Mikey headed into the store. I started pumping the gas, making very, very sure not to go over two dollars. All the petty cash was gone.

I pulled the Camaro up to the front of the store. Mikey came out holding the ginormous cup filled with blue raspberry Slush Puppie. He got in and we drove off.

I eased the Camaro into the school parking lot. I made sure to drive really, really slow, wanting to avoid any teacher entanglement. Teachers were known to police the parking lots in the morning, throughout the day, and in the afternoon, just looking for an excuse to bust you and take away your parking privileges – the kiss of death for us out-in-the-country kids. That would mean I would have to ride my mom's bus. Blech! It wasn't a large lot and seniors got priority. I'd had my license since the tenth grade but wasn't able to score a parking permit mainly because I didn't play sports and because I didn't kiss the principal's ass.

Our previous principal was a sports booster, and if you didn't play sports he would never remember your name, you got no privileges, *and* he would constantly harass you and ask you why you didn't play a sport. Any sport. Judging by his attire, the only sport he played was golf, and he musta been really worried about being hit by a ball because you could spot his pants from five miles away. Lime green. Bright pink. You name it, but it was always bright. He was most definitely not a child of the '60s, but he wore the colors. Luckily the new principal, who had just arrived my senior year, *was* a child of the '60s and "into the arts," as he would so often point out. He didn't care if anyone played sports. He was ok if you did, but it wasn't a prerequisite to be a teenager in his high school. But even with a more moderate in charge, the teachers would still prowl the parking lot, so I took it slow.

I parked the Camaro in the back of the lot, closest to the road. It was here that Mikey and I could mix our breakfast concoction of Slush Puppie and rum, away from prying eyes.. We dumped out a bit of the blue stuff and topped it off with Bacardi – everything a growing boy needs. Mikey stirred it up, and we both took big gulps.

Mike grabbed his head. "Argh."

"Too strong for you?"

"No. Brain freeze."

Brain freeze was no joke. And nearly every time you drank a Slush Puppie, you got it. Bad.

I laughed. "Slow down, cowboy."

"Can't. Gotta get going. Don't want to be late."

I took a swig and I myself felt the early effects of brain freeze. "Ok, let's go."

"Let's go? What do you mean 'let's go'? We get caught with this shit and it's my ass. We got lucky last time. Really lucky."

"It'll be fine. We'll finish up before we get to the end of the tennis court fence. There's a trash can right there."

Mikey looked down the fence line, about fifty yards, and scanned the parking lot to make sure no teachers were standing around. "Ok, let's go."

We both exited the car and started walking down the sidewalk, right down the fence line that went around the tennis courts. We drank and laughed, with a few brief brain freeze pauses in talk and in step. Once we got about halfway down, we saw a teacher emerging from between two parked cars.

"Oh, shit," Mikey exclaimed in a loud whisper. "Oh, shit. She's coming this way."

I saw her and grabbed the cup, mostly empty at this point, and smoothly placed it behind the front wheel of a beat-up, shit-brown Ford Bronco. I jumped back to Mikey's side before Ms. Mitchell could notice. "You boys better hurry up. First bell is about to ring."

"Oh, yes, ma'am. We're hurrying," I said.

Mikey and I picked up our pace and turned our heads so Ms. Mitchell couldn't see our blue lips, tongues, and teeth.

"Man, that was a close call," Mikey said nervously. "Whose car is that?"

"Hell if I know. But they're gonna get quite a surprise when they pull outta here this afternoon."

We both started laughing as we entered the school via the side door just as the first period bell rang.

A few hours later, coming out of third period and heading to lunch, my buddy Bob saw me walking down the hall and tried to flag me down. We usually ate lunch together – us two, Mikey, our friend Ron, and a few other rockers and outcasts.

"Hey, man! Wait up!" Bob called out as he exited his third period biology class. He caught up to me, a bit out of breath. "Do we have practice tonight?"

"It's Tuesday, isn't it?" I fired back.

"Uh, yeah... I think so." He thought hard. "Yeah, it is."

"It is. And, yes, we do."

"Ah, shit, I totally forgot, what with yesterday being Memorial Day and all. Shit! Shit. You know, I think I forgot to tell my parents… again. You know how they get. They like to have everything… boom, boom, boom." Bob made a karate motion, signifying that his parents were very by-the-book people and everything had to be documented in triplicate.

"Bob – first off, it was Labor Day, not Memorial Day," I said.

"Shit. Yeah, you're right. I always get those two confused."

"Second, we've been practicing at your house, on Tuesdays – most Tuesdays, hmm, well, *some* Tuesdays – all summer. I'm sure they know and, if not, they should."

Bob looked a little sheepish. "Yeah, you know how they get though. They need to know everything. Remember when they put lines on the Jack Daniel's bottles in permanent marker after they caught us drinking their booze? They think we're hoodlums."

I laughed. "They're not wrong."

We entered the cafeteria, and in this light Bob noticed a slight blue hue on my lips. "Speaking of which, looks like you and Mikey are up to no good – as usual."

I laughed again. "I have no idea what you're talking about."

We grabbed our lunches and sat down. Mikey, Ron, and Ricky were already at the table. Bob sat across from Mikey and looked inquisitively at his blue-tinged lips.

"Uh-huh," Bob said, shaking his head.

"'Uh-huh' what?" Mikey fired back and then smiled to show his bright blue teeth.

After school, Bob and I headed to the school parking lot, Bob toward his Toyota Corona, me toward the Camaro. Mikey ran after us. "Hey, man! Wait for me."

"No can do, rump ranger. Got practice tonight," I said.

"Shit. On the first day of school? Shit. Ok," Mikey said, sounding mildly disappointed.

"Practice waits for no man," I said, halfway joking.

He turned quickly and looked for anyone else he knew heading for their car. "Hey! Wait up!" he yelled after a girl that lived close enough to him that he could walk the rest of the way home.

Mikey went running after her. Nobody wanted to ride the bus. Ever.

3

LACK OF COMMUNICATION

THE CAMARO AND I screeched to a halt in front of Bob's house. Bob was right behind in his Toyota Corona. Bob and I rolled out of our cars, and there were a few folks sitting on the stoop waiting for us.

Our friend Todd was the first to greet us. "Geez, guys. Where have you been? We've been waiting for like ten minutes."

Todd was one of my oldest friends. We got our driver's licenses together and went on the same job interviews. We had applied to the same places, restaurants mostly, because we wanted to work together. Didn't work out that way. We ended up working at different restaurants on opposite sides of town. When I had put out the call for band members in middle school, Todd was one of the first to sign up and, to his credit, he actually got his parents to give him a drum set for his birthday one year. He'd been practicing and was pretty good.

Todd and the others – Ali, Harold, and Scott– had been hanging out for years in this particular housing development right down the road from the school. I had to come in from the country. Back in the old days, we would all congregate in Todd's or Bob's basement, not to *play* music but to stay up all night talking about it and, of course, to play video games or D&D. We spent many hours competing in Track and Field games on Atari VCS, beating the shit out of the controllers and then complaining because we had carpal tunnel syndrome before we even knew what that was.

Today was not about Atari. Today was about music.

Bob and I were the founding members of Lost Talent. Harold had conjured the name and it was a little too on the nose, but what we lacked in talent we made up for in comradery. It was a good group. A fun group. It was a group five years in the making, from the middle school recess area to Bob's basement. It took a long time to get here, and we had very little to show for it.

In addition to Todd on drums and me on vocals, Harold and Bob played guitar, and Ali played the trumpet (yes, trumpet). Scott didn't play anything but showed up for moral support and to hang out, along with the rest of the regular crew. Band practice was mostly a hangout with a little (very little) music thrown in for good measure.

Todd got behind his kit and started hitting the drums while the other kids set up their amps and plugged in. The basement became a noise factory. No one was playing the same song (they actually weren't playing any songs). Scott dropped his ass into a '70s-style, dull orange beanbag chair, where he remained for the entire practice.

I plugged my bright blue Radio Shack (of course that's where I got it!) special microphone into a shitty little Realistic speaker, turned it on, and tried to get the rest of them to shut up. I'd had this microphone for about a year. It wasn't fully professional grade, but it did have an XLR connection rather than a quarter-inch jack, which meant it could be ready for a bigger event if I needed it. I really wanted to upgrade to a Shure SM58 Beta but lacked the funds. The PA was my top priority. Didn't matter how good the mic was if no one could hear you.

I tried to get the group's attention and put an end to the cacophony of pain. "Alright. Alright. Stop. Stop. Stop! Did you guys work on the new song?"

Harold looked up from his Sears & Roebuck guitar. "What new song?"

I just shook my head. "The new song? 'Detroit Rock City,' you know? Kiss. We talked about this."

Kiss had been one of my favorite bands going all the way back to the third grade, when I'd landed on their *Destroyer* album as I was thumbing through a Columbia House promotion (ten records for a penny!). Back then, I chose records for a variety of reasons but mostly because of the covers. I'd never heard Kiss, but, man, the *Destroyer* cover was one of the coolest. I went on to join the Kiss Army and even dragged a Kiss lunchbox to school – in the third grade. I was obviously very popular with the elementary school teachers. I had acquired every Kiss record to this point mostly through begging sessions with my grandmother or as gifts. Most of my family didn't know what to think when they went to the store to procure these albums.

"Oh. I didn't know we were doing that this week." Harold shrugged it off.

Todd chimed in, "Yeah, me either. Let's work on what we got."

I dropped the mic with a big thump – not the first time I'd done this, evidenced by the fact that the microphone's mesh mouthpiece was beat to shit. "What we got? What we got? We know two songs. We know 'You Really Got Me' from Van Halen."

Scott looked up from his *Dungeon Master's Guide* he'd been reading since he plopped himself down into the beanbag. "The Kinks," he said.

"What?" I said, looking at him incredulously.

"That song is by the Kinks. Not Van Halen."

"Yeah, I know," I said, rolling my eyes in a very exaggerated fashion. "But we're doing the Van Halen version."

"Hell yeah we are!" Bob exclaimed excitedly and noodled a guitar riff to emphasize his point. He had been a big Eddie Van Halen fan ever since he really started to get serious about playing the guitar. And really, who wasn't in the '80s? Eddie represented the pinnacle of guitar-playing virtuosity.

Ali, who was sitting on a crate to the side of Bob, added, "Don't forget the second song is" – he made a drum roll sound and flailed his arms as if he was playing the drums – "'Raindrops Keep Falling on My Head.'"

"Yeah. 'Raindrops Keep Falling on My Head.'" My voice was a plate of disdain with a side of sarcasm. This was the only song that Ali knew on trumpet. So being the team players we were, we had all decided to learn it. "C'mon, guys. We want to be a real band. We want to eventually get out there and play a show," I implored. "We've been working on these two fucking songs for a fucking year."

"Well, yeah, but we've had SATs and we're all in AP classes and have tons of homework," Harold cried.

"I'm in some of those classes too, you know?" I shot back.

"Yeah, but you never do any homework," Ali said with a smirk. We all laughed. Including me.

"Well, yeah, that's true," I had to admit. "Alright. First song. Let's go."

The band muddled through the beginning of "You Really Got Me."

I started waving my arms. "Whoa, whoa. Stop." The band screeched to a halt like a car accident. "You guys gotta turn down. I can't hear myself."

"We can't turn down," Bob shot back. "This is rock and roll. You need to be louder. When are you getting the new PA?"

The new PA. The current bane of my existence. I'd had it on layaway at Music World for about a year, slowly (very slowly) paying it down.

"Shit, I dunno. Never? I still got four more payments on that thing. I was hoping to have it paid off by now, but who knew taxes would be such a bitch. Plus, I'm supposed to get tips at the Captain Hook Inn, but the waiters and waitresses are greedy bastards and keep it all."

"You mean 'bitches,'" Harold chimed in.

"Yes, *and* bitches. They won't share anything."

"Well, I don't know what to tell you. If I turn down any lower, you won't get to hear this baby growl." Bob rubbed the top of his knockoff Stratocaster. The band sighed and exaggeratedly turned down their amps. Ali pretended to turn down his trumpet.

The band started again with "You Really Got Me."

Just as we got going, Bob's mom yelled down the stairs. "Bobby! Bobby! Turn that rock and roll music down! I can't hear myself think."

The band stopped – again. Collectively sighed – again. And turned down the amps – yet again.

After running through both songs too many times, the band was out of music to play. The guys were independently noodling on their instruments, and it was just a wall of noise. Finally Scott spoke up. "Hey, you guys wanna play some D&D?"

We all looked at each other, and it was obvious we weren't going to get anything else done musically. Playing D&D after practice had become a kind of tradition.

"Sure. Why not," said Bob.

"Great. I just picked this up." Scott held up a D&D advanced module: *S1 - The Tomb of Horrors*.

"Shit, dude! I love *Tomb of Horrors*! One of my favorites," I blurted out.

Scott looked a little disappointed. "Oh, you know this one?"

"Yeah. I have it. I have S2 too. Waiting to get *S3 - Expedition to the Barrier Peaks*. It's got aliens and shit. Gary Gygax is the fucking man!"

"Good. I haven't read it yet, so that makes you the dungeon master."

"Sweet! You got it!" I was excited, even if we weren't doing what I came there to do – play music.

The guys put away their instruments and moved to the other side of the basement, around a card table that Bob had just put out.

"Hey, Bobby, you got anything to eat?" Harold said, making puppy eyes at Bob.

Bob rolled his eyes. "Yeah. Be right back."

After band practice, everyone started carrying their gear to their respective cars. Bob and I were sitting in the basement packing up the remaining things and winding up cables.

I dropped down on the big beanbag with a huge sigh. "Ugh. What are we gonna do?" I put my hands on my head, fingers interlocked. "We can't keep doing this. One year? Two songs? And one of those songs isn't even a good song. It isn't even a rock song. And as much as I love D&D, and you know I do, we gotta get the music going."

"Yeah, I know. Not sure what we're gonna do, but you have to get that PA outta layaway or we'll never be able to hear ya," Bob said sympathetically.

"I know, I know. Just gotta make a bit more cash. It ain't easy driving from where I live, to work, to school, here to practice, and back. Most of my money is going to gas and keeping that fucking car on the road."

"You need a more fuel-efficient car. Like my Corona." Bob started singing, "M-m-my Corona!" to the tune of the Knack's "My Sharona."

"And get rid of the Camaro?" I protested. "Never!"

We both laughed.

"Hey, you wanna go see *Purple Rain*?" I leaned over and put my microphone in its protective case.

"Again? Is it still playing?"

"Yeah, it's back in the theater. Some rerelease shit. Guess they wanna keep milkin' it. Plus it's two-dollar Tuesday, so it's a bargain."

"How many times have you seen that movie? Two? Three? That's all we did last summer."

"Four. But who's counting? It's a great movie."

"It is cool, but it's a school night."

"Oh, c'mon. Pretty please? I'll buy."

Bob gave me a little sly, sideways glance. "You just wanna go see that girl."

"No!" My face was turning a little red, I could feel it. "Pfft, no. I just want to see the movie."

This was true, but Bob was also right. The girl who worked at the movie theater was a legit babe – the prettiest girl I had seen around our little two-horse town. And while I did love to go see movies, I also didn't mind standing in line at the concession stand, where she worked, and staring at her. "C'mon, man, I'll buy."

"You just said it was cheap."

"I know. That's how I can buy. Oh wait. Umm… I actually don't have any cash," I said sheepishly. "You'll have to buy."

"Really?" Bob stared at me with the 'You're not going to let me get outta going, are you?' look. "Shit, ok. Let's go," he said, finally relenting.

We laughed and headed out to our cars.

"Oh, umm, hey. Can you drive? I only have enough gas for school and work this week."

"Sheesh. Ok. Fine," Bob said reluctantly, as we climbed into his babyshit-green Corona. "Hoodwinked again."

4

MAGIC POWER

"HERE WE ARE," Bob announced as we turned into the theater entrance of the mall and parked. We both got out of the car and walked toward the mall. It was unseasonably warm out. Maryland weather was a crapshoot, and tonight was full-on Indian summer. It was hard to believe it was September 3rd. As we entered the mall, we were hit with the stale, cool, conditioned air. You could tell that they had been getting all set up for winter when the Indian summer hit and had to reverse course. The windows were all fogged up, which was the first tell.

"It's fucking cold in here," Bob said, rubbing his arms. Neither one of us were dressed for the chill. We had prepared for the opposite, thinking the A/C would be off.

There wasn't much to do in our little country town. The mall, the skating rink, cruising 'the circuit,' and that was about it. Because of this we'd spend a lot of time in the mall. It had a decent selection of food options – Dairy Queen, Long John Silver's, Roy

Rogers, Pappy's Pizza, and Friendly's ice cream parlor – as well as lots of shopping. Most of my time was spent in the movie theater, the record store (Sam Goody), and the Radio Shack. The mall had big department stores on either end, a Montgomery Ward (where Bob worked) and a JC Penney. On the weekends, the mall would be teeming with people of all ages. In the evenings, on a school night, it was a different story.

Tonight, it was dead. We walked up to the movie theater ticket counter (no line) and bought our tickets. Or I should say Bob bought our tickets. Once we had our tickets in hand, we headed toward the concession stand.

"There she is," I blurted out in a half whisper from one side of my mouth while trying to subtly motion my head toward the counter.

"Yep, there she is," Bob replied, trying to match my whisper.

We approached the counter, and I could immediately feel my heart in my throat.

"What can I getcha guys?" the blonde behind the counter enquired.

She was wearing jeans, a brown-and-yellow smock top covered in what appeared to be popcorn butter (or whatever they put on the popcorn), and a tag with the name "Susan" on it.

"Susan," I thought. "So that's her name."

Bob and I stared at her for what seemed like an eternity – long enough anyway for her to notice we hadn't been able to answer.

"Hello? What can I get for you guys?" she said again.

"Uh, hmm," Bob sputtered and reached into his pocket and pulled out a handful of change covered in lint, with a few guitar picks mixed in. While Bob was fumbling and I was drooling, the blonde noticed the guitar picks in the change pile mounting in Bob's hand.

"Oh," she said, perking up, "are you guys musicians?"

"Uh, yeah. Yeah we are." I was finally able to get a few words out, but they sounded a little froggy.

"Oh, cool. Hold on a sec." The blonde grabbed a large empty tub, scooped it down into the popcorn, and plopped it in front of us. "One large popcorn."

Then, quick as a shot, she popped over to the fountain drink machine, filled two large cups with ice, and proceeded to top them off with Coca-Cola.

"Two large Cokes. What kind of candy do you boys like?"

Bob and I were dumbfounded. Bob kept looking back and forth between the pile of change in his hand and the mounting pile of refreshments with a look of horror on his face. The blonde gave us a very kind yet let's-move-this-along kind of look.

"Oh." Bob finally got the word "Raisinets" out of his mouth.

"Milk Duds for me," I added.

The blonde went to the display case and pulled out the two boxes of candy and plopped them on the counter next to the Cokes. "There you go."

"Umm… We don't have… uh… that much." Bob was nervously fumbling through his change pile. The blonde lifted one finger as if to tell us to hold on and went to the back of the counter and pulled out what looked like a very official form, along with a pen. She started writing on the pad. Bob and I looked at each other, wondering what the hell she was doing.

She finished writing in the notebook. "There you go."

"Umm." My heart was in my throat, but I managed a few words. "Yeah, that's cool and all, but we don't have the money to pay for this."

She shot me a bless-your-heart kinda look. "Hey. My boyfriend is a musician, so I know y'all spend most of your money on that. You see" – she waved her hands over the large concession pile before us – "all of these things are damaged. Anything that's damaged gets thrown away. We just have to keep track of it." She patted the notebook and shot us a wink. You could've knocked me over with a feather. "You guys better hurry or you're gonna miss your movie."

Boyfriend? My heart sank back down into my chest as the word penetrated my brain. Of course she had a boyfriend. A knockout like her had to have a boyfriend. Made sense. We thanked her and moved away as a young couple approached the counter. I could hear her voice, more and more distant as we walked into the actual theater. "What can I get you guys?"

Susan. I had a major crush on Susan. Susan with a boyfriend. Fuck.

We had missed the movie previews and sat down just as the opening song, "Let's Go Crazy," started over the title credits. The theater was empty. This was not much of a Prince town, and very few would venture out on a school night when the movie wasn't even a new release. As soon as I sat down, the hair on the back of my neck stood up, and it wasn't just due to the icebox we were sitting in. This movie did that to me. It was so powerful that I started singing along, much to Bob's dismay. I knew this movie like the back of my hand. Every word. Every scene. Every note. This movie about a poor kid, an outcast, trying to escape his reality using the only thing he had to give, his music, resonated with me. Deeply. This was what I wanted and the path I wanted to take. I was hoping against hope that I could use music as the vehicle to get the fuck outta there. To knock off the dust of this rural existence and head west to the land of the metalheads.

The fact that Prince was able to use his hometown, Minneapolis, as a backdrop was interesting to me. His world looked like an urban version of my world. A world full of less-than-sincere adults and people trying to crush your dreams. Even today, I watch this movie at least once a year, and every time I do I am transported to this time. To this dream. Yeah, I wanted to be David Lee Roth, but I also wanted to be Prince. If you could've wrapped those two together, that would've been my superhero.

I sang every song, including the Morris Day and the Time tunes, and by the end I was exhausted. Bob was always a good sport. I am sure there were many other things he wanted to do after the first day of school and the first practice, but he was a good partner.

After watching *Purple Rain* for the fifth time, I exited the movie theater with Bob, still talking about it – and about how I wanted a real band. Bob had heard this before, so many times. I wanted a band that could play real rock and roll songs. Like Prince. I loved the guys in Lost Talent, but to them it was just a hobby, a hangout. They weren't motivated, not like me. Not even like Bob.

We walked by the *Purple Rain* promotional poster. "That's what I want to do." I pointed. "I want to play. Play live in front of a crowd."

"You just want girls that look like that hanging all over you." Bob pointed to Apollonia in the poster.

I laughed. "Well, yeah, that too," I admitted. Sure, that's why guys get into rock bands, but it's not why we stay. We stay, ultimately, for the music.

This was the absolute truth. If fifty-year-old me were to add up all the money spent on this hobby, on this obsession, I would've been able to buy a second home, or a third home. In the end you don't really do it for the girls, and you certainly don't do it for the money. It is the love of music that eventually drives you. But in the beginning? Yeah, it's the chicks.

We walked through the mall a bit and stopped in front of the Radio Shack. Bob pointed to the computer in the window. "Hey, do you still have that TRS-80?"

"I do. But I just got an Atari 800. It's in color and I can cruise BBS and download sick games. I just got a floppy disk drive for it. Loads games sooooo much faster. Minutes not hours, my friend." We noticed a bunch of '80s new wave kids who sneered at us, so we kept walking.

We also saw a few long-haired guys. "Hey. How about those guys? Wonder if they can play an instrument? They look like rockers." Bob pointed to the group.

I laughed. "Ned? No way. That guy looks like a rocker but can't play a fucking chord. Trust me. I saw him trying to impress this girl in the music store a few weeks ago. He walked in with her on his arm. She was staring up at him like he was a Greek god. He grabbed this Les Paul off the wall, sat down, mere feet from me, and started strumming. He said something like 'I'm not that good,' and he sure wasn't. Dude was god-awful. I kinda felt bad for him. The shine was off. The girl made a face and walked out. Poor guy. But no, he can't play."

We walked further, down toward Sam Goody. My friends and I would spend long hours there, mostly looking since we rarely had money. Today was no exception, for me at least. We browsed around the aisles, looking at all the cool album art. Sometimes (most times) the album art would sell the record. This was the time before MTV, at least it was at my house. My house wouldn't get cable until the late 2010s, long after my family had moved away. Sometimes this was the only way to 'see' a band, even before you heard them. And most of the bands we listened to were not being played on popular radio stations. I moved down the aisle and landed on one such band – Iron Maiden.

I held up the *Killers* album, which featured the skeletal madman, Eddie, wielding a bloody hatchet in the gritty streets of London. "Now this is a rock band. Look at this cover."

Bob recoiled. "My mom would shit if she saw that."

"I know! That's the point," I said, with more than a tinge of satisfaction mixed with rebellion.

Rock and roll was rebellion, and heavy metal took this up to eleven. The music, when played loud, would scare any parent and make them believe that their kids were full-on devil worshipers. But it was the album covers, the art, that really made parents recoil in horror, while simultaneously attracting disaffected youth like moths to a flame. Iron Maiden was great for this. *Number of the Beast*, the follow-up to *Killers*, was even more gruesome, with its depiction of purgatory and the devil being puppeteered by none other than the skeletal madman himself. Metallica's *Ride the Lightning* featured an electric chair surrounded by a lightning storm. *Blizzard of Ozz* showed Ozzy in a church, about to smash a crucifix into the ground.

Twisted Sister's *Stay Hungry* featured Dee Snider in full transvestite mode, about to sink his large teeth into a severed limb. Was it human or was it bovine? We couldn't tell and didn't care. We ate it all up (no pun intended). These album covers were the gateway to our heavy metal experience.

Bob headed to the end of the alphabet, where he eventually landed on Triumph's *Allied Forces* record with its electric flying V on the cover. "Now this is my kinda rock record," he exclaimed, running his hand over the front cover. "The other Canadian trio."

I looked over at it. "Huh. Yeah. Looks cool."

We headed toward the cash register, Bob holding his latest vinyl acquisition. "You gonna buy something?"

"The PA, remember?" I said begrudgingly.

"Ah yeah, that's right."

"You can dub me a copy of that one though. I don't think I have any of their records."

"You will not be disappointed. I picked up *Never Surrender* over the summer. Didn't have this one and figured, eh, might as well get it."

While we were walking toward the counter, we saw a long-haired kid in the back stocking shelves. We gave him a look but didn't pay him too much mind. We got to the counter and Bob laid down the vinyl.

The manager of the store was a lady named Karen. She was in her forties but might as well have been sixty as far as we were concerned. She looked us up and down in the most inappropriate way as we stood at the counter.

"Hey, fellas. Love the hair." Karen made a hair-flipping motion to me, blew me a kiss, and winked. "You boys just hanging around the mall, eh?" Karen looked us over again.

"Yeah. Yeah, we are." Bob gulped, not sure what else to say.

"On a school night no less. Lucky me." She gave us a big smile full of teeth yellowed by cigarette tar. We scrunched up our faces in a serious did-you-see-that-shit? expression.

Karen rang Bob up and put the record in a bag. "Y'all come back now, ya hear?" she said, giving us another big smile.

"Uh-huh. Thanks," Bob said as we turned and walked away. As we walked out of the store Bob made a yuck face. "What the hell was that about?"

"Hell if I know. Crazy old stalker." I laughed.

Bob and I headed back toward the mall exit.

"Hey man, I almost forgot," Bob remarked as he jetted his finger into the air. "My sister said that they started doing an all-ages night at the Rabbit's Foot on Sundays."

"Sunday? A school night?"

"Yeah, but they end early. Like eleven or something. Could be pretty cool. They've been having some real rock bands play. You know, like Kix and Wrathchild. Some really good bands."

"Yeah? Cool. We should definitely check it out."

We headed out through the exit doors, into the darkness of the night, and climbed into Bob's Toyota. It had gotten a little bit brisk in the two hours we had been in the mall. "Fucking Maryland weather," I thought to myself. We could see our breath in the car as we waited for it to warm up.

"She's just about there," Bob said as the breath clouds finally started to disappear. "It was pretty cool of that girl to give us all of that free stuff, right?" Bob put the car in gear and backed out of the parking space. "What was her name?"

"Susan," I said dreamily.

"Awww... Someone's got a widdle crush." Bob started laughing.

"Fuck you. She's cute, that's all."

She was more than cute, and Bob was half right. I had a crush, but it wasn't a little one. I changed the subject because I could feel myself blushing and knew I would never be able to live that shit down. We continue discussing girls in general and our love lives in particular, which was a pretty short conversation since neither Bob nor I had a love life at the time.

Bob pulled the Corona into his driveway and shut off the engine. I hopped out and headed to my car. "Mañana, man."

"Yep, see you in the a.m.," Bob replied as he opened his front door. Just before the door closed, I heard Bob's mom yell, "Bobby Book, do you know what time it is?!"

I sat in my car, knowing full well I was gonna hear the same thing when I got home. After this year, I would be out. Outta that house. I loved my family, but it was time and I was getting antsy. I had a lot of plans that didn't involve cutting wood, picking corn, or baling hay. I couldn't wait to get off that farm.

5

FLAMING YOUTH

I HAD SURVIVED THE first couple of weeks of school relatively unscathed. My classes were alright. AP History, AP Lang & Comp, AP Chemistry – the rest were fuck-off classes (gym, art, etc.). I was hopeful that I could sail my way to graduation with minimal effort.

On Monday, I pulled the Camaro into the school parking lot and parked in my usual spot, toward the back of the lot, and cut the engine. I stretched, trying to get back into school mode after a weekend of nonstop work at the Captain Hook Inn and at the farm, finishing up the sweet corn season.

"Ugh, back to the grind," I exclaimed to Mikey, who was crushing some Pez candy in the front seat. "What the fuck are you doing?"

"I'm crushing Pez," Mikey said, his tone of voice asking, 'What the fuck do you think I'm doing?'

"I can see that. Why the fuck would you want to do that?"

"To snort it."

"To what? You say to snort it?"

"Yeah. Me and Bernie. In shop class. That class is fucking boring."

"Does it get you high?" I said, disbelieving.

"Eh. Nah. Mostly just burns and tickles your nose. But it's something to do."

"Good Christ. Ok."

Now before anyone gets the wrong idea here: Mikey was not and never had been a druggie, but when you grow up in the middle of nowhere, you get bored. And Mikey was more bored than most. He was always doing stupid and usually very funny shit like this.

Mikey changed the subject. "Hey, you going to detention today?"

"Detention? I don't have detention."

Mikey laughed. "Ha, yeah you do. Remember last Thursday? We nearly got caught with the blue stuff and Mr. Hopper said he knew we were up to no good and gave us detention anyway? Probably wanted to suspend us, that fucker, but didn't have enough just cause."

"Aww, shit. Fuck! Yeah. That bastard is always out to get us, man."

"Yeah he is," Mikey said with a grin.

I had been so busy over the weekend that I had forgotten about our little run-in with 'the management.' "Fuck. I have to work. Fuck! Shit! Fuck! I'll think of something."

We heard the first bell off in the distance.

"Shit!" we yelled at the exact same time. As we scrambled to get our shit together, Pez dust billowed all over the car. "Damn, dude!" I yelled as I wiped Pez dust off the dashboard. We both ran out of the car and down the long sidewalk. Right about then I was wishing we had parked a little bit closer. We were in full stride when Mikey shouted out, "I'll see ya in the library at 3:30, dude!"

I ran to my first period class, AP Language and Composition.

The teacher was not my biggest fan. I'd had her for English in the tenth grade. I never really did any homework (who has time for that?), but I managed to get decent grades, and this drove her crazy. Today, she was writing on the board as I came in and didn't even turn around. "Mr. Frazier. Maybe if you got a haircut you could hear the bell."

The second late bell rang. I pointed up to acknowledge the bell and made a face.

"I saw that," she said, still not turning around.

I mouthed "what the fuck" to Bob, who was smiling and shaking his head, and dropped into a seat next to him, panting. Not the first time that I'd made it into class by the skin of my teeth. I looked to my right and saw a pretty girl. I popped my brow. She looked at me and then looked away in disgust. I shrugged. "Oh well. At least she acknowledged me. Progress!" I thought. She was on the cheerleading squad and I, of course, knew her name, but I'm sure she couldn't pick me out of a police lineup.

The rest of the day was pretty typical – in other words, uneventful. We gathered at the lunch table as usual. It was "Pizza Monday," which meant that most of us had bought school lunch. The pizza was pretty terrible but, hey, it was still pizza – barely. I put down my tray where I always sat, next to Bob, across from Mikey and a couple of his friends. The only things on my tray were two rectangular slices of pizza (the cheese was barely melted; you could still see the unmelted chunks) and a chocolate milkshake.

"What, no vegetables?" Mikey snickered. "You only got two of the food groups there."

"Three. The pizza sauce. You know, tomatoes." We all laughed.

Mikey pulled a cassette tape case out of his pocket and motioned to me. It was the case for Metallica's *Ride the Lightning*. "Hey, notice anything missing?" he asked, opening up the case to reveal no tape inside.

"Yeah, so? It's in my car. You left it in there."

"Uh-huh. So you could listen to it. Not keep it."

"It's only been a week, you idgit." I smiled at Mikey, and he gave me a sly smile back. It wasn't the first time I had 'borrowed' a tape from Mikey for an extended period of time. Last year, Mikey had bought Mötley Crüe's *Too Fast for Love* and made the mistake of popping it into my cassette deck for an evening of cruising the circuit. Mikey never saw it again. It was the perfect record for cruising. Lots of upbeat, in-your-face music with a few slow parts where I could belt out the tunes with the windows rolled all the way down.

Well, on with the show
Going on with the show
Come on baby
No, no, no
Oh my, my, my
My, my, my

'The circuit,' as it was called, was just a bunch of teenagers and some older assholes driving their hot (and sometimes not so hot) rods around town in what was basically a large square of downtown roads. It started at the McDonald's on Route 40, where the kids would gather and spend their spare change on fries and milkshakes and then proceed to drive through downtown in a never-ending loop. They would hoot and holler and sometimes stop and try and pick up chicks or pick a fight, whatever they were into. It wasn't a highbrow event, but if you were young and lacking in funds, it was a great way to get your socializing in for very little coin. It was way cheaper than going to the movies, the arcade, or roller skating at Skate Haven, which were the only other things to do in our small town. If you had a car, the circuit was where you'd hang out. If you didn't, you did your circuit walking around the mall. With no money, there wasn't much else to do. Besides, you'd sometimes get lucky, either with a girl or with a kindred spirit. This could take the shape of another car nut or another music nut or just another nut that was into the same shit you were into.

Mikey, Bob, and I – sometimes with our other friends, – were known to spend many Saturdays engaging in this local ritual, but there always had to be a soundtrack. There was always music, at least for us. Music set the mood, always. We lived it and breathed it. Others brought their soundtracks too. Most of the cars blasted AC/DC, Black Sabbath, or Led Zeppelin. All legit bands. But we always brought something a little different to the party. For us it was Mötley Crüe, Van Halen, Ratt, Black 'N Blue, Iron Maiden, Queensrÿche, Rush – a crop of new bands, most from the LA strip, a few from the Pacific Northwest, and a few from Canada and the UK, basically all over. Depending on our mood or who we wanted to piss off or impress, we might play side one of *2112* in its entirety while enjoying all the other kids looking on and making faces as the song played out its highs and lows, culminating in the decidedly sci-fi climax:

Attention all Planets of the Solar Federation
Attention all Planets of the Solar Federation
Attention all Planets of the Solar Federation

We have assumed control
We have assumed control
We have assumed control

This was a real head-scratcher for most of the riffraff that spent the time cruising around in their pickup trucks or vintage muscle cars adorned with Confederate flags, or the old fucks in their Corvettes that cruised for young girls. Everyone hated these fuckers – you know, the perverts with money.

But with all the differences in musical tastes, there was one band that everyone held dear, and that was our hometown heroes, Kix. Kix had come up during the era of Aerosmith, AC/DC, and Led Zeppelin, while you could tell there were some influences there, they had a sound all their own. But the kicker was that they were from here, our town. Or at least very close by. Everyone, and I mean everyone, had the Kix records. The first two, *Kix* and *Cool Kids*, were the staples of the circuit scene. You couldn't make the round without hearing Steve Whiteman's ear-piercing "Cool Kids" ripping out of at least one vehicle. There were some Saturdays when all you heard was Kix.

While the first two records were amazing, combining the rock-and-roll sounds of their major influences, the third record, *Midnite Dynamite*, was a wholly different animal. When it came out, it changed the direction of the band but also put them in the same class as bands in the LA music scene. These guys could hold their own, and this album proved it. It also didn't hurt that you could run into these guys from time to time, since they were still very local. It wasn't a surprise to see the guys at the local carnivals during the summer or at the mall in the winter. They always wore their 'rock star' personas everywhere they went, but that was just fine. They were rock stars. At least the closest thing we had in our little town. It also didn't hurt that they were (and still are) one of the best live rock-and-roll bands out there. They could put on a show and the music didn't suffer. You couldn't say this about a lot of hair metal bands. Most of them, whether due to drugs, lack of talent, or lack of work ethic, sounded like shit live. Not these guys. They actually sounded better live, and that mattered. At least it did to us.

Of course, Mikey would eventually get that missing Metallica tape back. When he first put it in the Camaro's shitty Realistic cassette player early one morning and it launched into "Fight Fire with Fire," I was not a fan. I loved the guitar intro. Very satisfying. But when the first loud, fast guitar hit, I pinched up my face. "What the fuck is this shit? This sounds like four cats fighting in a garbage can." The fact is, I had never really heard anything like it.

"Give it a chance, man. You gotta give it, like, three or four listens," Mikey replied, almost offended.

"Three or four listens? I'll have a headache in two." I didn't like it all. I just didn't get it. Not at first. It was safe to say it was not love at first listen. But Mikey was right. When he left it (or forgot it) in my car, something happened. It didn't leave my cassette deck for three months. I couldn't stop listening to it. Songs like "Creeping Death" and "Ride the Lightning," not to mention "For Whom the Bell Tolls," were not only literary and smart (one of the reasons I was so drawn to Iron Maiden), but they were also brutal. Punch-you-in-the-fucking-face brutal, and I loved it. "For Whom the Bell Tolls" didn't even have a guitar solo. Who writes a metal song with no guitar solo? The truth is, it didn't need one. It was heavy and when played loud was oh, so satisfying. When I was in a particularly angry mood (and let's face it, what teenager isn't?), 'the circuit' would get the Metallica treatment. I never got so many stares and yells. No one was listening to it and nobody understood it – yet. But they would. It would just take time, like most things do. Eventually, Metallica, Megadeth, Anthrax, Testament, and Slayer would emanate from most vehicles on the circuit. It was a great time to be alive, musically.

At the end of the school day, Mikey and I had served our detention quietly and without incident. On the way out, Mikey saw his mom's station wagon parked right in front, with music blaring so loud you could make out every single word Vince Neil was screaming.

"Damn, dude, your mom sure does love Crüe," I said sarcastically.

"Ha. Not my mom. It's my bro. You can tell. His hair is longer."

"Yeah, I know. He's also uglier. Much uglier."

"True, true." Mikey laughed.

Mikey jumped in the car, and it tore off like a shot before he could even close the passenger door. His brother, Sam, had graduated a few years ahead of our group. He was also a metalhead and had the hair that we all envied – straight, jet-black, and reaching all the way down to his ass. You could always spot him riding around town, usually in his VW Rabbit, not in his mother's Caprice station wagon. He was the one with the metal music cranked, and at every stoplight all you could see was two hands beating on the dashboard and hair – nothing but hair, filling up the entirety of the driver's area. It was amazing.

As they sped away, I picked up my walking pace (why did I always park in the back of the fucking lot?). I was late – really late

– for work, and my boss was an asshole. This wasn't going to be a good shift.

6

WORKING MAN

I SCREECHED THE CAMARO into the Captain Hook Inn parking lot, found a spot around back, and snuck into the rear entrance. As I walked around a corner, I heard a loud, familiar voice – it was my jackwagon coworker Wesley. Wesley and I had never seen eye to eye on anything. Wesley was a good ol' boy who wasn't that good. He was a shitty waiter and an even shittier person. A week earlier, this shitheel got pissed off at me and, knowing my passenger door lock was, let's say, unreliable, dumped an entire can of food trash into my front passenger seat.

The car still stunk, even after two thorough cleanings and an added pine-scented air freshener. I had retaliated by taking small butter packets and smashing them on Wesley's windshield. The greasy little fuckers were hard to get off, and I knew it. In typical Wesley style, he then complained to our boss, Mr. Willis, who himself was a total douchebag. Mr. Willis had called me into his office and read me the latest riot act.

"You know I could fire you for this?" Mr. Willis fumed.

"Yes, sir," I'd responded, trying my best to sound respectful and contrite. "But you know, he started it, he—"

"I don't give a goddamn who started it. You pull that shit again and you're out of here. Get me?"

"Yes, sir," I'd replied sheepishly.

"Good. Now get to work."

Mr. Willis was pretty transparent about which side he landed on in this dispute. He had constantly heaped praise on Wesley for doing subpar work on just about everything he did. I wasn't sure, but I felt like they might be related. Mr. Willis even went so far as to say his actions were excused because he had a girlfriend and a baby on the way. "Who gives a shit?" I thought. I didn't care if he had a baby on the way. Besides, if he was that concerned about having a baby on the way, then maybe he should try to be less of a fuckup. I was pissed when that all went down, but I needed a job. I had to keep gas in the car, otherwise I would have to ride the bus and hitchhike to band practice, and I had a PA to pay off. I had to get that PA.

Today, I was just late. And Wesley was there to memorialize the occasion. Of course he was.

"You're late, cock-knocker."

"Yeah, I know, Wesley. You don't have to broadcast it to the world."

But it was too late. Mr. Willis had heard the whole thing. Wesley probably called him over before I even got there.

"Mr. Frazier. Come into my office."

I slunk into Mr. Willis's office. I had been through this before.

Many times. I figured I was gonna get his usual talking-to. That's what I thought.

"Close the door." Mr. Willis motioned toward his makeshift plywood door.

I closed the door.

"Have a seat." Mr. Willis pointed to a metal swivel chair in the corner of the office. I grabbed it and dragged it across the floor. Its rusty wheels squealed out in pain, as if they hadn't moved in years. I sat down.

"You know, we've had some trouble from you for some time now. Do you have anything to say for yourself?"

"What do you mean, 'trouble'?" I was fidgeting with my thumbnail. I tended to do this when I was nervous.

"Well, that incident last week with Wesley."

"You mean the one that he started? Which by the way, I have no idea why he did it or what it was about," I said defensively.

Mr. Willis shook his head. "We're not going to go through that again."

"You brought it up," I said, as my nervousness turned to anger.

I was more than a little pissed and more than a lot tired of this shit. I didn't really like working there anyway. It was a creepy old place with creepy old people. And the people who weren't old were just assholes. The waiters and waitresses never shared their tips, and they were always fucking up and doing dumb shit. If I had a dollar for every time I saw a server drop a hush puppy on the ground in the kitchen and then put it back on a plate, I would've been able to buy ten PAs. It was disgusting. I remembered my mom talking about how this place was the fanciest, nicest restaurant in the area back in the day. Well, it was shit now. The food was crap. It was dirty and old, and it smelled bad. Not only that, the place was haunted. Haunted as hell. Nobody liked to work after-hours cleanup. Not even Mr. Shoemaker, the ninety-year-old caretaker. Even he was scared of this place, and he wasn't scared of anything.

Mr. Willis continued, "Anyway, I don't think things are working out for you here. I think it would be best if we were to part company. Your insubordination, your constant tardiness—"

"Constant tardiness? I've been late twice." It had actually been three times, but who was counting?

"Regardless, I don't think you're a good fit here. You can pick up your final check from Ms. Doris. She's in the upstairs office."

Obviously he had been planning this if my check was ready to go. Probably since the 'trash incident.' The fact was that Wesley (or Weasel-y as he was known by just about everyone who worked with him) had been late dozens of times. Always excuses about his girlfriend or doctor appointments. Always different crap. "But no, he doesn't get fired. Prick," I thought to myself.

"We're done here," Mr. Willis said coldly as he put on his reading glasses and picked up a paper off of his desk, blocking his face from my view.

"Fine." I stood up, turned around, and headed out of Mr. Willis's office, closing the door behind me.

"*Fuck!*" I thought as I walked through the center of the restaurant. "What the fuck am I going to do now? I'm never going to get that PA!" My shoulders slumped more and more as I started to resign myself to the fact that this was going to put a serious wrench in my plans to play out. It was going to require me to get another job, which wasn't going to be easy. Us teenagers were competing with a lot of older folks for what we considered to be menial jobs, but the economy being what it was had forced those older folks downstream in the job market. It had taken me forever to find this one.

I plodded up the stairs of the main building and into the business office. Ms. Doris was sitting at her desk typing while the local radio station, Z104, was blaring out of a little desk radio to her right. They were talking about this year's bathtub races at Culler Lake.

Yes, the bathtub race was a real thing. It was the brainchild of local Z104 DJ Kemosabe Joe, a local on-air personality who was our town's wholesome answer to shock jocks Howard Stern (who was on DC101) and his heir apparent, the Greaseman. Once a year, in the fall, folks would show up at the downtown lake and try to practically will their bathtubs, built up with floatation equipment and decorations, across the lake before they sank. The prizes were Z104 T-shirts and mugs and other crap tchotchkes, but if you won, or came close – basically, if you didn't sink – you got your picture (decked-out bathtub and all) on the front page of the local paper. It was a town tradition.

As I approached Ms. Doris's desk, she looked up and, without saying a word, snatched an envelope from her desk drawer and handed it to me. I grabbed the envelope, muttered, "Thanks," and turned and walked out. She still didn't say anything. I heard the soothing, baritone voice of Kemosabe Joe fade as I ran down the stairs and out the back door.

I hopped in the Camaro and closed my eyes and took a series of deep breaths. "Ok, Sean. You'll figure this out," I said, trying to relax myself. It sucked getting fired but, hey, I didn't particularly like the job anyway, or the people for that matter. I opened my eyes and ripped open the envelope to reveal my final paycheck. I stared at it for quite a while.

"Hmm," I said, "this can't be right." I kept staring. The *Net Pay* field had a number a little north of five hundred dollars – $509.95, to be exact. "This can't be right," I said again.

Apparently the Captain Hook Inn paid in arrears. I had no idea what that meant at the time, but the thing I did know was that with this check and the money I had already saved, I had enough dough to get my PA outta layaway. After all, this was the only reason, at least the primary reason, I kept that shitty job in the first place.

"Woo hoo!!!" I yelled at the top of my lungs. "Baby's coming home today!" I threw the key into the ignition and turned it. Nothing.

"*Fuck!* Not today. Not today!" I slammed my hands against the steering wheel so hard that my glove box popped open and all kinds of shit fell out onto the floor. I could've cried. "Of all days, you pick this day to fuck me over." I was always negotiating with her. I sat there for quite a while. The sun was low in the sky; it was almost six o'clock, and I wasn't looking forward to going back into the restaurant and trying to find someone to give me a jump. I had to do something though. The bank closed at seven, Music World closed at eight o'clock on weekdays, and I couldn't wait another day to lay my hands on that PA.

I got out of the car and went back inside, taking great care to avoid Wesley and Mr. Willis. I didn't want to give them the satisfaction of knowing I was in trouble. They would've reveled in it. I was able to track down Mr. Shoemaker, the caretaker, and ask him if I could get a jump off of his F-150.

"You got any jumper cables?" he said in his sandpaper-y smoker's voice.

"Of course I do. This happens a lot," I said sheepishly.

"Alright then. Let's go."

We went outside, and Mr. Shoemaker gave me a jump. It took the car roughly five minute to get up enough juice, but she finally turned over and I was on my way. I arrived at the bank at ten till seven. Just under the wire. I left the car running in the parking lot so as not to chance a repeat performance of her not starting. I ran in, got my money, and squealed wheels outta there to head to Music World to liberate my PA.

7

WHERE EAGLES DARE

I PULLED UP OUTSIDE, jumped out of the Camaro, and headed into Music World, which was a small mom-and-pop shop run by a guy by the name of Reg. I was sure he had a last name, but to the local musicians he was just plain old Reg. Reg was a good guy. Tall, slightly balding on top, with long hair (always in a ponytail) running down his back. He was a deadhead right out of central casting and looked like he perpetually existed on a beach in Maui and simultaneously in the taping section at a Dead show in Red Rocks.

As I entered the store, the usual bell that announced visitors rang – an '80s version of the annoying alarm sensors that would fill retail stores for years to come.

"Hey, my man! What it be? Or should I say, what it is?" Reg called out from behind the front counter. This was usually where you'd find Reg. Standing behind his big black glass front counter, which acted as a showcase for his more expensive items (wireless mics, high-dollar recording gear, etc.) so he could keep an eye on them, and for local area musicians to sell their cassettes (and later CDs). Reg was a big fan and supporter of local music.

Reg's hippie vibe also belied the fact that he was a shrewd negotiator and businessman, though one with a big heart. He was a little spaced-out, but he was good to the local musician types and treated everyone with respect, even the longhairs. Especially the longhairs. This wasn't true of most adults, and all the hair-metal kids loved him for it.

I swaggered up to the counter. "Well. The day has finally arrived, my good man. I'm here to pick up my PA."

Reg slapped his hands on the counter glass. "Well alright, man. Far out. Let me get it for ya." Reg headed toward the back of the store and stopped to talk to a skinny kid wearing the musician's unofficial off-stage uniform: black T-shirt, jeans, and Chucks. He looked up from the drum kit he was putting together.

"Hey, Billy boy!" he said. "Go back there and grab that Peavey XR-600 with the two speakers. It's got a red tag on it that says 'Shawn.' S-H-A-W-N."

One of the other banes of my existence. For some reason, no one ever knew how to correctly spell my name. And when they saw my name they nearly always pronounced it "seen." I'm sure in bigger towns, people knew that S-E-A-N was Sean, but this was not a big town.

The skinny kid stood up straight and replied, "Ugh. Ok." He didn't seem too particularly thrilled to go load up this heavy PA system. Either that or he was a drummer and liked to put kits together better and mighta been in a groove. Billy slinked off to the back room, and Reg walked back up to the front of the store toward me. "Billy is gonna grab that for ya." Reg stepped behind the counter again and started filling out a sales pad, talking to himself.

"Alright. Alright. That PA amp is $399. Each speaker is $149." He grabbed a calculator and started tapping the keypad.

"That's $697. And then there's the tax. Gotta pay the man." Reg kept tapping on the calculator keypad. "Alrighty. Your total comes to $731.85 with tax, and with the hundred-dollar down payment subtracted" – *tap tap tap* on the calculator – "you owe me $631.85."

In the background, Billy brought the PA out, piece by piece. It was a heavy thing and he was struggling a bit. "Shit, dude! Use the hand truck," Reg barked out, pointing to the back room. Billy gave him an exaggerated shrug with his eyes bulged out as if to say, 'I don't know where the hand truck is.' Instinctively, Reg answered his shrug. "It's in the back. Near the door." Billy launched himself though the back room door.

I reached into my pocket and pulled out my red-checked Vans wallet and started slapping bills on the counter, counting them out. "One hundred, two hundred, three, four, five, six hundred. Twenty, forty. Here you go."

Reg took the money just as Billy finally found the hand truck and brought out the last speaker. Reg then ripped off the top page of the sales pad and handed it to me.

I walked over to the PA and rubbed my hand over the top of the head to the red tag that read 'HOLD for Shawn' and then down the side. "Finally," I said quietly. I didn't even mind that my name was spelled incorrectly. It was always spelled incorrectly.

Just then, Reg motioned to me. "You got the cables you need, man?"

"Uh. Doesn't it come with cables?" I stuttered.

Reg laughed. "Nah, man. That's how they get you. It's like razor blades, man."

"Shit. No. Sorry. I didn't know. Um, I don't have any money left."

This wasn't exactly true. I probably had some loose change in the Camaro. But I was pretty tapped out at this point. And I would still need to get gas.

Reg looked at me, then looked at Billy.

"Hey, Billy boy! Go grab two twenty-five-foot speaker cables. Quarter inch to quarter inch." He looked back at me. "You're gonna need a mic cable too, aren't ya?"

"No. I have the XLR to quarter inch I'm using now."

Reg gave me a dismissive look. "Nah, man. You gotta go XLR to XLR. Gotta get the fidelity, man. You gotta get the best outta this thing."

He yelled back to Billy, who was pulling cables off the wall, "Grab a twenty-five-foot XLR male to female while you're back there, buddy." Billy came back up and slapped the cables on top of the XR-600. I looked at the price tags. Each cable was twenty-five dollars. An extra seventy-five bucks!

"Reg, I don't have the money for these."

Reg waved his hand. "Pft. It's all good, man. You get me next time. You need the cables. The PA isn't any good without those."

This was why we local musicians loved him. He wasn't all about the money. His adult customers could afford to pay top dollar, but he knew us kids were flat busted most of the time and what little money we had we would spend in his shop. He also knew if these kids kept playing, they'd grow up to be musical adults who would spend even more money in his shop. If not for themselves, for their kids as the next generation started their own bands. Reg was in it for the long haul. He was special.

I got a little teary-eyed. "True. Thanks, Reg. I really appreciate that."

"Us musicians gotta stick together, man. It's a cold, hard world out there, and we need to rock it," Reg said with a chuckle. He was a businessman but also didn't mind poking 'the man' in the eye from time to time.

"Ha. Yes, we do," I replied.

Reg slapped the counter again. "Billy, help Sean get this fine gear into his car."

Billy dropped his shoulders and rolled his eyes again. "Ugh… ok."

This was Billy's typical response. He wasn't thrilled to do all this heavy lifting. He thought it would be cool to be a musician working in a music store. Not only that, but this was the only real music store in our town (Sears and Montgomery Ward didn't count even though they sold guitars). The only other music stores in the area were Veneman's or Chuck Levin's, both an hour away.

Billy piled the two speakers and the head on the hand truck and helped me load the whole mess into the trunk of the Camaro. It was a tight fit with all the junk that was already there, but I was determined. I had been waiting for this day for a long time, and the PA was finally in my possession. After stopping at High's to put the obligatory two dollars' worth of gas in the Camaro, I drove right to Bob's house to drop off the Peavey.

When I got there, I knocked on the door and Bob's dad answered.

"Oh. What do you want – it's late, isn't it?"

It wasn't, but Bob's dad always thought it was late. Or at least too late for Bob's musician friends to be visiting.

"Yes, sir, I know. Sorry, Mr. Book. Is Bob here?"

Bob's dad gave me a long sigh and looked me up and down. "I don't think so. I thought he was with you people?"

By 'you people,' he meant us longhairs. He would much prefer it if Bob hung out with the chess club or the marching band. Bob was, in fact, a part of both, but that wasn't where he spent most of his free time, much to his dad's dismay.

Bob's dad and I stood there for an awkward moment, until Bob's mom came into the foyer. "Oh hello, dear. Come on in, he's downstairs."

Bob's dad shot me a withering look and waved his hands as if to say, 'I didn't know he was here, but if I did, I still wouldn't tell you.'

Bob's mom moved to the basement door, opened it, and yelled down in a louder version of her very polite lady voice, "Bobby? One of your friends is here."

Bob clunked up the basement steps and came to the door. "Hey. What's up?"

I waited for Bob's parents to mosey on out of the foyer. "I got it!" My eyes were wide and lit like a fire.

"You got it? Holy shit!" Bob stopped himself and looked around sheepishly to make sure his parents didn't hear him say "shit." He started again with a whisper. "Holy shit! Where is it?"

"It's in the trunk." I motioned toward the Camaro. "Wanna help me bring it in?"

"Fuck yeah! Let me get my shoes on." This time he didn't worry about his parents hearing him and totally forgot to whisper. Bob threw on his Chucks and then proceeded to help me lug the PA into his basement.

Bob's parents looked on in horror as we carried the two large speakers down the stairs, *clunk, clunk, clunk* all the way down. Bob's mom turned to his dad and exclaimed, "Oh dear." Bob's dad just looked at her and headed back to the living room and straight to his liquor cabinet.

After we got it all down into the basement and set up, we stood there admiring it for what seemed like a very long time. Bob put his hands on his hips, a little out of breath from lugging this thing down the stairs. "This thing is sweet!"

"Yeah. It's got built-in reverb and everything. Six channels, three hundred watts. This thing is badass!"

Bob looked up at the ceiling and frowned. "How loud is it?"

"It's loud," I replied, shaking my head slowly up and down. "Oh yeah. Can we try it out?" I was anxious to plug it in to hear what it sounded like.

Bob looked a little scared. "Fuck no! Not tonight. I'm gonna get the third degree about this over dinner as it is. I need to break it to them gently."

Just at that moment, as if on cue, Bob's mom yelled down from the top of the stairs. "Bobby! Dinner!"

"Ok, Mom. Be up in a sec."

"Tell your friend it's time to go home."

"Ok, Mom," Bob replied in his 'geez, Mom' voice. He turned to me and smiled. "Apparently you have to go home, friend."

I flashed him a puzzled look. "'Your friend'? She doesn't know my name yet? I've only been coming here for, like, over a year."

"Oh, she knows who you are, but this rock-and-roll stuff is hitting them pretty hard. They love the marching band – not such fans of the rock-and-roll band."

I patted the top of the XR-600. "You think it's hard now." I smiled.

"We better be careful with that. Otherwise we'll be practicing at your house."

"Good luck with that," I laughed. "Unless you like playing on a dirt floor basement in an old farmhouse."

Bob chuckled. "No, I suppose not."

We both walked upstairs, and I headed home.

8

THIS BOY NEEDS TO ROCK

I STILL DIDN'T HAVE a job. So I drove around town for a bit, hitting all the standard establishments – mostly restaurants, plus a couple of spots in the mall. The mall would be ideal. For one, I spent a lot of my free time there and, two, Bob worked at Montgomery Ward in the far end of the mall. I figured we'd get to hang out and hatch our secret plans for world music domination. I had put in an application at Long John Silver's and Friendly's, and as I made my way down the mall, I noticed a help-wanted sign in the Radio Shack window. "Radio Shack. Of course," I said to myself. I spent a lot of time (and money) in this particular Radio Shack. Between my love for music and my love for computers, this place would be ideal, *plus* all the aforementioned benefits of being in the mall. Plus, plus... I wouldn't have to serve or clean up food. It would be a win-win-win!

I strolled over to the Radio Shack and walked inside. The annoying electronic bell rang and a fat, balding man, alerted to my presence, wandered slowly to the front of the store.

"Can I help you?" the man blurted out in a nasal, almost feminine voice.

"Um, yes, sir. I noticed you have a help-wanted sign in your window and I, uh… wanted to see if I could apply," I said, a bit more nervous than I expected.

The man looked me over in a very skeptical fashion. As he did, I in turn noticed that he was not only short and fat but also had dandruff to beat all hell. His shoulders looked like the bottom of a snow globe after everything had settled. "Do you have any retail experience?" the man asked.

"I do. I've worked in several establishments." By several I meant one. I'd only had one job. Although I'd been working on the farm for years, getting up at the ass crack of dawn to pick sweet corn and then selling it on the side of the road for the last several summers. That had to count for something.

"I've also got a lot of computer experience. I've got that one at home," I blurted out as I pointed to a TRS-80 Model III that was sitting on a little desk adjacent to the front counter area. "I do a fair amount of basic programming on that and another computer I have, an Atari 800."

The man looked really skeptical now. He was looking at a skinny kid with long, curly hair, wearing ripped jeans, checkered Vans, and a camo jacket. I didn't look like a retail-store-working, basic-programming type.

"Is that so?" the man said, and I could tell he wasn't buying the story. "Ok, show me." He pointed to the TRS-80 Model III and made a dramatic, sweeping gesture.

I sat down at the keyboard and bashed out a simple BASIC

program that cleared the screen and scrolled 'I love computers' diagonally across the screen in a repeating fashion. This took me all of two minutes. I stood up, feeling quite proud of myself. The man looked in amazement at the scrolling text. "I see. Please make it stop."

I hit the Esc key, and the program stopped to again show the seven lines of BASIC used to create the trick. The man huffed for a second and then turned and headed behind the counter and pulled out a sheet of paper. "Here. Fill this out." He handed me a job application. He then scrounged around in a drawer and pulled out a pen. "Here you go."

I filled out the form and handed it back. The man looked at me. A little softer this time but not much.

"You know, we've gotten a lot of interest. But we do have the holidays coming up soon. If it doesn't work out in the first round, maybe there is some seasonal work that would be available."

Shit! Seasonal work – the programming magic must not have been as impressive as I thought. I sighed. "Ok, whatever you could do. I would love to work here. And I really need a job."

"I'm sure," the man replied. "Have a blessed day."

"Oh shit!" I thought. Now I knew I wasn't gonna get the job. Short, fat, effeminate, and probably a Bible-thumper. Definitely a self-loather. He and I wouldn't see eye to eye on much. Oh well. Plenty of other places to apply.

On my way home, I stopped at a few other food service establishments to hedge my bets. First Pizza Hut, then the other usual spots. I hit McDonald's last, put in an application, and then grabbed a quick, cheap lunch – my usual, double cheeseburger and a filet-o-fish sandwich, fries, and a Coke. I was a growing boy, after all.

I was in no hurry to get home. My job prospects looked pretty slim, and I was feelin' a little down, so I made the decision to take the back roads through two adjacent planned-community neighborhoods that had popped up in the late '70s. As I did, I drove past a house with the garage door open and heard music barreling out from the open garage. At least, it was supposed to be music, but the guitar and the vocals sounded rough. Very rough.

I pulled the Camaro up to the curb in front of the house and stopped. I listened for a while, then hopped out of my car and approached the open garage. I was pretty sure they were playing the end of Ratt's "Lack of Communication." The singer was bad, and it was hard to fuck up Stephen Pearcy. Turned out the group was auditioning the singer, and it didn't seem like he was making the cut. He was god-awful. I made a quick assessment of the rest of the group.

The bass player was ok, as was the guitar player. But the drummer – the drummer was exceptional. The band stopped and talked a bit, giving the singer some words of encouragement. After a few minutes, the bass player acknowledged me standing in the garage opening. "Hey, man. I've seen you around school. Are you in a band?" he asked.

"Yeah… kinda. I mean, I'm kinda in a band but don't seem to really be going anywhere," I replied.

"What's your name?"

"Sean. You?"

"Hey, Sean. I'm Jeremy. My friends call me Jer." He pointed to the drummer. "This is Ron." He pointed to the guy sitting on a stool playing the guitar. "This is Andy." He then pointed to the short kid holding the mic. "And this is..."

The kid rolled his eyes. "Phil. My name is Phil."

"Phil, right. This is Phil."

I nodded to the group. "Nice to meet y'all."

"What do you play?" the guitar player asked me.

"I sing," I said, trying not to make eye contact with the kid holding the mic. He was visibly nervous and started squirming around a bit.

"You sing, huh?" the bass player said inquisitively. "Hey. You wanna sing one now?"

"Sure," I said. "I'm always game to jam."

"What do you know?"

"I know lots of things. Priest. Maiden. Mötley Crüe. You name it. I also know that song you were just doing."

At this point the drummer chimed in, "Well, alright! Let's do it!"

I replied, "Yep. Let's do it." I walked over to the mic and held out my hand to the short kid. "May I?"

The kid dropped the mic in my hand. "Sure, why not."

The band plowed through the Ratt song. Drums were on point, guitar and bass were ok. The vocals were decent. I knew this song cold. The bandmates looked at one another. Phil sulked out of the garage, got on his bike, and rode away.

The bass player turned to me. "Hey. You're pretty good. You looking to join a band?"

"Yeah, I guess. Me and this guitar player are trying to start one, but I think we could certainly join forces if y'all are up for it."

The other guitar player chimed in. "Other guitar player, huh? He any good?"

"Yeah, he's pretty good," I replied.

"Who's the other guitar player?" Jer asked.

"Bob. Bob Book. You know him?"

"Bobby! Yeah… a bit. Seen him around school. Cool. What are y'all doing tomorrow?" Jer seemed excited.

"Sunday?" I asked. "Not a damn thing. I'll call Bob and we'll come over. What time?"

"Noon."

"High noon it is," I said. "Ok. I have to run. We'll see you guys tomorrow." I headed out of the garage, hopped in the Camaro, and turned the key. Nothing. "Not again," I said under my breath. "This is fucking embarrassing."

The kids in the garage came out just as I was getting out of the car, cursing a blue streak.

"You ok?" Jer asked.

"Yeah, it does this sometimes. Can you give me a jump?"

"I'll go get my mom's keys." Jer ran into the house.

Ron walked over to the car and put his hands on his hips. "Hey! I've seen you around the mall with this heap before. Getting jumps. Ha!" Ron laughed hysterically, exaggeratedly slapping his thighs.

"Yeah, I know," I said, more than a little embarrassed.

Jer gave me a jump, and I was finally on my way.

The next day, Bob and I arrived at Jer's house separately. Andy, Jer, and Ron were all noodling around on their instruments. Bob dragged in his Peavey amp and set up. I did a bit of a warm-up. The group was all ready to jam on some tunes. We played "Lack of

Communication" and then jumped into a spirited, if loose, version of "Breaking the Law" by Judas Priest. The drummer fit perfectly, but the two guitar players didn't see eye to eye on much.

As the Priest tune rolled to an end, Andy turned to Bob. "Hey. On the verses, you're playing my part."

Bob looked up from his fretboard and locked eyes with Andy. "Uh, I think the verses are in unison."

"No, no… I'm pretty sure there's a harmony and you're not playing it right."

"Are you sure there's a harmony there?"

"Yep. I'm sure."

Bob shook his head. "Ok , if you say so. I don't know the song that well." The two guitar players seemed like they might not work well together, but Jer was a decent enough bass player.

After thirty minutes or so, Jer's mother came into the garage and yelled, "Jer, if you guys are gonna keep practicing here, you need to turn it down and you can't practice every gosh darn day. Sheesh. Besides" – she pointed out the garage door to the next-door neighbor's house – "Sissy is having conniptions. She's eight months pregnant and the vibration is driving her nuts!"

The band looked around at one another, and we all rolled our eyes. Another parent who couldn't stand this 'rock-and-roll rubbish.' Go figure.

We took a break, putting down our respective instruments (me, my microphone), and went inside. We headed to the living room and were just about to sit down when we heard a loud, high-pitched screeching voice bellowing from the other room, "You boys can't sit on those couches. Why don't you stay in the garage?"

This obviously wasn't going to work. "She's a nightmare," I thought to myself. Bob and I looked at each other like 'what the fuck?'. I realized maybe Bob's parents weren't so bad after all.

After an afternoon of noodling around on a few songs, we decided to call it a day. Jer's mom had given me a headache anyway.

"So? What do you guys think?" Jer asked as Bob and I were packing up our gear.

I looked at Bob with an unspoken, 'Yeah, this might as well happen.' He could sense my thoughts and he finally replied to Jer. "Yeah. It sounds cool. Are we in?"

"I guess so," Jer said. "Andy? Ron? What do you guys think?"

"Hell, yeah! It sounds great!" Ron was the first to reply, rather enthusiastically. This gave Bob and I a good feeling.

After a few moments of what must've been very careful consideration, Andy finally agreed as well. We had a band.

We all got together a few more times over the course of the next two weeks, but between Jer's overbearing mother, the tension between the two guitar players, and Jer's insistence that the band play radio hits, Bob and I realized that this wasn't going to be a long-term solution. Not in its current form. There had to be something else out there.

The drummer was a definite bright spot. A few practices in, I noticed another bright spot – the blonde. We were sitting in the garage listening to a Krokus song we wanted to learn ("Eat the Rich," of course) and this girl, *the* girl, showed up right in the middle. She walked straight back to Ron's kit and handed him a Gatorade.

"Thanks, babe." Ron snatched the sports drink and guzzled the whole thing in one gulp.

I knew her right away. It was the girl from the movie theater. She was wearing tight jeans ripped at the knees and a ripped-up Def Leppard shirt over a white undershirt. Simple, yet perfect.

She scanned the faces in the room. "Oh, hey," she said as she landed on my face.

"Uh… hey. Umm, hi, Susan." I felt pretty proud of myself for remembering her name.

"Susan?" Ron said, laughing. "This is my girlfriend, Lonnie."

"Oh shit," I thought. "You dumbass. Dumb, dumb, dumb." I was so embarrassed.

I cleared my throat. "Oh, I thought… when we met you at the theater, you had this name tag…" I pointed to my chest area nervously.

She laughed. "Ahh, I see. Well, I had forgotten my name tag at home and, well, we get in trouble for that sort of thing, so I had to borrow one from my friend Susan. My boss doesn't know any of our names, so it always works."

"You two know each other," Ron interjected in a very serious tone.

"Umm, yeah… Well, yeah, we've met. At the movies. I mean Bob and I…" I was sputtering and spitting, and I was sure my face was turning bright red.

"I'm just fucking with you. I know where she works." Ron turned to Lonnie. "Hey, I have something in my car for you." He got off his kit throne and came around and planted a big kiss on her lips, put his arm around her, and dragged her out of the garage.

"Well, that went well," I said to myself. I had never been more embarrassed. She'd said she was dating a musician. What were the odds that he would be in *my* band. This was going to be pure fucking torture.

Ron's girlfriend came to a bunch of rehearsals, and I was having a harder and harder time not staring at her. She was very nice and friendly, and I kept thinking that maybe there was something. Something between us. "Sean, you're an idiot. She isn't looking at you that way, she's just too nice to tell you to fuck off." I had this constant dialog, this battle in my mind. "Did she like me? Did she not like me?" I had no idea, but I knew she was off limits. I couldn't blow up this band for a girl and certainly not a girl dating the drummer. Dating Andy? Maybe.

Boy, did she look good. But it wasn't just the way she looked. There was more to this girl. She was funny and kind and smart. Smart as a whip, with a wicked sense of humor. I could tell right away she was special. I started noticing her around the school too. She had the reputation of being a little wild, but from what I could tell, she was just adventurous. She also knew her music. She was a fan of bands that I liked (like Def Leppard, of which she would've been considered a super fan) but also many other genres, like folk, country, blues, and '60s and '70s soft rock. She was also into photography and took all the artsy photo classes at school. She was by far the prettiest girl in school, but getting to know her in and around the practice house, I was definitely coming around to the fact that she was special. There were many occasions when she needed a ride home, and I would instantly volunteer. Or if I needed a ride home when the Camaro wouldn't start (which happened a lot) and I couldn't get a jump, she always returned the favor, both because we lived near each other and because the drummer's driving situation was always 'on restriction.' We had gotten to know each other on these long-ish drives, and it turned out she wasn't the wild, ditzy groupie chick that some people assumed she was.

It was reaching a point where I couldn't take my eyes off of her.

9

YOU CAN'T STOP ROCK AND ROLL

PRACTICES WITH THE NEW band were going pretty well, but Bob and I still hadn't let the Lost Talent gang know that we had moved on. The good news was that the rest of the guys were always so busy with schoolwork, they barely noticed. Knowing we couldn't keep the Lost Talent crew in the dark anymore, Bob and I called a band meeting. All the folks assembled on the front steps of Bob's house.

I presided over the meeting. "Hey, guys. So, I think you've all noticed that we haven't been practicing much lately, and—"

"Yeah, about that," Harold interrupted, "I'm not sure I can do this anymore. I mean, my grades aren't the best. I'm heads-down on the SATs – I just don't have the time."

Scott chimed in, "Yeah, me either."

Bob laughed out loud. "But you don't actually do anything."

"Well, I'm here, aren't I? Geez."

"Yeah, I'm kinda in the same boat," Ali said as he looked down at his feet, expecting to be chided by his fellow musicians and friends.

Now this was actually great news to Bob and I since we were feeling bad about dissolving the band. But still, we were a little bummed that the rest of the guys seemed to lack commitment.

The group sat in silence for a few seconds before I broke it down. "Fine. So basically you can all go fuck yourselves." The group looked astonished, then Todd started laughing. The rest of the group started laughing too, including Bob and I. They weren't really musicians, but these guys were very close friends and they weren't going to let one little band breakup blow that up.

"You know we're all gonna miss jamming," Harold said.

"Yeah, and we're really gonna miss playing 'Raindrops Keep Falling on My Fucking Head,'" Bob said with a smile.

We all laughed.

Scott threw his hands up. "Anyone up for some D&D?"

"Hell, yes." Todd stood up from the porch.

"Let's do this," I said, rather relieved that it had gone so well.

We all headed inside, slapping one another on the back. This group of guys had formed a tight bond in many areas. This bond would last for decades, and it continues to this day.

The new band had landed on the name "Exodus," not knowing at the time (hello, there was no internet) that this was Kirk Hammett's old band in San Francisco. Exodus practiced pretty regularly for the next few weeks, and we managed to learn a few songs. Unfortunately, the bass player and his mom were becoming too much to take. Jer had started dropping little hints that he wanted to be the lead singer, but he just wasn't that good and the rest of the guys knew it and would just ignore it when he talked about it. I was ok if he wanted to sing lead on a song or two – hell, that would give me a break to talk to chicks. But I had not realized that he wanted to be *the* lead singer, or that he wanted to change the musical direction of the band. Besides, his mother was driving the rest of us crazy. Constant refrains of "turn it down" and "you're too darn loud" and "those guys are eating me out of house and home" had left the band with a strong desire to get the fuck out of there.

At this point, though, there was no better place to go. Not at the moment. So we sucked it up and kept playing because at least we were playing. Maybe we hadn't made it out of the garage yet, but we would. I had the PA. We were getting really close to having the music to play an actual show. And even with all the shit we had to put up with, it was worth it. No pain, no gain. Eventually, the pain got to be too much and with tensions already running high, at the next practice Jer's mother decided to throw a match on the kindling.

She called him inside for the eleven millionth time. "Jer! Come in here pleaaaseee." Her drawn-out New Englander "please" was like nails down a chalkboard.

Bob yanked off his guitar, placed it in the stand, and sat down. "At this rate we are never gonna get a fucking thing done."

Ron was sitting back on his drum throne, twirling his sticks. "Yeah, she's getting worse. She yelled at me for coming in to get a glass of water. She clearly has issues."

It was getting late in the day anyway, and after what felt like thirty minutes going by without Jer coming back out to the garage (it was probably only ten, but teenage boys have zero patience), I flipped the power switch on the back of the XR-600 and started to roll up my cables. "I don't have time for this shit, I have to get to work."

I had just gotten the job at the Radio Shack in the mall. Turned out my BASIC magic did the trick and impressed Mr. Carter enough to get me the job. Mr. Carter was my new boss's name. Turned out computer skills were important and no one else knew how to do anything with them. They tried to sell the computers like they sold the phones or the remote-control cars, but they couldn't even answer any of the most basic (no pun intended) questions. I had only been at my job for an hour when I was able to prove my worth to Mr. Carter. A mom came in looking for a computer, and I was able to steer her to a TRS-80 color computer with all the accessories and answer all the 'programming' questions that her son was curious about. I was also able to upsell her on a home accounting package and knew how to set the whole thing up. The lady thought I was a frickin' genius. All this on my first day!

Today was only my second day, and I didn't want to be late, so I worked quickly to get my PA together and into the Camaro. Jer's mom didn't want any evidence of a band practicing in her garage, so she forced us guys to load in and out for every practice. This alone was reason enough to blow this joint. I hated carrying equipment. I was a singer, after all.

Once all my cables were wrapped up, Bob helped me load the PA into the Camaro (as he always did). I slammed the trunk, opened the passenger door, and snatched up my work clothes. I quickly threw on a button-down shirt with a tie dangling from the pocket.

Bob laughed. "Welcome to the mall madness. You gotta wear a tie. Ha!"

"Ugh. I know. Don't fucking remind me." I gave him a smile and quickly hopped around to the other side of the car, threw open the door, and jumped in. I said my typical prayer, turned the key, and it started. Whew.

"Yes!" I exclaimed as I pumped a fist. "Later 'gator."

"See ya!" Bob yelled back.

I was about to put the car in gear when I heard yelling. Ron was walking quickly out of the garage, waving his arms in the air. "Fuck this!" I heard him say before he ran across the street to his car.

"Where is everybody going?" was the last thing I heard coming out of Jer's mouth as I threw the Camaro into D and took off down the road. As I did, I looked back in my rearview to see Ron doing the same thing. Jer was standing in his driveway with his hands on his hips, and Bob had this 'oh shit' look on his face. I had no idea what just happened, but I didn't have time to find out. I was late as it was.

Later that evening, Bob walked into the Radio Shack wearing his work garb, which consisted of a pair of brown corduroys, a mustard-colored shirt, and a brown clip-on tie. He spied me, looking dapper in my grey woven tie, short-sleeve white shirt, cargo pants, grey leather shoes, and long-ass hair. We both laughed when we saw each other, at the absurdity of these outfits. Who would want to wear this shit? On purpose.

"So this is the new gig," Bob said with a grin on his face as he looked around. "Nice. Nice outfit, dude."

"Fuck off. I hate wearing this shit. I look like a creeper. You don't look much better, Mr. Mullet."

"Hey now. But yeah, you do."

"Do what?"

"Look like a creeper."

"They want me to tie my hair back. This ain't no food-service job. I look ridiculous with my hair tied back. The Jewfro was meant to flow."

"And flow it does." Bob laughed. "So… you want the good news or the bad news first?"

"Does it matter?" I was stocking the latest thing in technology: giant cellular telephones that were as big as bricks.

"It might. So, we don't have to deal with Jer's crazy-ass mom anymore."

"That is good news. I guess," I replied.

"Definitely good news. The bad news is we no longer have a bass player or a place to practice."

"Hmm. Figures. So did fancy pants quit?"

Bob burst into laughter. "Who you calling fancy pants, fancy pants?"

"Laugh it up, fuzzball. Seriously. I figured something happened. It didn't look too good as I was leaving."

"You don't know the half of it. When you left, all hell broke loose. He gave us an ultimatum, and we kinda told him to go fuck himself."

"Nice. Guess he wanted to do the singin', huh?" I said.

"Yeah. *His mom said so*," Bob replied, using his best baby voice. He started laughing again. I, of course, joined in.

"So, seriously," Bob continued, "what are we gonna do?"

"Same thing we always do, Bobby boy. Look for other musicians. Better musicians. I just wish half the kids around here who dress like metalheads could actually play a goddamn instrument."

"I hear ya. Hey, have you talked to that long-haired dude that works up at Sam Goody yet? I bet he can play. At least he really looks like it."

"Nah. That dude scares me. Have you seen his eyes? That's one intense motherfucker right there."

Bob threw up his hands, "Just thought I'd ask. We gotta do something."

"We'll figure something out. We always do." I sighed while staring down at a Radio Shack cellular telephone, which was as big as my whole head. Including the Jewfro.

10

ON WITH THE SHOW

THE EXODUS BAND MEMBERS had started to meet near the water fountains on the far side of the cafeteria every morning before the first bell. It was a way to catch up on with each other and just bullshit before classes started. We had also started wearing our outlandish band attire so that everybody in school knew we were in a band. The image was, in some cases, just as important as the music.

On this particular day, we were one short. Jer had decided that since he wasn't in the band, he didn't need to attend the morning band ritual. Ron rolled up last with Lonnie in tow, as per usual. This girl was starting to get the better of me. It was getting to the point that I was thinking about her a lot, and it was starting to interfere with my attitude toward the band. I couldn't help it. Every time she came around, my heart felt like it was gonna jump out of my chest. I was falling for this girl. Hard. But I also knew that this kind of band drama, while very common, was also the kiss of death for a band. Just look at John Lennon and Yoko Ono, or the blonde chick in *Spinal Tap*! I didn't want that to happen. Had to keep the old hormones in check. I knew it was hands-off, but I also got the sense that she was feeling something too, and that scared the shit out of me.

Ron was always the most boisterous in the morning. None of us could be considered morning people, but of all of us, Ron seemed the most 'awake' during our morning meetings and was also quick with a word or a joke or just a bust on someone or something. We all greeted him this morning as we had on so many mornings before. "Hey, Ron!" in unison.

"Hey, bitches!" he threw back with his patented machine-gun hand move.

"What's up, Ron? You look like the cat that ate the canary," Bob asked, suspiciously.

"Tell 'em. Tell 'em what you told me," Ron said as he poked his girlfriend in the side. It was playful, but you could sense she didn't like it – didn't like being poked and having this skinny, long-haired dude in her personal space, even if he was her boyfriend.

Lonnie turned back to the group. "Well… my parents are letting me have a Halloween party. And I asked them if I could have a band play… and, well, they said yes."

"They said yes!" Ron jumped in, completely overtaking the sharing of the good news. "You know what that means? We have a gig! A fucking gig!"

We all started smiling and high-fiving each other and arching our backs in a very prancy, peacock style. Now we not only looked the part, but we could *play* the part, and everyone in the school would know we were rockers. For real. We would be the rock stars of the school – finally.

Lonnie continued after Ron's testosterone-filled interruption: "I'm inviting everyone from school. Jenny's boyfriend is gonna buy the beer. He's older. A lot older. It's gonna be so much fun."

I was staring at her. I could feel myself staring at her. But I was always staring at her. And all I could muster was, "That's awesome! It'll be neat." Neat? *Neat?* Where the fuck did that come from? What an idiot.

Bob, practical as always, got right to business. "I guess we better figure out the music part. Practice at my house tomorrow. After school. My parents are going to be so pleased to have the band back in the basement." He smiled a bit, and the rest of us chuckled and waved our hands in a very 'oh, Bobby, you're so funny' kinda way.

The first bell rang and we all scattered. Bob and I started walking to our first period class. My favorite class of the day. Not really. Not even close. On the way, we discussed the elephant in the room. We had no bass player.

"We need a bass player." Bob stated the obvious as we walked.

"I know. I have an idea about that," I said as I was racking my brain on who might be a good fit.

I didn't know any good bass players, but I knew a pretty good guitar player who was already in the band – Andy. I also knew he wouldn't be thrilled to give up all the axe work to Bob, but he'd be better off playing bass. Bass has two fewer strings, and besides, what else was he gonna do? There were no other bands at the school. I just needed to find a bass guitar. It wouldn't be fair to demote Andy *and* make him buy a new axe. Luckily I had a line on one. Weeks ago, my good friend Harold (guitarist from Lost Talent) had told me that he had acquired a bass guitar. He was thinking about switching from guitar to bass, but as it turned out he didn't have time for either. It was your typical, wood-grained, Sears and Roebuck bass, but it would do the trick in a pinch. I just had to find out if he still had it and then figure out how to get it. I sat behind Harold in second period chemistry class. Perfect time to ask him.

I got to my second period class and plunked down in my seat right behind my good buddy Harold. My savior. As the teacher droned on and on about the quiz that I had neglected to study for, I knew this was my chance to get the goods.

"Psst." I put my face right behind Harold's head.

Harold didn't turn around.

"Psst. Psst." Louder this time. Harold stirred a bit.

"What do you want?" he whispered without turning around.

"Hey. Do you still have that bass guitar? The wood-grained one?"

"Yeah. Why?" Still not turned around.

"I need to borrow it."

By this time, the teacher had heard us whispering. It would have probably been quieter if we had actually talked in normal indoor voices, but we thought we were being stealthy. At least I did. The teacher turned around and glared at me. This was a look that I was quite used to.

"Mr. Frazier, is there something you'd like to share with the class?"

"Uh… no… Sorry, Ms. Harris."

Ms. Harris was a short, stocky, short-haired woman in a brown polyester pantsuit, which was kinda the uniform at this school.

Pantsuits, I mean. Most of the time she was cool, but she could turn on a dime and become a raving lunatic, so I knew better than to press her too hard. But I had to get the bass. It was a matter of life and death.

I whispered again, "I need to borrow it."

"You can't borrow it. But you can buy it. I'm not using it anyway and I could use the money."

I thought for a moment. "I haven't gotten my first check yet. I've got no m-o-n-e-y. No dinero. No coin."

Harold sat quietly for a moment. I was thinking he'd fallen asleep. That was the other thing Ms. Harris was good at. Putting people to sleep. After being in her class, I knew exactly where they got the voice for the teacher in the Charlie Brown cartoons. It had to be Ms. Harris. Finally, after what seemed like forever, Harold leaned a bit over his right shoulder, away from the teacher.

"You still have that extra floppy disk drive? You know, the one for your Atari 800?"

"Yeah?"

"Well, then. Let's make a deal. I'll trade you for it. Even steven."

By this time, Ms. Harris was getting really annoyed. Even though we were 'whispering,' we were still very loud. She walked over and stood over me with her arms crossed, a scowl on her face. I had seen this look before. Not fun. I didn't need another detention.

I slunk forward. "Ok. Even steven," I said and then popped back up straight in my chair with a big grin on my face. "Sorry, Ms. Harris. You may continue."

"Thank you for your permission, Mr. Frazier."

She smiled a bit, turned, and walked back up to the front of the class. "Whew, dodged a bullet on that one," I thought. She was in a good mood today.

After class, Harold and I worked out the details of our trade. I would bring my floppy disk drive to school and he would bring the bass guitar. We would make the swap in the parking lot after school, which was perfect since we had practice that night. I would bring the bass guitar to practice and break the news, gently, to Andy. It was all going to work out. At least I hoped it would. Crisis averted. This crisis. For now.

The next day after school, the trade went off without a hitch, and I headed over to Bob's house for practice. I wasn't looking forward to seeing the disappointed look in his parents' eyes. The disappointment that most parents feel when they think their kid is heading down the wrong path or hanging out with the wrong friends. Many years later, I would find out that in fact Bob's parents were very proud of the music he was doing, and they weren't nearly as disappointed in our merry group of musicians as I had thought at the time, but when you're a teenager, you are full of angst and fight. You fight 'the man' and at that age, parents are most definitely 'the man.' This is part of the teenage ritual, and we were in the thick of it.

Everyone arrived at Bob's house in their standard order. Ron was late, as usual, because he had been grounded, as usual, and had to negotiate a way to come to practice or just sneak over, which was his usual MO.

Bob got there first. After all, it was his house. Andy and I were next. We started setting up. It felt like coming home. Luckily, Bob's parents were not there. His dad was at work and his mom was shopping or playing bingo or doing whatever moms do when they are not home riding their kids' asses.

We got all set up, and Andy sat down on his amp and fidgeted with his guitar pick. "So what are we gonna do about a bass player?"

Bob and I looked at each other. I had let Bob in on my plan the day before. His face was a little apprehensive. I think he knew, instinctively as a guitar player, that Andy was not going to be happy.

"Funny you should ask," I said, with a nervous chuckle. "Hold that thought."

I ran to my car and grabbed a guitar case from the trunk. It was more than a little beat up. I ran back inside and clomped down the wooden stairs. Slightly out of breath, I took the wood-grain Sears and Roebuck bass guitar out of its beat-up case and held it, with my arm outstretched toward Andy. "Ta-da! Here you go, my good man. You are our new bass player."

Bob shot me an apprehensive look and smiled at Andy.

Andy looked horrified. "Whoa. No way, man. Fuck this! I'm a guitar player. I want to play six strings, not four."

"Dude, I know, but we're in a bind. The show at Lonnie's house is in three weeks. We have to learn two sets worth of songs *and* we don't have a bass player. After that gig, you go back to guitar and we'll start looking for another bass player. I promise."

Andy would never go back to playing guitar. It turned out he was a pretty amazing bass player and out of the whole crew was the only one who 'made it' in the music biz. Years later, Andy would go on to play for several national and international acts and tour the world. Twice. Who knew this was the moment when that life trajectory would begin for him? We didn't at the time, and I don't think he did either. But at that point in time, he was not a happy camper.

"How come I have to do it? Why can't Bob do it?" Andy gestured toward Bob with a mix of frustration and reservation.

"Bob's been playing longer. Besides, I think you'll do great. You can do all the rock moves. You know, lick the bass and shit? All the stuff you can't do if you're focused on playing solos."

Andy wasn't buying what I was selling. He was more than a little disappointed. He shot up off his amp. "C'mon. We can find another bass player now. How about that guy who's always hanging out at the mall. What's his name... uh... The guy with the good hair."

Bob looked over. "You mean Ned?"

"Yeah. That guy. Ned. He says he can play—"

"That guy can't play jack shit and you know it. He walks around the mall looking like Stephen Pearcy and can't sing. Can't play. Can't do a goddamn thing," I said rather heatedly. "He looks good though. I'll give him that."

Andy took the bass and slowly sat back down. He plunked on it for a couple of minutes. Bob and I looked on with a slight gleam of encouragement. Maybe he'll do it? Maybe it'll work out.

At this point, Ron rumbled down the stairs, late as usual.

"Hey, dingleberries. What up? Sorry I'm late. The parents are On. My. Ass."

Ron looked over at Andy and saw the wood-grain Sears and Roebuck bass. "Whoa. Nice bass. Did you get that from your grandpappy?"

That didn't help. Andy looked up at him incredulously and then looked over to Bob and I with a bit of a scowl. "No. I got it from your mom," he fired back with a slight smile. He was gonna do it.

We all chuckled with relief, and I went on to explain the situation to Ron. It looked like Andy had resigned himself to the fact that he needed to take one for the team. Had this happened a month before or even a week or two before, I don't think he would have done it. But in that short period of time, the group had become close and, more than that, we had realized that we had talent. All of us. If we wanted to, we could make this work.

We all sat down and started going over the song list.

I scribbled some song names on a piece of paper. "Ok. So we have 'You Really Got Me,' 'Lack of Communication,' 'Eat the Rich,' and… that's it. We have four songs."

Ron, twirling his drum sticks as he always did, said, "That's three songs."

I looked down at the paper again. "Right. Three. Three songs."

Bob looked up from his warm-up noodling. "I want to do 'Eruption.'"

Andy threw his hands up. "Really? Can you play 'Eruption'?"

The tension between Bob and Andy was a little thick sometimes. With multiple guitar players in a band, you always have a high level of competition. Plus Andy was still more than a little sore about getting tossed into the deep end of having to learn how to play bass, so every time Bob chimed in on things he wanted to play, Andy got a bit defensive. Understandably.

"Well… yeah… kinda," Bob said with a bit of a huff.

"You can't *kinda* play 'Eruption,'" Andy said emphatically. "You either can or you can't. If you can't *play* 'Eruption,' then we can't *do* 'Eruption.'"

Bob was a little more sheepish now. "I mean, I have it mostly worked out. I can have it ready by the time we play the show."

I scribbled another song on the list. "Ok. 'Eruption.' Now we have four songs. We need two sets worth of material. If we have to play some songs twice, we'll do it later in the night when people are shitfaced and won't know it. So... what other songs do we know, or kinda know, or can learn in the next three weeks?"

The band started throwing out hair-metal tunes.

"Dio, 'Last in Line.'"

"Priest, 'Living after Midnight' or 'Love Bites.'"

"Mötley Crüe, 'Helter Skelter' or 'Shout at the Devil.'"

Ron shouted out above the crowd, "Loudness, 'Crazy Nights.'"

"Huh?" I said. "Who the hell is Loudness?"

"Roudness," Ron shot back in a terrible Japanese accent. "They are an awesome metal band from Japan. You gotta hear this song." Ron jumped out from behind his kit and barreled upstairs and out to his car.

Ron was always finding new and interesting music. He lived with us in the sticks, but his dad lived in the city. He would go to his dad's house for weekend visits, and he always came back with new, interesting music for us to listen to.

Ron came back down the stairs the same way he went up, flying. Skipping every other step and full of excitement. He had a cassette tape in his hand. He jammed the tape into Bob's silver Radio Shack monolithic stereo system, rewound the tape, then hit play. The first guitar chords from "Crazy Nights" ripped out of the speakers.

"Whoa." Andy acknowledged the great guitar tone. "This is heavy."

The high-pitched vocals of Minoru Niihara screamed out and pierced our eardrums. I loved it from the first listen. I actually went and bought the cassette, *Thunder in the East*, that weekend and wore it out. It remains one of my favorite metal records to this day. I heard that when they recorded this record, Minoru didn't speak any English and sang the whole thing phonetically. I was never sure if this was true or not, but there was no doubting that these guys rocked.

I continued to write furiously. "Ok. We have a list."

I passed around the piece of paper to make sure everyone got the songs they really wanted.

"First of all" – Ron slapped the paper – "I can't read this shit. Your writing is terrible. Second, it's gonna be hard as hell to learn all these songs in three weeks. Three months, maybe."

"Well, we don't have a choice. We just gotta do the best we can," I said.

"And I'd like to remind you," Andy chimed in, "I've never played the bass before, and—"

Ron snickered. "C'mon, man. How hard can it be? It's two less strings!"

Andy shot Ron a really dirty look, and Ron gave him his innocent smile in return, batting his eyelashes.

I tried to get the group back on track. "Ok. Let's run through the four songs we have."

Andy shot back, "Three."

"Fuck, ok. *Three*. The three songs we know."

We blasted through the three songs about five times each. When rehearsal was over, we all made copies of the list of songs to learn. Exhausted, we packed up and left.

We started rehearsing as much as we could without completely pissing off Bob's parents and losing yet another place to practice. We were only able to learn ten songs. Andy's transition to bass had slowed us down a bit, but frankly these were harder songs than we had attempted in the past, so we all struggled. We were always boxing above our weight class.

Something else was painfully obvious. I had thought we could get away with a single guitar attack, but I was wrong. We sounded really thin with only one guitar player. We had all noticed, but no one wanted to tell Bob even though it wasn't his fault. We had just gone through all this drama with Andy, and no one saw a way to put him back on guitar and find a bass player in time for the Halloween show. We didn't sound great, but we were hoping no one would notice. Unfortunately, we were all perfectionists and had worked hard, so this slight oversight was weighing on us. We could all tell.

Thankfully, lady luck intervened to help us out. Over the summer, a new family had moved in just a few doors down from Bob and his family. They had two teenage kids, a girl in tenth grade and a boy in twelfth. The girl had met Bob's sister on the bus and became friends. On one particular practice afternoon, she came skipping down the basement stairs to say hi to the band. Bob's sister had, for the most part, steered clear of us longhairs, partially because she knew what her parents thought of us but also because of the teenage sibling code: whatever your siblings were doing, it couldn't be that cool. But today was different. Bob's sister and her new friend had come down to hang out while the band took a break. We were all sweaty and this girl was kinda cute, which made it awkward. Guys got into metal bands to get chicks, but the reality was, being in a metal band was hard work. You'd spend hundreds and hundreds of sweaty rehearsal hours just to support a single, one-hour show. It was grueling, real work, and we had all the sweat to show for it. This girl didn't seem to mind. She walked around the basement, looking at the set list and eyeing the guitars.

"You guys sound pretty good," she finally said. "You know, my brother plays guitar."

"Does he now?" Bob perked up.

"Yeah. He does."

"Is he any good?"

"Yeah, he's real good. Better than…" She stopped herself for a moment then continued, "Better than most."

Bob had seen her brother milling around in his front yard. Doing yard work. Sitting on his porch. The usual stuff. Skinny, long hair. He fit the stereotype. He wore tight, tight jeans and a band T-shirt most of the time. Bob had wondered if he was a musician. He sure looked the part, but then lots of kids did. And most didn't or couldn't play.

"Why don't you go get him and tell him to come on over here," I chimed in. "Tell him to bring his guitar."

"Sure." She lightly whisked her way up the steps with Bob's sister right behind her. Bob's sister shot him the typical sibling look. The one that says, 'Don't you dare ruin my day, Bobby. You and your hoodlum friends.'

After the girls left, the band got back to business, running through the songs. After roughly twenty minutes or so, we heard the rumbling of multiple pairs of feet scuffing their way down the stairs. It was Bob's sister, the new girl, and her brother. We instantly realized why it had taken him so long to get there. He was full-on metal. He was wearing tight jeans alright (tight pants were definitely his thing), but he also had a ripped-up Bon Jovi T-shirt showing from behind a rocker leather jacket. It was definitely a Sears and Roebuck leather jacket, but it was still a leather jacket. It was still cool. His hair was spiked to the heavens. I couldn't even guess how much Aqua Net that guy was using. Musta been the whole bottle. But he was smart. He knew an audition when he saw one and, so far, he was hitting all the right notes even before he strapped on his guitar. He had swagger too. He knew he was cool.

The girls settled down in the beanbag chairs, and the new guy swaggered right up to us.

"Hey," he said with a slight chin lift.

"Hey," we all said back.

He put down his guitar and introduced himself. "I'm John," he said, as he reached out his hand to me. I didn't do much hand shaking back then and this wasn't a standard high school rocker greeting, but hey, I was game.

I grabbed his hand and shook it. "I'm Sean. This is Bob, Andy, and Ron." He proceeded to greet each with a hearty handshake. We were all a little shocked and even more impressed. John didn't act like a kid.

John and his family had moved here from Jersey. An army brat, he was able to reinvent himself for this stop. Prior to showing up in Maryland, he was a little geeky with Coke-bottle glasses and pearl snap button shirts. Now he was a rocker, and we didn't have many rockers in our town so we were destined to cross paths and be friends.

John shrugged off his leather jacket, draped it over a small kid's chair, and proceeded to pull out his guitar, a cool-looking Flying V clone. He started to move his fingers over the fretboard until they were flying faster than we had ever seen. "Whoa," was the only thing I could think. I couldn't hear his playing yet, but I knew it had to be good if he moved that fast. He attached the strap and threw the guitar across his body. It looked very natural on him. Almost like it was meant to be there. I could tell he spent many long hours looking at himself in the mirror with that guitar.

"Can I plug in somewhere?" he said, looking around.

"Um, sure," I said. "You can plug right into the PA. It doesn't really have any effects. Just basic reverb."

"I don't need any effects. Effects are for pussies who can't play."

"Wow," I thought. This guy didn't think much of himself. At this point, I was thinking that he better be good to carry all that ego. Otherwise he was just a dick. It turned out he *was* that good. He already knew most of the songs we were playing and would learn the others in short order. We knew from the first clean chords of Dio's "Last in Line" that this guy could play. Really play. His level of talent would make us all better. Competition inside a band is a real thing. Most people don't want to be the weak link. If someone comes in that good, it drives the others to be better, and that's what John did for us. The next few practices were hectic and stressful, but also so much fun. We sounded like a real metal band. But we still had a lot to do and not a lot of time.

All this time, I had noticed that Ron's girlfriend hadn't been to as many band rehearsals lately – boy, did I notice. We'd always see each other in school, usually from a distance. This was ok with me because I got really, really nervous around her and didn't want to create any waves with the band. I was sure that everyone could see how much I liked her. I felt like it was tattooed on my forehead.

I was walking down the hall one day, and she jetted out of a nearby classroom as I walked by. I didn't even see her coming.

"Hey, stranger," she said as she dropped in stride next to me.

"Hey, you. Sorry yeah. Been super busy. Between school, the new job, and getting ready for this gig, I've been slammed. How are you doing?"

"Doing ok. Are you excited about the party? Everyone is going to be there."

My stomach sank a bit. I knew that the band was not totally ready and we didn't know nearly enough songs to play all night. Plus we were playing in front of our school peers. It was more than a little stressful. "Yeah. Very. It's gonna rock."

"It better!" She chuckled. "How is Ron doing?"

"Why are you asking me? He's your boyfriend."

"Yeah, I know. It's been hard to see him these last few weeks. He got grounded again, and I think he's sneaking out for band practice. Probably doesn't want to try his luck by seeing his girlfriend too."

"He's always grounded," I said. "What's the deal with that?"

"His parents are super strict… and honestly? He can be kind of an idiot." She changed the subject. "So you dressing up?"

"Dressing up? For what?"

"For my party, silly!"

We both laughed.

"Ha. Yeah, I'm coming as a rock star," I said with a sly smile.

She flashed a smile back. "Uh-huh. I hear ya. You know that's cheating."

"How about you?" I said, redirecting back to her. "What are you gonna dress up as?"

"Me and some friends are gonna dress up like Vanity 6."

Now this was something I really wanted to see, but at the same time, I didn't. I was having a harder and harder time controlling my staring as far as she was concerned and didn't want to betray my feelings. Also, I didn't want to piss off my friend. Besides, I wasn't even sure if she felt the same way.

She was a little flirty, but everyone was in high school. I didn't want to risk finding out that she didn't have those same feelings. We walked together in uncomfortable silence until we reached the front of the school and pushed open the heavy doors, heading to the parking lot.

She turned to me and smiled. "Well, I have to run and find Ron. I'm supposed to drive him home. See ya later, alligator."

Before I could get out "after a while, crocodile," she was off like a shot. I watched her leave before I headed to the Camaro and jumped in. Said my prayer and turned the key. Nothing. I hit my head against the steering wheel. I sighed and tried a few more times. Sometimes she was just finicky. Not this time. This time she was dead. It looked like it might rain. That must be it. "Ugh."

Just then, Bob drove up in his Toyota Corona. Sad, yet reliable. "You need a jump there, slick?"

I gave him a defeated look. "Yeah. Sure."

We proceeded to jump the beast, waved at each other, and headed home.

II

i WANNA BE SOMEBODY

HALLOWEEN WEEKEND, AND the day of the big show, had arrived. We showed up early at Lonnie's house and started setting up our equipment on the outside deck. It was a little brisk, but there was plenty of room for the band, drinks, and many raucous teenagers. Lonnie and I had been joking around with each other since I got there. This was making it hard for me to concentrate, and we had a lot to do. We loaded the drums, PA, and all the amps out onto the deck. Bob had his Peavey amp, same with Andy. John had an old-as-fuck Fender amp that was a total pain in the ass in every way possible.

No one could afford any Marshall gear, not at this point in our musical careers. We had been struggling with John's amp at rehearsal as well. It had this inclination to feedback. A lot. I was sure it mostly had to do with the fact that John liked to turn that thing all the way up in Bob's low-ceilinged basement. His parents really loved us now. It was probably also due to the fact that the tubes in this amp were older than John. He said they were vintage. I said they were just old. On top of all of this, the amp was heavy. Really heavy for such a compact rig.

We had decided to open with "Last in Line" due to its slow-build structure, but every time we played it, it was all great until the heavy guitar kicked in. That amp sounded amazingly clean, but when John hit the verse chords it would feedback like a bitch.

We're off to the witch
Screeeeeeeeeeech.
We may never never never come home
Screeeeeeeeeeech.
But the magic that we'll feel is worth a lifetime
We're all born upon the cross
Screeeeeeeeeeech.
We're the throw before the toss
Screeeeeeeeeeech.

It was ear piercing. We had all implored John to turn it down, but he said he couldn't do it. He would lose the little harmonic parts at the end of each line. He might have been right, but it was driving us fucking crazy, and we all worried it would feedback at the show and the audience would screech, with their hair standing straight up like a scene from *Better Off Dead*.

We got everything set up and sat down around the deck, all sweaty, admiring our work. It looked like a rock stage. Lonnie's siblings had put orange and black streamers, paper pumpkins, and all manner of decorations around the deck. It looked pretty awesome.

Ron rolled up with a beer in his hand. "This is gonna rock, my dudes."

Bob looked at the beer in Ron's hand and then back to Ron. "You better pace yourself, my dude."

Ron gave Bob a slight *pfft* and a 'don't worry about me' face. We all headed off in different directions, Ron to drink his beer and Bob to find a place to change into his spandex.

The sun made its hasty retreat behind Sugarloaf Mountain, and the guests were starting to arrive. We band members sat down on the deck to go over the set list.

Lonnie walked up to us. "Ok, boys. I have to go in and change. You guys need anything before I go?"

"No, babe. We're good." Ron leaned in to give her a kiss. She gave him a very brief peck and then moved away. Ron was already lit, and you could smell the beer from ten feet away. She pulled her face away and caught me looking at her. I didn't look away. I was stuck in a stare. She didn't look away either. There was something there. I could feel it.

"Ok then. See y'all in a bit." She headed in the house to get ready.

After a few seconds I could breathe again. "What the fuck was that?" I thought. "Oh boy. I'm in big, big trouble."

I snapped out of it and turned to the guys. "Ok. We'll put the five songs we know really well in the beginning."

The band mumbled and nodded in agreement.

"We'll put these other five at the end. And we'll just play them all again for the second set, in reverse order. No one will know the difference."

"What about 'Eruption'?" Bob broke in with a slightly offended tone.

Andy rolled his eyes. "Oh, here we go…"

I looked at Bob. "What about it? Can you play it? Did you learn it?"

"Yeah. I got it down last night."

"Then play it. Now. Show me," Andy said disbelievingly.

"I can't play it here. Everyone will hear it. It won't be special. It won't be fresh."

"It's gonna be like a fish. It ain't gonna be fresh later either." Andy snorted.

"Ok. If Bob wants to play it he can play it," I continued. "We need all the songs we can get. It's kinda like a guitar solo anyway."

"Hey. If Bob gets a guitar solo, can I do a drum solo?" Ron was kinda slurring his words at this point. He had started drinking a bit during load-in, and we really hadn't noticed how bad he was getting. Until now. This was our first show and it turned out Ron was really, really nervous so he was trying to take the edge off. He took it off alright.

"I tell ya what," I said, "you stay sober and you can do a drum solo. We need filler anyway." Oh geez, did we need filler.

"So what do we do for the second set again?" Andy looked puzzled.

"We play the first set over again. In reverse order. We take a thirty-min break in between and hopefully everybody is so shitfaced, no one will notice."

"Or maybe even an hour break," Bob chimed in with a chuckle.

"Yeah sure, maybe an hour. If Ron can make it that long." I snorted.

"Don't you worry about me. I'm cool. Cool as a cucnumber!"

"You mean a cucumber?" Andy laughed.

"Yeah, a cucnumber."

Andy stood up and let out a big sigh. "We're so fucked." He looked over at John, who was noodling his fingers up and down his fretboard. "You good?"

John looked up for a brief second – "Always" – and went back to noodling.

This is what he would always do. He would spend hours in his bedroom watching a small black-and-white TV with his Coke-bottle glasses, smoking, and noodling on his guitar. He was only infrequently interrupted by his mom, who would crack the door, poke her face through, and ask John if he (or his friends, if they were there) wanted anything to eat or drink. "Y'all want any ham sammitches?" she would say in her sweet southern Virginia accent. An accent not quite southern but also not quite northern. "Y'all want any soda pop?"

She was a sweet lady and always talked in the most calm, gentle manner. We used to joke all the time that John could be rolling down the road in his car and if his wheels fell off the vehicle, his mom would stick her head out the door and in the most calm, collected fashion possible, tell him, "John, your wheels fell off." We would tease him with his mom's calm, soothing voice. She never wavered. She was always so good to us longhairs.

We started making set lists and taping them around the stage (or deck, as it were). After we completed this task, we headed into the basement to change. As we did, we saw Lonnie and the other Vanity 6 girls.

Bob was the first to acknowledge this and seemed to be having a hard time picking his jaw off the ground. "Holy shit."

All our jaws dropped in succession. We looked like Y&T in the "Summertime Girls" video. Ron embraced his girlfriend and gave her a sloppy smooch. She kinda turned away. The beer odor was much stronger now.

"I love that shirt." I pointed to Lonnie's red, leopard-print shirt. It was the top half of a leotard she had cut to make it look more 'rocker.'

"You like this, huh?" She took off the shirt, exposing what she had on underneath, which was only a Frederick's of Hollywood black lace bra. This time it wasn't just my stomach that was doing backflips. She tossed the shirt to me. "You should wear this tonight. It'll go with your pants."

I was wearing black-and-white spandex with a stripe down the sides. She was right. It did go with my pants.

I kept looking at her. All of her. In my mind, I heard Pat Morita saying his famous line from *The Karate Kid*. "Look eye. Always look eye…" But my brain was saying, "Look boobs. Always look boobs." She looked good. Really good.

All us band guys took turns getting ready in a small half bath in the corner of the basement. We all Aqua Netted it up. When it was my turn, I tried on the shirt that she gave me. It looked good but not metal enough. I took off the shirt and dug around in the bathroom drawer until I found a small pair of scissors. I cut some zigzags in the waist section and enlarged the neck a bit. I put the shirt back on over my 'rocker' outfit and looked at myself, up and down in the mirror.

"Perfect."

The band emerged from the basement. The deck was full of kids, some dressed up in costume, some in the standard jeans, T-shirts, and sneakers uniform that most high school kids wore.

This was a real crowd. It was probably only forty or fifty people, but it might as well have been a thousand. Which made us more than a little nervous. The deck was packed! There was a keg in the corner with a long line of teenagers. People were having a good time. At this point, it was completely dark and it was time to rock. The outdoor lights were pointed at the stage.

"Showtime!"

We had worked out an instrumental intro but it was a little over-ambitious, and combined with the fact that we were super-nervous and our drummer was super-drunk, it didn't come off as we had planned. The intro sounded like a bunch of pans clashing together, a cacophony of noise, but the crowd didn't seem to mind. These were drunk (or nearly drunk) teenagers, and they were ready to rock. The crowd went wild.

I screamed out, "We are Exodus!"

The entire band erupted into yet another cacophony of noise as every member hit as many notes or beats as they could, all at once. And just as quickly as it started, it ended. The entire deck went silent and dark.

"You blew a fuse, you numbnuts!" someone shouted from inside the house. We later found out that this was Lonnie's little brother.

"Oh shit," I said to Bob as I turned around, my back to the crowd, more than a little embarrassed.

"I've got this," John said as he dropped his guitar into its stand. He ran inside. "Where's the fuse box, you little shit?" he said, fading away as the little bro led him to the back room of the basement to flip the circuit breaker. After what seemed like an eternity (it was really five minutes) the lights came back up and the crowd cheered.

"Whew," I mouthed to Bob, with an exaggerated brow wipe.

John came running out of the house and high-fived all of us. The crowd was still hootin' and hollerin.'

"Nice work, dude!" I said to John, more than a little surprised he was able to pull that off.

"No sweat," he said, shrugging his shoulders as he whipped up his guitar and slung it back on his arm in one smooth motion. "My dad's an electrician. You ready?"

"Ready," I said. I lifted my arm into the air and dropped into a body crouch. As I did, the band lit up again into the same wall of noise. This time, the power stayed on. Bob, John, and Andy jumped around, throwing the necks of their guitars left and right, and at one point Andy even licked the neck of his bass guitar. It was so metal!

The loud noise of the intro faded to a stop, and John started the clean, beautiful beginning of "Last in Line." I joined in with the clean lines of one of my heroes, Ronnie James Dio.

We're a ship without a storm
The cold without the warm
Light inside the darkness that it needs, yeah
We're a laugh without a tear
The hope without the fear
We are coming… home!

We got to the loudest part of the song, and it sounded amazing. I guess being outdoors on the deck had solved John's feedback problem. The guitar's sound was overdriven, naturally (as he liked to say), and the song sounded fantastic. When the song was over, we blasted right into "Lack of Communication" without missing a beat.

We only got to play three songs.

As Bob started ripping into Eddie Van Halen's "Eruption," there were sirens and flashing red lights everywhere. The cops had arrived.

Kids went streaming down the steps. Over the railing. Getting out any way they could.

Bob was still going. Playing his little heart out. He was gonna play this damn song even if he went to jail for it. Nero fiddled while Rome burned.

The cops were chasing kids everywhere. Some were waiting in the driveway for the kids to try and get to their cars. I was never sure if anyone actually got busted or not, but the cops sure scared the shit out of everyone. Once the dust settled and Bob finished "Eruption" (impressively, I might add – even Andy thought so), we surveyed the damage. There was no one on the deck but the band. The rest of us started clapping for Bob.

Lonnie came up the stairs, breathing heavy and a little shaken up. This was her first police bust, after all. Her parents had to come out and say the party was over.

Ron yelled from behind his kit, "The party ain't over. I still have to do my drum solo."

Ron proceeded to play the shittiest drum solo of all time. Turned out the alcohol had caught up with him. After he finished playing, he leaned to his right and puked all over his bass drum pedal – and his foot.

"Ah, shit. Bob, grab him," I yelled. "We have to get him to the yard."

Bob and I dragged Ron out onto the grass, where he continued puking. After he was done, we dragged him back into the basement.

Lonnie's friends and the rest of the band were down there playing pool and listening to music. Billy Idol's "Rebel Yell" was playing. Lonnie walked over to us. She looked more than a little concerned. "Oh my god. Is he ok?"

Bob chuckled. "Yeah, he will be. He's just gotta sleep it off."

On cue, Ron raised his head up, and in one final act of defiance, lifted his fist into the air and yelled "Blota!" He dropped back down and passed out.

"Blota. What the fuck is Blota?" John said.

We all looked over to the speaker. "Rebel Yell" was still playing.

"Ahh. Billy Idol," John and I said in unison.

Once all the commotion had completely died down outside, we loaded all the band equipment into the basement. When we were done, I saw Lonnie sitting down by the steps. I headed down and sat down next to her. "Hell of a party," I said.

She laughed nervously, not sure if I was kidding.

I continued, "We'll have some stories on Monday, won't we?"

"Yes, we will." She looked down at my chest. "By the way, you cut up my shirt. You owe me."

"Do I now?"

She shot me a sly grin. "You do."

"What do I owe you?" I asked in a very sarcastic tone.

We both laughed, then sat in awkward silence for a minute. Finally, I got up. "I better go help them get the gear out," I said. "I don't want them to think I'm the stereotypical singer. Won't help carry equipment. Even though I really do hate that shit." I smiled and headed out to the rest of the guys.

Once we were all finished up and I'd loaded my PA in the trunk of the Camaro, I went back up to the deck to check for any forgotten odds and ends. Ron was staying at Andy's place that night, so he and Bob got Ron to his feet and walked him down the deck and out to the car. They poured Ron's inebriated body into the passenger seat, and Andy got in and drove away. Bob and I headed back inside to find Lonnie's girlfriends sitting around the TV watching a Bon Jovi video.

"Man, that guy has good hair," Bob said, staring at the TV.

"Yeah, he does," I said as I approached the pool table in the middle of the rec area. "Hey, you wanna play a game of pool?" I started to rack the balls.

Just then a little kid, couldn't have been more than eight or nine, and only about four feet tall, came around the corner. "I'll play ya!"

"You?" I said, shrugging him off. "You can't even see the top of the table."

"You wanna play or not?" the kid said.

"Sure, kid. I'll play," I said, determined to teach this little squirt a lesson.

"Oh boy. This ought to be good," Bob said, copping a squat on a stool nearby.

"Rack 'em, bitch," the kid said.

"Whoa, son, you kiss your mama with that mouth?" I replied. He just laughed.

As I grabbed the triangle and finished racking the balls, the kid chimed in again. "A dollar a game."

"A dollar a game? Look kid, I don't wanna take your money."

He laughed. "I'll be ok. A dollar a game."

I was starting to get a little pissed. "Fine. A dollar a game."

I wasn't sure if this kid even had a dollar tucked into his Scooby-Doo pj's, but he needed to be taken down a peg or two and I was ready to do it.

Well, it didn't turn out that way. Not at all. The first game consisted of the little fucker running the table. The second game, I managed to sink two balls. Two. I lost the third game too. After that, I had to cry uncle. I turned to Bob. "You wanna shot at this kid?"

He laughed hard. "Hell, no! I saw that comin' from a mile away. That's Lonnie's little brother. He lives here and it's his pool table. You got played."

"Yeah, I did." I laughed, but I was also a little embarrassed. That little son of a bitch kicked my ass. But good.

"I gotta go anyway," Bob said. He jumped off the stool and gave me a wave. "Later, tater."

"See ya, Bobby boy."

He headed out the French doors of the basement and into the night.

"One more game?" The kid never quit.

"No way, friend. I'm done for tonight," I said, feeling exhausted.

"You owe me three bucks." The kid held out his hand.

Just then Lonnie came around the corner. I was wondering where she'd been. "Davey! What the hell are you doing down here?" The kid dropped his hand and put his arms behind his back and kicked the carpet with his bare feet.

"Just playin' pool," he finally muttered.

"You better get upstairs and get to bed. If Mom or Dad find you down here, they will whip your ass!"

"Oh man," the kid said with a huff. He turned and walked

toward the stairs before suddenly turning around and pointing at me. "He owes me three bucks."

She held up her fist and shook it. "I'll give you three bucks."

"Oh *man*," he said again. He turned around and quietly walked up the stairs.

"Whew," I said. "You saved my ass. I didn't have the three dollars."

"Don't worry about it. He's not supposed to be hustling my friends anymore."

"Anymore?" I said.

"Yeah. Both of my brothers are pretty good at pool, and they've been known to hustle my friends for candy money. Or fireworks or whatever the fuck else they're into."

I was sure I was staring at her, but I couldn't help it. The tension between us was something at this point. I felt sure I was going to explode, and I was pretty sure she felt the same thing.

"It's time for me to get going anyway," I said reluctantly. "I'm an hour past curfew as it is."

"I'll walk out with you," she said quietly.

She looked amazing in the moonlight. She was wearing an old Def Leppard shirt, jean shorts that had been cut off super short, and no shoes. We got to my car and I stood there, for quite a while, not opening the door. I didn't want to leave. Ever. I leaned against the door and looked up at the sky.

She jumped up and sat on the hood.

"Be careful. You might scratch my primer." I grinned and she smiled.

I moved over to her and kissed her. I couldn't hold back any longer. Band be damned. She slid her arms around my shoulders, and we made out for what seemed like forever. By now, it was getting really late, or you could say early since the sun was due to come out in less than two hours. It was getting pretty cold too, so we got inside the car. I turned the key and it started right up. "Fuck!" I thought. The one time when I would've wanted the car *not* to start. "I don't want to leave." We sat in the car talking for another hour. Once it got too late for me to drive home and for her to go inside, I turned off the car and we climbed in the back seat. We wrapped up in one of the blankets I used to cover the exposed foam and fell asleep in each other's arms.

The next morning, she and I woke up super early, around 5:00 a.m. "I've got to go," she whispered in my ear. We exited the car and she went running into her house. I couldn't say I minded watching her dash in, short-shorts and all. Once she was safely inside, I headed home.

I had gotten really good at sneaking back home. This skill would prove very useful in the months ahead. I shut off the car's engine and glided down the end of the long driveway. I didn't want to make a sound and wake up my mom, or even worse, my stepdad.

I parked the car, got out, and ever so quietly climbed the wood pile on the side of the house and into my bedroom window without making so much as a peep. I quickly took off my shoes and pants and got into bed. "Whew," I thought. "I made it."

I put my hands behind my head and stared up at the Iron Maiden poster on my ceiling. I had the biggest smile on my face. Even though last night was my first rock show, I couldn't stop thinking about her. What a fucking night.

I was finally able to doze off just as the sun peeked above the purple mountains on the eastern side of the farm. All of a sudden, I was jolted awake by my mom screaming bloody murder. "Sean! Telephone!" followed by the maniacal thumping of a broomstick on the ceiling below me.

"What?" I yelled, not at all awake.

"Telephone!" She was even louder this time.

"Ok, ok. I'm coming." I threw on a pair of jeans and stumbled down the stairs, still half asleep. I turned the corner in the kitchen to see my mom holding the phone receiver with her hand cupped hard over it.

"It's Ron. He's called about five or six times. Starting at eight o'clock." She was speaking in a weird, loud whisper. "He woke your dad!"

Step. Dad. "I can't talk to him. Tell him I'm not here, or asleep." I was matching my mom's odd whisper, hoping Ron didn't hear any of this.

"I will do no such thing. He obviously really needs to talk to you."

I took the receiver from my mom and stood there staring at the phone. I had no idea what I was going to say. I felt about an inch tall. I finally mustered up enough strength and spoke, quietly, very quietly, into the receiver. "H-hello?"

"Where have you been?" The voice that came across the tiny speaker of that phone was angry. Very angry, and it didn't sound like Ron at all. Not at all.

My throat got instantly dry, and I was stumbling over what little I could manage to say. "I was asleep. What's up?"

"Is it true?" Ron said sharply.

"Is what true?" I knew exactly what he was talking about but wasn't one hundred percent sure he did, so I wanted to see what he knew before I copped to anything.

"Don't treat me like I'm fucking stupid." Ron's voice was cracking. It went from pure rage to heartbreak.

Now I really felt like shit. If there had been a bridge anywhere near me, I would have taken a running leap off of it. How could I have done this? How could I have done this to my friend? Tears were starting to flow down my cheeks. "I am so sorry, man. I didn't mean for anythi—"

"Fuck you, dude!"

"It just happened."

"It just happened?" Angry Ron was back. "Shit like that doesn't just happen. You don't do that shit to your friends. *Fuck you!*"

Just as I was about to agree with him, I heard a loud bang and the phone went silent. He had hung up on me. I stood there while a few tears left my cheeks and torpedoed toward the floor. I finally hung up the phone and started walking toward the stairs. I could see my mom in the living room, standing there with a very concerned look on her face. "Are you ok?" she asked as I ascended the stairs.

"No, I'm fine," I said, wiping the tears off of my face.

I went upstairs and lay on my bed listening to music for the rest of the day and into the night. I didn't eat lunch. I didn't eat dinner. I just lay up there thinking about what a colossal mistake I had made.

12

BRINGIN' ON THE HEARTBREAK

THE NEXT MORNING, I was playing up not feeling well in order to avoid going to school. I couldn't face anybody. Not the guys, not Lonnie, and certainly not Ron. My mom was wise to my game, however, and told me that if I didn't go on my own she would load me into the bus herself and drive me in. That was all the incentive I needed.

When I walked into school, I felt like everyone was looking at me. It was like they knew. I had read *The Scarlet Letter* in the tenth grade (I hated that book), and now I knew exactly how Hester Prynne felt. I felt like I was wearing a 'I just fucked over one of my best friends' T-shirt. I avoided the water fountains and the cafeteria or anywhere where I thought there might be a good chance of running into Ron. I sat in my car at lunch time. I had managed to make it all the way to fifth period before seeing any of the guys, but as I turned the hall corner where my locker was, I saw Andy and Bob standing there. They had obviously been looking for me.

"Hey, man," Andy said somberly.

"Hey," I said, equally somber.

Andy tried to lighten the mood. "So. I got grounded hard after Saturday."

Andy's parents were very strict religious types, and he and his sister were adopted so I got the sense that his parents were never really sure how to interact with their kids. Spare the rod, spoil the child was definitely part of their philosophy.

He flashed a little smile. "But, man, it was so worth it. Kim talked to me on the bus today. She never talks to me. Anywhere. She said we were awesome. She wants to sit with me at lunch. Can you believe it?" His eyes started to beam, but he reined it in when he saw I wasn't reciprocating.

"It was pretty awesome," I replied.

We weren't really that awesome. We got really lucky. And the songs we did play were full of mistakes, but it didn't matter. We played rock music in front of an audience. Sure, it was a small audience of our peers, but it might as well have been the Capital Centre. We had proven something to ourselves mostly. That we could do this. And from that standpoint, my transgressions notwithstanding, it was pretty fucking awesome!

Bob finally spoke. "You ok, man?"

"Yeah. I'll be ok. Did you talk to Ron? Is he ok?"

"Look" – Bob raised his hands to stop me – "I don't know what happened and I don't think I want to know, but apparently he is pretty pissed. He stopped by my house yesterday and picked up his kit. I wasn't there since Mom thought I needed a slight god infusion, so she took my sister and me to church, which sucked.

My dad was home, said Ron stomped in, packed up his kit, and stomped out. Didn't say more than a couple words. But the words he did say weren't great. Something about quitting the band and never playing with us again and you" – Bob pointed at me – "being an asshole."

Andy was kinda shocked by all of this. "Well, that's just fucking great." He turned to me. "What the fuck did you do?"

"I'm sorry, guys. I…"

My throat was super dry at this point, so I walked to one of the nearby water fountains and took a drink.

"This might actually be my fault." I was still struggling to get this out. I'd really fucked things up. "Well… we made out," I finally blurted out.

"You and Ron?" Andy said, again trying to lighten the mood.

"No, not me and Ron. Geez. No, me and Lonnie. After the party."

"When? While Ron was passed out?" Andy was confused.

"No, no… After you guys left. It just kinda happened." I was full-on blushing at this point.

Bob looked a little shocked but not completely surprised. After seeing what she was wearing on Saturday night, he was pretty sure, if given the opportunity, he would've done worse but he was still pissed at me, and for good reason. This is the kinda shit that always blew up bands. I knew better.

"Whoa… dude! Not cool. Not cool at all. Dick move," Bob finally spit out.

"Yeah, I know. It wasn't cool. Yeah, a total dick move. I'm so sorry, guys."

Andy blurted out, "Don't be sorry to us, you gotta tell Ron."

"He called me yesterday. He doesn't wanna talk to me." I was looking down at my shoes in shame at this point.

Bob sat in silent contemplation for a moment. "Ok. Well, that certainly fucks things up quite a bit now, doesn't it?"

They both gave me hard stares, and I could feel how pissed they were. Luckily for me, the bell rang.

"Ha! Saved by the bell!" I said and gave a halfhearted laugh.

Neither laughed. They both gave me a look, turned, and walked toward their respective classes. Frankly, at that moment I was wondering where Lonnie was. Of course I was. I couldn't think about anything else. I assumed she was lying low, which was what I wanted to do.

I couldn't wait for that school day to end, but in typical fashion, the last half of the day seemed to drag on for an eternity. I hadn't run into Ron or his girlfriend (was she still his girlfriend?) all day, and that was just as well. I was not sure I could handle it. I wasn't a hundred percent sure where we all stood at that moment, but I knew that I'd torpedoed the one thing I wanted to get right my senior year – the rock band.

I walked straight out the front door of the school and made a beeline to my car in the parking lot. When I got there, Lonnie was sitting on the hood of my car.

"Can we talk?" she said quietly.

"Of course."

She looked around the lot. "Not here."

She jumped down and got in the passenger side. I got in and started the car. Didn't even get to say the prayer. I was too nervous. Luckily, the car started right up, like it knew this was serious and it better not fuck with me.

"Where to, m'lady?" I said, trying to break the serious tension a bit.

She looked around outside and then looked at me. Her eyes were a little watery and her hands trembled a bit. She grabbed a pack of cigarettes from her jean jacket pocket and banged one out on the side of her hand. "Remember that park we used to go to after practice sometimes?" she finally said.

"Of course I do." Every memory with her was etched in my brain. We used to go sit there after band practice when Jer's mom would kick us out early, or after dropping Ron off at his house. We'd talk for hours, about anything. Sometimes long after the sun went down.

She popped in the cigarette lighter and I had to remind her that it, like most things in this car, didn't work. "Hey, I think there are some matches in the glovebox," I said and gave a forced chuckle. "Mikey is always playing with fire on the drives back and forth to school."

"Does anything in this car work?" she said.

I had to look to see if she was really pissed, but she flashed a very slight smile. "Whew," I thought.

"Can we go?" she said, again very quietly.

"Your wish is my command." I slammed the car into drive and headed out of the parking lot.

I drove to the park, pulled up into a parking space in front of the playground equipment, and shut off the engine. We both got out, and she headed to her favorite spot, the monkey bars. I remembered many times she would hang on those bars and look stunning, with her blonde hair flowing down. She would tell me about her family (they had issues) and trouble with Ron (they had issues too), and I would tell her about my family (you guessed it, we also had issues!), but it seemed so long ago now.

Now I was looking at her a little differently. I still admired her beauty, but now there was way more to her than that. She seemed older somehow. Wiser.

She climbed up on the bar and sat. "So Ron stopped by yesterday."

"He did, huh?" I felt a tinge of jealousy. Were they still together? What was going on? Why was he stopping by her house?

"Yeah. He was very upset."

"He called me," I said quietly.

"Yeah, I know. He told me." She hesitated a bit and then continued. "Well. One of my 'friends'" – she used very exaggerated air quotes – "saw us making out, and she told Ron. She's liked Ron for months and I knew it. She's always trying to be around him." She continued, almost breathlessly, "Every time we go to the movies or to Skate Haven, she would just show up. It's fucking annoying." She finally stopped to take a breath. "Anyway, she's always liked him, and I guess she thought that this was her opportunity. Bitch."

"Fuck," I said, but I was thinking, "Ahh, so that's how he found out."

"No, it's fine. Anyway, we talked and he calmed down and apologized."

"Oh, here it comes," I thought. "They are gonna stay together. Path of least resistance and all." I had the feeling I was about to get my heart crushed.

"He knows that we've been drifting apart lately," she continued, "and we've been doing our own things, but he wanted to tell me that he loved me and wanted to try and work it out."

Shit. Here comes the heartache. Wait for it… Wait for it…

"But I told him I couldn't keep pretending anymore. I don't want him."

She stopped and looked right into my eyes. At this point, I was pretty sure this was a good thing. The sky was spinning.

She looked me dead in my eyes and said, "I want you."

Boom! There it was! My chest pounded, my throat was instantly dry.

This line was right out of *Purple Rain*, and I couldn't help but think about the ending of "The Beautiful Ones," which started playing in my head.

I was staring into her eyes for what felt like an eternity. I had never seen eyes so blue.

I moved over to her and started kissing her gently. I felt exactly the same way.

13

i WANNA ROCK

THE SPARK OF MY LOVE life had been lit. Unfortunately, in the process, I had torpedoed the only thing that mattered up to that point. We had somehow managed to get five guys together, build the chemistry and comradery, learn some songs, and I fucked the whole thing up because I couldn't control my libido.

With all of the tension I had created in Exodus, it was no surprise when Bob, Ron, and John decided to move on without me, and I really couldn't blame them. While I was busy with my existential crisis, they had gotten my ride-into-school buddy Mikey to sing for the group. He wasn't very good, but neither was I when I started. He started taking vocal lessons at the local community college and was really taking it seriously. Over the years, Mikey would become a world-class singer and a pretty decent drummer. At the time, I was more than a little jealous though that he was playing in 'my' band.

I was living in a self-imposed musical exile. Ron wasn't speaking to me, and I couldn't blame him. I'd broken the bro code. I would see him from time to time in the hallways, but he would always shoot daggers at me and turn around and head the other direction. I rarely saw Andy around school. He and I didn't have any of the same classes and, outside of music, didn't hang out with the same kids. I saw Bob and Mikey on a regular basis, but they wouldn't share much, if anything, about what Exodus was up to – mostly to protect Ron but also partially to protect me. They knew that the events that had transpired had taken their toll on me, but they also knew that Ron was really hurt, and they were trying to execute the balancing act of staying friends with both of us.

While this was going on, I needed to do something musically. I needed something to take my mind off of what I had done and what I was missing out on. So I did something kinda rash. I agreed to be the frontman for my stepdad's work buddy's band, filling in, like a hired gun, after their singer quit. It wasn't a long-term situation, but it was something to do to salve my musical, self-inflicted wounds. They had a couple gigs lined up, which would give me an opportunity to work on my stage show.

It turned out to be a pretty terrible idea. Practices involved jamming for a song or two and then sitting around and drinking for two or three hours, which didn't really interest me. Bob knew I would regret it, and he had warned me that playing with the old guys would have its downside. Bob always saw things like this more clearly than I did. I didn't always look before I leaped.

I had two gigs (and lots of, ahem, practices) with the "old fogeys," as I called them, under my belt. The last of the ones I had signed up for was coming up, but I still had to work to put gas in the car and pay for incidentals. Cassettes, movie tickets, and blue Slush Puppies.

You know, the important things. Money wouldn't be a problem for a little while at least. I was working plenty of extra hours because it was November and the mall was in full holiday swing.

Bob walked into the Radio Shack as I was ringing up a customer buying a TRS-80 color computer. Mr. Carter was helping a customer nearby but hovered a bit, which was what he always did. Bob waited for me to finish and then spoke up. "Dude. Where ya been?" I must have looked tired, because I was. I was burning the candle at both ends, and twice in the middle.

"Dude, I've been right here! I don't know whether I'm coming or going. Mr. Carter has been killin' me with the hours. Fuck Christmas."

"Yeah, it's been pretty busy the last couple of weeks," Bob said. "Haven't seen you in school much either."

"Yeah, I've been late a lot lately. This other band thing is killin' me. Those guys want to play all the time, which, on one hand I love, but they only do gigs on weeknights because they suck. I haven't gotten a good night's sleep in two weeks."

Mr. Carter left his customer to come over to the counter. He gave Bob a disapproving look and then turned to me. "Mr. Frazier, I'm sure you can see we have customers."

I let out a loud sigh. "Yes, sir. I sure can."

"Well, then. Chop-chop." Mr. Carter clapped his hands and pointed to browsing customers on the sales floor.

I looked at Bob, bleary-eyed. "My break is in an hour. I'll come get ya."

"Cool," Bob said as he gave me a very sympathetic look.

An hour later, I told Mr. Carter that I was taking my dinner break. The store still had customers so Mr. Carter was not pleased, but he knew there was a law about these things so he reluctantly shooed me away. I headed out into the mall and down to Montgomery Ward. The mall was teeming with Christmas shoppers as far as the eye could see. I wove my way through the throngs of people, past the McCrory's, which seemed to be literally bursting at the seams with people shopping and sitting at the food counter taking a snack break as they prepared for round two of their all day shop-fest. I passed the arcade, practically willing myself not to go inside, but luckily it was so busy (I could see lines of people four and five deep waiting for their turn to play some of the stand-up games) that I didn't dare go in. "Oh my god," I said quietly to myself as I approached the Waldenbooks. There was a large crowd pulsating out of the door. "Excuse me... Excuse me... Excuse me," I kept repeating as I tried to make my way through the crowd. I finally got to Montgomery Ward, which, luckily for me, was so huge it didn't look nearly as busy by comparison. I found Bob in the appliance department listening to one of his coworkers bitch about pay, overtime, Christmas, everything.

I walked right up and interrupted the conversation. "You ready?"

Bob looked at me, then over at his coworker. "More than ready."

We headed back out into the mall. Bob pointed to Long John Silver's. "Fried fish?"

"Oh god no. If I eat another hush puppy I'm gonna puke. Let's do Roy Rogers."

"Are you sure we're gonna have time?"

Roy Rogers was on the other side of the packed mall, and we'd also have to navigate the Christmas extravaganza, including a very lengthy line of kids waiting to sit on Santa's lap.

"Yeah," I said. "We can make it – if we go outside."

"Outside? Are you mental?" Bob asked. "It's frickin' cold out there."

"I know it is. But if we go that way" – I pointed to the mall, full to the gills with people – "we're never gonna make it in time,"

"Oh, for fuck's sake. Ok, let's go."

We took a sharp turn past the Peoples Drug Store and hit the outside.

"Holy fuck, it's cold!" I screamed.

"I told you," Bob said as his teeth chattered together.

Neither of us were dressed for this, but we moved as quickly as we could past the outside walls of Eyerly's department store and back into the mall next to Roy Rogers. This side of the mall wasn't as insane as the other, so we were able to move through the line pretty quick. We got our food and sat down. "Jesus fuck me Christ. I am so tired," I blurted out as I took out my roast beef sandwich and stood back up. I walked up to the sauce dispensers, drowned the sandwich in horsey sauce and BBQ sauce, and sat back down at the table. "How is Ron doing?"

"He's good. We haven't been practicing much because, you know, he's grounded all the time. You should talk to him."

"Pfft," I spit out. "He doesn't want to talk to me."

"Sure he does. You guys are good friends. Girls happen, man. Nothing we can do about that."

"I guess."

"You guess? I wake up with a boner every single day. We can't control it." Bob started laughing. "Anyway, so how's the new 'band'?"

I managed a tiny smile. "Huh. Fine, I guess. The guys are ok players. Not great, but ok. They're just so old. They do drugs and drink – a lot. I can't believe they can even play as well as they do, and they're really not that good."

"You gonna stick with 'em?" Bob asked between bites.

I took a bite of my roast beef sandwich and thought for a second. "I guess so. I dunno. Nothin' better to do. I keep trying to get them to play newer, current metal songs. All they want to play is Led Zeppelin and Black Sabbath and shit. Don't get me wrong, I love to listen to those, but play them? Not so much. It's not my cup of tea and, plus, it's old shit. I've gotten them to play one Judas Priest tune, but they're always bitching about it. 'Breaking the Law' is a fucking easy song, but they don't want to learn anything new and they're always fucked-up at practice. I'm tired of it, frankly."

"At least you're playing. We've only managed to have a couple of practices, and it's been hard to keep it together."

"Yeah, but I'd rather be playing with guys my own age. I want to play songs from bands like Queensrÿche, Iron Maiden, Krokus. Current stuff. Cool stuff."

I took another bite. Bob was full-on shoveling fries into his mouth but managed a little shrug.

"Anyway. What are you doing Tuesday night?" I asked, my mouth still quite full.

"Well, Ron is grounded so practice got cancelled. Again. Plus, not sure I'm gonna keep playin' with John anyway. He thinks he's god's gift to the guitar, and it's kinda pissing me off. So I guess it'll just be me and my homework, I'm sure. Oh, and Harold and Todd are coming over to play D&D."

I sank back in the molded plastic seat. "Ahh... D&D. I miss D&D."

"You should come over. Harold has put together this kick-ass campaign. At least he says it is. You should come."

"I wish I could. The old fogeys are playing Tuesday night. At the Southern."

The Southern was one of the shittiest dive bars in town. It smelled like stale beer and desperation. The floors were sticky, and the crowd was a mix of cowboys, bikers, criminals, and hard-looking old women.

"The Southern?" Bob looked shocked. "Holy shit, dude! That place is a D.U.M.P. Dump. My dad has talked about that place. He used to go there when it was a country bar way back in the '60s."

"Yeah, I know. I'm sure it hasn't changed a bit. The place sucks. But their staff is high most of the time, so I can probably sneak you in, and they let me buy drinks so I can probably slip you a few."

"Hmmm... what about Harold and Todd?"

"Bring 'em along. We go on at eight. Come to the side door in the alley at 7:30, and I'll let you guys in. You can see what a shithole that place really is."

"Ha. Not sure they'll want to go, but I'll ask them at school tomorrow." Bob paused, "You gonna be there?"

"Yes, Mom, I'll be at school tomorrow."

Bob laughed and then looked at his watch. "Time to make the donuts."

We cleaned up our table and dumped our trash, then headed

into the mall to fight through the Christmas shoppers to get back to work on time.

The following Tuesday at school, I was swapping out books at my locker, which was central enough – barely – that I could avoid carrying around forty pounds worth of books all day. My mom had wanted me in all the smart classes. She was adamant that education was the best way out of this place and, while she wasn't wrong, I had convinced myself that there was another way – a cooler way. I wasn't all that interested in all the schoolwork. But I did my part. I took the smart classes and carried the heavy books.

Bob saw me cussing the books at my locker and ran over. "Hey, I talked to Todd and Harold."

"Well, hello, Bobby," I said in a very official-sounding voice as I closed my locker. I shifted into my Jewish accent. "Well, what did they say? I'm on pins and needles here."

Before I got my license, my job, my social life, I spent most weekends with my Jewish grandparents who lived in Washington, DC, right over the border from Silver Spring. It was one of my favorite places in the whole world. My grandparents were two of the best people I've ever known and being at their house felt safe, at times when I didn't feel so safe. It also allowed me to spend time with my extended family, on my mother's side, who were all Jewish to the extreme. Jewish stereotypes exist for a reason. While most people make fun of it, I embraced it. Even my Great-aunt Nina, who was seventy but acted like she was ninety. She would complain to my grandmother that her chicken was always dry (it wasn't) or that she wasn't feeding her brother, my grandfather, properly (she was). Complaining and arguing were an art form, and they were the masters. Because of this, I was known to slip into Yiddish from time to time. This went over well in a rural area where some of the folk were either outright racists or closet racists.

Bob replied, "They're in. We'll meet you at the Southern's side door at 7:30."

This made me happy. I was missing my friends, and this was a great chance for them to see what I'd been up to these past couple of weeks.

"Good deal," I shot back happily. "You'll have fun. They serve booze to anyone in there, so bring some cash."

"I can't drink, I'll be driving."

"Then tell Todd and Harold to bring some cash. They can buy me drinks."

"Don't you get free drinks?"

"Are you kidding? I think they charge the band double. They let me drink, but I have to pay!"

We laughed a bit, but I was serious. That bar was full of tightwads. The place always reminded me of that scene in *The Blues Brothers*, the one at the country bar, Bob's Country Bunker. Every time we left the Southern, I always heard in my head, "Well, the band made two hundred dollars' but y'all boys drank three hundred dollars' worth of beer."

That evening was a cold, cold November night, and I had heard on the radio that they were calling for sleet, or at least a little bit of freezing rain. That was always fun in the Camaro. Rear wheel drive, light rear end. Not a good combo in bad weather. I parked the Camaro on the street in front of the Southern. So far, no sign of the bad weather to come, but the clouds looked a little ominous, plus it was early and the weather had a way of changing in a matter of seconds. I got out and grabbed my gig bag from the back seat, locked the car (sometimes that worked), and walked into the bar. "Holy fuck!" I thought. The place smelled worse than usual, and that was bad. Really bad. Bad enough to put a pucker on my puss. I ran my bag backstage, and by backstage I mean the back room with the pool table. I dropped my stuff and came back out and joined the rest of the band, who were already at the bar.

"What's up, guys?" I belted out as I sat on a bar stool and slapped my hands on the bar. It was sticky, probably from the night before. Yuck. Monday night was pool tournament night. All kinds of low-lifes on Monday night. Hell, who was I kidding, there were lowlifes every night in this shithole.

Eddie, my stepdad's work buddy, looked over for a quick flash and got back to his beer. "What's up, kid? How was school?" Clever. The guys all laughed. They thought this was hilarious. They always gave me a lot of shit about my age, but they knew I was better than their old fat fuck singer. Still, I kept waiting for the hazing to subside. It never did.

I smirked and gave it right back to him. "Fine, Dad. How was work?"

That didn't elicit the laugh I was looking for, but I didn't give a shit at this point. I was just about done with these guys. Time to get my drink on – the only way I was gonna make it through this shitshow. I turned to the bar mistress, who looked like what would happen if Aunt Bee from *The Andy Griffith Show* went on a meth bender. "Can I get a Long Island iced tea?" This was my drink of choice. My jam. I hadn't quite acquired a taste for beer yet, so I found a drink that tasted a bit like a lemon-sour but it would knock me on my ass and get me through these nights.

"Are you old enough to drink, kid?" she shot back. I had seen her in there before and she had served me in the past, but I was guessing she didn't remember much of anything, so I was not really surprised by the response.

"I'm with the band," I said, puffing my chest out a bit. She looked me up and down in that uncomfortable old lady way and smiled. She started making the drink. I figured she was just giving me shit. She was probably a friend of Eddie. They looked like they were the same age.

Speaking of Eddie, he continued to give me shit. "By the way, thanks for bothering to show up." The band had been a little miffed that they had to load in without me. They had gotten there at 5:30, right after work. It was now 7:00. Truth be told, this was one of the reasons why I wanted to be a singer. To just show up and sing. All I had to bring was a mic and some cool clothes. I had initially wanted to play drums until I figured out how expensive it was and how much shit I would have to carry around, not to mention trying to fit all of that shit into a '68 Camaro. I made up an excuse about school, but truth be told there was another reason I was late. I had driven Lonnie home after school, and her parents were still at work. We had found a great use for her Halloween costume, even though it never stayed on long.

The bartender set the Long Island iced tea in front of me. I took a sip, and my nose crinkled up. "Sour," I said. But it tasted good and, more importantly, strong.

"Alright," Eddie mustered as he dropped off the bar stool. "Time to get this show on the road." This must have been his favorite line because he said it every time. I could imagine that someday when this dirtbag had kids, he'd load them up in a station wagon to head out for a miserable road trip, declare, "Time to get this show on the road," and his kids' eyes would roll just as hard as mine did then.

The rest of the crew rolled off their bar stools and headed toward the right side of the stage (stage left). I looked up at the clock. 7:15. My friends would be outside the side door in fifteen minutes. I took a quick glance out the front set of windows and noticed that it was starting to rain, but it sounded a little louder than water – more like Tic Tacs hitting pavement.

"Great," I thought, "fucking great. I hate the cold." Freezing-cold rain was coming down. Could even be full-on ice or sleet by the time we'd be done at midnight. I shook my head as I thought about what the drive home was gonna look like. I didn't even want to be here, not really. But I wanted to play music, and at the moment this is what I had.

A few folks came in from the rainy outdoors, but the bar was pretty empty. It wasn't a big place to begin with. Probably five or six people in the bar, ten or eleven if you included the band. Plus it was a Tuesday night. We had played here on a Tuesday a few times, and it was never much better than this. I was starting to worry that I might be a little too obvious letting a few teenagers in via the side door.

I finished my iced tea and looked at the clock again. 7:28. I headed toward the side door. Luckily, there was no clear line of sight from the bar to the door. I thought for sure that the old lady bartender would rat me out if she could see me, and there was a bouncer somewhere around here, but I hadn't seen him yet. I didn't wear a watch, but I figured that two minutes had to have passed. I slinked toward the door, looked around, and opened it.

Bob, who always wore a watch and was usually on time, was standing out in the rain with Harold and Todd. They looked like drowned rats with little bits of ice bouncing off of their soggy heads. A rush of cold air blew in. The boys were smiling, happy that at last they'd be able to come in out of the cold, possibly be served alcohol, and sit and listen to rock and roll music on a school night.

Best-laid plans...

Almost as if in slow motion, the smiles dropped from their mouths and a large, looming shadow moved across their terrified faces. "Oh no!" I thought. "The bouncer!" Well, now I knew where he was. He came up behind me and grabbed the door handle. As he shoved the door closed, I saw the disappointed look on my friends' faces and their hands went up in protest. Then *bam!* – the door slammed shut. Hard.

The bouncer only said one word. "Nope!"

He turned and walked away, and I was left inside without my friends, only a bunch of Southern Tuesday regulars. Old drunks, including my bandmates. The glamorous life of a rock and roller.

We managed to play one-and-a-half uninspired sets of music. The bar cleared out and we stopped playing early due to the shitty weather. I helped the band load out all of their gear. I was an asshole, but not a total asshole. After load-out, I was drenched and cold. I got into the Camaro and turned the key. Nothing. Of course this was gonna happen. She didn't like the rain and liked freezing rain even less. A jump wouldn't help tonight. I flagged down Eddie. I loaded myself and my gig bag into his truck, and he drove me home.

We didn't talk the whole way. We had nothing to talk about – we existed in two different worlds. Plus I was beat. When he pulled up in front of my house, I jumped out quickly and went right inside, showered, and went to bed.

The next morning I was sick and decided to stay home from school. I needed to recuperate and think about what I really wanted to be doing with music. I was so done with the old dude band. I knew it was time for something else.

14

MIDNITE DYNAMITE

THE FOLLOWING SATURDAY, the mall was Christmas madness as usual, but Radio Shack was surprisingly dead. I sat at the counter, with my chin on the back of my hand, watching throngs of people walking by in the mall. I was bored so I fired up the game Defender on one of the display computers. My boss, Mr. Carter, came from around a pile of TRS-80 color computer boxes to admonish my laziness. "Hey. Have you finished putting prices on the CB radios we just got in?"

I responded without looking away from the screen. "Uh... no... uh... I'll do it in a sec."

"You'll do it now, mister. Those are gonna be hot sellers. Just in time for the holidays! We can't have people waiting while we look up prices when the mad rush hits. It's not professional."

"Not professional?" I thought. "This guy is lecturing me on what is 'not professional'?" He had nudie magazines in the employee washroom and plenty of hand lotion and Kleenex. Odd. Lord only knew what he was doing in there. I certainly didn't want to know.

"10-4, good buddy," I quipped.

I turned off the game and slowly stood up and headed to the back of the store. When I emerged from the Radio Shack's back room dungeon with an armful of CB radios, the bell dinged and Bob came into the store. I started quickly stocking the shelf.

"You take a break yet?" he asked, grabbing a box and looking it over.

"No. Let me get the rest of these CB radios out here and then we can go grab a bite. They *are* hot sellers, you know?" I said, very sarcastically.

We both laughed. CB culture was in full swing in the '70s, but at this point in the '80s it was definitely out, and Bob and I knew it was a fucking joke. In its time, though, it was just another way for people to communicate, long before cell phones saved/ruined the world.

I finished up and yelled back to my boss. "Hey, Mr. Carter, I'm taking my dinner break now."

I heard Mr. Carter's muffled voice as it emanated from the bathroom. "Is there anyone in the store?"

I looked around and saw a couple of kids messing with the RC cars.

"Uh, no," I said as I shrugged my shoulders to Bob.

"Oh... ok then. Thirty minutes," Mr. Carter fired back in a garbled, out-of-breath voice.

"Thirty minutes. You got it," I yelled. I turned to Bob. "Let's get out of here quick before he comes out."

We stepped into the madness of the mall and looked both ways. Bob looked across at the Long John Silver's. "Fried fish?"

"Fried fish? Ugh, yeah, might as well," I said, looking down the mall at the wall-to-wall bodies. I didn't want to go back outside and go around again. Plus I only had thirty minutes. "Fuck it." We headed across the mall to Long John Silver's. "Let's hurry up and eat – I want to get some Dragon's Lair time in," I said, taking in the sounds of the arcade as we walked by.

"Dragon's Lair?" Bob made a yuck face. "That game is a rip-off. It's fifty cents a play, and the controls are weird. I can't make it past the oozy room level. It sucks."

"Sucks? That game is the future. Have you seen Space Ace? All games are gonna be like that." It turned out all games were not going to be like that, but I loved the game and especially the Don Bluth artwork, so I was a bit of a die-hard fan.

We entered Long John Silver's and ordered the usual, fish and chips with an extra side of hush puppies. Balls of fried dough. What could be better than that? At least here they didn't drop them on the floor. Or if they did, at least I didn't have to see it. We sat down to eat, and Bob jammed a piece of fish in his mouth and proceeded to talk with his mouth full. "Oh shit, totally forgot to tell you, guess what?"

"You're pregnant?"

"Har har. Very funny, asshole. No, I'm not pregnant. I just found out that Kix is playing the all-ages show tomorrow night at the Foot. We have to go."

"Sweet. Hell yeah, we do. We need to call John, Andy and…"

I nearly said Ron. He and I still hadn't talked. Hadn't cleared the air. Frankly, I was scared of what he would say to me. I felt like total shit for what had happened and anything he would say to me, I thought, I would totally deserve.

"Have you seen Andy lately?"

"Come to think of it no, not in a while. Why?"

"He is full-on Captain Caveman."

"What the hell? Captain Caveman? What the fuck are you talking about?"

"He's been jamming with this band called Lynx. Up in Middletown. They are heavy with a capital *H*."

"He's been playing? I didn't know that. Huh. Well, I guess since we don't have anything going on, it makes sense. Guitar or bass?"

"Bass."

"I knew it. I knew he was gonna be a bass player," I said, somewhat vindicated.

"Yeah, he's getting pretty good," Bob said proudly.

"How do you know?" I said, puzzled.

"He gave me a tape. Oh, that's right. I also forgot to tell you that Andy and John just started working at Wards. With me. I got 'em jobs for the Christmas season. Well, at least I got 'em interviews."

"Wow. I had no idea. His band has a tape?" I felt a tinge of jealousy flash up my spine. Exodus hadn't reached the we-have-a-tape phase before I blew it all to shit with my inability to control my hormones. I wanted a band with a tape.

Bob continued, "Yeah. We hang out in the music and electronics section during our break, and he's banging out some tunes. He's not too happy with the job though."

"Why is that?" I asked.

Bob started laughing. "Well, he's the FNG, so he has cleanup duty every time a kid pukes in the store."

"Ewww. Gross!" I said, disgusted.

"You'd be surprised how often that happens too. Every time there's a call over the loudspeaker, he has to go grab a bucket and a mop and clean it up." Bob broke into his CB radio voice. "*Chhk*, cleanup, aisle five. Ladies' lingerie. *Chhk*." He snort-laughed. "He *hates* it."

"I bet he does. What does John do? I thought you guys were fighting?"

"No, he's fighting with the lady in the garden section at Wards." Bob laughed. "She's been there since the beginning of time, and she and John don't get along. She's always yelling at him. I don't think she likes boys with long hair."

"And John definitely has long hair," I shot back with a laugh. "So you and John are good?"

"Yeah, we're good. You talk to Ron yet?"

"Shit!" I looked up at the clock on the wall. "I have to get back."

"Yeah, me too. You didn't answer my question."

"I will. Just have to find the right time."

We got up, threw away our trash, and headed back out into the mall, me toward my prison and Bob toward his.

"See ya, Bobby."

"Later, dude."

I passed by the arcade, Time-Out, stopped in front and looked over. No Dragon's Lair for me today. No time left. Also not much money. Bob wasn't wrong about that game being expensive, and your plays didn't last very long. It was a good way to waste ten dollars in as many minutes. Plus Time-Out was doing triple babysitting duty today for all the Christmas-shopping parents. I was not going in there.

I kept walking and picked up the pace to make sure I wasn't late. "Andy is playing," I thought. "When the fuck did this happen?" I guess I was just so preoccupied with what was going on in my life that I didn't notice him not hanging around the fountain, or not seeing him coming out to the mall. Good for him. We were all a pretty hard-working, committed group, but out of all of us, Andy was the most committed.

I turned the corner and into the Radio Shack. Back to work.

• • •

CARS WERE STARTING to roll in at dusk for the all-ages show on Sunday night at the Rabbit's Foot.

I pulled the Camaro alongside Bob's Corona. He, like everyone else, was fussing with his hair. We got out of our respective vehicles and congregated at the back of our cars.

We were both dressed head-to-toe in the full-on rock regalia of the day. Ripped-up jeans, ripped-up band shirts, with bandanas around our arms and legs. Hair was big – really, really big.

I greeted Bob with the obligatory cool head nod and a "Hey."

"Hey," Bob gave back. "So, when you see Andy, do not laugh at him. You know how he gets. He'll spend the rest of the night in the bathroom looking in the mirror, trying to figure out what to change."

"I won't. I wouldn't do that," I said, but I didn't always abide by this rule. We used to make fun of Andy. Hell, we all made fun of each other, but Andy was very sensitive about his hair. The rest of us had managed to grow flowing manes pretty quickly, but it took Andy a lot longer. The irony was that once his did grow out, he definitely had the best hair, but the damage had been done. After months of ribbing, Andy was more than a little self-conscious.

"Sure. Sure you wouldn't." Bob grinned. He knew better.

I gave him a big 'who-me?' shrug for good measure.

A large group of teen wannabe rockers was starting to gather. Out of the corner of my eye, I spied the kid from Sam Goody. He was standing with another long-haired kid and a dumpy kid with short hair, all wearing bangles and torn-up clothing.

I motioned over to the new trio. "Hey, I'm gonna go talk to those guys."

"Is that the kid from Sam Goody?" Bob asked, squinting to get a good look.

"Yeah, I think so." It was hard to tell since everyone was all done up rather than wearing their daily street clothes.

"I thought you said he was scary?"

"Out here we're all scary," I said slyly.

I gave Bob a big grin, and he followed me over.

"Hey, man. What's up?" I said to the group of rockers.

The Sam Goody kid gave a head nod and a slight hair flip. "Hey."

This kid was too cool for school. He barely acknowledged us. He was surveying the crowd, seeing if there was anyone else, anyone cooler that he might know. I noticed his aloofness and tried to strike up a conversation. "You work in the mall, don't you? Sam Goody?"

"Yeah, that's me. I'm there all the time. Helps me with my record fix."

He laughed. Very cool though. More like a *heh, heh, heh* kinda laugh. Slow and deliberate.

I kept going. "I hear ya. I'm Sean, and this Bob. He plays guitar. I sing."

You had to introduce yourself with your musical talent right up front. There were so many wannabes in this group that it was hard to separate the wheat from the chaff, as folks would say.

He looked us over for a second, trying to surmise from a glance whether we were full of shit or actually knew something, anything about music. "Is that right? I'm Jak, with just a *k*. This is Mike and Dave."

"Jak, with just a *k*?" I asked, confused.

"Yeah. J-A-K, Jak," Jak said, seeming somewhat perturbed to have to repeat himself.

I shrugged. "Sure, why not," I thought.

We all shook hands and exchanged pleasantries.

Now it was my turn to become the interviewer, figure out what they were all about, musically speaking. "Are you guys in a band together?"

Sam Goody dove right in. "Yeah. Straight Jacket. Mike plays bass, Dave plays drums. Our singer isn't here. He had to work."

This Jak character seemed to do all the talking for the group. He was wearing a leather jacket under a jean jacket with the sleeves cut off. The jean jacket had an American flag sewn on the back, and he was wearing ripped-up jeans. His hair was longer in the back than the front. It wasn't quite a mullet, but it flowed and bopped around his head as he swaggered around. He definitely had cool down. Mike was also wearing a leather jacket and ripped-up jeans, plus wrestling shoes, and had jet-black hair down past his shoulders. He also looked cool. Dave was the odd man out. He was wearing new Wranglers, a T-shirt, and a few metal bangles, and had super-short hair. He had spiked it up with gel, but you could tell that his street clothes look would be decidedly tame (or lame). He was no rocker.

After a few seconds of sizing each other up, I continued, "Bummer. I mean, about the working part. Cool band name though."

"Yeah. It is." Jak must have come up with the name. He seemed pretty proud of it. He got a quick burst of excitement, almost like a kid. "Hey, we're playing a show next month if you want to check us out. Hold on a sec."

Jak went to his car (a beat-up, white Chevy LUV mini pickup with a camper top), opened the driver's-side door, and reached in so far that his ass was pointed up in the air. He pulled out a homemade flyer, brought it over, and handed it to me. While I was looking it over, he pulled out a pack of cigarettes, grabbed one from the pack, and lit it.

Mike pulled out a cigarette and motioned toward Jak. "Hey, man, give me a light."

These were the first words we heard come out of Mike's mouth. Bob and I looked on in awe. We weren't smokers. We never hung out with people who did, not really. Lonnie smoked, but only when she needed to calm her nerves. We'd kinda hang out with the 'heads' who sat outside the locker hallway doors on the far side of the school. At recess, that place was lit up like a chimney, both by the heads and by the FFA'ers, the farm kids. Other than hanging around those kids, we kinda lived a sheltered life, mixed-drink breakfasts and snorting Pez notwithstanding.

We both looked at Dave.

"Oh hey. I don't smoke," Dave said, waving his arms as if to say, 'I would never, ever do something like that!'

We watched in childlike awe as these two leather-clad rockers coolly let out mountains of billowing white smoke. Just then, Bob saw something out of the corner of his eye and quickly moved in and whispered in my ear.

"Don't look now. Two o'clock. It's Captain Caveman and the zoo crew."

I didn't know what "two o'clock" meant, so I looked around furiously, wondering what the fuck Bob was talking about. Bob could tell I was struggling, so he discreetly pointed to a group of hairy men – and by hairy I don't mean body hair, I mean fur – making their way toward us. There he was, our buddy Andy with three of his bandmates. Four 'cats' from the band Lynx, dressed head-to-toe in fur. Fur boots, fur pants, fur pelts around their waists and necks. This look was as cool as it was ridiculous. Totally over the top.

"Holy shit. You weren't kidding. Captain Caveman." I started to laugh.

Jak, Mike, and Dave looked at us, kinda puzzled.

Bob leaned over to me with a very stern, clenched-teeth whisper. "*Do not* laugh!"

"It's gonna be kinda hard. They look fucking ridiculous."

"I know they do, but *do not* laugh. You know how he gets."

Andy and his group of Neanderthals walked up to our group. Andy greeted us old band buds and the new friends. "Hey, guys. Sean, Bob. What's up?"

"Hey, Andy. You guys look… good," Bob said.

It was hard for me not to laugh, but they did look pretty good once the initial shock wore off. It was bold and, more importantly, their band was really, really good, which I found out when I got to hear them a few months later. It was hard for them to get shows because they were *so* heavy, which we kids of course loved, but club owners and private party folks wanted the same old shit played night after night. They wanted people to come, sometimes pay a cover, and drink. Drink *a lot*.

Most of our friends were nowhere close to drinking age. We could make the trip to Georgetown to drink and then suffer the hour-long drive back home, drunk. Or we had to sneak to drink. It wasn't easy for us to get into clubs, so bands like Andy's lived on the outside. They played places like the Braddock Mountain Roller Rink, which was where I would eventually see them. Their shows were amazing. Not only for the music, but also for the fact that they wore their caveman get-ups on stage. During a show. I couldn't imagine how much those guys would sweat or how bad that would smell! Eventually they would be cool, but tonight they looked like Billy Joel on the cover of the Attila record. They actually looked too good for this crowd.

"Hey, Andy," I blurted out. "I guess this is what you've been up to, huh?"

"Yeah. Been jamming with these guys for a bit. This is Mike, Jeff, and Dave."

I thought, "Too many Mikes, too many Daves. I will never keep 'em all straight." We all hung out and played in the same circles, opening up for each other, and playing shows together. We would eventually land on last names. It was just easier.

We all said hi to each other in cool, rock star ways, a nod or a muttered 'what's up?'.

"You guys should come check us out. We're heavy. Like really heavy. Kinda like…"

As Andy started to describe the band, people began filing into the club.

I quickly replied as we all started walking toward the door. "Yeah. Definitely. I'd love to come check it out."

After a few moments of navigating the queue, we all walked up the steps and into the front door. The hallowed hall of a rock club lay before us. I had never been to a real club before. Immediately I was hit with a strong odor. It smelled like vinegar. It was the stale beer, but I didn't know that at the time. It was a full-on olfactory assault. My nose quickly became accustomed to the smell – it had plenty of time since the queue of kids was taking its time getting through the entrance of this fine establishment. While lingering in the foyer, I saw a glass cabinet full of pictures. Pictures of bands. Some signed, some not. Some well-known acts, like the one we were here to see tonight, and some not. But all looked pretty much the same. They were all wearing tight clothing of some sort, some leather, some spandex, with their hair as big as they could get. Most of the bands and band members looked like girls. The hair. The makeup. The seductive poses. That was the thing in the mid-'80s. The more you looked like a girl, the more likely you were to pick up a chick. It was weird. I never really understood it and still don't.

We finally made it to the doorman, and I produced my ID. He gave it a good look, handed it back, and barked out, "Right hand!" I held out my hand, and he put a humongous *X* on it with a big, black permanent marker. Apparently the clubs still needed to make money on an all-ages night, so they were serving alcohol if you were over twenty-one. If you were under twenty-one, they needed a way to tell, right away, in a dark and dingy club, so the big fucking *X* was the best thing they could come up with. "This fucking thing is gonna be there forever," I thought. Not forever, as it turned out, but a few days. It would have been there a week if I hadn't scrubbed the shit out of it.

As we made our way into the main room of the club, people started filing into the few tables on the sides. The floor was already jam-packed with kids. They were the first ones in. This was where the action was, but it was mostly for dancing and we didn't dance. The tables had filled up pretty quickly, so I moved to the far wall and stood behind a row of tables. Bob followed me. I was gonna stand for the show anyway. I wasn't gonna sit down at a rock show, but I also wasn't gonna get up close and personal with a bunch of sweaty kids on a ten-by-ten-foot dance floor. I always stood. It was the excitement of it. Bob stood next to me, though I think he would have preferred to sit. Jak, Mike, and Dave got a table on the opposite side. Andy and the zoo crew were sitting at the table behind them. How they sat down in those outfits I had no idea.

The lights went down and the room went nuts.

Kix hit the stage with a power that nearly knocked me down, playing their opening song "Midnite Dynamite," the title track from their most recent record. Now the place was really going ape shit.

"This. This is what it's all about," I thought.

Kix was an amalgamation of many of the bands that had come before them. Steve Whiteman's skinny-chic vibe, always talking about sex and singing in his signature high-pitched, histrionic style always reminded me of a mixture of Robert Plant and Steven Tyler, but he brought those influences out in his own, very unique style. Beyond Prince, Steve, to me, was the best rock singer in the biz. He still is.

The double guitar attack of Brian "Damage" Forsythe and Ronnie "10/10" Younkins was what gave Kix its soul. The two players couldn't be more different. The combination of Brian's Keith-Richards-meets-Joe-Perry-meets-Duane-Allman riffage and Ronnie's silky-smooth, blues-roots rock was something special. Unique. And then there was Donnie Purnell. The main songwriter and the sloppy, almost punk rock bassist who would flop around the stage as if he was a rag doll on some invisible string. He would bounce in between the other players effortlessly. He and Jimmy "Chocolate" Chalfant were the heart of this band, banging out sexy, gut-punching rhythms that you could feel down to your shoes.

I leaned over and strained to yell into Bob's ear. "I can't believe they're playing here. On an all-ages night. Holy fuck!"

"Why not? Look at this place! It's packed. It's wild! We are the next generation," Bob said with more than a hint of pride.

We were the next generation. We were wild. I looked on in awe. Kix was (and still is) one of the best live rock bands on the planet. They put everything into a show (still do) to give the audience their money's worth.

"I want to be like that," I yelled, my voice not nearly getting over the guitars ripping out their chords.

Bob looked over at me. "What?"

I said it louder, really screaming now. "I said, I want to be like that. I wanna do that!" I pointed to the stage.

Bob didn't turn around this time but muttered, "Uh-huh."

Bob didn't hear a word I said. He was in his own rock fantasy world.

The entire room pulsated to the song. It was like magic. I spotted Jak sitting at his table. He was wearing the same look on his face that I was – the same one that everyone in the room who actually played music was wearing. Jak looked across the room, and our eyes locked. He gave me the Jak nod. The nod that said 'this is cool' and 'this is what we were born to do.' This was the nod that would kick off a thirty-plus-year friendship based in music but extending to many parts of our lives. We had that shared dream, that goal of playing music. It didn't matter how, it didn't matter where. It was what we wanted to do beyond all else. We would play music together, off and on, and write many songs together over the next couple of decades. We never really made it, although Jak got close a couple of times. But that stopped being the point, at least for me. The fact was that most didn't make it. Most did their time as garage bands and moved on when it was time to get a job or raise a family (or both) and never looked back. We weren't like that. We weren't built that way. Music got inside us like an incurable virus and never let us go. And even though we would never really made a living doing the thing we loved most, that didn't stop us from playing. It never would.

On this night, we had our whole musical lives in front of us, and this was all we wanted. Was all I wanted. To us, it wasn't just a dream. It was *the* dream.

As Kix's stage show raged on, my mind kept racing. I didn't want to play with the 'old fogeys' anymore. I wanted to play metal with kids my own age, with my friends. I wanted us to be like them, Kix. A bunch of cool kids up on the stage making music and making girls scream. That was never going to happen at the burned-out shitholes I was playing with the old guys.

15

INTO THE FIRE

THE MONDAY MORNING AFTER that life-altering rock show was hard to deal with. The alarm went off, as it did on every school day, at 7:30 a.m. It was too damn early. I had been out pretty late the night before, at least for a school night. I tussled around in bed for a while, not wanting to get up and thinking if there was any way I could pull a sick card today. Today, of all days, I needed it. I looked at the big black X on my hand. "It really happened," I thought. It almost seemed like a dream. The X. The tattoo of being underage at a local club. This wouldn't be the last one I would have. Far from it.

"Raised on the Radio" by the Ravyns was playing on my clock radio. Time to get up.

The Ravyns were another band of local heroes. Or they were mostly local. They were from Baltimore, which was only about a forty-five minute drive from our small town, so they might as well have been local. They had landed a song (the song I was listening to) on the *Fast Times at Ridgemont High* soundtrack, which shot them into the national spotlight.

I really liked that movie. I had identified with the film's anti-hero, Jeff Spicoli. So much so that I wore his shoes (black-and-white checkered Vans) and continue to wear them to this very day. "Raised on the Radio" was also featured on their first, full-length, self-titled LP, and while that song was great, so was the rest of the album. Songs like "No Regular Woman," "Don't Leave Me This Way," and many others would earn space on my playlists for decades.

The song ended, and I slowly got out of bed, took a long, hot shower, and headed downstairs for my ever-so-brief interaction with the 'rents before I left. My mom was at the stove and my stepdad was sitting at the kitchen table. A typical morning.

"Can I fix you something?" my mom said over her shoulder as she eyed the eggs frying in the pan on the stove.

I had never been a fan of fried eggs. Ever. "Nah, I'm running late," I responded quickly as I made my way toward the door.

This time she didn't look up from the eggs that were now popping. They smelled disgusting. "You were out kinda late last night."

"Yeah. We went to see Kix at the Foot. It was an all-ages night," I added to make sure she knew that I didn't sneak into a club to drink beer.

She chuckled a bit. "Wow. Is that place still there? It used to be called something else. What was it?" She stood there contemplating her own question.

Just then, the stepdad chimed in, "The Cross Keys. It was a biker dump."

Mom turned to look at him, sliding eggs out of the pan onto a plate. "Oh, that's right. It was a dump, wasn't it?"

I laughed a bit. "Still is. But the music was good."

I got into my car, and she started right up. Thank god for small miracles.

I picked Mikey up on the way, as usual, and we headed to school. No drama, no rum – not today. I was tired and also broke. It was dead quiet for the first twenty minutes of the ride. I was guessing Mikey was only half awake as well. After a while, he spoke up.

"Hey, my brother and his roommates are having a party this weekend. We should go."

"Roommates?" I said. "I thought he lived at home?"

"Nah, he moved out a while ago. He's living in a townhouse in that cookie-cutter neighborhood, right down the road from Bob's house."

"Hmm, sounds interesting," I said. And it did. Mikey's brother Sam was a wild man. I couldn't imagine what kind of mischief we could get up to at one of his parties.

We got to the school, and I pulled the Camaro into its usual spot. Mikey and I headed down the sidewalk, past the tennis courts, through the side door, and straight to the water fountains at the end of the cafeteria. Bob was the only one standing there.

I slapped Bob on the arm. "What's up, Bobby boy?"

Bob held up his right hand – you could see a slightly faded but still very noticeable black X.

I held up my right hand with the same X. We both laughed.

Mikey shot us a very disappointed look. "Hey, man. I wanted

to go to that but nobody called me and offered to give me a ride." He looked right at me and exaggerated his delivery.

"You said your mom wouldn't let you go," I responded, more than a little peeved.

"I know," Mikey said nonchalantly as he started unwrapping a Pop-Tart and shoving it in his mouth.

Bob rubbed his hand. "I can't believe they put this big fucking *X* on everyone's hand. It's an all-ages night, for chrissake. Everyone is underage. Doesn't make any sense."

"They're bouncers, not rocket scientists. Plus I did see some people getting beers. I think they still serve alcohol – the *X* is just a way to tell the kiddies from the a-dults."

"I guess so. Man, that show was epic," Bob said as his face lit up. "Those guys are so fucking good."

"Yeah, they are," I replied.

"I hope we're half as good as that someday," Bob continued. "I think the singer is dating my sister's old babysitter."

"No way!" I exclaimed.

"Way. They're from around here, you know?"

"I knew that. Yeah, I guess I just never thought that would mean they know people we know. Cool."

Mikey, ever the wiseass, blurted out, "He's lame."

"The fuck you say. He's NOT lame," I said.

Bob jumped in, slightly offended. "No fucking way. Do you know how many girls he's probably—"

At this point, Lonnie approached the three of us, and Bob choked off the end of his last sentence. She was dressed in tight jeans and a

Def Leppard T-shirt (as usual) with a flannel shirt tied around her waist. She looked good. She always looked good.

She walked right up to me and planted a big kiss on my lips. I guess that cat was outta the bag.

"Hey, stranger. Where were you all weekend?" she asked.

"Working mostly. Oh, and then Bob and I went to see Kix at the Foot last night."

"You should've called me. We got back kinda late, but I would've come out. I had to take my stupid sister horseback riding all day. My parents made me. The bitch wants a horse, so Mommy and Daddy have to buy the bitch a horse," she said in a mocking tone.

She and her sister didn't get along. No one got along with her sister. She was three years younger and a total nightmare, a monster created by her overcompensating, absentee parents.

"Oh. I know. That would've been awesome. I knew you had a lot of shit to do this weekend though."

The truth was that I wasn't used to dating. I wasn't used to checking with someone else about my schedule. Plus, these were the days before cell phones, so it was a lot harder to track people down.

"They were really good," I continued. "Next time they play, we'll definitely go. They ain't no Def Leppard, but they'll do," I said with a slight smirk.

"Uh-huh. I hear you. Well, I have to bolt. I've got this paper due and I need to go negotiate a new due date."

"Hey, wait," I said, kinda stuttering. "Mikey's brother Sam is having a party on Friday if you wanna go. I mean, if you aren't busy or doing anything." Oh geez, I sounded like a nine-year-old.

"Um, sure. I'm not doing anything," she responded.

"Great," I said nervously.

"Great!" She smiled at us and took off across the cafeteria. "You boys be good," she said over her shoulder as she walked away.

I always liked to see her walk away. That girl could move her ass. While I was watching her ass intently, I could feel Bob giving me a stare down. "When did that happen?"

"When did what happen?" I replied.

"That?" Bob said, pointing to Lonnie as she faded out of sight down the center hallway.

"Oh. You mean her?"

"Yes, I mean her. Are you guys an item now?"

"Yeah. I guess we are."

It hadn't really been discussed, it just kinda happened, but certainly she and I were now an item. We were spending all of our free time together.

The bell rang, and off to class we went.

The rest of the school week was uneventful. A monotonous cascade of get up, go to school, be bored all day, go to work, go home, watch TV or play on the Atari, go to bed and get up the next day and do it all over again. The same old dull routine. And then Friday came along. "Finally," I thought as I heard the dismissal bell. I jetted out to the parking lot and straight to the Camaro. Mikey was already there waiting.

"Hey, bro!" he yelled. "Thank god it's Friday, motherfucker!"

"You ain't kidding," I shot back as I jammed open the door and threw my books on the back seat. Mikey climbed in. I never did understand why he always waited for me to get in the car. He knew that my passenger-side door didn't lock. Courtesy, I guess. We headed out of the parking lot and on the main road toward home.

Mikey was squirming in his seat. "Oh man. Tonight's gonna be awe-some. My brother scored some grain alcohol and there are gonna be chicks there and… and—"

"And it's going to be awesome," I interjected.

"Yeah, awesome!" He could barely contain himself. I pulled up in front of Mikey's house and he got out. He then leaned back into the car through the window. "Alright. Pick me up at 8:00."

"I'll be here," I said emphatically. "But, hey. You be ready at 8:00. I'm not coming in there in case your parents don't know where we're really going. Like last time."

Or really most times. Mikey was always telling his parents bullshit stories about where he was going, and they always kinda suspected he was full of shit. So they always tried to get a corroborating story. It was awkward when I didn't get that memo and had to survive the parental third degree.

Mikey banged the inside of the door panel as he turned to walk away. "Yeah, yeah, no sweat. I'll be ready."

"Uh-huh," I yelled after him. By this time, he was already at his front door. That skinny little fucker could move when he wanted to.

I got home and managed to avoid interacting with the parental units. Mom was outside doing something with the animals, and the stepdad wasn't home from work yet. I had a little time to kill but decided to take a shower and get all decked out in my rocker clothes. I was out the door at ten till 8:00. Plenty of time. I hopped in the car, closed the door, and jammed the key into the ignition. I needed to get out of there before my mom noticed I was leaving and asked questions about where I was going.

I turned the key. Nothing. "Oh shit!" I said under my breath. "Not now. Not *now!*" I closed my eyes and said the prayer. I took a deep breath and turned the key again. She fired up. "Holy shit!" I screamed. The car gods were with me. I threw the car into drive and headed down the driveway, kicking up dust and gravel like a stampede of ponies. I got to Mikey's at 8:00 on the dot. This was unusual for me. I was late most of the time, but tonight we had a mission. We were going to drink with the big boys, and I didn't want to be late for that. Plus, after my little lecture to Mikey, I knew I would be a fucking hypocrite if I rolled in at 8:15 or, worse, 8:30. As I pulled up I saw Mikey already waiting, standing at the end of his (considerably shorter) driveway. He was wearing a black sweatshirt, black jeans, and white leather Converse high-tops with black lettering. He was carrying his camo jacket. It was a little warm but you had to be prepared for it to turn quickly.

Mikey jumped in, and I tore off down the road.

Mikey started rummaging around in my console and dug out a tape. "Oh yeah, time for some pre-game music!" It was TNT's *Knights of the New Thunder*. This tape in general, and the song "Seven Seas" in particular, was sometimes used as our partying rally cry or driving music. We would jam this one loud whenever we were heading down to the bridge or out to Harp Road or anywhere else local teens would gather to blow off steam, consume alcohol or whatever they could find, and generally get lit. Mikey popped the tape into the player, rewound the first side, and let it rip. The first guitar chords from "Seven Seas" blasted out of the speakers and caused me to drive just a little faster. "Fuck yeah!" I yelled. Mikey gave back a hoot and a holler. We listened to the song three and a half times, and this got us to the entry of the neighborhood where the party was. Bob's neighborhood. I turned down toward the townhouses and noticed there was no place to park. There were cars everywhere. This was gonna be one heck of a party.

I finally found a place to park, two courts over, and Mikey and I walked through all kinds of brambles and weeds and finally emerged next to Sam's townhouse. The front yard, a tiny front yard, was full of people. I couldn't believe his neighbors were ok with this. Little did I know, they weren't. Sam and his douchebag jock roommates from the local community college would only last two months in this place.

Mikey and I walked through the throng of people and entered the front door, which was wide open. The house was equally full, packed wall-to-wall with people. I saw Lonnie in the corner talking to Mikey and Sam's little sister. She was deep in conversation but caught my eye as she looked around. She kept talking but smiled a bit. I could tell the smile was for me. She and I had been on the phone Thursday night – hell, we were on the phone almost every night – and she had reminded me of my invite to this party. I'd had to call Mikey to get his brother's address but he didn't know it, so the directions I had given her were not very helpful. But hey, she'd found it. How could you not with all the cars?

Mikey headed off to the kitchen, and I walked over to talk to my girl. It took me about ten minutes to get through the sea of people. When I finally did, I greeted her with a big hug.

"You made it!" I said as I held my hands out.

"No thanks to you. Those directions were shit," she said, half joking.

"Yeah, I know, sorry. Mike didn't know his own brother's address."

"Not surprising since this is about the fourth place he's lived in as many months," his sister chimed in.

"Nope. Definitely not surprised," I said. "How are you doing, Sally?"

"Not bad. This place is a madhouse though. Think I'm going to go outside. I'll see you guys in a bit."

"Ok. See you soon." Lonnie turned back to me. "Do you have a drink?"

"No. Just got here. Where are they?"

"In the kitchen." She grabbed my hand and led me into the kitchen through the wall of sweaty bodies. The kitchen was quite the sight. There was no furniture. Anywhere. Only four fifty-five-gallon galvanized trash cans, lined with trash bags filled with jungle juice. Jungle juice, for those who do not know, is pure grain alcohol (190 proof) mixed with an assortment of 'fruit' juices. Two trash cans were Hawaiian punch, two were grape drink. There were also ten watermelons, which had been injected with pure grain alcohol, taking up the entire kitchen counter. The kitchen looked like a science lab with the kids hanging over the trash cans like monkeys, filling up their red Solo cups with the nectar of the gods. As we walked through, our shoes stuck to the floor, which was covered with a mix of Hawaiian punch and grape drink and mud from people's shoes. It was disgusting. But hey, I wanted a drink. Lonnie grabbed me a red cup, and I became one of those monkeys scooping out my grog.

The night ended up being a bit of a blur after the first few cups of jungle juice. Lonnie had to go home – she was babysitting her siblings all day Saturday. At some point Bob showed up, and we ended up in the backyard sitting around a fire with the music blaring really, really loud. The song "Into the Fire" by Dokken came on, and Bob, Mike, and I were banging heads when, all of a sudden, this super-drunk douchebag jock stood up and literally walked into the fire while singing the song.

"Into the fire!" the jock yelled as he ran back and forth through the fire. It was awesome. Embers flying everywhere, the fire melting his high-top leather sneakers. Twenty or so people in the backyard were yelling, "Into the fire!" and cheering him on.

This was a townhouse. We had no business doing what we were doing in a single-family backyard, let alone this postage stamp. I had no idea how the cops had not shown up yet. People were inside punching holes in the walls, holes in the doors – it was chaos. It turned out that this was kind of a thing for the jocks that lived there. There was a whole stack of interior doors in the basement, so I guess that was the ritual. Punch the doors on Friday and Saturday, hang new doors on Sunday. It was crazy.

While all of this was going on, Mikey's brother Sam was walking around and reading the Bible to folks. He was shitfaced drunk. His entire face was glowing red from the punch he'd been drinking, and his eyes were all big and crazy. He was not at all religious, but when he was on the grain train, he got wild – really wild. It scared us a bit. Mikey, Bob, and I managed to find a quiet room away from the crowd. I think it was a bedroom, but it didn't have any furniture. It also didn't have kids in it, either drinking, smoking weed, or having sex. We sat down on the floor with our red Solo cups full of jungle juice and proceeded to belt out the entire *Too Fast for Love* album, a cappella. I mean the whole thing, from the first note of "Live Wire" to the last note of "On with the Show."

We knew this album by heart. Frontward and backward. Backward and forward. Bob mouthed the guitar parts, including the solos, and Mikey banged out the drum parts and sang along on the whole thing. He looked like the crazy Animal character from the Muppets, sloshing his 'juice' on his pant leg and all over the floor. Just as we were finishing up our concert to no one, Sam burst through the door. He was shirtless and shoeless, wearing only pants and a flower lei around his neck.

His hair was a wild, half-braided mess. Apparently a drunk girl had tried to braid it in the living room, but Sam couldn't sit still long enough for her to finish it. He kinda reminded me of that voodoo doll on *Night Gallery*. That doll gave me nightmares for weeks, and that's exactly how Sam looked now.

"Hey!" he said with a very pronounced slur. "Hey. Hey. You guys wanna go to Denny's?"

Fuck yeah, we did. We were starving. Who knew what time it was. Bob had a watch on, but he was too drunk to read it. But how were we gonna get there? There wasn't a sober person in the whole house.

Bob looked up in slow motion. "Who's gonna dr... Who's gonna... uh... who's gonna drrr..." He couldn't quite get it out, so he took his hands and made like he was driving a car and moving the steering wheel back and forth. "Who's gonna do that?" he finally got out.

"Shit. I'm driving. I got this. C'mon, you fuckers, let's go." Sam stumbled through his response.

That was good enough for us. We were more than a little stupid and very hungry. We stumbled through the house. The crowd had thinned a bit, and there were only about ten or fifteen people left. Everyone looked like they were only a few seconds away from passing out, including us.

"Ok. Who's going?" Sam yelled out.

"Me, me, me," came from all corners of the room.

"Ok. Who can drive?" Dead silence. Truth was no one there had any business getting behind the wheel. Finally, Sam said, "Fine. I'll drive. C'mon." He headed outside and we all followed. His minions. He started counting, "One, two, four, six, seven. Ok, seven." We all stood there and looked back and forth between Sam, the group, and Sam's car – a green 1979 Volkswagen Rabbit.

Bob, being ever the smart guy, finally chirped, "Hey. We can't all fit in there."

"Sure you can," Sam said.

"Uh, I don't think so, man," I chimed in.

"Look, the Denny's is only a few minutes up the road. It's gonna be a little tight, but we can make it." Sam seemed to be a little less slurry now and getting a little peeved. "Just climb in there. We'll fit."

We did as we were told and all crammed into the car. Four of us in the back seat, two in the passenger seat, and Sam in the driver's seat. Luckily, we were all pretty skinny. The biggest part of our bodies was our hair. It wasn't at all comfortable though, not by a long shot. But like Sam said, the Denny's was only a few minutes away, so we figured, eh, we can do this.

Sam fired up the car and "For Whom the Bell Tolls" was in its second verse, which was instructing us to look to the sky before we die, it might be the last time we do…

I thought, "Well, I hope that's not prophetic." The song was heavy and loud, so by the time the Rabbit left the neighborhood, the entire car was headbanging. Nothing but flying hair in every direction. We must have been a sight.

It definitely caught the attention of the patrol car we passed when we turned onto the main road. The sirens came on and the lights lit up as soon as we drove by. Sam pulled over quickly and reached over and shut off the music. The headbanging stopped abruptly. We were fucked. There was no way that we weren't going to spend a night in jail. We were freaking out. Except for Sam. He was a cool customer. The officer approached the car, walking slowly, shining his flashlight into the back hatch, then the back seat, and then finally in Sam's eyes.

"Will you step out of the car please, sir?" he said, courteous but firm.

"Yes, sir, officer," Sam replied. He did as he was told. He stepped out and accompanied the officer back to his patrol car. He was in that car a long, long time. It was probably only ten or fifteen minutes, but to us it seemed like hours. I was sure we were screwed. We were all sure. "Oh god! My parents are gonna kill me," Bob said, his drunkenness obviously shattered by the sudden police presence. "They are gonna fucking kill me!"

"Hold on there a sec, Bobby boy," I said, trying to calm him down. "We weren't driving. Worst case we'll have to walk back to your house. Your parents will never know."

"Uh-huh. Unless we get arrested. Did you think about that? What do you think my parents will do when they get a call from the police station? What will your parents do?"

I thought for a moment and then responded, "Yeah, you're right. We're fucked."

There was no way we were getting out of this unscathed. After what seemed like an eternity, Sam finally emerged from the patrol car. His walk back to the Rabbit was brisk, but measured and unaccompanied. He opened the driver's door, jumped in, closed the door, and let out a big sigh. The patrol car turned off its lights, pulled out into the road, and buzzed by us. As it did, Sam gave a slight wave and started up the Rabbit. The entire car was quiet.

Bob broke the silence. "What the actual fuck? What just happened? I thought you were going to jail. I thought we were all going to jail. Holy shit. My heart."

He wasn't the only one. The passengers sat in stunned silence. Finally Sam chuckled a bit and slapped the steering wheel. "Nope. Just a warning. Now, who's hungry?" he said as he all at once turned back on the Metallica, threw the Rabbit into drive, and got us back on the road.

I never did find out what happened that night. We have all talked about it and joked about it over the years, but I never got the full story. The fact was we were dumb kids who sometimes did dumb things, this being one of the dumbest. My guess is that either Sam wasn't as drunk as he let on or he knew the cop. I guess we'll never know.

16

SCHOOL OF HARD KNOCKS

THE FOLLOWING THURSDAY, I was at school and the day was half over. That afternoon, I was pulling my usual duty as the aide for an AP chemistry class. They had me making copies, grading papers, and acting as a general errand boy, running memos around the school. It turned out that Lonnie was an aide at the same time for Ms. Mitchell in the special ed department. We timed our memo runs to coincide with each other and meet in the library where we'd sneak away between rows of books to make out.

On this particular day we emerged from the book rows and saw Ron standing and talking to the library aide. She was a junior, like Ron. We didn't know her name, but we had seen her around. I was wondering what Ron was doing in the library but quickly realized that if there was a cute girl, Ron was going to be around, somewhere. He had a sense for those things.

Lonnie looked over at me and said, "I've got to get back or Ms. Mitchell will send out a search party."

"Ok, see ya later?"

"Yep. Bye." She planted one last kiss and darted off. Just as she headed down the hall, Ron looked over and saw me standing there. He walked over. "Hey."

"Hey, man," I said nervously. We hadn't really spoken since that phone call, when I had torpedoed Exodus, at least the version that included me, and broke Ron's heart. "Hey, I'm really sorry things…"

Ron held his hand up and stopped me. "Hey, man. I'm sorry. I said some nasty things to you, dude."

I was relieved to hear him say that. I continued anyway. "Nothing I didn't deserve. I'm really sorry, man. I'm sorry everything happened the way that it did. That wasn't cool."

"It wasn't cool. But shit happens. You know… it kinda worked out for me. I wasn't good at being tied down. I didn't treat her right. Made her drive me around. Kept her on the line. Plus, I have been getting so much pussy since that Halloween gig. It's ridiculous."

I was a little shocked. I guess I had thought Ron and his girlfriend (now my girlfriend) were in love. Besides, after his drunk drum solo performance, I was sure no one would talk to him, let alone sleep with him. But these were teenagers, and for all I knew, the girls thought that solo was awesome.

"Ok. Um, glad to hear it?" I stammered. "I mean, cool!"

I wasn't really sure what to say, but I was glad that we were talking. After all, Ron was a good friend and, besides, he was the only decent drummer within a fifty-mile radius.

"Alright," Ron said, changing the subject in his usual swagger-with-a-hair-bounce kinda way. "How's the new band going? I guess it's not really new anymore, huh?"

He meant the old fogeys. "It's ok, I guess. We've been playing out quite a bit, which is good." I think he could tell that I was less than enthusiastic. But he seemed happy for me.

"That's cool." He quickly changed the subject again and all of a sudden got really excited. "Hey, I don't know if you heard, but Heather just told me—"

"Heather?" I said.

"The girl I was just talking to." Ron pointed over to the desk in the center of the library. "Anyway, Heather told me that there is a bit of a scandal going on that we may be able to use to our benefit."

Heather was one of Ron's many conquests since the big Halloween gig. She worked on the prom committee and was a little too highbrow for the rest of us, but Ron was a good-looking guy and he knew it. The girls would flock to him.

I was intrigued. "Do tell," I said. As much as teenage boys hate to admit it, we long for gossip just as much as the girls.

"Yeah. So apparently Shelly, the prom committee chair, was having an affair with Mr. Williams."

"The business teacher?" I asked.

"Yeah."

"No shit. Gross."

Ron looked down contemplatively. "Yeah. It is gross." Ron was then back to his upbeat story. "Anyway, they got caught makin' out in one of the closets near the staff break room. Big shitshow. Well, anyway, they took off. And she took off with the money that they had raised for the prom. Remember that big-ass fashion show and the flower sales—"

Ron had a tendency to ramble, so I cut in, "Yeah, yeah. I remember. Anyway?"

"Anyway. They're broke, dude. Outta dough. They don't have money for any food, or decorations, or hiring a band for the prom. Nothing. Zilch. Nada."

At this point, I assumed that Ron was going to volunteer putting the band back together to play the prom for free. Imagining us, all dressed up in puffy blue tuxedos with our long hair, activated my gag reflex. "No way," I said, "We are not playing a fucking prom!" I equated this to being part of a wedding band. Nothing could be sadder or more embarrassing to seventeen-year-old me. Fifty-year-old me has a different opinion... kinda.

"No, dude, listen. I don't want to play a prom. Wow. Lame. No, I think we should throw a concert to raise the money back. You know like Live Aid or Farm Aid. We could call it Prom Aid. We could play in the auditorium. It would be huge. It would be epic."

My face lit up. Now this was something. It *could* be huge. It *could* be epic. All kinds of thoughts were running through my head. A real live rock and roll concert. Not a gig on somebody's back porch, but an honest-to-god concert.

I was high on the thought, and then reality set in. "But we don't have a band. Not really."

"We could do this. We could put the band back together for this." Ron was holding out the olive branch, and I would be an idiot not to take it.

My wheels started turning. "I'm sure Bob would be in. But Andy... he's playing with those cat dudes."

"The caveman guys?" Ron snorted.

"Yeah, them."

"Bummer. Huh…"

"Yeah. We'd have to find a bass player – at least," I said. "And maybe another guitar player. This might be too big for just Bob. We could get John."

Ron shook his head no and took a breath through his teeth. "Not sure that'll work. Bob and John haven't really been seeing eye to eye lately, if you get my drift."

"I do. That makes it harder. Did you already tell Heather we could do it?"

"Well, no. Didn't know there was a 'we.' Plus, not sure they'll go for it. Seems a little ambitious."

I laughed. "Yeah, a little. When is the prom? When would we have to do this?"

My wheels kept turning. This was ambitious alright. But this, playing a big show, is what we had all been dreaming about for years. If we could pull this off, nobody would ever forget it.

"It's in the beginning of May. I think. Or April."

I gave him a sigh with a side of eye roll. "April? May? Big difference."

"Fuck, I don't know, dude. I don't remember exactly. I'll ask Heather when I see her."

"Ok, cool. I'll talk to Bob."

That afternoon in the school parking lot, Bob, Lonnie, and I were standing around my car talking. Ron saw us and ran over.

"Hey, hey…" Ron was out of breath. He leaned over, his hands on his knees. He looked over at Lonnie. "Oh. Hey."

Ron and Lonnie hadn't really spoken since their breakup, as teens tend to not do.

"Hey, Ron. How are you?" she said.

"I'm good… good. You?"

"Good. Really good," she said a bit nervously.

Bob and I looked back and forth between them like it was a tennis match.

I finally tried to get Ron on topic. "Um. Hey, Ron, what's up?"

"Oh… hey, yeah. So I talked to Heather. The prom is Saturday, May 3rd. We would need to do something in January or February. I hit her with the band concert idea. She thought it was a great idea. She's gonna run it by the committee, but they're pretty desperate so I know they'll do it."

Bob looked puzzled. "Do what?"

I hadn't had a chance to tell him yet.

"You didn't tell him?" Ron looked at me incredulously.

"I didn't. I was about to when you showed up." I looked at Bob as if to solicit some confirmation.

He just shrugged and put his palms up.

"So the idea is we are going to play a concert in the school auditorium to raise money for the prom. You know, like a *Prom Aid*!"

"Potentially," Ron interjected. "Heather can't give us permission to play at the school. You'll need to ask Mr. May."

Bob looked a little skeptical. "Prom Aid? Really?"

I looked at Ron. "What do you mean, 'you have to ask'? She's on the prom committee. She should ask." I turned back to Bob. "And, yes. Really."

"Well, I'm definitely not asking him. He doesn't like me," Ron said as he backed up with his hands in the air. "Heather won't ask either. She said we have to do it. Something about if her mom found she was cavorting with metalheads she'd get grounded. And apparently Mr. May and her parents go to the same church."

"What do you mean he doesn't like you?" I asked, ignoring the bit about Heather, which was ridiculous.

Ron chuckled nervously. "I'd rather not get into it here and now."

Turned out Ron had been busted for setting off M-80s on the side of the school where the heads congregated. Mr. May had seen him, so he was caught red-handed and got a week's worth of detention. He was also forced to scrub the big black marks off the bricks next to the steps.

I turned to Bob. "Bob?"

"Oh hell no. He doesn't know me and I'd like to keep it that way."

Bob could tell from my face I was not happy about this. "Fuck. So I guess this leaves me then. Ok, fine. I'll go in tomorrow. It's a Friday. Maybe he'll be in a good mood."

Bob was happy I was the one going to go talk to the administration, but he was still more than a little skeptical. "We have a bigger problem. We still need a bass player and preferably another guitar player to share the load. We don't have much time, and if we're gonna put on a real rock show we need to learn a shitload of tunes. Or play a shit-ton of solos. Or both."

Bob's wheels were turning now too, and the anxiety was showing on his face. This could be huge in a *good* and a *bad* way.

A lightbulb went off in my head. "Oh shit. Hold on a sec."

I jumped into the Camaro and started fishing around on the passenger-side floorboard, which was a mess. Hell, the whole inside of my car was a mess. I was digging around for a while. After a few minutes I pulled out a crumpled-up piece of paper. "Ah ha! Here it is."

I hopped out of the car with the paper and straightened it out. I handed it to Bob, who looked it over intently. "Oh yeah. I remember this. You got this from 'Sam Goody.'" He couldn't remember Jak's name. He looked over the paper while Ron and I looked over his shoulder. Lonnie had wandered away to talk to a friend in another car.

Bob's eyes lit up. "Holy shit. It's this Saturday."

"Lemme see." I grabbed the paper out of his hand. "Holy shit-balls! Karma. Kismet. Maybe it's meant to be." We all 'cool nodded' and looked at one another.

Ron stopped nodding when he realized he had no idea what we were talking about. "What is meant to be?" He'd been grounded during the Kix concert.

I tried to catch him up quickly. "We met these guys a couple of weeks ago at the Foot's all-ages night. The guitar player works at Sam Goody in the mall. And the bass player looks like Steve Harris. They look like legit rockers. We need to go see them play. If they're any good, we need to ask them if they'd be willing to play the show. Hell, even if his band is still a thing, he might be willing to loan himself, and the bass player, out to us for this show. This is a big fucking deal. It could be huge."

Ron pumped his fist. "Epic!"

I returned the gesture. "Epic!" It was good to be talking to Ron again.

Bob, ever the skeptic, said, "Maybe. Let's not put the cart too far ahead of the horse. You still have to talk to May."

"Yeah. Hee-hee, you do." Ron laughed.

I gave Ron a dirty look. "Ok, ok. Fine. I'll talk to May tomorrow. If we get the green light, we can talk to 'Sam Goody' this weekend."

The next day, Friday, D-Day, I walked into the principal's office. On purpose. I had never been there on my own volition before, and it felt odd. Very odd. I approached the office secretary. I was very nervous, to put it mildly. "Uh. Hello. I'm here to see Mr. May."

The secretary was a short woman with a bouffant hairdo. She was typing hard on her IBM Selectric, which didn't need her to be hitting those keys with so much force, but that didn't stop her. I guessed she was an old-school typer.

Without missing a key or looking up, she barked at me, "Do you have an appointment?" She sounded as if she'd been a smoker since she was nine. I was a bit startled but should've realized how this was gonna play out.

After a few moments, I got myself together and finally spoke up. "Uh… no. No, I don't. I just need to see him for a minute. It's important."

"Isn't it always." She finally stopped banging her keyboard and looked up and at me over her bifocals. "Well, Mr. Frazier. What's this all about?"

I was very surprised she knew who I was. Well, not too surprised. I had been in the office a few times during the previous regime, and this lady had probably been there since Eisenhower was president.

"Um, yes, ma'am. I need to ask him something. It'll only take a second."

She was still looking at me over her bifocals. Still as a statue. She didn't say a word.

"I need to ask him about using the auditorium. For an… um…

event. Um… like a show. You know?" I was starting to stumble over my words and, boy, was I nervous.

She stirred a bit now. "An event? A show? What kind of show?"

"Well." I gulped as I tried to think of something benign. I was having trouble with that. Her gaze was burning right through me. "Well. You see," I continued, "we want to hold a concert. To raise money for the prom."

"You mean like with violins and horns and such?"

I thought, "No, not like that. At. All." But out of my mouth came, "Yes, yes. Just like that. With violins and horns. Bob, Bob will be helping me. You know Bob. Bob from the marching band?"

I was stuttering and tripping over all my words. This lady made me nervous. Bob actually was in the marching band though. He had stuck with the saxophone while I had abandoned mine years ago.

"Ahh, Mr. Book." Her face lit up a bit, and I thought, "Whew. She likes Bob. Everyone likes Bob."

She managed a smile. "He's on the phone. He'll only have a few minutes when he's done. Have a seat over there." She waved toward the couches. "He'll see you when he comes out."

"Perfect. Thank you," I said graciously.

I sat down on one of the orange couches that looked like they came off the set of *2001: A Space Odyssey*. Seventies modern. I started to wonder, why orange? The school colors were gold and blue. I sat there for about ten minutes. It seemed like ten hours.

Mr. May emerged from his office and flailed his arms toward the office lady. "Can you get me the swimming pool cleaning schedule?"

"Yes, of course, Mr. May. There's a student here to see you." She motioned toward me, and Mr. May looked over.

Without missing a beat, he said, "Mr. Frazier. What can I do for you today?"

He knew my name too? Now that wasn't a good sign. But, well, I was there, so I stood up and began, "Yes, sir. I—"

"Come on in." He motioned me into his office. "Have a seat."

I quickly moved into the office and sat down. Mr. May closed the door behind me. He was probably in his mid-forties but looked older due to his receding hairline, glasses, and portly build. Though, hell, when you're a teenager, everyone looks old to you.

This was his first principal gig. He'd transferred from another school where he was vice principal and in charge of the drama department. He was a total drama nerd. This was a good thing. The previous principal was a total jock who loved all things jock-y.

His first conversation with me and every other longhair who came into his office had started the same way: "Do you play a sport?" And if the answer was no, his follow-up was, "Why *don't* you play a sport?"

That was not Mr. May's style. He was a big fan of the arts and was also known to act in plays put on by the local community theater. He was every bit a thespian. I was hoping all of these things would work in our favor. I was squirming in one of the chairs across from his desk, another orange *Space Odyssey* chair. Mr. May sat down in his big black leather chair. It was showtime.

"Well, young man? What can I do for you?" he said as he folded his hands on his desk in front of him. He managed a pleasant smile. This wasn't so bad.

"Well, sir. You see..." I hesitated. "C'mon, c'mon, keep it together. Spit it out," I said to myself. I was so nervous. I continued,

"We were thinking. My band and I. Our band. We were thinking. Well, we were wondering."

"Well, spit it out, Sean, I haven't got all day."

Oh shit. He knew my first name too. Oh, not good. I took a deep breath and kept going. "Yes, sir. Well you see, we were thinking of holding a fundraiser for the prom. We know that they've had some issues with funding lately, and we talked to the prom committee…"

They sure had been having some issues. Mr. May knew exactly what I was referring to, and he really, really didn't want to talk about that. He moved me along with a wave. "Yes, yes. True, true. Go on."

"Yes, sir. Well… we have a band."

"A band? What kind of band?" he interrupted sharply.

I knew that I couldn't pull the same Jedi mind trick with Mr. May that I had with the secretary lady. I figured I better be up front this time. He would find out one way or another, sooner or later.

"Well, sir. A rock band."

"A rock band? You mean like Elvis? Or the Who?"

Wow! I was pleasantly surprised he knew who the Who were— not so much Elvis.

"Yes. Kinda like the Who."

Mr. May's face showed more curiosity than disgust. This was a good sign, I thought.

I continued, "We wanted to put on a concert to help the prom committee. They're out of ideas and time is running out. They don't want to beg for money, but they're getting desperate. They can't do another fundraiser since they've already had two. We've talked it over with them, and they're cool, er, I mean good with it. We could really help out here."

The more the prom committee was mentioned, the more uncomfortable Mr. May seemed. He really didn't want to have a conversation about the scandal that was being discussed in the school hallways, classrooms, locker rooms, and at dinner tables in homes all over our town. He must have been hoping that the story would die down. But this was a small-town school. And it hadn't.

He was very interested in moving this along, quickly. "Ok, what do you need from me?"

"Just your permission, sir. We'll take care of everything. We'll set everything up and clean up after ourselves. You'll never know we were there."

"Uh-huh. I find that hard to believe. Who is helping with this 'event'?"

"We have a whole team of people," I said confidently. We didn't. But we knew lots of folks who could and would help.

Mr. May sat back in his chair and drew his hands above his head, rubbing his balding spot. "Hmmm. Well..." he said, after what seemed like minutes of him staring at me, rubbing his head. All at once he sat up suddenly and started flipping around in his desk calendar, without looking up. "When were you thinking of putting on this rock concert?"

"Well, sir, we were thinking February or March. The prom is in May."

"It can't be March. We have our spring play going on. Ah, yes, here it is. *Gypsy*. Mr. Hardford would have a conniption if we got in the way of that."

"Of course he would," I thought. Mr. Hardford was good at having conniptions. "Yes, sir. I see," I managed.

"So it would have to be February."

This was a positive sign that he was even entertaining the idea.

"Yes, sir. February would work," I said, trying not to sound too upbeat.

"You'll have to do this on a school day. That's the rule. Assuming you'll want to do a Friday evening?"

We really wanted to do a Saturday but at this point, beggars could not be choosers. "Yes. A Friday evening would work."

Mr. May landed his finger hard on a square in his calendar. "Here we go. February 28th. How does that sound?"

"Perfect," I said, again not trying to sound overly anxious.

Mr. May wrote in his calendar. "This is tentative. You'll need to talk to Mr. Farley and Mr. Hardford and Mrs. Stevens and…" He paused for a moment, looking up and to the right, tapping the butt of his pen on his lips. "I think that's it."

"Yes, sir. I'll get right on it. Thank you, sir." This time I didn't have to stop myself from sounding too upbeat. Talking to those three? That was gonna be rough.

"Anything else?" he said curtly.

"No, sir. Nothing else. Thank you." I popped up out of the *Space Odyssey* chair and dashed out of the office before he changed his mind.

17

ARMED AND DANGEROUS

WE HAD GOTTEN THE buy-in from all of the teachers in question. It was actually a little easier than I thought, and everything was falling into place rather quickly. With the concert locked and loaded with the faculty and the school, minus a few odds and ends that needed to be firmed up, mostly on our end, the gang and I were jumping head-first into solving the most critical problem. Finding more musicians. Specifically a bass player (again) and another guitar player (again) to round out the band for what we hoped would be an epic show.

The guitarist and bass player we were looking to court were playing a house party in a very small town where I had happened to attend elementary school. It also happened to be very close to where I lived, so that made it super-easy for me to shoot up there to check them out.

I picked up Mikey as usual, and we headed over the winding roads between Union Bridge and Woodsboro. It was about five miles as the crow flew, but that didn't mean much given the few roads in those parts. It would take us the better part of half an hour to get there. Mikey, as usual, brought the tunes. This time it was Twisted Sister's *Come Out and Play*, the follow-up to their immensely successful *Stay Hungry*. The record had just come out and, of course, Mikey already had it. We were both *huge* Twisted Sister fans. While we identified with the teen angst anthems "You Can't Stop Rock 'n' Roll," "I Wanna Rock," and "We're Not Gonna Take It," this band had depth that few others among our peers could see. Not even the musicians.

It wasn't just the music, which was awesome, it was also the attitude and the intelligence of it. That year, Dee Snider, the lead singer of Twisted Sister, had testified before Congress during all the hoopla surrounding music decency. The PMRC (Parents Music Resource Center) was trying to put warning labels on albums that contained graphic lyrics pertaining to sex, drugs, and violence. Basically trying to protect kids from themselves. It was a shitty idea, not least because us disaffected youth would flock to a record with that label like moths to a flame. The same way I decided to buy my first Kiss record or my first Iron Maiden record based on the cool cover art, kids would swarm to these records because they knew they would contain good shit.

But that wasn't the awesome part. The awesome part was that, as Dee Snider rolled into the nation's capital in his ripped-up jeans, rock-and-roll tank top, and crazy-ass hair, everyone expected him to show up, sit down, and tell the wannabe 'Mayberry Mamas' to fuck right off. He did that. Just not in the way anyone expected. He was smart, articulate, and made a good case for why this idea was not only silly but also a waste of time. Music censorship had never worked and never would. He became a hero to millions that day, and Mikey and I were firmly in the Dee-Snider-for-President camp. Twisted Sister songs like "The Price," "Burn in Hell," "The Beast," and the instant classic "S.M.F." were staples in my car. We could be seen and heard many Saturday nights, cruising the circuit blaring "S.M.F.," with Mikey's all-hair headbang playing out in my passenger seat. "S.M.F." had special significance for me. It was my go-to video game high score initials. I didn't have a middle name, so an *M* might as well be it – at least for the sake of tracking my video game prowess. The new record did not disappoint either. The title track, "Come Out and Play," is still in my top twenty playlist to this day.

Mike and I parked at the house where the party was supposed to be and saw Bob's green Corona on the side of the curb in front. We could see the silhouette of Ron's big hair through the back window. We all jumped out of our respective cars. "We made it!" Bob said as if he had just driven three hours to Ocean City. The town kids didn't like coming out to the sticks very often, but they knew if it took them a long time to get to these parties, it would take the cops just as long.

We could hear faint music coming from the back of the house, so all four of us walked around the side. It was dark, so we took our time and watched our footing in the mud. It had been raining, and nobody looked good in dirty rocker clothes. The band was set up to play in the basement apparently, and we could hear the music getting louder and louder as we got closer.

There were some kids outside smoking. We passed by them,

nodded, and proceeded to make our way inside. The band was playing against the back wall. It looked like a good crowd, mostly because it was a small basement. There were probably twenty or so people.

The band was pretty good. They were playing through the standard garage band staples, "Living after Midnight," "Breaking the Law," "Hells Bells," etc. The same songs most of our bands were playing at the time.

We noticed right away that 'Sam Goody' was pretty damn good. He had a style and a stage presence that was beyond his years. He was a very smooth player for a sixteen-year-old kid. Like he'd been playing awhile. He hadn't been. None of us had at this point, but what Jak lacked in technique he made up for in metal swagger and bravado.

The bass player was pretty solid too. He reminded us of Iron Maiden's Steve Harris. Not just his playing but the *way* he played. His moves. You could tell he wanted to rip out of those three-chord garage songs and let loose, but the songs he was playing just weren't made for that. Not these songs.

The drummer was ok. He had the same problem as ninety percent of the drummers who played around these parts. His meter sucked. He couldn't keep time to save his life. Which, if you're a drummer, is kinda the point. We had met him at the Kix show – the one with no style. We weren't impressed then and we definitely weren't now.

The singer was god-fucking-awful. He was flat, sharp, basically hitting notes that were nowhere near where they needed to be. As he hit the high part of "Breaking the Law," in the middle of the chorus, it was like nails down a fucking chalkboard. Ouch.

At that moment, we all looked at each other and made some

pretty sour faces. Like we had just sucked on lemons or something. Mikey, also an aspiring singer, made a gagging motion and pointed his finger in his mouth. Over the course of the night it was very apparent that 'Sam Goody' and 'Steve Harris' were really good and needed to join our band. They would make us a better band. We needed their talent.

Between sets, the band and the crowd rolled outside to smoke and to chat. Sam Goody and his bass player were surrounded by girls. Part of the job. He saw our group congregated by a rusty swing set and walked over. "You guys made it. What do ya think?"

Bob responded first. "Dude, you're a monster player."

Sam Goody acted all cool. He knew this. For his age, and for as long as he'd been playing, he was a monster player. He would become even better over the course of the next couple of decades. Becoming probably the best guitar player in the region. "Thanks, man," he said, trying to sound as humble as he could.

I jumped in, "Hey, man. This is Ron, our drummer, and Mikey. He's a friend of the band."

Sam Goody gave them the nod. "Nice to meet y'all." He had a weird sort of accent. It was kinda country but yet kinda foreign. It turned out his family was from Canada. His mom and dad were full-on French-Canadian, and a little of that accent shone through when he was younger.

We all shook hands, and Jak introduced himself to Ron and Mike. "Hey, I'm Jak."

Jak! That was his name. Not Sam Goody. We couldn't remember it at the time.

Ron was floored and had no poker face. "Man, you and the bass player are rippin'! How long have you guys been playing together?"

"About a year," Jak replied.

"Do you guys do any Maiden? He would be awesome playing that shit. He looks just like Steve Harris!" Ron pointed to the bass player.

"Ha. I wish. We'd both love to. The drummer would have a hard time and the singer? Well, let's just say, it ain't gonna happen in this lifetime."

We all gave out a chuckle as Mike, the bass player, approached the group and talked to Jak. "Hey, man. Dave wants to get playin.' He's gotta be home soon." Jak gave him a nod and then looked over and pointed to our group. "Hey, man, you remember the guys we met at the Foot? The Kix show?"

Mike looked the group over. "Oh yeah. How y'all doin? You diggin' the show?"

Mikey finally chimed in, "Oh yeah. Very cool. Very cool. Love your playing and your style." He made an air guitar, signature Steve Harris move as if he was pointing a bass guitar straight out and banging on the strings.

Mike the bass player nodded approvingly, then motioned his head toward the basement door. Jak acknowledged this subtly. "Alright, fellas. Back to the grind." He and Mike headed back for their fourth set of four songs. The crowd started to pile back into the tiny basement. I thought to myself, "We have definitely found our bandmates. They just don't know it yet." We heard the band start up again as the basement door closed.

Ron was jumping around. It was pretty cold outside, and he

hadn't dressed appropriately. He never did. "Yeah, ok, fellas. I have to get home. Supposed to be back by ten."

Bob looked down at his watch. "Dude. It's 9:55!"

"Yeah, so? I can be a few minutes late."

Bob shook his head. "So Ronnie."

We were all freezing at that point. Turned out none of us had dressed appropriately for winter, certainly not winter outdoors. I rubbed my hands together and called this meeting adjourned. "Alrighty, dudes, let's go. We've seen what we came to see."

We all hustled back around the side of the house. What was once wet, slick grass was now crunchy under our feet. The temperature must have dropped ten degrees in the last few minutes. Maryland weather was always a crapshoot.

We headed to our respective cars. Before opening his car door, Bob yelled over to me, "You want me to wait in case your car doesn't start?"

Bob knew my car well. Almost as well as I did. I licked my finger, stuck it up in the air, and looked up for a second. "Yeah, better wait a sec. Hold on."

Mikey and I jumped in the car. I put the key in the ignition, said my prayer, and turned my key. Nothing. Not even a click. I could see the smile on Bob's face through the fogged-up, icy windshield. I jumped back out.

"I told you," he said. "Good thing I said something."

"Yeah, good thing. I'll grab the jumper cables."

This always happened at the worst possible time. I found out months later, after buying three or four junkyard batteries, that the alternator was to blame. This car taught me a lot about working on cars, but it taught me even more about patience.

The next day Bob, Jak, and I were all working at the mall. It was closing in on Christmas, so we were all getting as many hours as we could handle. I didn't want to waste any time. We needed to get Jak and Mike onboard so we could start rehearsing. We had a lot to do and not a lot of time to do it. On my first break, I headed out into the mall and down toward Sam Goody.

When I walked into the store, I saw Karen working at the counter. She was reading a *Maryland Musician* magazine. This was a monthly magazine put out by a local publishing firm that covered all the local music events. Shows, record releases, etc. We would become well-acquainted with this rag in later years and specifically with its local music editor, Susie Mudd. She was a champion of local acts and would expend lots of ink and magazine real estate to champion the cause of us local musicians.

I stood there for a few seconds, and Karen finally looked up. "Well, well. What can I do you for?"

"Hi. Yeah. I'm looking for Jak. Is he working today?"

Karen looked puzzled. "Jak? Who's Jak? There's no Jak working here."

Now it was my turn to be puzzled. "Hmm. He has long-ish hair" – I made a big hair outline with my hands – "and he definitely works here."

"You mean Bob?"

Now I was really confused. "No. Bob works at Montgomery Ward." I pointed up the mall. "No. Jak. You know? Jak."

"Bob doesn't work at Montgomery Ward." She was growing a little impatient.

At this point I was very, very confused. This was a very Abbott and Costello who's-on-first moment. Just when I thought my head was about to explode, I saw Jak coming out from the back room carrying some records. I motioned excitedly as if trying to convince someone of the existence of Bigfoot. "There he is. Right there! Geez." I gave her a wide-eyed look and headed over to talk to Jak. Karen shrugged her shoulders and went back to reading the paper.

"Hey, man. You got a second?"

Jak gave the nod. "Hey. Yeah, just gotta put these records out, but you talk, I'll work."

"Cool. Hey so, good gig last night."

"It was crap."

"What? No, it was really good."

"It was crap. Dave can't keep time to save for shit, and Billy sounds like someone killing a cat. It was shit."

"Well, yeah," I thought but didn't say out loud. I continued, "But you and Mike were really good. You know, we're kinda looking for a guitar player and a bass player. How would you like to jam with us?"

"Who's us?"

"The group. The guys you met last night."

Jak stopped putting records out and looked at me with his serious stare.

"Are you guys any good?" he said apprehensively and then started putting records away again.

"Well. Yeah. We're pretty good." I didn't want to oversell us, but I knew we were good. Better to under-promise and over-deliver.

He looked even more skeptical. "Pretty good or good?"

"Good. Real good. Let's put it this way, if you wanna do Maiden? We can do Maiden. We can do lots of Maiden."

This got his attention, and he stopped working again. He and Mike had been trying to introduce Maiden slowly into their band, but it wasn't taking. Dave couldn't play it, and Billy definitely couldn't sing it.

"Really?" Jak said in a bit of a skeptical tone.

"Yeah, really," I said emphatically.

Jak was nodding his head slowly, and I could tell he was deep in thought. "Hmm... that could work."

"It gets even better," I said excitedly.

"Better than Maiden?"

"Yeah. We have a gig lined up. A *big* gig. We're gonna play our high school. In the auditorium. Like a real rock show."

"Get outta here. You can't do that. Nobody will let you do that," he snickered.

"They can and will. It's already a done deal. It's all worked out." It was sorta a done deal as far as the school was concerned, but we still had plenty of work to do. "We're playing to raise money for the prom."

"Ok. Ok. Interesting. Let's get together and see what's shakin'."

"What are you and Mike doing next Saturday?" I asked.

"Next Saturday? Fuck that. What about Tuesday night?"

I have always appreciated Jak's work ethic. Being in a band isn't easy. It takes a lot of work. If I sat down and calculated the amount of time I've spent over the years in rehearsal, learning songs, and in the studio, I would either laugh or cry. Most likely cry.

"Hmm," I said as I was thinking and rubbing my chin. "Well. Ugh. I have this thing I have to do with this other group," I said with more than a little disdain. It was frustrating working with the group of oldies. I was gonna have to get out of that mess. I was so done with them, but I couldn't leave them hanging. Not for a gig.

Jak shot back, "Thursday?"

"Thursday works," I said, excited but trying to keep it cool. "This is going to be fucking awesome," I thought to myself.

Thursdays were usually old fogey practice nights, but I would totally cancel for this. Hell, I would've canceled for a dentist appointment at this point. Besides, all they did at practice was drink beer and snort coke. I wouldn't miss a thing.

"We practice at Bob's house."

Jak gave me a quizzical look. "My house?"

I suddenly felt like I was back in that Abbott and Costello routine from a few minutes ago.

"Huh? No. Bob's house. I thought your name was Jak?"

Jak gave out a huge laugh. "That's what Mike calls me. My real name is Bob."

"Ahh, now I get it. That explains a lot. I bet there's a story there."

There was a story there. Turns out when Jak (er, Bob) met Mike in middle school, there was a hallway altercation. I heard at one point it was over a girl, but that was never confirmed. Anyway, Mike confronted Bob in the hallway, pushed him up against the lockers, and uttered something to the effect of, "You better stay away from my woman, Jack!" as a generic reference since he didn't really know his name, and it stuck. The two became fast friends soon after, however, and it turned out Bob liked the name Jack, but he preferred the cooler, rocker spelling of J-A-K. It fitted his metal alter ego, and he would use both names for most of his life. Bob to his family and work colleagues, and Jak to his musician friends. A good separation of lives.

"Well, we already have a Bob, so you're Jak."

"Heck yeah I am." He gave me a sly smile.

I walked over to the counter, grabbed a pen, and looked around for something to write on. I saw a band business card tray and grab the top card. "Monarch" was the band on the card. A local favorite. I flipped the card over and started writing.

"Here's Bob's address. We usually get together right after school. Around 4:00."

Jak looked at the back of the card with my shitty writing on it. "Is that an eight or a nine?"

I looked over at it. "A nine."

Jak grabbed the pen from me and corrected the nine. "It'll take us a little longer to get over there. Say 5:00?"

"5:00 it is. That'll give us, mainly Ron, a chance to set up."

"What are we gonna jam on?" Jak asked.

"The same stuff you guys played. Priest, Van Halen. Most of the songs you guys did, we already know."

"How about we up the ante?" Jak grinned and cocked his head to one side.

"Oooo-k." I was intrigued. "What did you have in mind?"

"How about some Maiden? You guys know 'The Trooper'?"

I had never sung it in a band setting before, but I had worn out my *Piece of Mind* tape. It was one of my favorite records, and Bruce Dickinson was one of my all-time favorite singers. Still is to this day.

"Yeah, I think we can do that." I wasn't sure about this, but I knew that this was a test. Bob, Ron, and I would learn "The Trooper." We weren't just sizing up Jak and Mike – they were auditioning us too. "Great fucking tune, man!" I said.

"Yeah, it is. Alright then. See you Thursday."

"Thursday. See ya then."

We shook hands, and I headed toward the store opening to the mall. I was at least twenty minutes late returning from my break, but I didn't care. This was more important. Music was always more important at this stage in my life. As I turned and made quick feet, Karen yelled out, "Y'all come back now, you hear?" as she always did. She was so creepy and weird. I rolled my eyes and sped up.

18

FLYING HIGH AGAIN

IT WAS FINALLY THURSDAY. Bob and Ron and I had been anticipating, and talking about, this rehearsal all week. When I got to Bob's house, he and I met in the driveway. Ron was sitting in his mom's Volvo station wagon, parked half in the grass and half in the road. Bob and I helped Ron carry his kit inside and down to the basement. Luckily Bob's parents weren't home, which made load-in a lot easier. We didn't feel as bad making noise and hitting the walls with the cymbal stands on the way down the basement stairs. Ron's kit was loaded in, and the guys helped me load the PA out of my car and into the basement. Thank goodness. For a small PA, that thing was heavy. Peavey didn't fuck around back then. The thing was solid. Solid enough to last through at least seven bands of my own, and several of my son's bands when he came of age. It's still resting in my storage shed some three decades later, and I bet if I dragged it out and plugged it in, it would fire right up and work like a champ. It was that well made. More than I can say for most things made after 1990.

We got all the equipment loaded into the basement and started setting up our respective gear. Felt like old times. I had called Bob and Ron as soon as I got home from work Sunday night to see if they could learn "The Trooper" prior to tonight's rehearsal. Luckily it was one of their favorite songs too, so everyone was game. It wasn't an easy tune by any measure, but I had faith that we could get through it. I got my speakers placed just so and started running my quarter-inch speaker cable. "So did you guys get a chance to learn 'The Trooper'?" I asked as I bent over behind the speaker. I plugged the cable into the quarter-inch hole with a satisfying *clunk*.

Bob had his Peavey amp all set up and was sitting on it while tuning his guitar. "Yeah. I kinda have it down."

"Kinda?" I shot back. "These guys are going to come prepared. I can feel it. Better not fuck it up, Bobby." I stood up and flashed Bob a smile.

"It'll be fine. I'll be fine. I'm more worried about you. Can you sing it?"

"Maybe," I said. We both laughed.

Ron was sitting on his throne behind his kit, adjusting his toms. "Yeah, it'll be fine. I've been playing that song all year. It's my warm-up record. Nicko is the shit! We got this." He did a ton of drum flourishes to make his point.

I was hoping they were right. We really only had one shot at this. One shot to get these guys on board. Otherwise it would be the 'Ron, Bob & Sean show,' and it would be terrible. We got all our gear set up and sat around and bullshitted for a bit. I guess Bob's mom must have gotten home, because at around 4:45 she opened the basement door and shouted down the stairs. "Bobby? You have some *more* friends here?"

She emphasized the word 'more.' She didn't sound thrilled.

Bob lifted his head from his guitar, which he had been noodling on for the past ten to fifteen minutes, and yelled back up at her, "Tell 'em to come down. Thanks."

The sound of plodding feet and guitar cases hitting the steps filled the basement. Mike and Jak emerged looking pretty metal, wearing the same outfits or at least a derivative of the ones they had on at the Kix show. They swaggered up and settled in the middle of the room with their guitar cases knocking together.

"What's up?" Jak said, giving the room a good once-over. "Where can we set up?" Jak was all business, very few pleasantries.

Bob pointed to the side of the drum kit opposite from himself. "Um. Well, you guys can set up over there."

Jak looked around again. "Hmm. It looks kinda tight. I'm usually stage right, and Mike is stage left. And since we can't have two guitar players stage right" – Jak looked over both sides of the room again and landed a head nod on stage right – "I'll go there. Mike will be over next to you." He pointed to a narrow spot between Bob and the drums. The power struggle had begun.

"Um, ok. Sure." Bob was a good sport with these kinds of things. It's what made him a valuable asset and a good friend. "Hey, Ron, can you move your kit over just a bit? It's gonna be a tight squeeze, but we can make it work." He was a solid guitar player without a lot of ego. It was a rare combination.

The band shuffled around, and Mike and Jak dropped their guitar cases on their respective sides and went outside to bring their amps in. Once their amps were all in position, they took off their heavy leather jackets, plugged in, and started tuning up. We noticed for the first time that Jak had a Marshall combo amp. We hadn't noticed him using that at the house party show, but it was cool. None of us had ever seen a Marshall anything up close. Mike's gear was more in line with our budget. He had a Peavey bass amp, and a speaker cabinet with two huge black widow speakers. "Wow," I thought to myself, "this is going to be loud. Bob's parents are going to shit golf balls!"

While the two new guys were setting up, Ron was running through the gig logistics in his kid-like, hyper-excited voice. I could tell from Jak's face he was getting a little annoyed. He probably wanted to set up in peace, but Ron was just too excited and really couldn't contain himself. "It's gonna be so cool. We're gonna get to rock out in the school auditorium. Everyone is going to be there. We get to play all fucking night long. Or at least until 11:00."

"You gonna stay sober this time?" I said, halfway joking as I got my mic and stand set up.

"Fuck you, man. I'll be ready. Don't you worry about me," Ron shot back with a smile.

Mike, the bass player, was looking around for power. "Hey, man, do you have an extension cord?" he finally asked.

Bob's eyes darted from wall to wall, looking for an outlet. "Here you go. Just plug in there." Bob motioned to his extension cord behind his Peavey amp.

Bob pulled a bright blue Kramer Voyager guitar out of a brand spanking new case, adjusted the strap, and plugged in.

Ron looked up and made a big *O* face. "Whoa, nice guitar, dude. Where did you score that?"

"Venemans," Bob said proudly. "I camped out at their big sale. I wanted a Flying V, but by the time I got in there this is all they had. I like this better though." Bob ran his hands across the top of his shiny new guitar.

"Sweet guitar, Bobby," I said. The guitar was definitely unique. I had never seen one.

Jak looked over as he continued to tune his Fender Strat. He and Mike were Fender guys. Jak with his Strat and Mike with his jazz bass with its extra-long neck. They even had matching Fender straps. "Cool guitar, man," Jak blurted out without missing a beat on his tuning, and then right back to business. "'K. So what do we wanna start with?"

"How about 'Breaking the Law'?" I suggested. "It's easy and it's a good warm-up tune for me."

Bob gave a thumbs-up. "Good for me too."

"Cool," Jak said. He turned to Ron. "Count it off, drummer man."

Ron did a four count, and the band dove right in. It sounded really good. Very full with both guitars. Jak's tone out of his Strat and Marshall combo was amazing – it didn't sound like a garage band guitar setup. When we were done, Jak gave a cool nod of approval. We'd all felt it and heard it. It sounded good and tight.

Without missing a beat, Jak belted out, "Sounds good. 'The Trooper'?"

Oh shit. "This guy doesn't waste any time," I thought. "All business." And he was. Always. He always wanted to work harder and to get the people around him to work harder. To sound better.

It wasn't 'out loud,' at least not always, but you just wanted to be a better player around Jak. He pushed himself hard and expected nothing less from the players around him.

Jak looked down at his guitar and over at Bob quickly. "Hey, what solo are you gonna do?"

"Um, excuse me?" Bob replied, kind of confused. "What do you mean, which solo?" Bob hadn't really thought about it. He wasn't sure which one was which.

"Two guitar players. Two solos. I was thinking I would do the Dave solo and you could do the Adrian solo. Does that work for ya?"

This would be the theme for all of the Maiden songs that we would learn for the show, and there would be a lot of them. Jak always did the 'Dave' solos and Bob always did the 'Adrian' solos.

Jak could sense that Bob was still confused. "Here, hold on." He walked over to Bob and they noodled for a bit, working out the solo parts. Luckily Bob had learned both, so he just needed to figure out which one he was actually going to play.

After a few minutes of them noodling and the rest of the band fidgeting, we got back to it.

"Ok. We're ready." Jak headed back over to his side of the 'stage.' He looked at Ron. "Count us off."

Ron sat up straight. "Right. Here we go. One, two, three, four."

Ker-blap! The snare hit and the guitars blasted the beginning of "The Trooper." It sounded fucking amazing. It sounded so good that I thought the grin on my face was going to break it in two. It was tight, and for a bunch of sixteen- and seventeen-year-olds it was pretty fucking good. We all really got into it and were having fun. The vocals were spot on and the solos were blazing. Mike put his foot up on a kids' chair and pushed his bass out, doing his best Steve Harris impression. He was loving this.

When the song was over, Jak had a great big shit-eating grin on his face. Hell, all of us did. But his was special. Us north county guys hadn't seen him smile like that in the little time we had known him, and it was apparent that Mike hadn't really seen it either. This band was going to work and work well. We were going to be good. There wouldn't be a band of any age playing this shit in our area. None. Period. All the elements were there. This gig was going to be epic.

We continued to play through the songs we all knew in common, over and over, and jammed for a couple of hours, with very few breaks in between. Before we knew it, it was almost eight o'clock and Bob's mom yelled down the steps, "Time to stop, Bobby. It's getting really late."

"Ok, Mom," he yelled back.

"Yeah, Bobby," Mike said with a *heh heh heh* behind it. The new guys were already part of the gang.

After practice, we all packed up our shit. Luckily for me, I got to leave the PA – I just had to jam it into a corner with Ron's drum kit. We could leave the heavy stuff behind, but it had to be out of the way to make room for whatever Bob's parents did in the basement, which was, from what I could tell, nothing. It seemed like the kids' domain, but that didn't stop them from imposing their rules on us.

I stepped out the front door and could see my breath. "Ah. Fuck this cold weather."

"Eh, it's not too bad," Mike said. He liked the cold.

"For you maybe. I'd rather be on a beach. In California. Fuck this place."

Bob had to go smooth things over with his mom *and* let her know that we'd most likely be practicing a lot to prepare for the show. He came outside last, without a coat. "Brrrr. So when are we gonna practice again? I have to run it by the parents."

Ron, freezing because he never wore a coat, and always wore shirts with the sleeves cut off, chimed in, "Yeah. Brrrr. Well, we only have about a month or a month and a half tops to get our shit together."

Jak sauntered back from his little Chevy LUV pickup and lit up a cigarette. "We're gonna have to get crankin'. We've got a lot of work to do, fellas. I think we should practice as much as we can. We have Christmas break coming up. We should plan on practicing every day during the break."

Bob got a nervous look on his face. "I think my parents are planning a Christmas trip to Ohio to visit family."

"Well. These songs ain't gonna learn themselves," Jak said, giving Bob the patented Jak look. The look we would come to know over the years. The look of impatience with folks around him not willing to 'step up.' It was a mix between a stare, a pucker, and a head bounce. "We can't half-ass this. Not with the songs we want to do."

Bob looked a little dejected and a little concerned about how he was gonna break this to his parents, but he knew Jak was right.

"So what songs are we gonna do?" Ron asked, as he rubbed his arms frantically.

I blurted out, "Queensrÿche! We have to do some Queensrÿche!"

Mike snapped his head around to me. "Can you sing that shit?"

I looked back at him, kinda offended. "Yeah. If you can play it, I can sing it."

Mike gave me a slight *pfft*, as if to say, 'That shit is easy to play. But it's not easy to sing.' He wasn't wrong. We did end up playing some Queensrÿche and I did it no justice, but it forced me way out of my comfort zone. It made me a better singer.

He changed the subject. "We have to do some more Maiden. 'Trooper' rocked."

"Definitely Maiden," Ron chimed in.

"How about "Aces High" and "2 Minutes to Midnight," Bob said, lighting up out of his stupor. He had recently gotten seriously into *Powerslave*.

"Definitely," Jak said, putting his cigarette out and grabbing a pad of paper from his mini-truck. "Hey. You got a pen?"

"Yeah. One sec." Bob ran inside to get a pen.

"So which Queensrÿche song do you want to do?" Jak asked.

Queensrÿche was (and is) one of my all-time favorite bands. *The Warning* is an all-time top ten album for me. "I'd love to do 'Take Hold of the Flame,' but that one is a real bitch to sing. Frankly I'd do anything," I said.

Mike kinda pooh-poohed the idea. "Plus it's slow. Doesn't rock enough."

"Oh, c'mon," I said. "It gets there. It's a powerful song."

Mike conceded, "Yeah, it is."

At that point, Bob had come back outside with a pen. He handed it to Jak. "Here you go."

"Thanks. Ok. So 'Aces High' and '2 Minutes To Midnight.' 'Queen of the Reich' is a bitchin' Queensrÿche song, we should do that one." Jak wrote these all down. "This is a good start. Saturday. Can we do Saturday?"

"I have to work," Bob said. "But yeah, maybe after. Like 5:00?"

I raise my hand. "Me too. 5:00 works."

"5:00 it is. Any objections?" He looked at Mike and Ron. Neither had jobs, so both nodded in agreement. Then Ron got an oh-shit look on his face. "I'm supposed to help my stepdad," he said sheepishly.

"Do what?" I asked.

"Fuck if I know. He always needs something done around the house. Stupid shit. You know? Fuck it. I'll be here at 5:00."

We all looked at Mike. "Hell yeah. I'm in."

"Cool. Here." Jak handed the list of songs, pen, and paper to Bob. "Make yourself copies."

We all split before we turned into Popsicles.

19

CALL TO THE HEART

THE NEXT DAY WAS FRIDAY. Thank god! As with most school days, I really couldn't wait for it to end, but it seemed to drag on forever. I had plans that night. I had a date! When the final bell rang I ran out to the Camaro, waited for Mikey, drove him home, and then headed home myself. Lonnie's parents were out of town for the weekend, so I was as giddy as a schoolgirl (or boy, as it were). After I got home, I ate a quick snack (bowl of Cap'n Crunch cereal, my go-to favorite) and hit the shower, again. I spent longer than usual primping and teasing my hair. I don't know why I ever bothered. My Jewfro was in full swing at this point, and it had a mind of its own. It was going to do what it was going to do, regardless of time or product. I was about ready to leave when I heard the phone ring.

Mom yelled up the steps. "Sean! Phone!"

"Who is it?" I barked back, still looking in the mirror and making sure I was presentable.

"I think it's Eddie. Your dad's work friend."

"Stepdad," I said under my breath. "What does he want?" And then it hit me. "Oh shit. Shit."

I had been avoiding Eddie. I had been avoiding the whole band. I was so past done with those guys at this point but hadn't actually worked up the nerve to quit.

"Tell him I'm not here," I said quickly. Yeah, that was thinking on my feet. "Idiot," I said to myself.

"I will not!" my mom fired back in her disapproving mom voice. "You've been avoiding him for over a week. He's called twice. At least, that I know of. You know he works with your father?"

"Stepfather," I said a little louder, although still muffled through gritted teeth. Certainly not loud enough for her to hear. "Sheesh. Ok. One minute."

I finished getting ready and snuck downstairs, which was very hard to do using a creaky wooden staircase in a two-hundred-year-old farmhouse, but I made it past the parents without getting on the phone.

The Thin Lizzy song "Jailbreak" popped into my mind for some reason.

I headed out to the Camaro. Quietly.

The parents were watching TV and completely oblivious to the fact that I had left. The phone receiver was still sitting on the counter. Who knew how long Eddie stayed on the line waiting for me. It was a dick move, but I didn't care. I got into the car, started her up (yes, she started!), and headed down the driveway. As I was cresting the hill I looked back and saw my mom standing on the porch with her arms crossed. "Shit. I'm gonna catch hell for that when I get home." And I did.

I pulled the Camaro up outside Lonnie's house, just down the street so as not to be seen by any spying eyes. Mainly Lonnie's brother or sister. She was supposed to be babysitting them both. I got along with the brother well enough even though he was a little leprechaun pool shark, but who knew what secrets he would spill to her parents about the weekend's activities. Her sister, on the other hand, was a whole different story. She was a terrible person, inside and out. Any ammo that you gave her was sure to wind up right in your face. She was a vindictive little shit and rotten to the core. So rotten that even her parents were scared of her. I never could imagine growing up in a house with that power dynamic.

Lonnie's bedroom was in the basement, which made it pretty easy to sneak in unnoticed. I got to the back window and tapped on it. She came to the window, looked out, saw me, and burst into a big smile. She opened the window and I started to climb through.

"Shhh. If my sister hears you, my parents will find out and I'll never hear the end of it."

I continued my awkward climb through the open window, and she closed it behind me.

With the window closed, I finally got to stand up straight and I was looking right at her. She looked so good. She always looked good, but tonight she looked especially good. I had known for a while that I had fallen in love with her, although I hadn't admitted it to her yet. We had been 'together' a few times, but this night was going to be special, and I could tell she thought so too. She had the bedroom lit with candles and Mötley Crüe's song "Piece of Your Action" was playing on the turntable. This had become our song for when we were... um... hot and heavy, so to speak. She was ready, and boy howdy was I glad because I was ready too. I had been waiting for this all week and couldn't think of anything else.

We started making out and one thing inevitably led to another and we were quickly in her bed, naked and sweaty in full-on foreplay mode when she looked over and the ecstasy left her face.

"Get out of here, you little perverts!" she yelled toward the window.

I jumped up instinctively, not knowing what was going on, and saw four tiny little faces pressed up against the glass of her bedroom window. It was her brother and his little neighborhood group of hoodlums. They had big shit-eating grins on their faces for a brief second, but those smiles were dashed when Lonnie wrapped the sheet around her and in one swift motion jumped across the room, opened the window, and managed to smack one of them square in the jaw.

I was always impressed with her athletic ability and had always thought that if it weren't for her shitty home life, I mean with more encouragement, she could have played any sport or done anything in that realm that she wanted to. She was that talented. But on this night, her talent was scaring the shit out of a quartet of peeping toms.

She hadn't managed to hit her brother, but she did a good job of scaring all four of them. "You wait until I get my hands on you, Dave. Your ass is grass!" she yelled as the kids ran screaming up the hill away from the basement wall of the house. She slammed the window shut and put up the tapestry that served as a makeshift curtain. She had it there, obviously, for just such a violation. She then turned to me and in an instant her face went from anger to sex. "Where were we? Oh yeah." She dropped her sheet to expose her perfect body. She then slowly moved to me and at once she was on top of me. "We were right here," she whispered in my ear.

After we finished our coital entanglement, we lay in bed next to each other, looking into each other's eyes and talking. She was running her fingers through my crazy hair, which at this point looked like something that a pack of wild beavers might live in.

"How is the new band coming along?" she said without missing a stroke.

"It's good," I said. "Intense. But good. That guy Jak is no joke. Great guitar player but a bit of a taskmaster. But it's good. We kinda need that. Ron is feeling the brunt of it though. He can't phone in some of the drum parts that he used to do. Jak likes everything by the book or 'like the record,' as he is so fond of saying."

She chuckled. "Not surprised. Ron's a really good drummer, but he can be a little lazy."

She knew Ron pretty well, obviously.

"Yeah. Yeah, he is. It's good though. He's still having issues with his parents. I don't know what their problem is. They ground him for the dumbest shit."

"Did you ever stop to think it's not all them? You hang out with Ron. He could drive Jesus to drink."

I laughed. "Yeah, sometimes. As usual, you're probably right."

We both sighed. She was still running her hands through my hair as best she could, and I started running my hands down her breasts toward her stomach. I was thinking that it might be time for round two when she removed her hands from my hair and sat up quickly. "Hey. Do you wanna get outta here?"

"Um, sure. Where do you wanna go?"

"I want to go out. I want to skate. Can we go to Skate Haven?"

Skate Haven was the local roller-skating rink. It was one of the few places you could go in our town to do something like hang out or go on a date. It was also next to the Putt-Putt mini-golf course, which had a little arcade attached to it. The arcade wasn't as big as Time-Out, but if you got tired of skating or miniature golf, it was a decent place to hang out. Of course, she was an amazing skater. Me? Not so much. I could skate well enough on the carpet, but I was terrible on the actual rink. I was always on my ass, but for her? I would go anywhere.

"I thought you had to babysit?" I reminded her.

"Those fuckers can fend for themselves for an hour or two. That bitch never listens to me anyway, and my brother? He's probably looking in windows halfway around the neighborhood. They'll be fine."

The kids in her family were used to being on their own. They'd spent most of their childhood that way. I was game. "Alright then. Let's go."

We both got up, dressed, and headed to the Camaro. I got in and turned the key. Nothing. It was just the typical click. "Oh no! Not again. C'mon, not now. You motherfucker." I was quite flustered. Not a great way to impress a girl.

She started laughing. "Does this thing ever work?"

"Yes, most of the time," I said a little defensively but not very convincingly.

She gave me a look that said 'oh, really?' and rolled her eyes.

"Well, some of the time," I admitted.

She was still staring at me with that dubious look on her face.

I finally conceded, "I know, I know. It sucks."

Her face changed back to her happy, bubbly self. "We'll take my car." She bounced out of my car and over to hers, a worn out, shit-brown Ford Bronco that her grandfather had given her. This car was also a piece of shit, but it was her piece of shit and it was a tad more reliable than my piece of shit.

We hopped in and she fired the truck right up. As she did, "Piece of Your Action" started playing out of the stereo. She looked a little embarrassed and her face turned red. It was easy to tell when she was blushing. She was a very fair-skinned blonde and had no poker face. Eventually she mustered an excuse. "What? I was getting ready for tonight," she said and flashed me that sexy smile that I knew and loved. A split second later, she threw the car in drive and we were off.

On the road, once the Crüe song was done, we let the rest of the tape play out ("Starry Eyes" was next) but turned it down a bit so we could talk. Twenty minutes later, she turned in to the Skate Haven parking lot. It was packed. It took us more than fifteen minutes to find a spot – we had to wait for someone to leave. It was Friday night, after all. She parked the car and we started walking toward the door, stopping every few feet to greet all of her friends. She was not exactly a regular here, but she seemed to know everybody.

We finally made it to the front door. Skate Haven was run more like a nightclub. You had to pay a 'cover' to get in, and you had to pay for however long you were planning to skate. Depending on whether you planned to skate eight to ten, ten to midnight, or all night, they took your money and then gave you a colored wristband so they could easily pick you out when it was time for you to get the fuck out.

She knew the doorman (of course she did) and managed to finagle an all-night pass for the same price as the eight-to-ten pass. Five bucks each. It always pays to know people.

We walked over to the skate desk to get skates, and I looked nervously at her. "You know I can't skate, right?"

"Sure you can," she said. "Anyone can skate."

"Nope, not me. I'm pretty sure I can't skate. I have this inner ear thing. Bad balance."

She gave me her signature smile. "Don't worry, you're with me. I've got you."

The inner ear thing was real. I had ear issues my entire childhood. It was one of several catastrophic health things that I navigated as a child. I don't know how anyone survived the '70s.

We got our skates, put them on, and went out to the rink, where I fell. A lot. But true to her word, she helped me up again and again. She held my arm and we skated around for a few songs.

"See. You can do this," she said with an encouraging smile.

"Sure, when you're holding me up." I let out a nervous laugh.

"Nah. I just want your arms around me."

She was so beautiful. "Yeah, me too." I couldn't skate, but being with her made it worth it.

Giuffria's "Call to the Heart" came on, and they announced a couple's skate. We skated for the duration of the song with Lonnie holding me up. We kissed from time to time, when I wasn't losing my balance. Every time we kissed, I felt like I was going to fall and she had to steady me, but I wasn't nervous anymore. She was there holding me up. The song transitioned into Sweet's "Love Is Like Oxygen," signifying that the couple's skate was over. The floor was overrun with little kids flying around proficiently on their skates. This made me nervous again.

She could sense this. "Hey, would you mind if I skate around fast a few times? I don't want you to fall."

I was ready to be off the floor anyway. "Not at all. Just point me toward the snack area."

She guided me in toward the snack area, pointed me in the right direction, and gave me a push. I waved my arms to stay up. Once I finally make it to the carpet, I could skate better. I quickly dropped into a booth. "Whew!" I thought to myself. "Made it."

She skated around the rink like a pro for a song or two. When she was done, she sat down in the booth opposite me. I had managed to make it up to the counter and purchased two drinks and two soft pretzels. They were waiting for her when she sat down.

"So tell me more about the band stuff," she said as she tore off a piece of pretzel and popped it in her mouth.

"The band. Right. It's tight. Very tight. Hard to describe it, but we all just seem to click. We are playing some pretty tough shit, and it sounds really good. Better than I expected actually. There won't be a band in this town that can touch us. At any age."

"What songs are you guys playing?"

"Lots of cool stuff. Lots of Maiden. We knew we only had a limited time to learn a shitload of songs, so when we compared what we already kinda knew in common, it was a lot of Maiden. Doing some Queensrÿche, Krokus, Accept – they are one of Jak's favorite bands, but I could take 'em or leave 'em. Some Dio, Priest. Good shit."

"Wow. Maiden. That stuff seems pretty complicated, and very literary."

Iron Maiden was and still is well known in metal circles for having many, many literary influences. I was impressed that she knew this, but I was a little more oblivious at the time, although I did know that "Rime of the Ancient Mariner" was from a poem written by Samuel Taylor Coleridge. The song was over thirteen minutes long, so we had to play it.

"Yeah. They're hard songs," I continued. "But we're pulling them off. They sound really good. We're also starting to delve into some Metallica and Anthrax. More heavy stuff."

"Anthrax? Like the disease?"

"Exactly! Great band. We probably won't have those songs ready for the show. That's some next-level shit."

We both knew what anthrax was because Fort Detrick, located nearby, had had an anthrax leak and several buildings were closed off for many years. It was pretty cool that this was the inspiration for the name of a band that would inspire us over the next decade.

"I'd love to stop by to hear you guys some time," she said.

"Absolutely. We're practicing a lot, and it's gonna ramp up over Christmas break. We still have a lot to do."

"So I guess I won't be seeing much of you then. Between work, the old fogey band, and this one, you're not gonna have any time for me, huh?"

She sounded a little disappointed, but she knew this show was important, and the fact was, I loved spending time with her. She and I got along well and it wasn't just the sex, which was great. She was just an amazing person and when I wasn't with her, I found myself wishing that I was.

"Yes, you will. I get to see you at school, plus I'm quitting the old fogey band or may have already quit." I smiled since I really hadn't pulled the trigger on that. "That's been the plan all along. It was just something to do, but I can't do both, and frankly I don't want to play in that band anymore."

"Have you told them yet? I know they had some gigs lined up."

"Not yet. But I will," I said sheepishly.

"So what's the name of this super group?"

"Onyx."

"Like the stone?"

"Like the stone." I shoved a big piece of pretzel into my mouth.

She pondered it for a moment. "How did you guys come up with that?"

"Bob came up with it. He was hanging out with some band geeks up in Middletown and the kid's house he went to was on Onyx Court. Heh. We even went up one night after band practice and stole the street sign. It's hanging in Bob's basement."

"You bunch of hoodlums." She laughed. "You're lucky you didn't get caught. Sounds like something my family would do." She and I laughed.

"Huh, yeah. That's us. Hoodlums."

We sat quietly for a bit and finished eating our pretzels.

"You know... if you guys pull this off, it's gonna be huge," she said.

"Not *if* but *when*! And yeah... it's gonna be something."

We finished our food, turned in our skates, and headed outside. It was nearly 11:00 p.m. and the parking lot was still buzzing. We climbed into her Bronco and drove back to her house. When we arrived, we started our goodbye ritual that consisted of lots of making out and lasted for at least an hour.

"Do you want to stay here tonight?" she said, staring up at me with those deep blue eyes.

"I'd love to, but my mom would kill me."

She looks at me disappointedly. "Are you sure? It's late. Plus, what if your car doesn't start?" She shot me a very mischievous grin.

It *was* late – already past the time I was supposed to get home. This plus leaving my stepdad's coworker hanging on the phone meant that I was probably going to get an earful.

"Yeah, that car is always causing trouble," I said with a wink.

We went inside. I stayed the night.

When I got home the next morning, my mom's car was gone, which meant I had a reprieve from any lecture that was due. I walked into a quiet house and there was a note for me on the kitchen table, propped up so I couldn't miss it. "Eddie called three times. Call him! Today!" with a phone number on the bottom.

I sighed but remembered what Lonnie had told me. I owed it to these guys to let them know what was going on. She was right. She was usually right. I picked up the phone, dialed Eddie's number, and let him know that I had another band and wouldn't be able to sing for them anymore. He was surprisingly gracious and said that he understood. "No hard feelings," he said. "You can sing with us anytime." It wasn't nearly as bad as I had thought it would be.

20

DELIVERING THE GOODS

WE HAD BEEN PRACTICING all through Christmas break. Between that, school, and work, I couldn't tell if we were coming or going most days, and we were some tired teenagers. We took Christmas Eve and Christmas Day off, but we were back at it the very next day. Luckily everyone's work schedules slowed down a bit after the holiday and, since the school was still on break, we were able to practice during the day, which made it easier to not disturb Bob's parents. They had decided not to go to Ohio after all since Bob was busy with the band and they weren't about to leave five 'longhairs' alone in their house for a week.

On an unusually sunny day, Bob, Ron, and I decided to sit outside to wait for Jak and Mike to show up for practice. It was brisk but tolerable in the sun. "Another day, another dollar," I said, just to say something.

After a prolonged silence, Bob finally spoke up. "You got that right. Jesus. I've been so busy I can't see straight. Between work, school, and this shit, I don't have time to breathe." He made an exaggerated breathing gesture.

"Hey, guys." Ron finally joined the conversation. "So something I forgot to mention. I, uh, I invited Jer to come to practice today."

Ron was always conveniently forgetting things like this.

Bob and I let out an exaggerated sigh, and I gave him a huge eye roll. "What the fuck, Ron? Why would you do that? We have enough to do. No time for entertainin'."

"C'mon, guys. He's a good dude. His mom is just an asshole," Ron said, trying to defend Jer.

"No disagreement there," Bob chimed in.

Ron continued, "We don't need to entertain him. He heard we were doing this show and wanted to help out. Run sound, lights, whatever. He just wants to help."

I was still rolling my eyes a bit, but the fact was we all liked Jer. He could be a bit over the top sometimes and his mom was a jerk, but Jer was a good guy and he did have skills. He was way more organized than the rest of us, with the exception of Jak.

"You know he's pretty good at planning stuff," Ron went on. "Plus he knows people who work at Soundstage in Hagerstown. They're the ones that rent sound equipment to all the big bands that play the Capital Centre. He said he can help us with the sound gear and other stuff too."

I eased a bit as Ron spoke. We had talked about renting a sound system. Goodness knows we needed a much bigger system than my little PA to fill the big auditorium, but we'd been so heads down on the music part that we had sort of forgotten about it.

So I agreed. "You're right. We talked about that but we kinda dropped the ball."

"Exactly!" Ron got all excited. "And he can help with all that stuff. Plus he's a suck-up with all the teachers, so he would be kinda good at like PR or something. Keep us out of trouble."

We knew that we could use all the help we could get there. We had managed to keep the show on the books, even with some scrapes with the school law.

"Ok. Cool," I said.

Bob agreed. "Cool."

Just then, as if on cue, Jer rolled up in his mom's K-car. He got out, looking as preppy as ever, and bolted over to us. Jer was a bit of a chameleon. When we were jamming, he was rocking ripped jeans and T-shirts with the sleeves cut off. At this point he was back to his preppy New England self.

"What's up, fellas? Long time, no talk," Jer said as he bounded up the driveway.

"Hey, Jer. It has been awhile," Bob said, flashing him a friendly smile.

"Well, you don't count, Bobby boy. I see you in school almost every day." Bob and Jer ran into each other most days between third and fourth periods. They always said hi and exchanged pleasantries. The rest of us weren't exactly avoiding Jer – there just wasn't an opportunity to see him, which we were ok with.

"Now, *you*, stranger. Haven't seen you in ages," he said, looking at me.

Jer and I had had a bit of a tense relationship. Over the course of the last few weeks, Jer had been trying to run into Lonnie every chance he got, and she would give me the play by play. Apparently when she and Ron broke up, Jer thought that was his chance to make his move and started hitting on her. All the time. They had photography class together, and he was always trying to get her into the darkroom alone. She, of course, wasn't interested. At all. She was nice to him – she was nice to everyone – but Jer read that as one thing and it was meant as something completely different. All those moves he tried to make, even though he knew (it was a small school) that she and I were an item, were pointless. But this didn't sit well with me, and I didn't exactly trust Jer. Even so, outside of the relationship drama, I liked him and knew the band needed help. His kind of help. And lots of it.

"Hey, man. Whatcha been up to?" I finally responded.

"A little of this, a little of that. Looking forward to helping you guys get this show off the ground."

Jer could be a little annoying sometimes, and he always seemed to give the impression that if he wasn't involved in something it was bound to fail, but when he was motivated (and motivating) he was able to get things done.

"Cool. We can use all the help we can get," Bob said. He and Jer always got along better than most.

"Alright then," Jer said as he looked around. "So where are these wunderkinds from cross county?"

Apparently Ron had been talking up the duo to everyone at school, including Jer.

Bob looked at his watch. "It's ten till 1:00. They'll be here any minute."

The duo was always punctual. As much as our gang was driven, Jak was more so. To him it was about fun, but it was also business. And in business, time is money.

Just then, like clockwork, the little Chevy LUV rolled onto Bob's street.

"Here they are. Right on time." I pointed to the truck.

The group watched intently as the truck pulled up and stopped. Heavy metal with some severely operatic singing could be heard clearly even with the windows closed and the truck running. The truck had a hole in the muffler so it was kinda loud. Jak liked it that way. He was a car guy and liked 'em loud. The cab was completely filled with cigarette smoke, and we could barely make out the silhouettes of the two long-haired teenagers sitting inside.

The truck shut off and the music stopped. Cigarette smoke wafted out as the doors opened. Mike and Jak emerged with lit cigarettes in their mouths and with their hands full of Dr. Pepper and BBQ Corn Nuts.

These were their pre-practice snacks of choice. Every day it was Dr. Pepper and Corn Nuts. You would think that they lived in a 7-Eleven, and on practice days they kinda did. Gas, cigs, and snacks – the essentials. The two sauntered up to the group of us sitting around on Bob's front steps.

Jak spoke with the cigarette still hanging from his lips. Too cool for school. "What's up?"

We all greeted one another.

"Hey, guys. Corn Nuts! Sweet." Ron held out his hand, and Mike dropped some Corn Nuts in. This was a practice ritual too. Ron started munching and proceeded to talk with his mouth full, spitting out bits of Corn Nuts along with the words. "Hey, guys. This is Jer."

He pointed to Jer in a sweeping fashion. The duo were clearly less than impressed with Jer's look, which was less rocker and more extra on *Miami Vice*. He was wearing khakis, a pink oxford shirt, and a green polo shirt underneath that, with both collars popped. I bet the song blaring in his mom's K-car as he drove around was "Wake Me Up before You Go-Go."

"What's up?" Jak gave Jer 'the nod' as cigarette smoke rolled over his face.

"Hey, guys. Nice to meet you. I've heard so many good things, so many good things."

Jer was a bit nervous, which was interesting to see. He tended to talk like a game show host when he was nervous.

"Alright, Jer. Fill the fellas in on what you were telling me yesterday," Ron said, getting right down to business.

"So. Yeah. I can help you guys out. I know..." He looked at Ron and continued, "I know that you guys haven't lined up a sound system or a lighting rig. The show is gonna be here before you know it, and that little Peavey ain't gonna cut it."

He was referring to my still kinda new practice PA. "Don't get me wrong," he went on – Jer knew that I loved that PA and was starting to get a little offended – "that's a great little PA and it would be perfect as an onstage monitoring system. And that's what we'll use it for." Jer was already throwing around 'we,' and Jak and Mike, though still a little skeptical, were listening intently. They knew we needed these things, and if someone else could figure it all out, they were cool with it.

He went on, "So, I have this contact—"

"John," Ron interrupted.

"Huh?" Jer groaned.

"Your contact. It's your brother. John."

"Well, yeah. It's my brother, but he *is* still my contact."

"Everybody here has met your brother. Well, everybody except them." Ron pointed to Jak and Mike. "You can just say 'my brother John.' We know who he is." Jer had a way of making everything grandiose and formal and of droning on and on. Ron just wanted him to cut to the chase. He could tell that Jak and Mike were getting bored and were ready to play.

Bob and I definitely knew John. We had met him when Exodus (before it was really Exodus) was practicing at Jer's house. John was Jer's older brother, and he was the definition of cool. With his Joe Strummer looks and his wild taste in music and mind-altering substances, John had become one of the group's favorite party buddies. It was also cool that John didn't take any shit from their overbearing mother. If Jer was the apple of her eye, John was the worm.

"Ok, ok," Jer continued, a bit exasperated. "My brother John works at Soundstage in Hagerstown. Are you happy now?"

Everyone knew where Soundstage was, but whenever anyone said it, it always had to be followed by "in Hagerstown." Even though Hagerstown was only one town over, it was a different world, in form and substance. It was called Hub City due to the fact that several highways and railroad lines converged and put it at the center of all Mid-Atlantic commerce. It had a beautiful historic downtown that had been overrun by crime and decay. It wasn't the kind of place that was hospitable to anyone, especially after dark. But due to its location, it had many businesses that didn't exist in our town, Soundstage being one of them.

"Anyway," Jer continued, "he's gonna get us his employee discount. We're gonna get a sound system, a light rig, probably some drum risers and other miscellaneous stuff. You know, like maybe even a couple of smoke machines. The works!"

"What's this employee discount gonna look like?" Jak said, all business as usual.

"Well. If they're not using the equipment, it could be pretty substantial. Not free but pretty cheap."

Jak liked what he was hearing. He knew their gear and service by reputation, and it was legit. All the big bands used them when they came to town.

"But whatever it is," Jer said, "we can get the prom committee to pay. They've got a little money set aside for expenses. They'll just deduct the rest from the proceeds."

Jer was smart. Bob and I had no idea what he was talking about, but Jak did.

"And?" Jak wanted to know more.

"And whatever it is, it won't come out of your pay."

"Is that right?" Jak replied. "We're getting paid?"

My ears perked up. "Pay? Nobody said anything about pay."

We had been so excited to play a show that we had never even thought about the fact that we could be getting paid for this.

"We're not getting paid," I said, looking at Ron. "Are we?"

Ron shrugged. "Don't look at me. I just work here."

"You guys aren't getting paid? Well then, it definitely won't be coming out of your pay," Jer said as he laughed, a bit nervously. The rest of us didn't laugh. The fact was, it was ok that we weren't getting paid. We were in it for the show.

"So you say they'll cover expenses?" Jak finally said.

"Well yeah. When I talked to Heather, they had this all figured out. They were kinda surprised that up until this point you guys haven't had any."

Now I was recognizing that this was the part of the show we could really use his help on. Jer was good friends with Heather and the whole prom crew. Which was good since Ron had moved on to greener pastures, as he was wont to do, so we had lost that connection.

"Do you guys have any?" Jer asked.

"Any what?" Bob chimed in. He had only been halfway paying attention.

"Expenses!" Jer responded curtly.

Jak held up his hands with the Dr. Pepper and the Corn Nuts in them and made a 'duh' face. "Oh yeah, we got expenses. Mike and I have been schlepping our asses over here to your neck of the woods for weeks. We gotta eat. We gotta get gas. We're outta pocket."

"Well, there you go!" Jer made a grand gesture as if he'd just cured cancer. "Problem solved. I'll talk to Heather when school starts up again next week. You're gonna need receipts."

"Oh, I got receipts." Jak knew how to play this game. Mike and Jak looked at each other, winked, and nodded.

With all the high points hit and the details to be worked out later, Jak kept the show moving. "C'mon, fuckers, are you ready to play some music?"

I moaned like an old man getting off the steps. "Yep. Let's do this."

"Time to make the donuts." Bob's favorite saying.

As we headed inside I hung back to talk to Mike.

"What were you guys listening to when you pulled up?"

"Huh? Oh. Fates Warning. *The Spectre Within*. Great record."

"Dude. That sound was badass! That guy can sing. What song was it?"

"Yeah, he can. 'Kyrie Eleison.' The whole record is like that. Good shit."

"Note to self. Gotta buy that record with Jak's Sam Goody discount."

We all disappeared into the house and down into the basement to make some noise.

21

READY TO BURN

WE HAD BEEN HARD at work practicing – so much so that it seemed like practice was all we were doing. It was T-minus seven weeks to the show, which seemed like a long time, but school had started back and work was picking up again too. We had moved back to practicing on Tuesdays and Sundays only, which meant we only had a handful of practices left. Luckily we had made the most of our two-week Christmas break, and we had a lot to show for it. We had more than twenty songs pretty well down.

Mondays were always hard for me, and it was especially hard to get up and get moving this particular Monday. To add insult to injury, the Camaro was not being very agreeable today and it looked like it might rain, so I had to ride the bus to school. I hated riding the bus. Not only was it a ragtag group of miscreants, but it also ended up getting me to school a full half hour earlier than I needed to be there. I liked to slide in right before the first bell rang.

This particular morning, because I was early, I was sure I would be the first one at the water fountain and would be standing there by myself for at least fifteen minutes. Fifteen minutes! To a teenager that might as well be an hour!

As I rounded the corner from the bus drop-off hallway into the cafeteria, I saw her. The blonde was already at the fountains. She was crouched down against the wall to the far side, reading. She was always reading. I stopped and watched her for a bit. *Catcher in the Rye* I said to myself as I read the cover of the small red paperback book in her hand. "What the fuck is that? A cookbook?" I looked at her for a few more seconds. She was so beautiful and almost seemed oblivious to it.

She and I had been dating for a quite a while now, and even though it was hard to find time to see her, I found myself always wanting to do just that. I mean, sure, we would steal away some moments whenever we could – here at the water fountain, in between classes, our little teacher's aide rendezvous. But I was feeling like I wasn't spending nearly enough time with her.

I kept telling myself, "When this show is over, we will have time to do whatever we want," but the reality was, there was always a show, or an event, or a thing that had to be done, and I needed to figure out how to balance all of that. That was the reality. That was life. But right now, at this moment, I was just happy to see her. I stopped staring and approached the water fountains.

"Hey, you!" she said as she spotted me heading toward her. Her eyes lit up. This made me happy. It made me think that I wasn't the only one who felt this way.

"Hey!" I said. "What are you doing here so early?"

She stood up and slid the small paperback into her back pocket.

"I didn't want to be home. My parents and sister were fighting this morning, and I just had to get out of there." She walked over to me, moved in close, put her hands on my chest, and gave me a soft, sensuous kiss. She then pulled back a bit. "I was going to sit in the Bronco and read, but it's too cold so figured I might as well come in here." A sly smile hit her face. "Car wouldn't start, huh?" She switched gears, knowing me, and my car, well.

"Nope." I said, shrugging my shoulders and putting my hands up as if surrendering.

"Well, I can give you a ride home after school. It would be good to spend some time with you."

I felt the same way. After a few moments, Ron and Mikey walked up. Mikey's mom had dropped him off and Ron rode his bus, which luckily for him didn't get him to school at the ass crack of dawn. He did, however, live a lot closer to the school than I did, so I'm sure that had something to do with it. Lonnie headed to photography class early, leaving Ron, Mikey, and I to shoot the shit. I noticed Ron's eyes go wide – he was looking over my shoulder toward the school doors. As I turned around, I saw Bob walking toward us. He had gotten a perm. A super-tight Bob Ross–looking perm. Whatever possessed him to do such a thing, I will never know. We all gasped and stared, mouths wide open as he approached.

Mikey was the first to start laughing.

"Oh my god. I'm so tired and my fingers hurt." Bob stopped in front of the left fountain, oblivious to our stares as he looked over the guitar string calluses on the tips of his fingers.

Mikey, never one to mince words, was the first to comment. "Dude! What the fuck happened to your hair?"

I stifled a laugh. Ron had turned away from Bob and was full-on belly laughing.

"What? You don't like it?" Bob patted his head. First the sides, then the top. "I got a perm."

"No shit. Looks like a tribble crawled on your head and died," I screeched.

Bob gave me a dirty look. I tried to stop laughing. "Sorry." I put my hand over my mouth to block the coming snort laugh.

"Very funny. My hair was getting long, and it was kinda scraggly. I wanted to do something new with it. I thought a perm was a cool idea."

Mike made a 'wrong answer' game show buzzer sound. "You look like your mom."

It was true, Bob's mom had the same hairdo.

"Well, look at *your* hair." Bob pointed to me, defensively.

"What about my hair?" I cried out.

"It's curly too! Fucker."

"Yeah. It's that way out of the box, man. I've thought about straightening it. It gets on my nerves. It's got a mind of its own. But I wouldn't do *that*" – I pointed to Bob's head – "on purpose. Your hair was great before." I had never liked my curly hair. It was a menace. I just couldn't understand why someone would want to make their hair curly.

Bob looked and felt a little embarrassed. He thought this was going to be cool, but now he was all self-conscious.

At that point, Jer strutted up to the group. "What's up, fellas?" He glanced at Bob. "Whoa, Bobby. What the hell happened to you? Stick your finger in a light socket?"

We all started laughing again. Bob didn't. He had heard enough.

Mikey, ever the jokester, said, "Hey! Maybe that's why your fingers hurt?"

"Great. Just fucking great." Bob was getting really upset now and turned to walk away.

"Hold on there, my frizzled friend. I have news," Jer said once he stopped laughing.

Bob shot him a look and then turned back around. "This better be good."

"Oh, it's good," Jer continued. "I talked to Heather over break. We're good on the expenses. I ran over the equipment list with her, and she didn't bat an eyelash, so now the planning starts. I've got some drawings."

Jer handed out some xeroxed pages. On them he had drawn a crude representation of the stage layout, including locations of all the gear and all the cabling. There was going to be lots of cable. He had also drawn expected lengths and dimensions.

"These aren't to scale, but I'm gonna go do some measurements in the auditorium after school if y'all are interested in helping me out."

"Sure. Yeah, cool," I replied.

"Cool. See these lengths" – Jer pointed to the cables running between the sound booth and stage – "they're not accurate. But you get a sense for where they'll go." He looked at me. "I'll also need to measure your Peavey PA speakers. I'm gonna build some stands so they'll face up at an angle. So you'll hear what's comin' out of 'em. I'll stop by a practice this week and get the measurements. When you do guys practice next?"

"Tuesday," Ron and Bob said in unison, both with a hint of

exhaustion. We all had the practice schedule burned into our brains.

"You mean tomorrow?" Jer sniffed.

"Shit. Yeah, tomorrow," Bob said, still playing with his perm.

"Great. I'll stop by then. Gotta run. See you at 3:30 in the auditorium."

The bell rang, and we were all off like a shot. "Does it really look that bad?" Bob said to me as we were walking away.

"Of course not," I replied. It did. But I didn't want Bob to feel bad.

After the dismissal bell, Bob and I met in the hallway and headed to the auditorium. When we got there, Jer was already measuring and Ron was standing in the back watching. Next to Jer was our buddy Todd. Bob and I had science class with Todd.

Jer yelled from downstage. "I bet you're wondering why Todd is here. Tell 'em, Todd."

"Well. Jer said you guys wanted to do a killer light show," Todd said excitedly.

"Do we?" I said, looking at Bob.

"I don't know, do we?" Bob looked at Ron, who shrugged his shoulders.

"Of course we do. Just fuckin' with ya," I said. "Please continue."

Todd smiled, then went on, "I was thinking we could put together a laser show. I'm gonna get the science club working on this right away. We've been studying lasers in class—"

"Oh yeah!" Bob and I said in unison, our faces lighting up. We had been studying lasers in science, though we hadn't really been paying attention that much. Not like Todd, obviously.

He continued, "And the science club was wanting to put one

together anyway, so this is a good excuse to do it and to help you guys out."

Todd was the head of the science club. He was an über science geek. If anyone could put together a laser, it would be him and the science nerds. He went on, "I was thinking we could put it up there." He pointed up to the sound booth above our heads. "And the light will shine down there on the stage, where we'll have this massive screen. It'll be just like a Yes show. It'll be spectacular."

We all nodded in approval. "Yeah," I said. "That would be awesome." I had seen a few concerts (very few), and they all had some kind of kick-ass lightshow. The lights were a large part of the allure, the mystique. They would definitely set the mood, and this laser was just the sort of thing that would make people go crazy at a show.

Bob, Ron, and I walked down toward the stage, where Jer was looking at the orchestra pit. He was standing there, with his arms crossed (which he always did) and his chin in his hand, with his face scrunched up like he was trying to figure out a puzzle. He then jumped up onto the stage with one quick, fluid motion as if he'd figured it out.

"We'll run the cables down the center," he said as he pointed to the center aisle. "And then we'll run them through the orchestra pit, then up on the stage. From there we'll run them back to a snake under the drum risers." He ran a line with his finger from the front of the stage to the back. "Yeah. That'll work."

Jer looked very pleased with himself. We were also pleased since we wouldn't have to do any of this work.

"Where are the drums going to go?" Ron asked.

"They'll be back here." Jer walked to the back part of the stage. "We're gonna get a riser set from Soundstage and put it here. It'll take up this whole area," he said, stretching his arms out wide in either direction.

"Whoa! Cool!" Ron was impressed with the amount of room. Much bigger than anyplace we had ever played – those being Bob's basement and Lonnie's back deck.

"Yeah. It's gonna look so cool," Jer opined almost giddily.

I jumped onto the stage (not nearly as gracefully as Jer) and walked over to him. "We need to get a second tier. Behind Ron so I can go along behind him. Like Bruce does with Nicko."

"Um. Ok, I think we can do that. So, Bobby, you'll be over here," Jer said as he walked stage right.

"No. Jak is stage right. I'll be over here with Mike." Bob motioned toward the other side of the stage.

"Uh, ok. So you'll be over here with the bass player and the other guitar player will be stage right. Got it." Jer looked around again. "So we'll cut a hole here, in the orchestra pit, and run the cables back here." Jer motioned this way and that, flailing his arms around. He then walked toward the back of the stage again, looking up into the rafters.

Todd came up to the front of the stage. "Hey, guys. I gotta go."

Jer glanced at him. "Oh ok, Todd. Thanks, buddy. Looking forward to seeing that laser."

"Me too," I said, with a little skepticism. Hopeful, yet skeptical.

"Yeah, it's gonna be cool. I'll let you know as soon as we have a working prototype." Todd headed out up the center aisle toward the main doors at the back of the auditorium. He passed Lonnie as she was coming in. She looked around and saw Mikey sitting in the last row, doodling in his notebook. She slid past him and sat down.

Mikey yelled out, "Hey, man. Are we leaving anytime soon? I'd like to get home before the end of the week."

I looked out, my hand over my eyes so I could see the seats through the bright stage lights.

"Ask her." I pointed to the blonde sitting next to him. Mikey looked at her and she gave him a smile and a little tinkling wave.

"Oh yeah, I forgot." Mikey laughed. "That piece of shit. He's gonna need to get a real car. One that works. Alright. Back to work." Mikey continued doodling.

Jer walked back to center stage, looking up the whole time, and bumped smack into Bob. "Oh. Sorry, Bobby. Yeah, no. These lights will not do. Ten cans! Ten freakin' cans! This isn't a production of *A Christmas Carol*, this is a rock show." He walked side to side, looking up and scribbling in his notepad. He again walked to the back of the stage, looking up and taking notes.

Bob and I turned and faced the auditorium. All at once we had butterflies. We both looked around in awe at the room. It was a big room, and it looked bigger when you were on the stage looking out. While we were gazing out at the rows of seats, Ron came up between us, slammed his arms around both of us, and pulled us in.

"My dudes. This is gonna be the show of shows. This is gonna get us noticed. This" – he paused for effect – "this, gentlemen, is going to get us laid."

He jumped back, howled, and headed back toward Jer. Bob and I looked at each other.

"Like he needs any help with that," Bob finally said.

We both laughed.

I knew that Lonnie and Mikey were both waiting for me. "Alright. I'm outta here," I said loudly, to no one in particular.

"Hold on a sec." Jer stopped me. He went over to the side of the stage and opened a briefcase. He pulled out stacks of what looked like cards, wrapped with rubber bands, and started handing them around. "Here."

"What are these?" Bob asked.

"These, my good man, are the tickets for the show."

"We have to sell them? What the fuck? This isn't LA!" I said incredulously.

"Well, yeah, you have to sell *some* of them. The prom committee will sell them, I'm gonna sell them, and yes, the band has to sell them. You want to make sure your friends and family get tickets, right?"

"Well, yeah," Bob conceded.

"Ok, sure," I chimed in, backing Bob.

"Well, then," Jer continued, "this is how you do it. Sell them tickets."

He threw a stack to Ron, who bobbled and then caught them. "Right on," he said.

I jumped off the front of the stage and straight down the center aisle. I got to Mikey and my girl.

Mikey looked up from his notebook. "About damn time."

Mikey got up and headed out. The blonde stood up and gave me a big kiss, and we headed out of the auditorium. As we passed through the big double doors at the back of the auditorium, I slid my sweaty hand into hers.

"Geez. You're all clammy! Eeww!" she said, though she was smiling.

I was clammy. The weight of the whole show was starting to take hold of me. This was a big fucking deal. "Yeah. I guess you might say I'm a little nervous."

"You? No way!" She smiled again.

We passed the trophy case in front of the head office.

"But, hey, I guess the one good thing is... Ron said this is gonna get us laid." I shot her a sarcastic grin.

"You know, it just might." She winked.

We headed out into the cold night.

22

BEFORE THE STORM

WE HAD BEEN HITTING it hard. Practice, school, work – it was all becoming a blur. But it was only a week until the big show, and we were starting to see light at the end of the tunnel. All the i's were dotted and all the t's were crossed. It was Wednesday night so Bob, Jak, and I were hard at work at the mall. After a slow few hours, I decided to take my break early and head to my usual break spot, the Time-Out arcade, to get some game time in. I didn't have lots of cash, so I decided to stay away from Dragon's Lair and hit my other favorites: Tron, Tempest, and Pac-Man.

I was playing Tron when Bob suddenly came up behind me, drinking Coke out of a Long John Silver's cup. "How's it going?" he said with a big pat on my back.

"You know how it's going. I'm dying, this game is kicking my ass. I've been so busy with other shit that I haven't gotten my game on in a while. I'm rusty on all my arcade faves."

"Ha. I can't play this game. Light cycles get me every time," Bob said as the blue light of the game shot across his face.

I nodded and kept playing. I hit the spider sequence, level four. This one was so hard. I moved my body left and right like the tiny Tron character on the screen.

"Shit. Fuck you, spiders," I yelled, loud enough for the whole arcade to hear.

"Keep it down, man, you're gonna get thrown outta here," Bob said as he took a slurp through his straw. "Did you talk to Jak yet?" he continued.

"Shit, no. What time is it?"

Bob looked at his watch. "7:45."

"Shit shit shit." I had totally spaced and forgot. I was on break and was supposed to go tell Jak about the load-in schedule for next Thursday and give him his tickets, since we had forgotten to give them to him at practice. "Fuck! I forgot. Gotta run. Play this for me."

I moved away from the game and pushed Bob toward the console. I quickly ran out of Time-Out and into the mall, took a hard right, and nearly landed on my ass. I looked back to see Bob was struggling with Tron. He played for like five seconds and then derezzed. He looked at the screen in disgust and batted at the controller. "I hate this fucking game."

I kept running down the mall and into Sam Goody. I approached the counter and doubled over, out of breath. I raised my hand to ask where Jak was, but before I could, Karen motioned to the back of the store. "He's back there." I waved a big thank you and tried to catch my breath as I headed toward the back of the store. I saw

Jak doing his usual duty, stocking the albums in their slots in alphabetical order by band.

"Hey," I mustered, still more than a little winded.

"Hey," Jak replied. "What's up?" He looked at me, more than a little puzzled. "Where's the fire?"

I was all sweaty and my knit tie was hanging over my right shoulder. I was a mess. I stood up straight and was finally able to speak. "Whew. So I only have like thirty seconds, less than that actually – anyway we finally found out the logistics for next Thursday. Jer's brother is gonna show up at the school with the truck around noon. We have permission to get out of class for the whole afternoon. Which is awesome! We're gonna help him unload all the gear – the whole band plus a bunch of our friends who want to get out early too." I took a deep breath and continued, "And we're gonna help set shit up. If you guys want to show up then, that's great, if not, be there by the end of school, like 3:30 or 4:00 or something."

"Yeah, I think we'll come then. We'll try and get there earlier," Jak said excitedly. He and Mike wanted to get out of school early too, of course.

"Cool. So after we get all set up, we'll do a soundcheck and make sure everything is cool. Almost like a dress rehearsal."

Jak narrowed his eyes and cocked his head back. "We getting all dressed up for the dress rehearsal?"

We had all gone to the local cool shop in the mall and each bought our own spandex. It was a girls clothing store and the spandex was probably meant for girls, but we didn't care – we looked cool. Or at least we thought we looked cool. We looked like all those guys on the wall at the Rabbit's Foot, and that was cool to us. And frankly, if we were gonna pull off wearing those things, our sixteen- and seventeen-year-old selves were the best ones to do it.

I made a sour face. "You can if you want. I'm not gonna. So, we'll do the soundcheck and we'll get to test the lights and the laser and all that shit."

"The laser. Pfft." Jak made a 'get outta here' motion with his hand. "That fucking laser ain't gonna work. When they brought that to practice, the only thing that came out of it was smoke."

Jer and Todd had come to an Onyx practice to show off the laser, and it had nearly caught fire. It didn't work, but it did set off the smoke detector and scared the shit out of Bob's mom, so we had that going for us. I tried to reassure Jak. "Todd told us it's almost ready. We're gonna test it on Thursday so we'll know."

"Uh-huh. I'll believe that shit when I see it." Jak didn't suffer fools. Ever.

"We're gonna use it in the beginning. Picture this" – I was trying to sell Jak on the idea that it was going to be cool – "the room is dark, the fog machine is cranking out crazy amounts of fog. Then the beginning of 'Number of the Beast.'" I waved my arms. "'*Woe to you, oh Earth and sea*,' and the laser is gonna take up the entire back of the stage and be in sync with the voice. It'll be bouncing off the fog and going everywhere. Fire and brimstone, man. It's gonna be so metal!" I waved my arms even more wildly now. "It'll be so cool. So fucking cool!"

"If it works, it'll be cool," Jak said skeptically.

"Trust me. They're on it. It'll work. We gotta trust those science nerds. Ok, so you know when and where y'all need to be Thursday, right?"

"Got it. We'll be there."

"Sweet. I've gotta run. I am so late." I turned to leave but then spun back around. "Oh shit. I almost forgot. Next Friday. Before the show. Bob's uncle has a side business driving a limo. He's gonna pick us up at the school, drive us around for a while, and then drive us back to the school right before the show. So we have to be at the school five-ish."

"Now that's cool." Jak managed a smile. "That's some rock star shit!"

"Hell yeah!" I said, pumping my fist in the air. "We'll get to roll out of a limo in front of the school, with all the fans standing out there. Just like rock stars."

Jak nodded. "Oh yeah! That'll be sweet."

"Yeah, it will. Alright, definitely have to go. Oh shit, here, you'll need to sell some of these."

I tossed a bundle of tickets to Jak. He caught them, pulled one out, and looked at it.

"Ten dollars, huh? A bargain."

"Whatcha got there, Bob?" Karen snatched the ticket from his hand. "Ahh. Well, save one for me, fellas."

She was so creepy.

"Alright. You know about Thursday, the limo, the tickets." I counted off the items on my fingers to make sure I hadn't forgotten anything. "Ok, I think that's it. Now I really, *really* have to go. I am so fucking late. Later."

"Later," Jak shot back. Karen gave me a wave, but by that time I was out into the mall and burning rubber down to the Radio Shack. Mr. Carter was gonna have my ass.

23

HELLO HOORAY!

IT WAS LUNCHTIME ON the Thursday before the big show. We were finishing lunch, and the nervousness of the day was starting to hit all of us. By our small-town standards, this was a pretty big deal. It wasn't winning-the-state-title-in-football big, but for us, it might as well have been. It was certainly going to be the Super Bowl of our high school careers. We had everything ready to go, but we were all just waiting for one of us to slip up, to do one thing that would give any member of the faculty, or our parents, an excuse to shut this show down. Because of this we had all been on our best behavior for weeks. Not that we were used to raising a lot of hell, but a typical week for most of us consisted of at least two or three run-ins with the law. The school law, that is. The past few weeks we had been squeaky clean, and it made us all more than a little nervous.

The nervousness was warranted. It turned out that a massive shock was coming, and it would come from a place that we should've all expected – Ron. While we were all on our best behavior (including

Ron), he was only ever a split second away from being grounded. Mid-term grades had gone out on Tuesday, and Ron's weren't good. They usually weren't, but this time they were worse than usual.

Ron had had a dentist appointment before school so he wasn't able to break the news at the water fountain in the morning, which was just as well. I enjoyed a few extra hours of feeling like we might actually be able to pull this show off. Ron came into the cafeteria, and we could tell right away that something was wrong. He looked like he had been crying. He sat down next to Mikey on the opposite side of the lunch table from Bob and me.

He was hunched over. I had never seen him like this. I had heard his voice on the phone when he was upset, but I had not seen him. "Is this how he looked when I broke his heart?" I thought to myself as those memories rushed over me. I shook my head and snapped out of it. "Hey, man. What's wrong?"

Ron looked up like a kid who'd just lost his dog. "I got fucking grounded. Again."

"You're always grounded," Bob said at once, trying to lighten the mood and believing that it was no big deal because we had been living with Ron's parents' draconian rules for a year.

"No, man. You don't understand." Ron looked like he was gonna cry. "I can't play the show. They took the car. I can't go anywhere. Can't do anything." A lone tear streamed down his cheek.

"You can't play the show?" I said unbelievingly. "That's bullshit, dude! We've... You have worked so hard for this. This is fucking *bullshit*."

My voice was loud enough that Bob leaned over and whispered in my ear, "You better cool it or you'll be next."

Our buddy Mikey seemed oblivious to it all as he sat there shoveling tater tots into his mouth. Truth be told, it wasn't his ass or reputation on the line, but he was a big part of our group. If he was nervous or upset you would never be able to tell. His appetite was as huge as ever. For a little guy, that dude could put away some food, but then again who can't when they're sixteen?

"Are you gonna eat that?" Mike said, eyeing my stack of fish sticks.

"Nope. All yours, dude." I couldn't eat and didn't much care for those frozen fish sticks anyway. My stomach was already in knots, and this shit with Ron had put me over the edge to full-on stomachache.

Mike proceeded to grab the entire stack with one hand and drop them onto his plate. He took one, eyed it until he went cross-eyed, and shoved it in his mouth.

"We need to head to the auditorium," Bob reminded us. "We're supposed to finish setting up and do the dress rehearsal."

My mind was spinning. I was worried about my friend, but the life of the show was flashing before my eyes. We would never get this opportunity again, and we would never be able to live it down if we cancelled. We wouldn't be able to show our faces around the county, let alone our school.

"I'm sorry, guys." Ron was crying for real now. "My parents are such assholes!"

"Hey, man, don't worry about it. We'll think of something." Bob was always good in times like these. Not a hothead like me.

I racked my brain to think of a solution as we sat there watching Mikey consume all the fish sticks. "Bob's right. Let's just go in there, do our setup and soundcheck, and we'll figure something out."

We couldn't do anything at that moment. I turned to Ron. "Hey, don't tell anyone when we get in there. There are a lot of things to get done, and I don't want to slow any of 'em down. We'll figure it out… We'll figure it out."

We all shot up from the cafeteria table. "Wait for me," Mikey said as he shoved the last fish stick into his mouth and ran behind us. We all dumped our trays and headed toward the auditorium.

The four of us entered the auditorium through the main doors at the back. The place was in a state of frenzied chaos and looked like a busy shipping and receiving dock. Equipment was moving in and out, and people were running and darting in every direction. Jer was directing traffic like an orchestra conductor, and the drama teacher, Mr. Hardford, was following everyone around to make sure they weren't damaging anything in the auditorium.

Mr. Hardford was gay and everyone knew it, but those things weren't discussed so openly back then. He would bring in his partner, Renae, (a dude) to accompany the chorus, of which I was a member, and you could tell that they were an item. Some of us suspected and a few of us knew, but it had never bothered me or my friends. I grew up in a very accepting Jewish household. My family was all about live and let live, which is kinda how you have to be when your entire culture is threatened with extinction every hundred years or so. The fact that Mr. Hardford was gay was inconsequential to me and my group. Besides, we all liked Mr. Hardford. He and I had gotten along really well these four years of drama and choir. We later found out he'd been a big advocate for letting us do this show, even though he looked pained anytime anyone mentioned it. That was the way he was. He had also, in his younger days, taught David

Byrne of Talking Heads fame, so he had an appreciation for that side of the arts. For all sides of the arts, really.

But he was putting on his prize spring show in a month and didn't want to deal with any additional drama, apart from his own. This had to be at least the sixth time he'd put on *Gypsy*, and he could probably do it with his eyes closed. But he was a perfectionist – something I would appreciate from him over the years, but this particular afternoon it was annoying as shit. This particular chaotic afternoon.

I noticed him yelling back and forth to people carrying in some speaker cabinets. "Hey, don't put that there." He pointed and waved his arms and fingers dramatically. "You, you over there – this is not your living room." He jostled back and forth, his head on a swivel, and chastised stage left and stage right equally. He was following people around and micromanaging their work. It didn't help that these were all teenage boys loading in heavy equipment, audio, lights, etc. with all of the care and finesse of a bunch of linebackers. Hell, some of them *were* linebackers!

Just as Mr. Hardford looked fit to be tied, Jer walked onto the stage with a power drill. "Alright. We're gonna drill here and here and here." He pointed to three spots along the stage and one in the orchestra pit.

Mr. Hardford went apoplectic. "No, no, no, no, *no*!!! You can't drill! You can't drill anything!" He slapped his hands to his face in his best Edvard Munch impression.

Jer looked at him, flustered. "We've got to get the cables through and up onto the stage." He gave a sweeping wave of his hand that, in normal circumstances, would have made Mr. Hardford very proud.

"Well, run them *here*," Mr. Hardford said, pitching his voice at the end and waving his hand in equally grandiose fashion as he pointed to the outside wall of the orchestra pit.

"That won't work," Jer shot back. "This place is gonna be filled with a bunch of kids. You know, a tripping hazard! Fire hazard! All kinds of hazard!" He motioned to the row of seats against the orchestra pit walls. "They'll trip on them or, worse, pull them out and kill the show – something will happen."

"Well. You can't drill. That's all I can tell you," Mr. Hardford said, a little calmer, not wanting to match, or exceed, Jer's apoplexy. He then reached out and snatched the drill from Jer's hands. Jer looked shocked. "I'll take this, thank you very much!"

"Ok then," Jer said, resigned to the fact that there would be no drilling without a drill.

Mr. Hardford gave him a big-eyed look and cradled the drill like a baby. Jer turned to a couple of lanky kids standing over him on the stage. "Hey. Can we lift up one of the panels?"

One of the kids looked at the floor, put his hands on his hips and shrugged. "Yeah, I guess so."

Jer turned back to Mr. Hardford. "Can we move the pit panels? Do they come out individually?"

"Yes, they do, and yes, you can move them. Just don't scratch them. Be careful. And I want all of this" – he frantically waved his arms again – "back to the way it was before you showed up."

"Yes, sir. We'll put it all back the way we found it." Jer was good at dealing with adults. He was our secret weapon in this regard. Had any of the band members been forced to deal with the politics and sometimes small-mindedness of the adults, this show would've been over before it started. Mr. Hardford scampered off with the drill in hand. As he left, he yelled toward two kids on the stage: "Hey. You two. Be careful with those curtains. They're old!" His shoulders dropped and he sighed. "Lord give me strength. Or at least an aspirin," he moaned as he headed out of the side of the auditorium.

Jer, happy Mr. Hardford had moved on to torture someone else, turned back to the skinny kids standing on the stage. "Alright, you heard him. Pull this panel up. We need to prop it up and run the cables through here." He pointed to a junction box on the side wall of the orchestra pit. "And then back there." He pointed to the back of the stage, where a few people were setting up the drum risers. The boys got to work lifting the panel.

At this point Ron, Bob, Mike, and I approached Jer, who looked tired.

"Where have you guys been?" Jer barked. "Ron, will you help them?" Jer said, pointing to the two teens trying to figure out how to Tetris the drum riser.

"Sure," Ron said softly.

I walked with Ron and gently touched his shoulder as he got out of earshot of the rest of the guys. "It'll be alright, man. We'll figure this out. Don't worry about it."

"Easy for you to say."

"Yeah. I know. Just go do what you need to do for now."

Ron gave out a sigh and a resigned head nod. He jumped on the stage and started directing the listless young men.

"Is he ok?" Jer asked.

"Oh yeah... He was just at the dentist," I said, not lying but also not wanting to have that conversation with Jer.

"Ouch. That sucks. Hey, Bob, where is your rig?"

"In the band room," Bob replied.

"Go get it and set it up there. Wherever you're gonna be," Jer said, pointing to the stage left space, next to the drum risers.

Bob gave him a salute and enlisted Mikey's help. "Mikey? Give me a hand?"

"You got it," Mikey said enthusiastically.

They both headed off toward the band room to get Bob's amp rig.

Now it was just the two of us. "What about me?" I said, trying to get Jer's attention.

Jer thought for a bit. "Stay out of the way?" He laughed. "But seriously. Things are moving fast. If you want, go check out the backstage area and make sure everything is... well, the way you guys want it."

"Huh. Ok. Sure." Seemed like a bullshit task to me but, hey, it also seemed easy, so I took it.

Jer's brother, John, entered the auditorium from the side door as I walked by. "Oh, hi, Sean! Hey, Jer! Bringing the lights in."

"Shit. The lights. Shit!" Jer shouted back to me. "Hey! You wanna help do something? Help bring in the lights. Fuck. I forgot all about the lights." He yelled at the guys on the side of the stage. "The lights are coming in. Clear this area, and this area. Someone go get those big ladders back there."

As I headed out to help John with the lights, Mike and Jak walked down the center aisle, leather jackets on, guitar cases in hand as always.

Jak yelled up to Jer. "Where do you want our shit?"

"Hold on." Jer looked back and forth. "Once the lights are up, you guys can put your rigs in their spots. He pointed to stage right and stage left next to where Bob and Mikey were setting up Bob's amp. Jer had made up little paper signs that read JAK RIG, MIKE RIG, and BOB RIG. He'd printed these using his Macintosh and a dot matrix printer, which meant they were a little faded but still kinda professional looking.

After an hour or so of complete chaos, the place started to come to order. The lights were up and were being tested. All the rigs were on the stage, and the drum risers were up. Ron was tweaking and tuning his drums.

I stood at the back of the auditorium to look at the stage, and it was quite a sight. It looked like an honest-to-god rock show stage. The rental equipment we had managed to cobble together was pro gear, and it all came together nicely. And the lights. The lights! It was like a show at the Cap Centre. I couldn't believe it once I saw the whole thing put together. Just then, guitar sounds started to emanate from Jak and Bob's amps. Mike was having trouble with his. The bass amp was crackling in and out, and Mike was standing over it and hitting it with his fist. With every hit the tone changed and occasionally went out completely.

Ron was sitting on his throne with his feet up on the top rim of his bass drum. "Hey, man, I don't think that's gonna work," he said when Mike banged on his amp again.

Just then, Jak noticed the bass issues. He walked to the center of the stage and peered over to Mike. "Hey, man, what's that noise?"

Mike, without looking up, said, "I don't know. Fucking piece of Peavey shit."

Bob, sensing that Jak was getting a little perturbed, chimed in, trying to be helpful as always. "It sounds like a bad cable. I've got another one. Hold on."

Bob ran and got Mike a new cable. He plugged in and it was a little better, but it was still crackling. "Shit!" Mike was still fucking with it and the more he did, the more frazzled he got.

Ron sat up with an aha! look on his face. "Hey! We happen to know another bass player." He looked at me. "Andy."

"Oh yeah," I said, "Andy. Is he coming to the show?"

"I think so." Ron jumped off his throne and down off the risers. "Let me go call him and see if he can bring his amp tomorrow night. Just in case."

This caused Mike to relax a bit. "Ok. Thanks."

The only other amp Mike had was his practice amp, and he didn't really want to have to source one for the show this late in the game. Ron ran off to the office to call Andy.

Jer walked to the front of the stage. "Where is he going?"

Mike replied, "He's going to save my ass!"

"Very well then. Alright, gents. We want to give this system a run-through. We've got your clip tape queued up. We wanna make sure everything works here. Once Ron gets back, we'll run it."

The lights above were twinkling incessantly. Our buddy Todd, who we'd drafted to run the lights, was getting used to the controls. He was all over the place and it looked like we were gonna have plenty of light.

We all started squinting and covering our faces.

"Well, the lights are working," Jak said as he shaded his eyes with his hands.

"Yeah. Those are badass, aren't they?" Jer was obviously impressed.

"You know, that's one-quarter of the lights that Maiden rented when they played the Capital Centre!"

"No shit?" Jak said, as he always did.

"No shit," Jer said with a smirk. Just then, Ron ran back down the center aisle, breezed past Jer, and vaulted onto the stage. "Ok, let's get some levels," Jer said. He headed up to the sound booth up in the back of the auditorium.

Ron leaned over to Mike. "Hey, I talked to Andy. He's definitely coming and he said he will bring his bass amp."

Mike was more than relieved. "Thanks, man. You're a lifesaver."

"No sweat," Ron replied.

Jer's voice boomed out over the PA. "Ok, fellas. Let's check it all out." He sounded all crackly.

He directed the band to play through the instruments so he could get line checks on everything.

Grrchk. "Bob? You first. Give me a chord."

Bob played a chord and a few licks.

"Good." *Crzrgk.* "Ok. Jak?"

Jak did the same.

"A little more." Jak kept noodling and doing a bunch of sweeping arpeggios. Bob looked over and I could see him mouth the word "dang." He was pretty impressive for a sixteen-year-old guitar player.

"Ok. Mike?" Jer boomed out.

Mike played some bass licks. His bass was still crackly.

"What the fuck is that?" Jer said.

"I dunno. Fucking piece of shit." Mike walked over to his amp head and gave it a smack with his fist and the sound cleared up. "There!"

"Better," Jer said, pleased. "Ok. Ron? Give me a snare."

Ron hit the snare over and over for what felt like forever. *Grrchk.* "Ok. Give me kick."

Ron smashed the kick drum pedal over and over. Same deal. "Ok." *Jjzzzrcruck.* "Give me the whole kit."

Ron played a little drum solo that utilized all the drums and cymbals.

"Ok. Vocal mics."

We all talked and blew into our vocal mics and did the "check, check," and "check one, two, three, check one, two, three" until Jer was satisfied they all worked.

"Cooking with gas!" Jer said. "Great. Ok. Let's run through the beginning with the recording and see what everything sounds like. Ok. Here we go."

We had decided to open the show with the spoken-word intro to "Number of the Beast." This ominous, foreboding passage from Revelation, read by British actor Barry Clayton, would set the mood and let the audience know that we meant business. That this was going to be a heavy metal show with all the trimmings.

The lights went down, and Barry Clayton's voice boomed through the speakers. But the lights stayed dark and there was no laser and no fog. When it got to the point where the music was supposed to start, it didn't.

"Hold on, hold on." Jak started waving his arms. "I can't see a goddamn thing. And, hey, where's that fucking laser?"

"Ok, hold on," Jer came back, his voice crackling through the static. "Ok. Todd is ready. He just hooked the laser up. It'll be ready soon."

"Well, I'm gonna need some kinda light. I can't see my fretboard. I can't see anything," Jak said impatiently.

"Of course. Gotcha. Ok," Jer said. "We'll hit you guys with a little light before you start."

I walked out to the center of the stage and spoke into the mic. "Where's the fog?"

"This is just for sound and lights. We don't need fog."

I didn't agree with this. To me, 'dress rehearsal' meant doing it like the show. But since I wasn't wearing spandex, I let it go. As I was walking back away from the center of the stage, I tripped on the raised pit panel. When I did, the mic cable came loose from the mic and dropped to the floor.

"Motherfucker! What the fuck?" I yelled.

Jer clicked back over the PA. "Oh yeah. I forgot to tell you. We had to run the cables down through the raised panel. Be careful. Don't trip."

"Now you tell me." I bent over and picked up the mic cable and plugged it back in.

"Ok, let's run through this again," Jer said.

We ran through it again, this time without a hitch. Lights and sound were amazing. There was still no laser and no fog. My voice kept cutting out because the mic cable wouldn't stay plugged in. After the fifth time I yelled, *Fuck!* really, really loud.

We managed to get through the run-through, and the house lights came up.

"Ok. That was good. Sounds really good from up here," Jer said over the PA. "I think we're ready. Hey, Sean, no F-bombs. This is a high school event."

"Fuck that! This is a metal show," I said loudly into the mic as I gave him a little smile. "But FYI, the reason why I was dropping the F-bombs was because this damn cable won't stay in." I pulled the cable ever so slightly and it dropped out almost effortlessly onto the stage. I bent over, picked it up, and plugged it back in. Again.

"Ok. We'll fix it."

"Where's that laser?" Jak just couldn't let it go.

Jer came out of the sound booth and bounded down the center row. "Todd is having a bit of trouble. But we'll get it. It's gonna be great."

Jak smiled and shook his head.

"What about the fog machine?" I said.

"Hmm... good question. Ricky?" Jer said, looking around toward the back of the stage.

One of the teenage stagehands emerged from the darkness at the back of the stage. "Yeah?"

"What's going on with the fog machine?" Jer asked.

"Oh. Yeah. We can't find the juice."

"The juice?"

"Yeah, you know? The fog juice."

"For chrissake." Jer lifted his head up and yelled around the auditorium, "Has anyone seen the fog juice?"

Everyone kinda shrugged and nodded in the negative, and we heard a lot of muffled no's.

"Ok." Jer let out a big sigh. "I'll have to stop at Kmart and pick some up tonight."

We band guys slowly came down off the stage, one by one, just as Mr. Hardford entered the auditorium from the right. "Ok, boys." He looked at his watch. "3:30. Time to call it a day."

We all wanted to do one more soundcheck. There were a few songs that could really have used another run-through. We had most of the songs tight, but a few… well, let's just say we played them on a wing and a prayer. But we could only stay until the end of the school day, so we reluctantly acknowledged this fact and started to pack up. We band members congregated center stage as we waited for everyone else to clear out of the auditorium. Jer was still running around backstage with a flashlight. If nothing else, he was committed. We really could not have pulled off this show without him. We were beat.

Ron was looking extremely downtrodden. "Hey, guys. I have to go catch the bus. If I don't come off that bus at exactly 4:05, my mom is gonna send out a search party."

"Ok," I said sympathetically. "Don't worry about it, man. We got this. We'll figure something out."

Ron jumped off the stage and ran up the aisle toward the exit. He looked like a kid who had just been told there was no Santa Claus.

"What the hell was that all about?" Jak asked, a little concerned.

"Well," I said, "I have some good news and some bad news."

"What's the bad news?" Jak didn't want to fuck around with this.

"Ok. Ron got grounded again and he can't play the show." I braced myself for the inevitable explosion.

Jak thought for a moment. "What's the good news?"

"There is no good news. People just always say that, so…"

"Fuck!" he let out.

"There it is," I thought. The instant realization that all of our hard work was about to end up on the shit heap of history.

"That's bullshit," Mike chimed in.

"Yeah, it is," I agreed. "I don't know what we're gonna do. I told Ron not to worry about it, that we would think of something, but I don't think he believed me. Hell, I don't believe me."

We stood in silence for a moment and then Bob half-jokingly said, "Anyone know any drummers?"

"What about your old drummer? What's his name. Dave?" I interjected.

"No way," Mike said immediately. "He couldn't play this shit if he had a month to do it. A day? No fucking way."

"We have to do something. Do we know anyone else?" I said desperately.

"There isn't anyone else." Jak finally jumped back into the conversation.

He was right. Ron was an irreplaceable part of this band, the cornerstone. Without him, none of this worked.

"I have an idea," Jak said in his slow, mind-churning way. "We have to go talk to his parents."

"What?" I screeched. *"No. Way!"*

We didn't do parents, we avoided them. And Ron's parents were the ones we tried to avoid the most. They were strict and, frankly, a little scary.

"That is not going to happen," I continued. "Besides, they're not gonna listen to us. We're a bunch of kids. Hoodlum kids. Longhairs. That's a terrible idea."

"Hey, man, if you have a better idea, I'm all ears."

Jak was right again. I didn't have any other ideas except to maybe break Ron out of 'jail,' but I knew that would end horribly and put us in a much worse position that we were already in.

"I don't. I don't have a better idea. Fuck. Alright. Bob, you have the most responsible-looking vehicle, so you drive."

"Me?" Bob waved his arms as if he were tapping out of a wrestling match. "Y'all don't need me. I'm not going to Ron's house to talk to Ron's parents. No way."

"You have to. We all have to go. We are a band, and one of our bandmates needs our help. *All* of our help," I told him.

Bob relented. "Ok, ok. Let me get my shit."

We all collected our stuff and went out to put our respective shit into our respective cars. We met back at Bob's Corona and all piled in. We spent the six-minute drive to Ron's house discussing strategy. What we were gonna say, how we were gonna behave. Anything that would give us the best chance of convincing his parents that Ron had to play this show. *We* had to play this show. This all went out the window, however, when we parked in Ron's driveway and walked to the front door. We were all so nervous I could feel all thought leaving my brain. Jak was the only one who seemed to be even the slightest bit composed. He rang the doorbell.

After what seemed like forever, Ron's mom answered the door. She was slightly flabbergasted to find four longhaired boys standing at her door, bathed in the dusky late afternoon sunlight of winter. "Can I help you?" she said skeptically.

"Yes, ma'am, Ron's mom. I… um. My name is Sean, I—"

"I know who you are."

Wow. This was going to go worse than I'd thought, and that was hard to imagine. "Yesss. Um. We were wondering if you and um... Ron's dad had a few minutes to um..." I was stumbling hard over every word. Parents scared me. "We were wondering if we could talk to you for a minute."

She looked the group over and let out a big sigh. "I guess. Sure. Come in."

I actually couldn't believe we got past the front door. She escorted us to the family room in the back of the house, past the stairs and kitchen, and motioned toward the couches. "Please have a seat," she said pleasantly. "I'll get Ron's dad." It was really his stepdad – this was a pet peeve of mine.

"Stephen," she called up the stairs, "Ron's friends are here. They would like to talk to us." She came back into the family room. "Can I get you boys anything? Something to drink?"

We all responded in the negative. While we were waiting for Ron's stepdad to come down, I looked around the room. It was clean. Very, very clean. I had never seen a house so clean. There were no dirty dishes in the sink. No clutter on the countertops, no dust on any surface I could see.

"Who lives like this?" I thought. We were all sitting on a couch draped in a thick plastic cover that squeaked when we moved, and since we were all nervously squirming, it sounded like a mouse concerto.

Ron's stepdad bounded down the stairs and opened a door near the kitchen. He yelled down the steps to what I assumed was the basement. "Ron! Why don't you come up here?"

We heard Ron's voice, muffled, coming up from the basement. "I told you, I'm not hungry."

"Your friends are here. You might as well come up and hear what they have to say."

After a moment we could hear Ron slowly, methodically plodding up the basement steps. He reached the top and we saw him emerge from the basement doorway as his stepdad headed into the family room and sat on the love seat across from us, next to Ron's mom.

"Go ahead and pull up a chair, son," he said, pointing to a chair in the kitchen.

I could see on Ron's face the same expression I would have if my stepdad called me 'son.' In that moment, I thought about how unfair it was, for both the kid and the stepparent. Each trying to find a way to repair something that was broken, something they were attempting to put back together. The stepparents were the ones who were there and had to put up with all the hurt and all the pain that had been caused by someone they may have never met. But they stayed. They stuck with it, and it was never easy. Many years later, this would make total sense to me and I would feel bad for how I had responded to my step-situation.

Ron pulled out a kitchen chair, placed it at the boundary between the kitchen and family room, and sat down.

I watched a lot of TV as a kid and this setup – with us band-mates on one side of the room, the parents on the other side of the room and 'the defendant' in the middle – reminded me of a scene right out of *Perry Mason*. And for all intents and purposes, this was a hearing. We had to make a case for why Ron should be allowed to play this show in light of his many infractions.

"Alright, we're here, so spit it out." Ron's stepdad struck first.

Us band members looked at one another as if we were all trying to will the others to speak, to be the spokesperson for this little trial. After a moment, I finally spoke up. "Well, sir. We were hoping that we might be able to convince you to let Ron play the show. We've been planning and practicing and practically killing ourselves to get to this point, and—"

Ron's stepdad interrupted, "We know. That seems to be part of the problem. Ron's grades have taken a nosedive. Now, we have rules around here, and in our house an education is the most important thing. Ron didn't keep his end of the bargain."

"I understand," I said.

"Yeah, we get it, man," Mike interjected. Most unwelcomed by me.

"No, I don't think you do. If you 'got it'" – he made exaggerated air quotes – "you would have done more to encourage Ron to keep his grades up."

I was thinking, "Look, pal, it's not my job to worry about Ron's grades!" I was also thinking, "Mike, shut the fuck up, you are not helping!" But out of my mouth came, "Yes, sir..." I was struggling with a way to respond that wouldn't make things worse for Ron and for us. "My parents are the same way. I get it. It's just, well, this show is kinda important. We wouldn't be here if it wasn't."

I looked at Bob to see if he had any words of encouragement to add, but he looked mortified. If someone had clapped their hands, Bob would've shit himself.

"Well," Ron's stepdad continued, "if it were so damned important, you all should have thought about that before you slacked off on your responsibilities." Ron's mom reached over and gently touched his arm, trying to calm him as his voice rose a few decibels.

I was not winning this argument.

Just when I thought all hope was lost, Jak finally spoke up. "You're absolutely right. We've all been ignoring all of our other responsibilities. We've all put everything we have into preparing for this show. Mike and I have been driving from the other side of the county for rehearsals, and my parents aren't exactly thrilled about any of this either. My grades have suffered. My girlfriend broke up with me. I have invested every ounce of energy I have into getting this right. Doing a good job and making my people proud. Most of all myself. Proving to myself that I could do this. This is a once-in-a-lifetime show. We will never, no matter how old we get or how successful we are, play another show like this one. Have I let things slip? Grades. Chores. Sure I have. But those things will be there on Monday. This show won't."

Jak was on a roll. I noticed Ron's mom's demeanor soften, and even his stepdad was looking on in awe of the oratory prowess of this sixteen-year-old guitar player.

Jak continued, "Besides, it's not just about us. We are supposed to raise money for the prom. We've sold over a thousand tickets. We have a crew of over thirty people helping us pull this off." Jak was appealing to the business sense of Ron's stepdad. He was able to articulate, even if he didn't quite understand it, that it takes a mountain of people to pull off a show like this. It's never just about the band. It's the supply chain. "This is a big production and, frankly, we can't do any of it without Ron."

We all sat for a moment in fraught silence. I could've sworn I saw a tear in Ron's mom's eye. It was a monologue for the ages. I had never heard Jak say so many words together and have not since. Now, we hadn't sold a thousand tickets and Jak didn't have a girlfriend – these were for effect – but he got the point across. We *had* all sacrificed. Hours upon hours upon hours to do this show. But our secret was we loved every minute of it and I, at least, wouldn't have traded any of it, for anything.

"Give us a second, guys," Ron's stepdad said, very thoughtfully, followed by a huge sigh. He and Ron's mom stood up and went to the dining room. We could hear their hushed talk but couldn't make out what they were saying.

The jury was out for a very, very long time. I struggled to think about what that meant on *Perry Mason* episodes. Did that mean acquittal or conviction? Ron was nervously tapping his foot and staring at the floor. The rest of us squirmed on the plastic-covered couch. After what seemed like an eternity, Ron's parents emerged from the dining room.

"Ok." Ron's stepdad took a deep breath. "Ron can play. But…" We all sat up straight, with the biggest smiles on our faces! "But, Ron, first thing Saturday morning you are back on restriction, mister. Get me?"

"I get you." Ron stood up and gave his stepdad a hug and then hugged his mother as he wiped a tear from his eye. "Thanks," he said as she gave him the motherly 'it'll be alright' look.

We all stood up, and Ron's stepdad shook our hands and thanked us for coming over to talk to them. It made them feel better about the kids that Ron was hanging around with. He made a special point to give Jak a friendly pat on the shoulder.

As we walked out, Bob got a huge, satisfied grin on his face. "I can't believe we just did that. This is really happening. We're gonna play."

"What the hell did *you* do?" Jak spit out with a slight chuckle. "You didn't say anything."

"Well, yeah, but…" Bob sputtered.

I looked over at him and felt a tinge of empathy. "It's alright, Bobby boy. It was good that you were here. It was good that we were all here. This has been a long road, my friend. It's all on us now. We better not fuck it up." I laughed.

"Thanks. Like I needed anything else to make me even more nervous!" Bob said, half joking.

We all piled back into Bob's car, and he drove us back to our cars in the school parking lot.

As we got out, Mike asked, "Hey, what time do we have to be here tomorrow?"

"Limo picks us up outside the band room at 5:00. Don't be late or we're gonna leave without you," Bob responded.

We were all pretty relieved that the show was back on. I looked at Jak and gave him one of his own signature nods. "Thanks, dude. That was awesome."

"No sweat," he responded. He turned as he opened the door to his Chevy LUV. "I bet ya dollars to donuts that laser still ain't gonna fucking work."

We all laughed as we got into our cars. It was all over but the crying now, as they say. We had done all the hard work. Put in hours upon hours of practice. Horse-traded schedules with bosses, parents, and teachers. Acquitted Ron of bad grades, at least temporarily. I realize now how many things had to go right for us, and how few things would've had to go wrong for it not to happen, and it amazes me to this day.

I'm sure none of us slept well that night. I know I didn't. Well, maybe Jak, but I doubt he did either. Despite his 'all business' attitude, Jak was just as vulnerable as the rest of us. The next day was gonna make or break us in the eyes of our peers and even more importantly ourselves. The teenage ego can be a fragile thing; if we failed, it might cause some of us to hang up our instruments and our spandex for good. We had no way of knowing how it was going to turn out.

None of us were very religious, but I'm sure some of us were praying that night. I know I was. I was praying the show would go well. Praying I didn't get sick. It was February, after all! Also praying that enough people showed up. I knew we had sold a bunch of tickets, but that was no guarantee of attendance, especially if the weather turned bad. I was sure there were plenty of parents who wanted to help support the prom committee who bought tickets but had no intention of setting foot in the school on show night. It was nerve-racking, but it was about to go down either way. There was no way to stop it now, and we wouldn't have wanted to if we could.

24

SLICK BLACK CADILLAC

IT WAS FINALLY HERE. The day of the big show. It had seemed like our entire musical journey had all been leading up to this. I hadn't slept well the night before. I was worried about everything. Usually I slept like a baby, I always had, but this event was a big deal and apparently my body knew it. Today would start off like every other school day, sort of. I didn't have to pick Mikey up today; he knew how busy I was going to be, so he was taking the bus. I wasn't going home after school since I had so much to do before the show. He would ride to the show with his brother. Plus he needed to go home and change into his metal clothes before the show. No one wanted to be caught at the show in their street clothes. At least not if they could help it.

I did the normal routine. I got out of bed, showered, and got dressed. I had laid out my show outfit the night before – a meticulously crafted ensemble of ripped shirts (layered), my spandex (black-and-white stripes and leopard print), wrestling shoes, and an assortment of different-colored bandanas. It was a sight to behold with a decidedly '80s rocker vibe. I packed up the clothes and all my books while listening to *Powerslave*. We were doing several songs off of this record tonight, and I was going to need all the help I could fit in.

I got everything packed into my little duffle bag and headed downstairs. The adults were all at work, so I guzzled some OJ and wolfed down two pieces of toast and headed out to the Camaro still chewing my last bites. I hadn't really thought about the fact that if she didn't start, I would be totally stuck. Luckily, I didn't need to worry today. She started right up. I had thrown the duffle on the back seat and was fishing around for my show mixtape. I found it – where else? – in the center console. I popped the tape in and hit the rewind button. It would take a while since my tape deck was old and fairly shitty. I put the car in drive and headed down the driveway. When I reached the end of the driveway, the tape had still not fully rewound. I sat there, waiting at the end of the driveway for it to finish. When it finally did, with a satisfying *clunk*, Dio's "Rainbow in the Dark" started playing. "Goddamn, I love this song!" I said to myself as I headed out onto the main road.

Twenty minutes later, I was pulling into the school parking lot. I parked the car and headed inside. It was a weird day. I chalked it up to lack of sleep in anticipation of the show, but everything seemed to be moving in slow motion and the school seemed smaller somehow. I realized, on some level, that the school – with all its brick and mortar and bright yellow, orange, and brown lockers – hadn't changed. Not really. It was me. This show, the prom, and then graduation. That was it. In the quick span of five months, I would be done with this place, and it would be done with me. When you're young, it seems like time drags on forever, and there were points (many of them) when I thought that high school would never end. But things always end. As you get older, time picks up the pace to the point where it feels like you're holding on to a racehorse – and then one day that racehorse puts on a jet pack and hits Mach 5 before you even realize it. This day was the beginning of the end in a way. The end of this part of my journey and, somehow, I felt that.

As I was walking down the hall between classes, people were walking by and giving me the cool nods and saying things like, "Hey, man, have a great show," and "Hey, man, can't wait to see you guys rock tonight. It's gonna be so epic!" It made me feel good because I thought that if all of those well-wishers were actually coming to the show, it would be a decent crowd. One of my biggest fears was playing to a large room with only ten people in the audience and having pictures of that debacle show up in the school newspaper. The only saving grace was that Jer and Lonnie both worked on the school paper, so I was sure they would find a way to make it sound bigger than it was, even if it turned out to not be so well attended after all.

But I could feel that, on this day, the kids would show up. It was February and stinkin' cold outside and it was a Friday night. What else would they do? Go to Skate Haven for the fiftieth time this winter? Go to the mall? Ride the circuit and freeze their asses off? They could do all of those things any night of any weekend. This show was going to be special and, as the day wore on, I felt that, more and more. I was also feeling more than a little bit of pride. This show was a big undertaking and had taken us a long time and a lot of work to get here. The feeling that all of our hard work was going to pay off soon made me feel good. Really good.

I had been clock-watching all day. One of the side benefits of putting on this show was that we got out of class early to get things ready. Ironically, however, on the day of the show, everything was done. There was nothing to get out of class for. Not really. But I was never one to let a good excuse go to waste, so I convinced my sixth-period teacher, Ms. Henry, to let me go early. She had been through this drill before with me over the past two weeks, so she waved me off as if to say, 'yeah, yeah, get going.' I bounded down the hallway and stuck my head into Bob's math class. Bob was writing a complex equation on the board.

I cupped my hands around my mouth and shot a very loud whisper into the room. "*Psst. Psst.* Hey, Bob!"

Bob looked at the door, saw me, and finished writing. When he was done, he walked over to the teacher's desk. "Mr. Smith, may I be excused? We have to go finish setting up for the show."

Mr. Smith looked at Bob, looked at me in the doorway, and then back to Bob. "Fine. You'll need this." He filled out a hall pass and handed it to Bob.

"Ok, great. Thanks," Bob said as he snatched the slip of paper from Mr. Smith's hand. Bob gathered his things and headed into the hall where I was standing.

We started walking, and I slapped him on the back. "You ready for this?"

"Ready as I'm ever gonna be. By the way, Todd got the laser working last night."

"No shit. Did you see it?"

"No. But Jer did."

"That fucker finally did it. Jak will be so pleased," I said sarcastically.

We walked around the corner and into the side door of the auditorium. Jer was there (of course) and a few other folks, including our buddies Rick and Mikey, were entering from the side doors, getting ready to get down to business. They were all running around and making last-minute adjustments here and there. I hopped up onto the stage and looked around. The stage looked really good. I walked toward the back and climbed the riser stands, behind the drums, and found my mic lying on the riser. It was wrapped to the cord with what looked like an entire roll of duct tape. "Now that cord's not going anywhere," I said. "Nicely done, gents."

I headed back down to the main stage, and Bob and I milled around, pretending to look at things, but in fact there was really nothing for us to do. We headed back into the dressing room and plopped down on a pair of comfy chairs that had been moved in there. Mikey had 'borrowed' three or four chairs from the guidance office. They were the kind of comfy chairs meant to put you at ease when you are sitting in there talking about your future, but you have no idea what you're gonna do tomorrow, let alone next year, or five years from now. But, hey, at least the chairs sure were comfortable. We found out later that the guidance counselor was pissed that these chairs went missing and had a hell of a time locating them because Mikey never did take them back, so they sat backstage until *Gypsy* dress rehearsals started in March.

Someone had brought in snacks and drinks – probably Jer since he was all about attention to details. We had Funyuns and Bugles (my favorite) and all manner of candies, including M&M's. Bob would always say, "No brown ones! We can't have any brown M&M's in the dressing room!" I wouldn't find out why until many years later, but Bob was a huge Van Halen fan and knew that they had it in their tour rider that there were to be no brown M&M's in their dressing room ever. This gave the band a little bit of a reputation for being difficult, but the reason they did it made perfect sense. Their contention was that if they got backstage and there were brown M&M's, it meant that the staff had not read the rider. And while the brown M&M's were never the point, that would mean that other things that they wanted were probably also missing. Like sound gear or light gear or safety equipment. Today was the first time of many I would hear Bob proclaim, "I don't want to see any fucking brown M&M's in here!" I laughed, assuming it had something to do with brown being the color of shit. That's how a seventeen-year-old mind works.

Ron rolled in to find Bob and I gorging ourselves on junk snacks and reading *Circus* magazine. *Circus* was how we got our metal news most of the time. There was no internet back then and popular radio never played the shit we listened to, so it was this and word of mouth. Those were the only ways we knew what was going on in the world. The latest issue of *Circus* had just come out, and Vince Neil was on the cover, wearing pink lingerie. This was Vince from the *Theater of Pain* tour, and while we were all massive Crüe fans, none of us loved that record. *Too Fast for Love* and *Shout at the Devil* had been very influential records for all of us. We spent lots of time throwing hair around our cars listening to these records, but when *Theater of Pain* came out and "Smokin' in the Boys Room" became the first hit from that record, we had all had enough of Crüe. The only silver lining on that record was "Home Sweet Home," which wasn't a great metal song, it was just a great song. Period. But we had soured a bit on this new, softer Crüe and would come to realize that they would never get back the magic they had with their earlier albums. They'd come close. They'd have glimmers of the old Crüe, like "Kickstart My Heart," but they would be fleeting.

Ron plopped himself down and looked at Bob reading *Circus*. "Girly Vince Neil. Cool! Let me see that when you're done."

"Sure thing," Bob shot back, still flipping through the pages.

"Hey, guys," Ron said in a very somber tone. "Thanks for coming and talking to the folks last night. Honestly, when I saw you guys sitting there I thought I was royally fucked. Couldn't imagine there was anything you could've said that would change their minds. Jak is the man!"

"Jak *is* the man," I said with a smile. "Hey, man. No sweat. You would've done the same for us."

"Yeah, I guess so. Still. It was cool." Ron was truly appreciative. He had dodged a bullet. It wouldn't be the last time that we would be confronted with that dilemma but for now, for this show, we were locked and loaded.

Three-fifths of the band was there. The local crew. We were still waiting for Jak and Mike, and I was getting a little bored. "Are we getting dressed up for the limo ride?" I finally asked.

"Well, yeah, we kinda have to," Bob replied. "We're getting picked up at five and the show is at seven. We're gonna go grab dinner. Plus when we get out of the limo in front of the school, everyone will be there." When he finished his declaration, Bob tossed the magazine to Ron, put his hands behind his head, and rocked back in the comfy chair.

Ron caught the magazine and started flipping through it without missing a beat. "Well, yeah! We don't want to break the mystique, the illusion." Ron waved his arms in hippie trippie fashion and pointed to his legs. He was already all dressed up in his snakeskin-print spandex and a torn shirt. All he needed to do was to apply an entire can of hairspray to his hair and he would be ready to go.

"Uh, ok. Cool. Just askin'," I said.

Bob and I stood up and started to rifle through our bags to change as Jer walked in.

"So I hear Todd got the laser working last night," I said as I threw off my jeans to expose my tighty-whities.

Jer looked at me nervously. "True, true. He got it working." He started nervously shuffling around looking for something and quickly changed the subject. "Have you guys seen the bottles of fog juice? I put them in here, but they're gone." Jer's face was bright red.

"Oh yeah. Ricky came in and got them earlier," Bob replied.

"Ok. Great," Jer said as he shot back out the door.

"He looks stressed." Ron said, a little concerned.

"Yeah, he's been running around like a crazy person," Bob said as he pulled his black T-shirt with ripped-off sleeves over his head. Just then, Jak and Mike walked into the dressing room.

"The limo is here," Jak said as he and Mike put down their guitar cases and duffle bags.

"Oh shit. Really? He's early." Bob was getting flustered now. He quickly sat down and threw on his Chuck Taylor sneakers and sprinted out of the dressing room.

"Looking good, Ron. Looking good," Mike said as he watched Ron lean his head over and spray almost an entire can of hairspray into it, teasing it before flipping his head back up.

"Thanks, man," he said as he flipped his head upside down one more time and hit it with another blast of Aqua Net.

Jak looked at us. "Are we getting ready now?"

"Yeah," I replied. "We need to be dressed before we do the limo thing. We won't have time to change when we come back. Plus he's gonna drop us off by the crowd in front of the school, so we want the full effect."

"Is that right?" Jak said. This was his go-to response. You never knew if it meant "Cool, I understand" or "You're totally full of shit." I came to know, over time, that it could be either or both.

Jak and Mike start changing just as Bob came running back in, out of breath.

"Ok. So the limo is here. He is early. He's gonna hang out for ten minutes and then we have to get out there. Also, we were supposed to get an hour and a half, but he's only got an hour."

We had blown the leftover expense money on hiring this limo. The driver was a friend of Bob's uncle, and he was cheap. The fact that he was as cheap as he was should've been the first clue that this guy was a bit of a dirtbag and that his normal clientele were probably less-than-savory folk. But it was a limo and, to us, a limo was a sign of status, no matter how dirty it was. And this limo was *dirty*. We all hurried to finish getting ready and emerged from the dressing room in full getup. Lonnie was standing on the front of the stage, checking out the setup.

"There you are," I said as I headed over to her and gave her a kiss.

"You guys are all dressed up," she said, giving us all a good look over. "You look good."

"Thanks. Yeah, it seemed like a good idea at the time. We're getting ready to head out to the limo. Do you want to go with us?"

"Oh... I don't know." She looked over at the guys. "You guys go. It's a band thing."

"Hey, yeah. You should come with us," Ron chimed in.

"Yeah. You're part of the band, Lol. You gotta come," Jak said with a smile. 'Lol' was his favorite nickname for Lonnie.

She mulled it over for a second and gave me a questioning look.

"C'mon. It'll be fun," I said.

"Alright. Are you guys going now?"

"Yep. The limo driver is apparently waiting for us," Bob replied.

She nodded in the affirmative and slipped her hand into mine as we all headed out the side door of the auditorium. We hit the hallway, passed through the band room, emerged from the side school door, and headed toward the limo.

It was brown and pretty grimy on the outside, which was not a great sign. Bob opened the door for the group. We were immediately hit with the strong odor of stale beer and cigarettes. Lonnie stuck her head in briefly and pulled it back out just as quick. "Oh god. Uh... no. I think I'll ride up front."

I opened the front passenger door for her, as the other guys climbed in the back. I closed the passenger door and then climbed in back with the fellas and closed the door behind me. This thing stank. But, hey, it was a limo, so we started messing with everything. Putting the barrier glass and all the windows up and down. Turning on the lights. Messing with the drink tray. The drink bottles looked like they were many years old. This thing must've been an antique.

Just then, Ron noticed the entertainment center. "Hey, look. It's got a little TV and VCR." He hit the power button and the set buzzed to life. As the picture started to brighten, it was suddenly very obvious that there was a porno playing in the VCR. "Whoa!" Ron finally said with his mouth agape.

One at a time, we all started to notice what was playing on the tiny nine-inch color TV in the back of the limo.

Mike was shocked, yet excited. "Bob. What kind of people rent this limo?" he said, laughing.

Jak gave his patented *heh heh heh*. "People who wanna drink and fuck, obviously."

"Ewwww. Gross!" Bob muttered in disgust.

We were all enthralled with the porno. This must be what rock stars do. Watch pornos in the back of limos! The reality was that a true rock star wouldn't be caught dead in this particular limo. It was most likely the fat limo driver watching porn, by himself, whacking off. The car was disgusting. But that scenario didn't enter our minds at the time. This was the first time that most, if not all, of us had been in any kind of limo, so it added to the magic of the night. Even if it was a little gross.

We had been driving aimlessly for a little while, just taking in the sights of our small town from a different vantage point, hoping that some kid would be walking down the street and see us so we could hang out the windows and show him that it was us. Showing off that in fact we had made it. We *were* rock stars. We never did see any kids we knew on the meandering drive, and it was getting late and the porno was still in high gear. Bob looked at his watch. "Shit. Hey guys. if we're gonna get something to eat, we have to do it now. We have to be back to the school soon."

"Where are we gonna go?" Jak said as he perked up. He was getting hungry.

"I don't care," Ron said robotically, his eyes still glued to the porno.

Lonnie stuck her head back through the divider. "How are you guys doing back there?"

"Uh… we're fine," I said, a little embarrassed by the porno and its, ahem, effects.

"How much money do y'all have?" Bob asked the group.

We all looked at each other, except Ron because, you know, the porno. Mike finally responded, "I'm wearing spandex. Where the hell would I keep money?"

Ron finally looked up for a brief second. "Shit. Yeah, me too. Nada." His face was glued once again to the TV.

"Well, we really didn't think this one through, did we, ya fuckers!" Jak said, a bit cranky. Still hungry.

"Hold on." I leaned up into the front of the limo to talk to Lonnie. "Hey, how much money do you have?"

"Why?" she asked.

"Well, we were supposed to stop and get some food, but none of us have any money. We decided to wear our spandex and… well… no pockets." I gave her a sheepish grin.

Lonnie shook her head and smiled. "Let me look," she said, sighing and then tearing into her purse. After a few moments of fishing around, she pulled out a five and a wad of singles. "I've got ten dollars."

"Shit. That's it?" I was a little disappointed.

"Yeah, sorry. I wasn't planning on buying dinner for a bunch of broke rockers."

"Fair enough," I said. "Can we borrow it? Pretty please?" I gave her a cheesy smile. All teeth.

"Well... ok. I guess. For you." She smiled back. "By the way, what are you guys watching back there?"

"You don't wanna know." I pulled my head back through the divider and dropped down into my seat. "Well, she has ten dollars."

"Great. What are we going to get with ten dollars?" Bob said just as we passed a McDonald's.

Jak pointed out the window. "That!"

We all looked out the window with more than a little disappointment. Bob stuck his head into the front. "Hey, we just passed a McDonald's. Can you flip it back around and hit the drive-thru?"

The limo driver responded in a rough, smoker's voice, "I can flip it back around, but this thing ain't gonna make it inta no drive-thru."

"Hold on a sec." Bob retreated to the back. "He can go to the McDonald's but he can't do the drive-thru."

"So?" Ron said with a shrug.

"So!" Bob pointed down to his spandex and then to the porno.

All of us had massive hard-ons. There was no way Bob or any of us were going to go into the McDonald's like that. Ron maybe, Bob no way. "Ha. We've got boners." Mike practically squealed with delight and started laughing. Bob was a bit mortified.

"Well. Tell him to go park and we'll think of something," I said.

Bob popped his head back up front again. "Hey. Just go ahead and park in the McDonald's parking lot. Please."

The driver hung a sharp U-turn that knocked Bob back into his seat. The limo came to a screeching halt in front of the McDonald's. We sat there for a while. We all still had full-on erections and were hoping they would die down at some point. They didn't. We were sixteen or seventeen. These things would last for hours.

The blonde finally leaned her head through the back window. "We're here."

"We know," Jak said exaggeratedly.

"Yeah. We... uh, we can't go in," I said sheepishly. "We—"

"Why not?" she interrupted.

We all looked back and forth at one another, our faces turning red from embarrassment, and started snickering.

Jak smiled. "Well, dear, I'm not sure you really wanna know."

She looked around in the back. All us boys were crossing our legs and covering our privates. She noticed the porno playing. "Ewww. Oh, gross. Ugh, ok." She smiled a bit before asking impatiently, "What do you guys want?"

"Thanks, babe," I said, more than a little embarrassed.

Lonnie took our order and went into the McDonald's. About fifteen minutes later, she emerged with her arms full of paper bags and drinks. This wasn't exactly the high-class, night-of-show meal we had imagined, but who were we kidding. We weren't really the high-class crowd anyway. We were a bunch of poor kids from a rural area, and McDonald's was just fine with us.

We all started to shovel down our burgers, ignoring the stench of the limo. We were starving. When we were done, we threw the greasy cheeseburger wrappers and fry containers into the bags and dropped them right on the limo's filthy red carpet. As we were finishing our drinks, the limo pulled up outside the main entrance of the school.

Ron looked out the window. "Where is everybody?"

At this point, we were all looking out the windows. We didn't see anyone. We all climbed out of the limo and started to look around, but there wasn't a soul in front of the school. Lonnie sat down on a bench near a light pole and took a book out of her purse. She started to read while the band wandered around, looking in the big glass doors of the school.

Bob looked at his watch. "Well, since we didn't do a fancy dinner, and we ate in the car and we, uh, well, didn't really have anywhere else to go, we, uh, we're back early."

"Wait, that wasn't fancy?" Jak said with a sly grin.

I was a little relieved. I wasn't sure I wanted people to see me like this. Not until the show. Not in the light of day.

"What the hell? What does that mean?" Mike seemed legitimately disappointed.

"It means we're early," Bob snapped back.

"I know. But damn. Where is everybody?" Ron was disappointed as well.

"I think what Bob is trying to say is that they're not here yet," I said, slowly for effect.

"Yeah, that's what I'm saying."

"Well, shit, fellas," Ron said, still disappointed.

"Can we just wait in the limo for people to show up?" Mike asked.

Bob stuck his head in the passenger-side window. "Hey, can you drive us around the block a few times?"

"Ha. Yeah… sure, buddy."

Bob reached out to open the limo door, and the driver started laughing. "I was kidding!" And with that, the limo driver locked the doors. "I was told to drive you kids around for a bit, take you for food, and then drop you off. I did that. I gotta go."

The limo driver put it in gear and hit the gas. Bob just barely got his head out of the window in time. The limo tore off out of the parking lot, leaving five done-up, long-haired teenagers and one blonde alone in front of the school. To make matters worse, it was cold and we certainly weren't dressed for February. The wind blew right through our spandex and shredded T-shirts.

"Well, that's just fucking great," Ron said, which was what all of us were thinking. "This fucking sucks!" he yelled. We all tried to get inside quickly before we froze, but the main doors were still locked. We walked to the side doors, and to add insult to injury, the side doors were now locked too. So we had to walk back to the front entrance to the school and bang on the doors until the janitor let us in. We entered the front lobby with our teeth chattering. This was *not* the grand entrance we had planned.

25

CRAZY NIGHTS!

WE MADE OUR WAY TO the backstage area again to warm ourselves up. My fingers were still Popsicles. We sat in the dressing room, rubbing our hands together and blowing warm air into them. Ron was spinning his drumsticks, Jak was fiddling with his guitar, Bob was reading his *Circus* magazine. Again. There was nothing else to read. Mike and I were staring at the ceiling.

There are two facts about being a musician that people don't talk much about.

Fact 1. It's a lot of work.

Fact 2. There's a lot of waiting.

If you know these things going in, you'll do ok. As Tom Petty famously said, "The waiting is the hardest part." We were waiting and more than a little bored.

Lonnie entered with a can of Coke, sat down next to me, and gave me a little elbow nudge and a smile. A few seconds later, Jer entered the room, wearing his official stage manager headset, and said, "Dudes! You gotta come check this out."

He rushed back out. We all looked at each other and then slowly got up and headed out after him.

Jer was standing by the side of the curtain closest to the dressing room, looking out at the auditorium. We each slunk alongside him and peered out. The auditorium was full of kids. Kids dressed in their best metal regalia. Lots and lots of kids. The whole place was full to the rafters. The seats were occupied all the way back to the far wall of the auditorium. The floor seats were a sea of teenagers, moving and pulsating and talking and screaming. The place was one living, breathing organism. It was glorious.

"Holy shit!" Ron blurted out. He was always great at punctuating a moment. But he summed up what we were all feeling. 'Holy shit!' indeed.

"Would you look at that?" Bob said, rather shocked.

We looked out in awe and then pulled our heads back from the curtain. Our fears of playing to an empty auditorium were just that, fears. Everyone had turned out for the show. I mean *everyone*. "Even the back rows?" I thought. "I never would've guessed we would pack the whole place." We were nervous but also excited. "No going back now," I said, moving back away from the side of the curtain.

"Heh. Would you want to?" Jak replied in his typical dry, sarcastic way. "We're gonna rock this fucker."

As we walked back to the dressing room, almost in a state of shock, Jer approached us with a bunch of cords wrapped around his arms. "Ok, folks, here are the backstage passes."

"Backstage passes?" I said. "Whoa, dude. Where the fuck did you get these?" I took one and started looking at it.

"I made them," Jer said in an 'of course I did' tone. "Here you go." He handed one to Lonnie and then proceeded to hand them out to the rest of the band.

These were legit backstage passes. Laminated and everything. On the front it said "Onyx - VIP"; on the back it had a number. I had never seen a backstage pass before, but in my mind this had to be as good as any backstage pass at a Judas Priest or an Iron Maiden show. They looked really good and very professional. So Jer.

We all dropped the backstage pass lanyards over our heads and down they dropped over our T-shirts. We had arrived. We had made it. Backstage passes and all. It was almost too much.

We were all feeling the gravity of the show. The culmination of a hell of a lot of blood, sweat, and tears all coming down to this. We had given up nights and weekends and holiday breaks. We had spent most, if not all, of our money on gas, food, and gear. All in a long shot attempt to do something special. Something legendary.

But I was scared. Scared shitless. In the past two years, I had played quite a few shows. When I was with the old fogey band, I had even played in front of an audience at Shiley Acres, a farm field turned outdoor concert venue. We opened for the Outlaws, whose hits "Green Grass and High Tides," "Ghost Riders in the Sky," and "Highway Song" were damn good songs. The outdoor field party audience had to number in the thousands, way bigger than this auditorium, but this was different. This was an auditorium full of our peers. People we went to school with. We knew everybody in the crowd. That made us more than a little nervous, but it also made it way more special.

We were all sitting in the dressing room, feeling the weight of the moment and staring at our newly minted VIP passes. Mike was feeling the nerves too… a bit. "Wow. That's heavy. Heavy shit right there, man," he said, clearly thinking back to the crowd size.

Bob was kinda calm. More calm than I expected him to be and certainly more calm than I was feeling on the inside. "Shit," he said, "there are a lot of people here." His surprise was shared by all of us. This was exactly what we'd wished for, but now it was time to step up and do this.

As we sat there contemplating the crowd size, Andy stuck his head in the backstage dressing room door. "Hey, motherfuckers! Y'all ready for this? There are a crapload of people out there!"

It was good to see him and I was glad he was here. Andy might not have been an active member of the band, but he would always be a member of the band in spirit. He would always be one of us. "Hey, man, glad you're here. You got your backstage pass?" I finally said.

"Yep. Right here." Andy held up the laminated rectangle at the end of his lanyard with pride. "You guys are gonna kill it. Oh hey, Mike, before I forget" – he turned to Mike, who was leaning over his knees doing some breathing exercises and whose head shot up at the sound of his name – "I put my amp right out here, in between the second row of curtains. In case you need it."

"Thanks, man. Really appreciate that," Mike said, more than a little relieved to have the backup.

"No sweat, dude. You gotta hear this crowd out here!" Andy disappeared back into the darkness of the backstage area.

The noise coming from the auditorium was overwhelming. We actually could hear it all the way back in the dressing room now. It was just kids, but they numbered in the hundreds and they were amped up. Hundreds of teenagers talking and yelling and carrying on. Getting ready for the show.

Just then, Jer popped his head into the dressing room, all business as usual and trying to keep the trains on time. "Alrighty! Everybody, places. Curtain up in ten. Hey Sean! Break a leg! But seriously, don't trip and really break a leg!"

"Did Jer just make a joke?" I thought. I gave him an ok sign and then the middle finger. Loved that guy.

We all started to head to our places, which was quite a challenge. The curtain was still closed and the backstage area was pitch black. Luckily, Mikey and our buddy Ricky stood in front of us with little miniature flashlights to light the way as they escorted us to our spots. Mikey guided Bob to the front of his amp. Mike was right beside him, looking like he was praying. Mike wasn't religious – none of us were, not really – but I'm sure he figured it couldn't hurt. We needed all the help we could get. Jak was in front of his amp, noodling on his fretboard. He actually looked a little nervous, which surprised me. Ron and I headed back to the drum riser with the help of Ricky and his flashlight. Ron sank down onto his drum throne, and I stood next to him on the top riser.

I knelt down to my mic, which was there on the ground, right where I had seen it earlier. Right next to it was a High's half-gallon plastic bottle of orange juice. It was my live drink of choice until I realized later on that it didn't really help me sing any better.

I picked up the mic and held it in my sweaty hands. I looked at

Ron, and he gave me a big shit-eating grin and a thumbs-up. "Not gonna fall out this time," I said, pointing to the mic.

"Nope. Don't think it will," he said. We smiled and nodded to each other. Not believing this was really happening. Ron started to spin his sticks. He was actually pretty good at the ol' stick twirl. Better than most. He was exercising his butterflies.

The fog machines kicked on, and the stage started filling with smoke. Ron made a yuck face. "Is that... is that strawberry?"

"I dunno," I said taking in a big whiff. "Uh. Yeah. I think it is. Fucking gross."

Ron was now waving his hands in front of his face to try and dissipate the fog. "Yeah, it is. Nasty."

The lights were nearly nonexistent at this point, except for a faint set of purple cans. Just enough light so everyone could see where they were and find their instruments and – just as importantly – to find their notes. We didn't see the house lights go down, but we didn't need to. We could hear it. The room erupted into the loudest cheering any of us had ever heard, except for maybe at an Iron Maiden concert, but this time the cheering was for us. The anticipation was palpable. It was like being on a roller coaster, cresting the first hill before the big drop. You kinda knew what was coming, but you couldn't make your stomach stop doing summersaults.

The curtain started to pull apart slowly, and we could see the throngs of teenagers. They had already started rushing the stage. This was a rock show, and the kids were into it. Boy, were they into it.

I turned to Ron with the largest *'oh my fucking god!'* look on my face. "Holy shit, this is really happening."

"You better believe it, brother. Better hold on. Gonna be a wild ride!" Like the roller coaster ride, Ron was raising his hands above his head and ready to scream.

Suddenly the recorded intro started playing...

"Woe to you, oh earth and sea, for the devil sends his beast with wrath because he knows that time is short..."

Ron and I looked back and saw the laser bouncing along with the words. The laser, it turned out, was a puny little scraggle of green glowing lines no bigger than a man's head. It was the least impressive thing ever and certainly not befitting of this show. I could see Jak laughing through the fog, shaking his head with his 'I fucking told you so' laugh.

He started pointing at the laser, and Ron and I couldn't help but laugh either. It was a very Spinal Tap moment. The recording continued...

"Let him who hath understanding, reckon the number of the beast. For it is a human number. Its number is six hundred and sixty-six."

This was it!

Jak started playing the first guitar notes, and they sounded glorious reverberating throughout the auditorium and bouncing off the walls. The crowd went nuts. I started singing as I stood on the top drum riser.

I left alone, my mind was blank
I needed time to think, to get the memories from my mind
What did I see? Can I believe that what I saw
That night was real and not just fantasy?

I quickly descended the steps to the next level down on the drum riser. The entire floor of the stage was covered with an eighteen-inch layer of fog. It looked evil. It looked ominous. It looked so fucking metal.

Just what I saw, in my own dreams, were they
Reflections of my warped mind staring back at me?
'Cause in my dreams, it's always there
The evil face that twists my mind and brings me to despair

I hit the high note, *"Yeah!"*

I then dashed down the final flight of steps out across the stage and, without being able to see my feet, tripped on the raised panel from the orchestra pit. Everyone knew I was going to do it. Everyone had warned me about it, and here I was.

I did it.

The guys looked on in horror, but without missing a beat I shot up, mic in hand, and I continued the song without missing a fucking beat.

"The night was black was no use holding back, 'cause I just had to see, was someone watching me."

The crowd either didn't know the trip was an accident or didn't care. They roared.

My jitters were gone in an instant. I had left them on the stage floor. When I popped up, I was staring right into the eyes of all of our schoolmates. Arms raised, mouths open. I knew these kids, but somehow they were transformed. They were now metal fans. All of them. The lights were so bright in my eyes (we had really outdone ourselves in the lighting department) that I could only make out the faces in the first few rows. The rest were a blur of silhouetted hair, arms, and fists for as far as I could see. I had never experienced anything like that, before or since. The first time you look out on a crowd of people screaming in your direction, screaming as if their lives depend on it, is special. It was like a drug, and I was high.

We went on to finish "Number of the Beast," ripped right into "Queen of the Reich" and kept going from there. Like a group on a mission. And we were.

I wouldn't say we played flawlessly, not even close. But for a group of sixteen- and seventeen-year-olds playing Iron Maiden, Dio, Queensrÿche, Scorpions, Accept, Krokus, Ratt, Mötley Crüe, Black 'N Blue, Quiet Riot, Judas Priest, and Van Halen, we held our own.

We played for nearly two solid hours with no breaks, at least no breaks on purpose. Mike's bass amp did end up taking a shit in the middle of "Eat the Rich." Right in the beginning of the song, we knew something was up. The bass was crackling and wheezing so loud we were sure everyone in the audience was wincing as badly as we were. Mike went back to his amp and started beating it with his fist. He looked like a crazy old man trying to get his TV to work. He was cussing up a storm and we were all mortified. The rest of us kept playing and pretending like nothing was wrong, knowing full well there *was* something wrong. Was this going to end the show? Would we have to take a break? We didn't want to lose the momentum we had built. We had hit the stage like a freight train and hadn't slowed up one bit.

Luckily Andy kept his head, jumped on stage from the side, and helped Mike swap out his bass amp head. It was done in the dark, in mere seconds, and it was doubtful that anyone noticed. Hell, I didn't even notice! All at once the low end blasted through the speakers, rich and deep. Mike was back! Heck, he didn't even miss the bass solo in the middle of the song! As a matter of fact, his bass roared back to life literally three or four notes before the solo. The timing couldn't have been any better. Andy was our hero.

The whole show was magical, with lots of interesting moments. The biggest one for me (beyond falling on my ass at the start of the show) was the fact that I never had any idea what song was coming next. We had shuffled around the song list several times and, yeah, I had two printed setlists. One was taped to the top riser next to Ron's drums. I had asked Jer to put another one down on the floor, center stage. He taped it to the raised orchestra pit panel. Well, the setlist on the riser wasn't visible during the show. At all. Apparently it was in a dead spot for the lights so I could never see it. And the setlist on the floor, centerstage? Some kid grabbed that setlist about two songs in, so I never saw it again. During the course of the show, Jak would either try and mouth the song to me or, if he were close enough, whisper it in my ear. There were many occasions when I didn't know the song until the gang started playing, but yet Jak would want me to make an announcement. So more than once my announcements were "Hey! We got another song for you!" and "Hey, we're gonna do another for ya." Very vague because, most of the time, I had no fucking idea what was coming next.

It was also interesting that the two sets of fans from rival schools segregated themselves. Jak and Mike fans were stage left; Ron's, Bob's, and my school chums were stage right. It was almost like a sporting event, but this allowed me to do a few competing cheer sections in the middle of songs like "Ten Seconds to Love" or screaming the chorus to "Big City Nights." The crowd did not disappoint. Every time they yelled, I was floored at how loud they were. I don't remember if these interludes were planned or spontaneous, but it was amazing to hear hundreds of kids screaming out lyrics at my command. The crowd was wild, from the first note to the last. I'm sure everyone in that room left exhausted.

Shitty laser notwithstanding, and even that ended up being pretty damn funny, the whole night was spectacular. At one point, Jak and I dragged a student on stage to synchronize rock back and forth with us during Judas Priest's "Green Manalishi." It was apparently this kid's favorite song, and he was really into it. So much so that Jak and I couldn't help but smile the entire time. The entire front row was screaming and throwing their hands in the air, and the kid stage dove right back into the roaring crowd. I didn't even know what stage diving was back then. It was full-on rock and roll.

It felt almost like as soon as it started, it was ending. Two hours breezed by as if it were ten minutes. When we got near the finale, I didn't want it to end. Ever.

The last song of the night was Iron's Maiden's "Powerslave." At the climax of our nearly two hours of playing, singing, jumping around, and headbanging, we erupted into a protracted ending and Todd went wild with the lights. He hit us with every light he had in his arsenal. The band and the crowd were treated to an explosion of light, nonstop strobes, and every last bit of the strawberry fog juice. The place was electric. Fucking electric. When the song finally ended, there was a roar from the crowd. The loudest of the night. I was amazed that they still had it in 'em, frankly. Goodness knows I had spent nearly every ounce of my energy.

Before the last note had finished ringing out through the auditorium, the house lights came up. We all joined hands and proceeded to the edge of the stage for our obligatory final bow before this boisterous crowd. We were sweaty. We were tired on one level, but on another level I think we could've gone on all night. The crowd fed us and we fed them. The ocean of cheering had not let up. We bowed once, twice – at least four times. At the end of all the bowing, each of us walked closer to the edge of the stage and started high-fiving the sea of kids that had descended upon the front row. Walking back and forth, making sure we didn't miss anyone. After a few minutes of this, we all headed to the stage left exit.

We didn't do an encore. We had exhausted our repertoire. We only had twenty-six songs (almost half of which were Maiden) and three solos – a drum solo for Ron and guitar solos for Bob and Jak – so we barely made it to the two-hour mark. Had we planned it better, we might have held a couple of songs back, but we just pushed on the gas for the entire two hours. Besides, we weren't even sure we were allowed to do one since it was a school night. Thinking back now, I wish we would've been able to do one. Or two. Or three. Hell, I wish we could've played all damn night.

As I headed offstage, I spotted Lonnie standing in the dark area between the two curtain rows. I made my way over to her and gave her a big after-show kiss. "I'm sorry, I'm so sweaty," I said apologetically.

"I think that is to be expected," she replied. "That was a hell of a show. Did you see that kid jump into the crowd?"

"Yeah, that was crazy!"

"You guys were amazing," she said, looking up at me with those big, blue, amazing eyes.

"Thanks," I replied. "I'm going to go back to the dressing room and see what the fellas are doing."

"Sure," she said. "Tell 'em I said they did great."

"You can come tell 'em if you want," I said.

"Nah. I only wanna see my smelly man." She shot me a very naughty grin, and I shot one right back.

I headed back to the dressing room. All the guys were in there hootin' and hollerin' and carrying on. We were still riding high on the energy we got from the crowd. I was beat, exhausted sure, but I couldn't sit down! Bob was chattering like a schoolgirl. I don't think I had ever seen him that excited. I sat down in one of the guidance office chairs and just watched for a bit. I had left nearly every ounce of energy out on that stage, but it was so satisfying to see these guys so happy. Hell, even Jak had an ear-to-ear smile and was mixing it up, back and forth, with Bob. It was good to see. Those two had bonded in the last few weeks and their interplay on the stage really hadn't translated to their personal interactions, until now. Ron was shaking up cans of soda and spraying the entire dressing room and all of its occupants. You would have thought we had won the Super Bowl. But hey, we were all high. High on the adrenaline of the show, high on a job well done, and high on the fact that what we had pulled off would lead us to bigger and better things. I watched as my friends interacted and just thought about all the great things that lay ahead for us and how grateful I was to be a part of this.

The rest of our senior year would pale in comparison to this night. It really was the pinnacle. The rest of the year rolled on as we went to class, played shows, and tried to figure out what we would do with ourselves once we graduated high school and became adults.

For a few hours, we all felt like rock stars. And for a brief moment, we were. Reality would hit us soon enough, but the high of that show lingered on for the rest of that year and would come back to visit me, from time to time, well into my adult life.

26

COMING HOME

I SIT, STARING OUT THE plane window for quite a while, thinking about Bob.

"Why? Why would anyone do that with so much going for them?" keeps playing over and over again in my head. "And his family. Fuck, dude! You have" – my thought pauses – "you *had* a family. What the actual fuck?" I'm still having a hard time processing the whole mess.

The pilot comes on the loudspeaker to announce that we are flying over the Rockies, and it wakes me out of my trance. "I don't give a shit!" I think as I shake off my stupor. "Do you know how many times I've flown over the Rockies?" I rub both of my eyes and look over at Lonnie. Beautiful as ever. She turns to me. "Have you texted the guys yet?" she says. "To let them know when we get in?"

"Shit. No. I forgot," I say, still a little out of it. "I'll do that now. Is the Wi-Fi working?"

"Seems to be," she replies. "The online TV thingy works, so I would guess so. You guys should get together tonight. Just the group. Before all the craziness starts."

"Yeah, that's a good idea."

I pull out my phone, head straight to my messages, and scroll back to *the* group text. We've had a group text going for a long time. The content stretches back years. We didn't always see each other, especially with me being on the other coast, but thanks to the wonders of modern technology we were able to keep in touch. And we did. Sometimes we'd go for months without nary a text to the group, and then one of us would text something inane, or childish, or both and the thread would roar back to life with spirit and gusto for the next several months. The last time we had a lull in the conversation, Ron texted the word "penis" to the group, out of the blue. We had the bodies of men in their fifties but the minds of thirteen-year-olds, and the thread came back to life for six months.

Ron was always good at kick-starting the reconnection. I stare at the open group chat. The last interaction was a few weeks ago. Ron had again, out of the blue, texted the group a picture of someone who he had run into. Someone from our past. The guy looked gaunt and old – truth be told, we all looked a little rough around the edges – and we spent several pages of texting trying to guess who it was. Ron wouldn't tell us. Typical Ron. Bob finally guessed it was our friend Ricky from high school. Ron had run into him at a local restaurant. Ricky had his kids with him, and he and Ron shot the shit for fifteen or twenty minutes. After Bob guessed who it was, Ron gave us the play-by-play of Ricky's life since high school. Taking up another few pages in the chat.

I stare at the end of the thread for a long time. At the top I can see everyone's name. Jak, Mike, Ron, Mikey, Jer, and Bob. Bob was still on the thread. I can feel the tears welling up in my eyes. I finally let out a huge sigh and send the group a note:

Hey, fellas. Just crossed over the Rockies. We'll be landing in Baltimore around 4:00. Should be to the hotel no later than 6:00. Anyone up for a quick bite and beverage at the Tavern? Say 7:00?

I click send.

After a few minutes, my phone buzzes. Jak is the first to answer. *Sounds good. Safe travels. See ya at 7:00.*

It's not a surprise that Jak is the first to respond. This is usually how it went. He was almost always first, then Mike, Jer, Mikey, and Ron were always somewhere in the middle (in no particular order), and Bob was always last. I realize I forgot to take Bob off of the distribution. Maybe he'll respond? Maybe this is all a big joke or a big misunderstanding? I could convince myself of this. It would sometimes take Bob days to respond to these things. I guess either out of his utter nonchalance or just the fact that he owned an Android device and didn't want to deal with the technology. Any technology.

The next to respond is Ron: *You got it. The Tavern at 7:00. See you fuckers there.*

Typical Ron response, but I'm glad to see he is going to make it. Mikey's response is hot on his heels:

I'll be there. Might be a few min late tho. Order me some cheese fries and a beer. Nothing foreign.

This makes me chuckle a bit. Lonnie looks over to see me monitoring the thread responses. I don't hear back from Mike or Jer right away, but that doesn't bother me. If Jak is coming out, Mike will be there – and Jer? Jer will show or he won't. You never know until it's time. I'm still staring at my phone. Somehow trying to will Bob to respond. "C'mon, Bobby boy. I know you're out there," I say to myself. "Just give us a sign, Bobby boy." But nothing. I know, in my heart, that he can't respond, not from where he is. This just makes me feel a little emptier. A lot emptier.

The plane lands a couple of minutes early (good tailwind), and the pilot gets us to the gate quickly. We all disembark, and Lon and I grab our luggage and then head out to the rental car bus. The bus takes forever to get there. I swear they must have only one rental car center shuttle working at a time.

After about twenty minutes of waiting, the bus finally appears and we're on our way to pick up the rental car. We pick out our car, an SUV in case the weather turns bad, and check out of the rental car lot. We're on the highway by five o'clock, so we're still on track to get to the hotel around six.

My phone buzzes. I look over at it and then look at Lon. "Can you see who that is?"

"Sure," she says. "It's Jak. He says that Mike is coming tonight."

"Good," I say. "I hadn't heard from him. Anything from Jer in that thread?"

She taps on my messages and scrolls around a bit. "Nope. Nothing."

"Ah. Typical," I say.

We get to the hotel, park, and unload the car. I've already done the pre-check-in, so there's no need to stop at the front desk. Room 212. We whisk our way up to our room, open the door, and throw our shit on the couch in the entryway. It's a suite. One of the perks of traveling so much. I look over at the clock on the desk. 6:15 p.m.

"I better get ready," I say. "I'm meeting the crew at the Tavern at 7:00."

"The Tavern, huh?" she says. "That place is still around?"

"Oh you betcha," I respond.

The Tavern is a little dive bar in our home town. What it lacks in character it makes up for in filthiness. It's dirty. But it's also cozy and quiet and a good place to go if you want to have a drink and some bar food and not be hassled by pick-up artists and the usual, young bar patrons. You can actually have a conversation in this place. Which is what I'm looking for. Some beers, some friends, and a little quiet conversation.

I take a quick shower and throw on some jeans and a T-shirt. Lon is sitting in a comfy chair in the corner. She looks like she is meditating.

"Do you want to come too?" I ask. I should have asked her earlier, but my head hasn't been right since yesterday.

"No, no. You go on. You guys need to catch up. I'm gonna shower, crawl into bed, and watch a movie. And by watch a movie I mean fall asleep. I'm exhausted."

It has been a long day and I don't blame her. Crawling into bed next to her sounds perfect to me too, but I have to go do this. We have a lot of catching up to do. "I don't blame you. Wish I could stay and cuddle up with you," I say.

"I'll be right here. Cuddle me when you get back."

And she will be right there. She is always right there and she has always been my rock, my conscience, and my sounding board. "Sounds like a plan," I say. I slip on my checkered Vans, kiss her, and head out of the room. Luckily the Tavern is within walking distance of the hotel. A few hundred yards down the city sidewalks, I find myself standing in front of the Tavern. It looks exactly the same. We had had so many good times and conversations in this place over the years. This was one of Bob's favorite places to go after we graduated and could legally drink. Mostly because it was so low key. Just like him.

I stand outside for a few minutes, looking at the front of this fine establishment, thinking of my friend. I can see several familiar heads and faces through the wavy glass. They are all there, even Jer, laughing and yelling, with arms waving. They look older but yet, just like I remember. The only one I can't see is Bob, but he's here. I can feel him. He will always be here. I take a deep breath, open the door, and walk inside.

EPILOGUE

THE SHOW DID WHAT we thought it would do.

Not everyone was thrilled with the show, or more to the point, the aftermath of the show.

The following Monday, Mr. May called me to the office and escorted me to the auditorium to show me the damage done to the first five rows of seats on the 'visitors' side of the auditorium. Turns out all of Mike and Jak's friends from their high school were pretty rowdy and had managed to rip all five rows out of their concrete footings. There was broken concrete lying all around, and the seat rows were all limp and flopped over.

"I think this rock-and-roll experiment is over," Mr. May confided in me. "I don't think we'll be seeing anything like this for a long, long time. And definitely never again on my watch."

His voice was firm and not without a little regret, but I got the message. I knew that side of the crowd had been rowdy. They were rockin' all night long. The damage wasn't even the worst part. When all the dust settled on the accounting, it turned out we hadn't raised any money for the prom. As a matter of fact, the prom committee owed Jak $17.50 for Dr. Pepper and Corn Nuts.

Mr. May's last words to me were, "This was unfortunate."

As he walked away, up the center aisle of the auditorium and back into the cafeteria, I stood there in silence for a moment. "No," I said to myself, "this was rock and roll."

After that show, we were in demand and were playing out a lot through the rest of the school year and through the summer. We opened for national acts, in clubs where we had no earthly business being since we were a bunch of sixteen- and seventeen-year-old kids, but we did it, *and* we held our own there too. We were one of the few bands in our town to play the heavier songs and once we did, nearly every other band followed.

Not only did it give us legendary status in our schools, but the tale of this concert spread far and wide, inside and outside our county. This show was a launch point for an amazing summer. We secured management and were opening up for bands like Wrathchild and Child's Play in clubs all over the DC, Maryland, Pennsylvania, and Virginia area. At this point, we had ditched the spandex and gone down a bit of a harder, heavier road. We started playing songs like Metallica's "Fade to Black" and Anthrax's "A.I.R." At that time, we were one of the only bands in our area, of any age, playing these songs. We played in clubs and bars and the occasional party. I would like to think we had some influence on the musical direction of other bands in our sphere, bigger bands than us.

We also had a few personnel changes. It's tough to keep a band together. It's like being married to four other people. Ron's constant grounding finally got the better of the band, so we had to let him go. Mike and Jak went to Ron's house again to try and talk some sense into his parents. You can guess how well that went. Fool me once and all. Ron was gone soon after. Bob and Jak got into a disagreement over a school marching band field trip to Canada that Bob wanted to go on, which happened to conflict with a show we wanted to do in DC. The band always took priority in Jak's mind, and mine too, so we replaced Bob and brought in our buddy John from our Exodus days.

We managed to continue and grow through the summer, but afterward we were all exhausted. We burned bright, very bright, but sometimes when you do, you tend not to burn very long, and that's exactly what happened to us. Lonnie and I were starting a family at light speed, so I had to cut my hair and get a real job. This took my focus for the next few years, and in the meantime, Ron joined another outfit after graduating high school and moved south. Jak and Mike joined another group as well and made the heavy metal pilgrimage to LA to try and make it big. After a few months, they had depleted their funds and, after realizing just how saturated and corrupt the LA music scene was, they came home.

Jak, Mike, and I would reunite a few years later and put together another group. Actually, Jak and Mike had put together the group as an instrumental trio but then decided they wanted to add a singer. At that point, I was up for jumping back into music, so it worked out well. I grew my hair back out, and we tried to make another go at it. We wrote a lot of songs and started doing the same club circuit we had done years before. Trailblazers once again, we were one of only a few all-original rock band playing the club circuit. And again, others followed. Everyone started writing their own songs. I would have to say though, we were the best, and yeah, I might be a little biased. This group was certainly one of my favorites. We wrote some great tunes that still, in my mind, hold up well today.

Jak, Mike, and I became much better friends as young men in our twenties than when we were high schoolers, even with bills to pay and kids to feed (both of which I had). Even after that band ended, we all managed to keep in touch over these many, many years. The music brought us together, but we've been in each other's lives so long I can't imagine ever not having them in mine. They will always be my brothers.

CPSIA information can be obtained
at www.ICGtesting.com
Printed in the USA
FSHW010511111220
76805FS

9 781735 581729